Peel still couldn't comprehend why a Humvee waited on the surface of an airless world hundreds of thousands, if not millions, of light-years from Earth, as if it expected them to show up. But then, Peel could ask the same question about himself. He was also an anomaly in this alien world.

BioOp-2793 said, "I'll look—"

"Wait—!"

Before Peel could prevent the cyborg soldier from acting, BioOp-2793 opened the side door.

Peel couldn't properly recall what he witnessed next, except that a black, light-absorbing blob emerged from the cabin and sucked the cyborg inside.

The door slammed shut without a sound. The Humvee rattled and shook. Parts seemed to move inside, barely glimpsed through the dark windows, like gears and pumps and pistons and pipes, moving, turning, all working together with some cohesive plan or agenda. The motion continued for perhaps thirty seconds.

Then it halted.

Then it started up again.

A minute later, a square hole about thirty centimeters across opened in the middle of the door. Several cubes popped out and bounced onto the rocky valley floor. The first cubes comprised metal, the same color and shape as their suits. The second cube was transparent glass, and inside, two eyes floated,

their nerve endings connected to what appeared as an unraveled human brain…

Peel stepped back, his stomach tightening against the horror he witnessed.

More cubes spewed forth. Forged from flesh, they quickly froze in the vacuum while blood simultaneously boiled away as crimson gases.

First Edition

ELDRITCH PRISONERS

A CTUHULU MYTHOS ANTHOLOGY

DAVID CONYERS

JOHN A. DELAUGHTER

MATTHEW DAVENPORT

DAVID HAMBLING

BROKEN SINGULARITY: SEQUENTIA PRIMUS

BY DAVID CONYERS

"**W**ake up, lazy bitches, lazy bastards! Time to work. Time to live!"

Eyelids fluttered in Harrison Peel's face. Dry air carried no scent. Icy chills prickled his naked skin. Frozen muscles shook without control.

"Move it! Move it!"

A metallic cocoon split like unfolding petals and tipped Peel forward and out onto a metallic ribbed floor. The impact hurt, but so did stiff muscles. He moaned, but his voice came out croaky.

Encircling light resembled a chilled halo. Rubbing hands on his chest for warmth, Peel staggered onto numb feet. Further halos lit three additional unclad humans ejected from their own egg-like cocoons, metal orbs suspended from ceiling-mounted cables and manipulated by robotic arms. Two women to his right thudded like discarded garbage, and an expelled man on his left similarly shook as teeth clattered against the subzero temperatures.

"You want to live? Then work to live."

Peel's companions were not the source of the disembodied voice. The mocking orders echoed from far away, suggesting a vast and shadowed chamber that imprisoned them. The impersonal tone reminded Peel of a drill sergeant, or a strict high school teacher.

The woman closest to Peel turned and danced on chilled feet. She, too, rubbed her hands across her white skin for warmth. Peel knew their efforts were futile. Temperatures were subzero. They would die in minutes if they didn't find clothing.

The woman looked to Peel for answers. He had none to offer, but carried enough wits to notice the skin on her arms and legs displayed geometric lines. Beneath the skin lay cyborg limbs, forged from metallic components, which left her stick-like.

"Bitches and bastards. Hesitation is a rookie mistake. Grab your suits. Work for a living."

Cocoons retreated into the shadowed ceiling like lizard tongues slipping back into an unwelcomed mouth, out of sight and reach. Concurrently, other invisible tubes in the shadowed ceiling slurped organic black blobs at their feet, dropped like turds from an anus. The blob next to Peel rolled over his foot, then unfurled and spread across his skin, enveloping Peel in a black, ribbed, carapace-like suit, leaving only his head uncovered. Soon the suit solidified into a rubbery substance. His body warmed, and his shaking subsided. Its texture wasn't fecal matter, but proper clothing.

The two women and the man watched, as if waiting for the organic suit to horrifically dissect Peel. After many seconds, as Peel remained unharmed, his companions gave into their fears and touched their blobs with their feet, and the viscous matter enveloped their bodies.

"Tools and tanks, boys and girls. Tools and tanks. Oxygen privileges expire in sixty seconds."

Spider-like chromatic limbs lowered new tech, spacesuit apparatuses comprising egg-shaped transparent shields for encasing heads, and pill-shaped air tanks for strapping to their backs. Rather than dropping to the floor, the robotic arms slipped these suits over each man and woman, where they fused with their black ribbed armor. Peel's own breathing reverberated inside his suit, while his pulse echoed inside his head. The temperature warmed to a comfortable level.

"Resting is for the dead, bitches and bastards. It's... work time."

Air rushed around them, or more precisely, escaped. In

seconds, they stood in what was presumably a vacuum.

A vast, metallic door, perhaps twenty meters wide and five high, grinded open from the center towards both the ceiling and floor. The door made no noise because no sound carries in a vacuum, but Peel felt the gears and motors as labored vibrations that pulsated through the metal floor.

Outside, the scene was a vast landscape of gray rock and jagged mountains stretched towards all horizons. A spiral galaxy that might have been the Milky Way hung motionless across half the sky, surrounded by multiple globular clusters and diffuse dwarf galaxies. A more distant but larger galaxy, which might have been Andromeda, seemed poised to race towards them.

Prominent was a broiling red dwarf, six times larger than the Sun in Earth's skies. The star moved with enough speed to track its motion against a backdrop of thinly spaced stars, therefore it gave the illusion it orbited their world, and not the other way around.

"Situation anomalous," observed the other male in their group, with an accent Peel didn't recognize. His voice confirmed to Peel they shared radio communications. The man continued speaking, "Conscious stream interrupted."

No one answered until the disembodied voice did. It spoke inside their suits and not with a direct answer. "Work time, boys and girls. The game's name is knowledge: observations, artifacts, speculations, translations, explorations. Don't come back until you have some. I don't reward lazy bitches and bastards. Comprehend-*eh?*"

Peel hesitated, standing firmly inside the chamber. His last memories were… underground, in a cave within Mexico's Yucatan Peninsula… early twenty-first century…

Those memories, however, felt like a million years and as many light years from this moment. Someone, or something, must have transported him across vast gulfs of space and time and brought him to this alien world… but why?

He shuddered and resisted the urge to vomit inside his spacesuit. No answer could be good.

"Bitches and bastards, wait inside and I'll turn off your air."

Peel looked again for the source of the voice.

He saw nothing.

Perhaps their tormentor wasn't a person, but merely a recording. An automated program that activated when humans came to life inside their cocoons.

"I've warned you. Air time is over. Plenty more slave fodder where you came from."

The vast doors started closing.

Peel ran, then jumped over the grinding metal lip until he stood outside. The others followed and soon the four stood together on the naked, airless surface of a dead world.

Behind them, the giant door sealed shut.

The silence was almost terrifying by its pervasiveness and eternalness.

Peel looked back, his breathing and pulse pounding audibly inside his transparent bubble headpiece. He noticed many box-shaped metallic contraptions like the one they had stepped from, arranged in a structured pattern, and presumably part of a larger human habitat. Or warehouses holding many more frozen prisoners.

Further afield, equipment and structures resembled a petrochemical refinery, but were likely operational plants required to power this airless base, to recycle water and make oxygen, and otherwise keep inhabitants alive—or prisoners as they no doubt were. At least the structures seemed human-made. Peel had witnessed his share of alien architecture in the past, and none of it ever proved welcoming. In fact, in his experience, most alien structures he'd explored had proved fatal to humans. Imprints of humanity here gave hope their captors held some sense of empathy to their plight.

At least that was what Peel told himself...

He turned and studied his three companions in their matching spacesuits. They seemed more mysterious than the human outpost.

The woman with the cyborg skin featured close-cropped lime green-hair and circuitry boards imprinted just under her skin.

The second woman appeared more natural, with

shoulder-length auburn hair and a white complexion. Then Peel noticed her eyes, how they shuttered regularly like camera lenses snapping photographs. Lines of digital text scrolled unendingly across her irises, too minute for Peel to read.

He turned to the other male, noticing his enlarged muscular frame bulging under his carapace suit. Otherwise, he looked normal enough, with dark, close-cropped hair and beard, but Peel suspected that like the others, he was more than flesh and bone.

"Do any of you know what's happening here?"

The three figures stared unblinking at Peel. Their expressions seemed uncomprehendingly cold and emotionless.

Then, as if emerging from a daze, the auburn woman stepped close to Peel. A beam of light shined from her eyes and scanned Peel's face. "Unmodified," she reported, "and ancient biotech." Her words reminded Peel of a governmental internal report title, boring and unimaginative, as if generated by a machine. Her artificial eyes seemed to zoom in on him. "Data anomaly. Historical throwback. I haven't encountered your kind before."

Peel furrowed his brows. "Would it mean anything if I said the same about you?"

Her eyes lost focus. "You lack the capacity to analyze statistically-relevant data. A voided statement."

Peel sighed. These people seemed more tech than biological, cyborgs with constructs that disallowed relatable emotions. Peel also recognized he was the primitive species here. But how did he know such things, when his last memory was of pre-space flight Earth, pre-cybernetics, circa 2010s? But somehow Peel knew that of the four, he originated from the most distant past.

"Okay, let's clear a few misunderstandings. I'm early twenty-first century. Earth. I'm a former soldier and intelligence officer." Peel watched their incomprehension or lack of interest in him, but he wasn't ready to give up engaging with these people from the future. "What about you?"

The man answered without emotion or empathy. "You are an anomaly. I've never encountered a replicant so ancient. I didn't understand clone tech existed back then?"

The three watched Peel, like he was the youngest kid in the playground by many years, alone and wanting to play with the bigger kids because there was no one else his age.

Peel puffed up his chest and said, "The name's Harrison Peel. I'm presuming like me, none of you know how we came to be here, why we are here, or what that disembodied voice is?"

Instinctively, the three cyborgs glanced around as if the voice might again order them into action. Peel suspected it listened to everything they said, even now. But he also suspected it was an automated response, a pre-programmed sequence of instructions and not a sentient being, and cared nothing for their discussions. Its input/output requirements would be minimal, like a non-player character on a computerized online role-playing game.

"Well?" Peel said with a shrug. "Do you have names? Roles? Histories?"

The man answered first. "I'm BioOp-2793. Vat-grown crop soldier seeded in Amazonis Planitia. Twenty-seven percent tungsten carbide."

Peel was about to ask what any of that meant, when the green-haired woman said, "Chusue.Net. Knowledge quantumist. Dweller-eliteus Shog City, circa twenty-fourth century. Third R'lyeh Singularity Event singleton."

"And I'm Narrella Sandstorm," said the woman with camera-like eyes. "Nighty-eight percent sentient simulator. Post-humanist, post-synthobiologist. Quasi-theoretical cosmologist. Algebraist-rated."

Peel processed what he heard. All that made sense to him were their names: BioOp-2793, Chusue.Net and Narrella Sandstorm. That would have to be enough for now. "Do any of you know where we are, or what this place is?"

The three cyborgs looked again at each other, then at Peel.

Chusue.Net said, "No. Do you?"

"No idea."

A deep recess of his mind felt that perhaps he should.

Narrella photographed the red dwarf star with her eyes. "Peculiar. Our stellar gravitational host moves rapidly through the skies against the galactic plane."

"What does that mean?" Peel asked.

Her eyes powered down and darkened. "Unknown."

Frustrated with answers that meant nothing to him, Peel grunted and took off at a brisk pace towards a horizon.

"Leaving? What is your agenda?" asked BioOp-2793.

Peel shrugged. "You heard the Boss Man. I'm off to find information. The Boss Man controls life support, so if we don't bring it what it needs… Well, you can guess the rest." He walked faster and focused on the sharp, airless horizon.

He hadn't waited for an answer, but one came to him in a few minutes when he noticed the three companions matching his pace, marching across the lifeless landscape with Peel.

"What purpose is this direction?" asked Narrella.

"I don't know."

"Then why choose it?"

"Better than choosing nothing."

"Illogical."

"Perhaps. Standing doing nothing is more illogical."

They covered approximately one kilometer before Peel looked back and noticed that the curvature of this tiny moon had already vanished the dead human settlement beyond the horizon. He wondered if the gravity should be lighter here than on Earth, because he didn't feel more buoyant than usual. Perhaps the core of this tiny planet comprised dense elements, therefore resulting in an Earth-equivalent gravity.

After fifteen minutes of further marching, they encountered a ravine half a kilometer across.

"What is that?" said Chusue.Net, as her finger pointed to a metallic object situated midpoint in the ravine.

Peel looked to where she pointed, and couldn't believe his eyes.

BioOp-2793 caught Peel's incredulous stare. "You comprehend?"

"That, my newfound friends, is a Humvee."

"What is a Humvee?"

Peel had trouble believing what he saw, so he had trouble explaining himself. "A late twentieth, early twenty-first century Earth military transport."

"What is it doing here?"

Peel raised his hands in the air. "I have no fucking idea, BioOp."

"That is not my name. My name is BioOp-2793—"

"Whatever, mate… I have no fucking idea… about anything here." His companions stared at him with the same blank, emotionless stares that never seemed to change, no matter how bizarre their circumstances became. "Seriously, people, why are we here? What is 'here'? I mean, I remember nothing. My last memories are Earth, pre-space flight and definitely pre-memory download tech. I have absolutely no knowledge of how I came to be in this airless world, or why a Humvee might be here, too. It's all too fucking weird."

The three partial-humans all looked at each other, then back at Peel.

Chusue.Net said, "I also remember nothing. My purpose was collapsing wave-functions of Jewish history circa Six-Day War. A Tel Aviv subroutine cross-pollinator localized to Baku Secondus. That is my last memory, and it was a day like any other. Unremarkable."

It was an answer but, like everything else his companions shared, useless to Peel and their predicament.

"Well then, Chusue, why don't we go investigate?"

"Chusue.Net."

"Fine! Chusue.Net. The Boss Man wants knowledge, right? We might learn something from the Humvee."

When no one answered him, Peel took off down the side of the ravine, finding the least steep path which still required significant efforts via scrambling on all fours to reach the base. The cyborgs followed without a word and again matched his pace. Twenty minutes later, the four stood before the United States manufactured Humvee, with an odd circular shadow cast underneath it. The last time Peel had seen a scene as strange as this one was a U.S. aircraft carrier wreckage rusting in the high ranges of the Himalayas.

While the Humvee appeared battered and battle worn, it was without significant damage or in need of repairs. It looked ready to drive off.

The windows, however, were dark and obscured by whatever hid in its interior.

Peel spotted no weapons on the hard points. It worried him that the vehicle didn't seem more 'alive', but then he asked himself, how could an inanimate object take on the characteristics of a living organism? Did Peel seek connection with familiarity in this alien setting because his companions were devoid of emotion and empathy, and naively believe a piece of tech from his era might achieve that? But why did the Humvee leave him feeling more chilled than when the cocoon had first expelled them inside the dead human habitat?

"It is a military vehicle?" BioOp-2793 asked.

"Yes."

"Are you qualified to operate it?"

Peel nodded. "I am."

"Then we should take it, commandeer it to traverse this planet with greater ease than foot mobility."

Peel wanted to agree, but he still couldn't comprehend why a Humvee waited on the surface of an airless world hundreds of thousands, if not millions, of light-years from Earth, as if it expected them to show up. But then, Peel could ask the same question about himself. He was also an anomaly in this alien world.

BioOp-2793 said, "I'll look—"

"Wait—!"

Before Peel could prevent the cyborg soldier from acting, BioOp-2793 opened the side door.

Peel couldn't properly recall what he witnessed next, except that a black, light-absorbing blob emerged from the cabin and sucked the cyborg inside.

The door slammed shut without a sound. The Humvee rattled and shook. Parts seemed to move inside, barely glimpsed through the dark windows, like gears and pumps and pistons and pipes, moving, turning, all working together with some cohesive plan or agenda. The motion continued for perhaps thirty seconds.

Then it halted.

Then it started up again.

A minute later, a square hole about thirty centimeters across opened in the middle of the door. Several cubes popped out and bounced onto the rocky valley floor. The first cubes comprised metal, the same color and shape as their suits. The second cube was transparent glass, and inside, two eyes floated, their nerve endings connected to what appeared as an unraveled human brain…

Peel stepped back, his stomach tightening against the horror he witnessed.

More cubes spewed forth. Forged from flesh, they quickly froze in the vacuum while blood simultaneously boiled away as crimson gases.

Then further boxes popped out, these forged from tungsten and bone.

"What the…" Chusue.Net responded, expressing an emotion Peel had not known she was capable of.

The cubes that weren't manufactured from dying flesh bounced and jumped around, as if invisible springs provided these living entities with locomotion. When they collided, they fused, then clumped, twisted, reshaped, and reformed. It took several seconds for Peel to understand what he was looking at… He stared down the barrel of a Mk 19, a belt-fed 40mm grenade launcher sometimes fitted to Humvees.

The launcher now bounced towards the Humvee.

"Shit! It's a weapon."

Peel was already diving for cover.

In the airless environment, he heard no noise but recognized the flash as a projectile sped through the vacuum and hit Chusue.Net in the upper left thigh. He expected an explosion. Instead, her leg sheared off and tumbled away. The woman fell, and Peel noticed the skin suit sealing off her wound. She screamed through their shared communications channel until some automated processes abruptly shut off the noise.

As for the leg, it flopped and bounced in the gray dirt until it folded and shuddered, and transformed into another cube. Then the cube burst apart, becoming a dozen 40mm grenades. Those grenades bounced towards the Mk 19, which in turned bounced towards the Humvee.

The Mk 19 hadn't fired again, but Peel knew it soon would. He had to act now, so he raced to Chusue.Net. Silent screams filled her face bubble. Sweat covered her. Peel tried helping her to her feet, but this proved ineffective as she continued to twist and contort in unnatural angles against the excruciating pain she must have endured.

Narrella, meanwhile, had sprinted back the way they'd come and now scrambled up the side of the ravine.

"Suit?" Peel spoke to the alien spacesuit protecting the futurist woman and felt stupid that he was, but what else could he do? "Can't you control her pain?"

In an instance, Chusue.Net's sweaty- and circuitry-covered face blanked, her eyes rolled up in their sockets, the lids closed, and she fell limp. The suit had forced her into an artificially-induced coma, but at least it took away the pain.

Peel dragged her behind a rocky outcrop just as the alien grenades slotted into the Mk 19 magazine. It fired again, not once but as a volley of grenades, and not at Peel and Chusue. Net, but at Narrella Sandstorm. She was the only target within the weapon's line of sight.

Peel watched helplessly as the dozens of grenades shattered her body, not as an explosion, rather she fell apart as if she were a block of ice taken to with a hammer. Narrella's broken bits comprising hands, feet, head, arms and legs, and bits of torso now bounced and sprung about, cubes ready to form into something new…

With enemies now on both sides of the rock, Peel knew his cover would soon be forfeit. Chusue.Net's limp form was too heavy to carry with any speed, so he spoke again to whatever passed as a processing unit inside both their suits. An idea came to him, but why it did so remained a mystery. "Suit, can you slave Chusue.Net's movements to mine?"

The cyborg flipped and stood tall, mimicking Peel like a mirror.

In a moment of panic, Peel glanced back at Narella Sandstorm's remains. Her newly-formed cubes bounced around each other, and looked to be forming a surface-to-air missile.

In desperation, Peel shouted, "Suit, send Chusue and me into orbit?"

Once again, the spacesuits surprised Peel, as they both launched like rockets into the airless blackness of space. The g-forces hurt, and Peel couldn't recall if he'd blacked out momentarily during the rapid acceleration. He soon recognized that Chusue.Net and he now zipped across the planet's dead surface, barely a kilometer up. Then Peel had enough sense to say, "Suit, ensure our trajectory doesn't take us back over the Humvee or anomalies like it." Their suits didn't respond in any meaningful way, but Peel sensed forces acting on his body from time to time, suggesting course corrections.

After a few minutes of hellish speeds over this airless world, Peel recognized that he and Chusue.Net had become satellites above this strange environment. They later passed over the human habitat where they had woken and did so again five minutes later. The world was tiny, moon-sized and perhaps only a few hundred kilometers in diameter and roughly spherical. The red dwarf star seemed to spin with them in dizzying motions, and the galaxies turned and tumbled in the inky skies, bringing a vertigo that caused his stomach to churn.

"Suit, can you gently return us to our starting point?"

It didn't answer, but again Peel felt forces slowing him, as their two bodies descended gracefully to ground level. As they dropped, Peel spotted what he considered might be some kind of rocket or spaceship parked deep inside the outpost's heart, with presumably fusion engines, landing gear and a metallic composition that didn't match the rest of the ancient refinery-like facility.

An escape out of here?

Not that he had any comprehension how to pilot or navigate such a craft.

Their suits dropped them before the gigantic door they had exited earlier, and again it ground open, providing access.

Peel shuddered, uncertain he wished to return inside.

"Bitches and bastards, back I see. Information you bring, better be good."

The voice again spoke inside Peel's suit. The Boss Man.

He looked to Chusue.Net. She remained unconscious, although her face expressed fear and pain. Peel suspected she lived on borrowed time, and the only location that might offer the medical support she required lay within their prison. He stepped inside and her slaved suit followed.

The gigantic door ground shut, sealing them in.

Air filled the chamber.

Metallic mandibles reached down to snatch their helmets and air tanks. Then their suits dissolved and slurped away along the floor and into holes that opened in the metal and swallowed them.

Peel and Chusue.Net were nude again, but the air was no longer frigid. Instead, a balmy, humid breeze wafted around them, reminding Peel of the tropical jungles of Mexico still fresh in his mind.

His unconscious companion still stood, and he saw why, for metallic tendrils had stretched from the ceiling and suspended her. The wound on her leg had frozen and died, looking ragged and painful. Then a cocoon dropped from the dark ceiling and scooped her up, and she disappeared above.

He waited for a cocoon to collect him, return him to his artificial slumber, but no shapes descended.

"Lazy bastards. Lazy bitches. Work time hasn't ended. Time to report in."

Peel looked around, identifying deep shadows everywhere. He considered the Boss Man might show himself at any moment. He shuddered when he realized he was the only member of their party to survive their expedition unscathed. How many more missions like today would he have to experience before he too lost his life?

The chamber stilled, oozing darkness and an aura of repulsive unease. Peel wondered what he should do, when he spotted an airlock dilate open like the shutter on a camera. Warmer light seeped from the room beyond.

He approached, realizing that his footsteps carried no noise in this place, but he heard sounds of distant duct fans and dripping water.

Once close to the new portal, Peel peered inside. The room

appeared tiny, only three meters square and two meters high, and forged of metal walls with structural beams and grills inlaid into the cladding. The only furniture comprised a metal desk built into the wall and one metal chair bolted to a pole jutting from the ground.

As Peel sat, the camera-lens door sealed shut behind him. A small hole dilated open in the wall. A tray appeared upon which rested a scratched translucent cup filled with chilled water, and a metal bowl with food that resembled cooked porridge.

He drank the water, not realizing how thirsty he was. Then he tried the meal, and while it lacked taste and its consistency was difficult to chew, he figured it was food designed to keep him alive. If the disembodied Boss Man wished to kill him, it would have easily done so already, rather than by poisoning him now.

Another panel slid open, revealing two robotic arms that telescoped outwards. The first ended in an arm of a slim woman, the second held a woman's shaved head and neck. Human eyes blinked open, as if she had just woken. The pale white face seemed to recognize him and smiled. "Hello, Harrison Peel." A keyboard appeared on the wall, allowing the fused arm to type words.

"You know me?" Peel asked. She looked familiar. He recalled the various women he had known in his life who had meant something to him: Nicola Mulvany, Joan de Molina, Donna Shelby and Zoe Isles. The head wasn't any of these women he'd once considered as friends, lovers or both, but he felt that he knew her at an intimate level.

The disembodied eyes looked away, bashful. Peel sensed a lie even before she spoke it. "I've read your file many times. That is how I know you."

Peel let the silence grow in the shadowy room for many seconds, before he said, "Where am I? What is this place?" Perversely, a conversation with a living, decapitated head was far from the weirdest experience he had ever undertaken.

"I'm sorry, Mr. Peel, I ask the questions."

Peel felt his jaw and fists tighten. "You do? What if I refuse to cooperate?"

She blinked and blushed. "It's not like you, Mr. Peel, to threaten like that."

"Is that what my file says? That I'm a threat?"

The head blushed. Her eyes looked away. "You know what will happen if you don't cooperate..."

He thought upon her words, and the intent behind them. He recognized the woman hadn't threatened him, rather expressed a conspiratorial warning. She was trying to help him. Their engagement seemed too familiar, too... intimate—and he questioned this.

"I must answer your questions, otherwise you'll turn off the air. And I'll die?"

"I won't turn off the air..."

"But the disembodied voice will? The Boss Man?"

She made an odd motion with her head, which Peel recognized as a nod.

Peel leaned back in his chair and remembered he was naked. Again, what could he do about it, or anything concerning his bewildering predicament? Nothing, except follow the instructions of this woman and see where it led. "What questions do you have for me?"

The woman asked him about today's mission, what he had discovered, observed, collected and interpreted. Peel answered, and they conversed for more than an hour as she probed every fine detail in his report. The alien threat masquerading as a Humvee, Peel thought she would explore with detailed interrogations, but they glossed over it as if she knew all about it. What interested her most was Peel's orbit around the tiny, airless world. She made him recount everything he had witnessed on the crater-pocked surface.

"Don't your suits record everything we look at?" Peel asked.

The head bobbed on its cybernetic arm, which Peel again interpreted as a nod. "It does, but it's not as smart as you. Can't interpret what you see as you see it. Only... human eyes... see what we need to see."

Peel snorted a laugh. "You give me too much credit."

"Mr. Peel, your track record suggests otherwise."

Leaning forward, he raised his eyebrows. "Track record? You mean…?"

"I mean your history, Mr. Peel. It's how we came to purchase your clone—"

Peel shuddered. "Clone?"

Again, the head looked away. "I'm sorry. I should not have told you that."

"You mean…?" Peel felt the world recede away from him, and his face and fingers became numb. "You mean… there are several of me?"

She wouldn't answer. Wouldn't look at him.

"We've spoken before, haven't we? In this room, under these circumstances. I mean, you've spoken with one of my clones?" Then a second thought occurred, as he remembered Chusue. Net's horrific wounds. "Wait a minute, you were once like me, held in those suspended animation cocoons, and released occasionally and sent out to explore this world. An accident, or one of those horrors, broke you. And now…"

Peel stared at what remained of this poor woman, nothing more than a head and an arm, inflictions that left her limited in her usefulness. Similar inflictions that Chusue.Net had endured today. Someone with authority had demoted this bodiless woman to a post-operations de-briefer and interrogator when she no longer possessed the required body parts to perform in the field.

He caught her stare and noticed tears rolling down her porcelain cheeks.

"You've been out there too," Peel pointed towards where the gigantic outside door lay, "with one of my clones, on a mission. And that Peel could only save this much of you?"

Until he witnessed it, Peel had never believed a disembodied head could shudder.

"Not exactly…"

The door that had let Peel inside now opened. He turned back to the head, now disappearing back inside the wall. She said before she disappeared, "The cable with the round socket… is sometimes faulty…" And then she vanished.

Peel stood for a long moment, feeling that he had missed

an important aspect of what the bodyless woman had told him.

He felt a chill behind him, as frigid air seeped into the main chamber.

"Want to sleep to live another day?" echoed the disembodied Boss Man from everywhere and nowhere. "Then don't stand around, bitches and bastards."

Peel stepped outside. Already the temperature was well below freezing and he soon shivered violently. His feet and hands numbed as icy vapor escaped from his breath.

A cocoon lowered from the shadowed ceiling and opened to welcome him inside.

It was then that Peel noticed the cables on its undercarriage, and one in particular with a round socket.

The socket didn't look faulty.

"Oxygen privileges expire in sixty seconds…"

Deciding that he had nothing to lose, Peel approached the cocoon and pulled the cable from the round socket. Lights blinked off, but the metallic cocoon soon encapsulated him. A gas filled his mouth and nostrils… and everything went dark…

THE PRISONER FROM BEYOND

A novella of The Esoteric Cavalry

BY MATTHEW DAVENPORT

Buford Cartwright, my brother and sometimes pain in the ass, was exercising his impatience with me. We had found a telegram office in the small town of Slimvale, in the Nebraska Territory. To call Slimvale a town was to use grandiose terms. It had a telegram office, a few houses, and a small saloon.

My name is Hiram Cartwright, and I am a member of the Esoteric Cavalry of the United States.

Or what's left of it.

In 1841, Arlington Fitz, a Brevet Second Lieutenant in the United States Cavalry, saved President Martin Van Buren from something that could only be described as "not of this world." Immediately following the demonstration of his calm demeanor when faced with a creature directly from nightmares, Brevet Second Lieutenant Fitz was promoted to Captain and asked to lead a secret branch of the United States Cavalry that would focus entirely on protecting America from the mysteries hidden in its still-untamed lands.

When the North and South went to war, an older Captain Arlington Fitz mounted up and brought his decades-old Esoteric Cavalry to the front. For five years, we protected America from the powers that both sides attempted to bring to the war effort. I was recruited at the beginning of the war and, aside from the captain himself, was the longest-surviving member.

When the war ended, about six months ago, our numbers

were down. The Esoteric Cavalry had fought hard and paid for it with our lives. With only a handful of us left we shifted our focus to two fronts: recruitment and the untamed lands further west. Captain Fisk asked me to recruit a new cavalry to move out west and continue our efforts.

Six months on, and my only recruit so far was my own brother.

I had sent the telegram to Captain Fisk yesterday morning, and since then we had been camping in the bushes just off the only path in and out of Slimvale.

The wait was aggravating to Buford, and he had taken to throwing his knife at a tree. His impatience wouldn't have bothered me, except he had started to hit the tree with surprising consistency. The repetitive sound of contact was starting to fray my nerves.

Before I could snap at him, he turned to me. "You think he might have responded, yet?"

I sat up from my bedroll and rubbed my eyes. While we were set up near the road, we were also only about ten feet or so from the door to the telegram office. Buford knew this.

"They know we're out here," I didn't try to hide any of my annoyance as I answered him. "They will come and tell us—"

"Telegram for Hiram Cartwright," a voice called out from the doorway.

"Thank God," I stood and went to the barred window.

The man behind it was smiling with all his teeth and, by the look in his eyes, it was obvious he had avoided the night shift. I took the telegram and read it over before turning and crashing into Buford, who had snuck up behind me to read over my shoulder.

"What's it say?" my brother demanded.

"Don't you know?" I grunted before just giving up and telling him. "Somewhere between here and the Indian Territory is a settlement that goes by the name of Barrenstand. A group of people there have a wild man living in their hills. Captain Fisk only described him as a wizard."

"Wizard?" Buford crossed his arms. "Like Merlin?"

I kept having to remind myself that Buford was only recently deputized to assist me in my efforts protecting the territories. He hadn't stood beside me during the war as the Confederate Army called up nightmares straight from the bowels of Hell to destroy us.

"No," I answered. "Not like Merlin. Wizards aren't ever like Merlin. Wizards use people to break the laws of nature."

Buford smirked and touched the star on his chest. It was a Marshal's star, but instead of the standard five points, it was shaped with the more stylized Elder Sign—a protective ward against the types of critters that the Esoteric Cavalry tended to come up against.

"Good thing we have badges, then."

Because of the limits of both the telegram and the people on each end of the wire, there was a lot of information that Fisk hadn't told us in that message. Because I knew the man, it was my job to interpret what his message actually meant. He had said that the people of Barrenstand had called this thing a wizard. That didn't mean that it was. Most people don't have a clue what they are dealing with, and I tended to walk into most situations blind because of it.

It was clear that this thing looked like a person and was doing questionable things, things that were questionable enough to get the Cavalry's attention.

I joined Buford in picking up our bedrolls and giving my horse, Antilles, a quick snack before saddling up. A glance at the map and a conversation with the man on duty in the telegram office and we had a general idea of where to head to find Barrenstand. We were looking at about six days ride to the south.

Perhaps Buford wouldn't annoy me as much, now that we had a destination.

For a settlement in the middle of nowhere, Barrenstand had a lot more to it than Slimvale had. For starters, the saloon had rooms and we didn't need to set up a camp. Something about our presence seemed to bring out the best in everyone, and our badges got us cheaper accommodations than we were expecting.

The town was carved out of a small plain on the edge of a short crop of trees. A wide road went through Barrenstand, and buildings lined each side. Aside from the saloon and the store, they were all one story. Everything in the town looked a bit windblown, which made sense given the location. There was a doctor's office and, to my surprise, a telegram office as well. They seemed ready for civilization even if the territory wasn't yet.

Aside from why we were there, the only strange thing in Barrenstand was the gatherings of people chanting at nothing.

Three people, one woman and two men, stood in the middle of the street as we worked our way across town. They would fall to their knees and then leap to their feet, chanting and pointing at things that weren't there.

"Traveler," the woman took me by surprise, grabbing at me while I rode by. Buford reached over and grabbed my arm before I could draw on her. The scars from the war rode deep on my spirit. My brother nodded at her sleeve, stained in blood.

"Traveler," she repeated, "live the righteous path and do not suffer as we do. Do you see the demons?" She waved around me, indicating the shared dream they were having, whatever it was.

"Not yet," I answered. I didn't slow my horse.

"Praise be," she fell to her knees and was almost trampled by my horse. "There is still time to save your spirit. Today we repent for ourselves and pray for you."

They returned to chanting.

"We are your messengers. We are your soldiers. Bringing the purple light to the dark corners of the world. Prepare, sinners. The devil has come to collect his debt."

Buford and I were shaken, but this wasn't where we needed to start our investigation. The religious tended to not understand what was really going on, and liked to drag you down to their level instead of rising to yours.

Any traveler would tell you that the best place to get information would be the saloon. Some might even tell you the sheriff's office, of which there was one on the edge of town. Normally, they would be correct in a generic sense.

Not every town had a doctor, especially in the unclaimed lands between territories. Doctors tended to live closer to where they could get their necessary supplies and a steady flow of money. Towns like Barrenstand were a rare thing. When you found one, it was a smart idea to skip over the saloon and the law and go right to the source. Everyone went and saw the doctor, even when they didn't want to.

Buford and I took the time to get our horses set up at the town stables. Our badges didn't afford us anything special there, but we weren't expecting anything. I made certain everyone there knew to keep their distance from Antilles if they liked keeping their fingers.

I was the first in and out of the bath provided at the saloon. It was nice to get the week of travel washed away and the time we took gave the town space to get their gossip started. Between us showing up and flashing our badges, the chatter would only serve to grease the tongues of anyone who might assist us.

Buford hung back to dredge up whatever gossip was sloshing around the patrons of the saloon. I had to beg him not to use the word wizard when he was asking around, and I can't say that he didn't just agree to shut me up. I also told him to hide his badge.

"Why? They already know we have it." Buford was tucking in his shirt as he asked.

"They know we have badges," I explained, "but they don't know we've got Esoteric Cavalry badges." I slid my pistol into its holster. I itched to be carrying my rifle, but that wouldn't do where I was going. "You need to be doing the asking, not answering their questions about monsters and funny badges. It'll be better if we let them think we're Marshals."

Buford accepted that and hid his badge where I always hid mine, on the inside of his jacket. The Elder Sign on our badges acted as protection against supernatural magics. We couldn't go without them without putting ourselves at risk, but we didn't need to show them to every wandering eye.

A shot at the bar was all I needed before leaving Buford and making my way to the doctor's office.

The office was on the opposite end of Barrenstand from the

saloon. I didn't know if I was looking for places for me to hide or looking for where someone else might be spying on me. I stuck to the other side of the street from the worshippers we had bumped into on the way in, and they ignored me for now.

The walk let me take in the town. My years with the USEC had me staking out high ground for ambush positions.

Old habits die hard, and some monsters carry guns.

The building was small with only a few rooms. Several windows were curtained, but they didn't need to be open for me to see the line going out the door. The sign out front read "Doctor Warren."

I pushed past the ailing and infirm by doing exactly what I told Buford not to do. Pulling my coat aside, I let anyone who gave me the stink-eye take a peek at my badge.

A young woman with a sense of authority about her slapped her hand against my chest before I could show her my badge.

"Sir, you cannot cut the line," she said. "You need to head home and come back tomorrow. The doctor is not going to have time to see any more patients after he gets through this batch."

"Miss—"

"Ward. Charlotte Ward. And you are leaving." Her hand pushed me back before she returned it to her side.

With my coat free, I pulled it open.

"What is that?" Charlotte asked. "Are you some kind of Marshal or something?"

"You could say that," I gave as an answer. I threw a look over my shoulder at the crowd. "What's with the plague?"

Charlotte wasn't quite that sure about me yet. "Why? You sick?"

"No, ma'am. The United States government asked me to investigate," I let out a sigh, "and I will need to see the doctor."

"The law doesn't have much say here." She wasn't wrong. The territory was sparingly cared after. It was likely that I was the first law Barrenstand had ever seen.

"Miss Ward," I leaned in to whisper, "I believe someone might be responsible for this and I am investigating as to put a stop to it. You can help me so that I can help you, or I can see about getting the law to visit more frequently."

Towns like Barrenstand tended to have prospered by staying out of the war, and continued to do so by keeping to themselves. The last thing Miss Ward wanted was to bring the law into town and earn the upset of her neighbors.

"The doctor is done for today," she called past me. The response was the overall complaint of the townspeople, some of them shouting that the demons would take me.

As she helped usher the people out, the door to the doctor's office opened and a small man stepped out and joined the group making haste to their other medical sanctuary: the saloon. Perhaps Buford would get the stories from them that the doctor hadn't.

Following the small man out was the doctor. He was about a hand shorter than I was and looked exhausted.

He thrust his hand out to me and I shook it.

"Doctor Warren," he said. "I assume you're my savior today?"

"Maybe yours," I answered, "but most certainly not theirs."

"They all suffer the same illness and I have no idea how to help them anyway," Doctor Warren explained. He shrugged. "This town is plagued. If it weren't for their homes, most of them would have left weeks ago."

He eyed me a little closer and I opened my jacket to give him a glance of my badge.

"Government sent me to figure out what was going on and put it right." I didn't want to call myself a marshal unless I was forced to. I preferred not to lie to people, but sometimes it came to that. It was better they think me a marshal than know that the world was filled with things that they couldn't understand.

"Government noticed, eh?" Doctor Warren snorted. "They don't tend to notice us unless there's something in it for them."

"Whatever they want here," I said, "they failed to tell me. I'm just here to make the sick go away."

The doctor eyed me again, focusing on the pistol on my hip.

"You planning on shooting this plague?"

I shrugged, "That depends on what you can tell me about it."

Doctor Warren nodded slowly and grabbed a cigarette from

his shirt pocket. I offered up a match and he took a seat on a chair in the corner of the room.

"The symptoms are unique," he explained. "First, the dreams." He shivered. "I don't know how to describe them. Worms? Tentacled things? Horrible things invade your dreams, and you find yourself doing everything to stay awake. Then you see these things when you're awake. Only every now and then at first, then constantly." He pointed toward the door to the waiting room. "Everyone out there is seeing these things all the time."

"Some of them were bleeding," I pointed out.

Doctor Warren nodded. "That's the next step. These hallucinations are making people hurt themselves. You ask them and they think these monsters they're seeing are biting them, but that don't make sense." He rolled up his sleeve and exposed a bandage covering his arm. It had bled through a bit. He peeled it back and showed a chunk of flesh missing from his arm. "This happened in my sleep, but you can't tell me that a monster bit me. I don't believe in no spookies. This was something I did to myself, I'm sure of it."

The doctor might have been sure of it, but I wasn't. I wasn't so sure that these were dreams, either.

"What can you tell me about the religious fervor I saw on my way in?" Monsters and dream worms were one thing, but things would get much more complicated if people were worshipping these things.

"People seeing things they can't explain choose to explain them the best way they can." His eyes drifted as he searched his thoughts. "When angels appear in the Bible, they come with plagues, famine, and destruction. We like to think of angels as pure beings of light and wings, but if the unexplained floats through your wall and bites you, you can't help but wonder if you've had a visitation."

I shook my head. "That's not where everyone's mind goes."

The doctor brought his attention back to the now and nodded. "No, it isn't. That's why not everyone is out in the streets praising the angels of the dream god."

"Is that all of the symptoms? Dreams of monsters and injuries?" I asked.

"That's all so far," the doctor said. "It only started a few weeks ago, the same time that the fog started."

"The fog?" I asked.

"A month ago," he took a long drag on his cigarette, "a fog started filling our town every evening. We don't usually get fog and never regularly. Shortly after that, people started getting the dreams."

I frowned at that. It wasn't the first time I had heard of an odd fog, but a fog that brings dreams with it was entirely new.

"What about the fog made it unusual?" I asked.

"Marshal," Doctor Warren's face paled, "I have never been one for superstition," he waved a hand in dismissal, "ghost dreams notwithstanding, but this all started the day Atticus Miller arrived."

"Is that the wizard everyone is talking about?"

The doctor nodded before shrugging. "From what I've seen, he's harmless, but if this is all his doing, then maybe he is a wizard of some kind."

"Harmless?" I needed this doctor to make sense. "If he's harmless, what makes the people think he's a magic man?"

He was scratching at his sleeve, and I saw some blood soaking through.

"You can't see them worms floating around without thinking they might be demons." Doctor Warren noticed the blood on his shirt and stopped scratching. "Atticus arrived, then the fog came, then everyone was seeing demons. Even if you had no schooling, that's simple math." The doctor looked to tire right in front of me, as if the conversation was taking everything out of him. "Then there's all the work he does. He's about half a mile out of town, but everyone hears him as if he was a blacksmith right in the center of Barrenstand."

"That all of it?" I asked. He didn't look like he was going to be up for too much more conversation.

He yawned. "Almost." Dr. Warren blinked his eyes a bit and said, "Two drunks, I don't remember their names," he yawned again. "I always saw them passed out near the stable. They wandered off. Anna Watts said she saw them with Atticus."

"Where can I find Ms. Watts?"

He raised his arm to point in a general direction toward where we had ridden into town. He moved weakly and I noticed the blood had soaked through his shirt and was pooling at his elbow. "At the shop. Her grandpa is the grocer. He's on in years and she takes care of him."

The doctor's arm fell to his side and his head started to roll around on his neck. I grabbed his arm up and tore his sleeve open until I saw the wound.

Directly center of his wrist and elbow was a large bite. It was almost a perfect circle with deep puncture wounds.

I called out to Charlotte and stood back as she rushed in and started treating the doctor's wound.

"We all see them," she explained. "We all see them, and we all get bit." Rage or frustration suddenly filled her eyes as she turned and stared me down. "If you're looking to fix this, then you had better get to it before you start seeing them too."

Leaving the doctor in what I hoped were her good hands, I made my way back to the saloon to find Buford.

My brother was sitting at a table with three other men. Chips were tossed across the table as he concentrated. He noticed me and nodded, and I chose to let him be.

Turning toward the bar, I flagged the bartender down and had him bring me a whiskey.

It was another half an hour of his card game before Buford joined me at the bar. When his drink came over, I filled him in on my visit to Doctor Warren's.

"These," Buford wiggled his fingers in the air, "invisible worms are real then?"

I nodded, "As far as I can tell." A memory that had been tickling the back of my mind came to the top. "It reminds me of an event outside of Vicksburg back in sixty-three. A gal was hiding in a cave with some sort of soundless music box. It was big, too, and as she cranked it the air shook for about a mile." I could tell that I lost Buford at the music box. "I wasn't there, but the way it was explained, you can peek under the curtain at other places if you get the vibrations right. This music box was filling the air with vibrations and those vibrations made people see things."

"Purple monsters?" It was an odd question, but Buford wasn't smiling.

I nodded. "Something like what these folks have been seeing. The Confederates were using them as a distraction, but I don't think that's what's going on here."

My brother took a big gulp of his drink and flagged the bartender down again. "This ain't no distraction. These things are biting people." He shook his head. "Are these things always right here?"

"Think so," I answered. "Reality keeps them and us apart. The vibrations bring us together."

The bartender set another drink in front of Buford.

"And the fog?" He asked.

This time, I shrugged. "I'm guessing the fog is acting like the music box somehow."

"How are we supposed to fight fog, Hiram?" Buford wasn't attempting to hide his frustration. Since joining me and the Cavalry, he had been discovering just how frustrating monsters could be. I sympathized but didn't have the luxury of letting myself get frustrated. We needed a plan.

"We can't fight the fog," I explained, "but we can look into where it came from. The doctor said there were two men that went missing after meeting with our," I lowered my voice, "wizard. He said that the grocer, a Ms. Watts, might have seen where they went. We should talk to her."

I eyed the bartender, hoping he had overheard me mention the local woman. He had and stepped closer.

"You know her?" I asked.

The bartender was a mousy looking man with wisps of hair on his head and barely any stubble. He seemed at least a decade older than me or my brother, and he answered us over round spectacles.

"Certainly, Marshals," his voice was higher than I expected it to be. "Ms. Watts opens her store bright and early every morning at six. It doesn't get busy until a little closer to eight. You can find her then about two doors down from here."

I nodded my thanks and pointed at my brother's drink. "Finish up. That will give us time to figure out where this fog is coming from."

We checked our weapons over in our room. The saloon owner was going to be upset when they saw what I did to some of their towels. It probably wouldn't help, but we needed something to stop us from breathing the fog.

When the sun went down, we started walking the streets with our homemade bandanas on. Nobody gave us notice. The zealots seemed to have melted away. We saw none of them. The fog was at the thinnest it had been all day and it was hard to imagine it returning as it had.

Most of the few townsfolk we saw were also wearing masks, which let us know they were expecting an unnatural return of the fog as well.

Buford and I split up and walked alleys on opposite sides of the street. Barrenstand was a small town, but it had its fair share of dark corners.

We had been milling about Barrenstand for a few hours before my brother signaled me to join him. He was standing in the shadowed space between the saloon and the barbershop. It was a slim alley with crates and barrels making it seem all the more crowded.

"Notice something?" I asked.

Buford nodded. "Five men." He nodded toward the other end of the alley where moonlight shone on the dirt behind the buildings. "All carrying buckets of something. They are trying hard not to be noticed. Think I saw one of them pouring the bucket on the ground under a window of the saloon."

I had been wondering if this was something made by man or leaking in from elsewhere. It could still be coming from somewhere else and just being collected by these men, but they were clearly placing the town in danger.

Men were easy. Men could bleed and men could talk.

I gave Buford some ideas on what to do and then drew my pistol as I made my way toward the moonlight.

What my brother must have missed was the large wagon about thirty feet back from the buildings. All five of the masked men were standing at the back of it and reloading their buckets from two large barrels. I made no effort to hide myself, and they stopped moving as soon as the light touched my face.

"I was sent here by the government," I spoke up, keeping my gun aimed at the ground as I approached, "to find out about this fog. Any of you want to tell me what you're doing here?"

As one, they set down their buckets and drew their pistols. I stopped walking but otherwise didn't move my gun from where it aimed at the dirt.

"God has given us our path," the one still standing in the wagon spoke with confidence. "We shall not be moved."

One of them smacked another and pointed toward the front of the wagon, where Buford had managed to sneak close enough that aiming his shotgun wouldn't have been necessary.

The one standing in the wagon smirked and aimed his pistol at my brother while the rest kept their guns aimed at me.

"You're a little outnumbered," he said. He had a wild look in his eyes as he added, "We are protected by divine might."

I shook my head. "There's no need for a fight. The townsfolk have enough reason to be afraid right now. We just have some questions."

The moon couldn't show us everything, but I didn't need to see to feel the shift in the mood. Grips tightened and my instincts took over.

My pistol came up and barked as the man furthest from the wagon fired his. His shot went wide and mine didn't. Before he hit the ground, Buford's shotgun took out the man standing in the back of the wagon. His body flew out of the wagon and into the men on the ground, scattering them.

One of them was up and aiming at Buford with almost enough time to shoot my brother. Buford ended him with a second blast from his shotgun.

That left the last two men to make some serious decisions. The first looked to be not much older than a child while the other looked old enough to be his grandfather.

The child kept looking back and forth between Buford and myself so fast that I thought his head was going to twist off. The old man had already made his choice.

With more speed than his age implied he should have, he brought up his pistol and took aim at my chest. My bullet took him in the eye before he could pull the trigger.

Buford took aim on the kid, but I stopped him by yelling out.

"Hold your fire," I shouted.

The boy was unsure what to do. His eyes were spinning as he tried to keep both of us in his sights. I gave my brother a slight nod and he turned away from the kid so that he could calm the horses and start checking on the dead.

Behind the boy and out of sight.

"We didn't want a fight," I said to the kid.

His chest swelled as he spoke through his mask, obviously trying to look tougher than he was. "Well, you found one, didn't you?"

I felt sorry for the kid. When measured in years, it wasn't that long ago that I was sporting for a fight everywhere I went. A war changed that.

Holstering my pistol, I raised my hands. Buford's look was noticeably concerned, but he didn't stop what he was doing.

I slowly pointed at his friends. "God isn't going to protect you from a bullet. Not tonight. The arguments of man are too small for His attention. Before you try and shoot me," he needed to hear what I had to say, "you should know that I fought in the war."

"What side?" With how quick he spit out the question, I figured he must have a vested interest in the answer.

Personally, I hated that question. That war pitted family against family and anyone asking that question was looking to start a fight all over again. I didn't want that with this boy. I wanted the fighting to stop.

"It doesn't matter," I gave as my answer, "because every damn day there was someone begging me for a fight, somebody who swore they were going to put me down, and every damn day I was the one still standing." I sighed and lowered my hands. "Now, you can try it, and maybe you will be just another bad memory that I carry with me until the next damn day," I nodded to the saloon, "or we can sit and have a talk. My brother and I can buy you dinner and we can all have bad dreams tonight."

He tossed a glance at the barrels of stuff that they had been pouring into the buckets. It was the first time he had taken his eyes from me since I had started talking. Putting his pistol away, he nodded.

It was late and the saloon had mostly cleared out except for the handful of folks who I assumed never really left. While for some the comfort of their homes was the only relief they could find from the dream worms, others saw it differently, and dove into their bottles.

Our masks had done nothing to protect us from the fog. Nothing was dancing before my eyes yet, but I could see Buford's attention drifting and that he was only an hour or so away from being bitten.

The boy pulled down his mask when he sat, and it was plain to see that the folks that poured out the fog were not immune to its effects. His jaw was scarred by a fresh bite mark that looked as if it had only recently stopped bleeding.

Buford brought us all glasses of whiskey before going on the hunt for the cook.

I was against pressing the kid before he was ready, and chose to sit there quietly until he came around.

My brother returned with a plate of beans, which was more than I thought he was going to find this late. We both sat silently as the kid ate. Buford poured him another glass when his meal and the drink were gone.

He didn't drink it so much as stare into it, and I saw that as the most opportune time to start.

"What's your name?" I asked.

He didn't look up from his drink. "Ben."

"Alright, Ben. Why were you making this fog?" It had seeped into the bar, as I could only assume it did every night.

Ben looked around at it, obviously noticing something that I was not yet privy to. He shuddered.

"Mr. Miller, in the woods, paid us to."

I nodded slowly. "What is in the barrels?"

"I don't know," Ben shrugged. "Just about everything. I've seen Jim mixing the stuff but ain't ever seen the recipe. Horrible stuff, animal parts, and things I ain't never seen before. Mr.

Miller gave him the recipe I think."

"Is Mr. Miller the same wizard everyone is talking about?" Buford asked.

Ben shook his head at the question, "I wouldn't know anything about that. I don't come to town much." He finally took another sip of his drink. "I only saw him once. He's got a weird way of walking. Might have hurt himself or something. Jim was the one who met with him on the regular. He would give Jim the stuff to make it and on Mr. Miller's orders, Jim would use it to do God's work." He stared down into his drink again. "I guess he won't be doing that anymore."

"Do you know where we can find him?" I pushed past acknowledging that I had likely just killed his friend.

"He was about a mile south of town the one time I saw him." Ben shook his head. "That won't do you any good, though. He asked us to meet him there, but I don't think Jim had ever been there before."

"That don't help us at all," Buford was getting frustrated again and I didn't blame him. It seemed like a dead end, but we at least knew where the fog was coming from.

"Do you know how this Miller was getting hold of Jim?" I pressed.

Ben nodded, "The bounty board outside the jail. The town never gets much in the way of crime, so it started being used for announcements. The day we pour out the fog, he puts up the next meeting for supplies." He shook his head as if he just recalled something. "That won't do you any good, though. The Prisoner wrote it in a code of some kind."

"Prisoner?" Buford asked.

Ben shrugged, "That's what Jim called him once. It sounded like a name." The boy smirked. "Jim thought that perhaps Mr. Miller was a Prisoner from down in Tartarus, released to absolve the wicked of their sins." He waved at something that I still couldn't see. "These things are the divine intervention of an angel freed from Hell."

I ignored the new name and the idolatry. "Is there a meeting on there now?"

"I assume so," the kid polished off his drink. Between the

whiskey and our earlier encounter, it was obvious that the day was catching up with him. I spoke to the bartender and got the kid a room for the night.

"Why are you being so nice?" Ben asked.

I pointed in the general direction that their wagon of fog still rested. "Nice was my intention from the start. Your friends decided to take it a different route."

He said nothing to that and left for his room.

Buford poured us another drink. "If we can't read the board, we can wait for him."

I agreed. "As far as this Prisoner knows, Jim dealt out the fog. He will have put up a new notice." I tossed the last handful of bills on the table. Buford and I had to travel to specific outposts to get our government pay and we were overdue. We had taken a few odd jobs on farms in the last few months to keep ourselves fed but even that was running out.

"Finish your drink and get some shut-eye," I told my brother. He hated when I told him what to do, but he also knew that when we were on a job I was in charge. "I will watch the board tonight. When I get the message for Jim, I'll head to bed too."

"What about the," he waved his hand around in the air, indicating the creatures that I still could not see, "things?"

"They bite you yet?"

Buford shook his head.

"Then maybe we stopped Ben and his friends before they got the full evening's fog out." I shrugged. "You should be fine for the night."

My tone was anything but reassuring.

"Are you seeing them yet?" Buford asked.

Shaking my head, I made an effort to look where he had been waving his hand.

Nothing.

"Why is that, you think?" he pressed.

The question had been on the top of my mind for a while now, and hearing it out loud failed to make any revelations appear.

"It could be for any reason," I explained. "While you were minding the family properties, the Cavalry was getting inoculated against all sorts of nasty business. Or maybe I am protected by my strong belief in my badge and what it stands for." I smirked at Buford. "The more likely option is that I just don't breathe as hard as you. You're bigger than me, you probably have to breathe twice as hard to keep that body moving."

"Shut up, you." Buford scoffed and dug around in his shirt for a cigarette, choosing to chew on the tip for a bit instead of lighting it.

"And what if the Prisoner makes a show?" Buford turned his attention back to the evening's plan.

He asked a good question. The answer depended on what exactly the Prisoner was.

"You mean Mr. Atticus Miller? If he's a person, then I will talk to him if he's willing to hear what I have to say."

Buford finished his drink and asked, "What if he's something else?"

My brother believed that people were the worst monsters, and sometimes he was right. I was not as sure as he was this time around. Fogs made from some sort of alchemy and making people see ghost creatures from another world sounded less like the person kind of monster and more like what the Esoteric Cavalry was formed for.

"Then we kill it," I said.

I didn't wait to see if Buford ordered another drink with our dwindling billfold or if he headed to bed. As I put the mask into my pocket, I let my hand touch the pistol at my hip. The fog would get to me sooner or later, and the mask hadn't helped Buford. I was of the thinking that if they could bite me, then I could shoot them, and was looking forward to testing my theory.

The jail was a small one-room building with a porch that looked like it was about to collapse. A light was on inside. It could have been the sheriff, but I doubted it. Normally, the local law would have introduced themselves by now. Barrenstand either didn't have a peacekeeper, or they were out of town.

Another thought hit me. If I was going to make an entire town see demons from the pits of Hell for whatever my plan was, then I might see a need to relieve the town of its sheriff.

The bounty board was anything but. A square board was nailed to the side of the left side of the jail. It was half covered by a run-down wagon leaning against the building. The board was covered in flyers about bake-offs, church gatherings, and daily menus for the saloon. There wasn't a bounty on the board.

The notice was harder to find than I had expected it would be. Underneath flyers and other papers near the bottom of the board was a torn corner of leather with a branded letter and number on it. It was held in place by a nail. I pulled up the edge to look at the back but left it in place so Atticus Miller wouldn't know I had been here. There was nothing on the reverse side.

The brand on the front read, "E3."

Coordinates or a code, probably. I had seen communications like this before, both inside and outside of the conflict. Whatever it meant, it would be useless to me without some key to solve it.

That left me with waiting for the Prisoner to arrive and replace the message. Perhaps then I could follow him.

I spared a glance toward the saloon. It had a porch with no light and an unoccupied rocking chair. It wouldn't be difficult to see the board from there and sit in comfort while I did it.

Pain filled my mind. I fell to the ground, clutching at my head. In the back of my mind, I faintly remembered that I had a badge.

It was in my grip before I realized I had let go of my skull. My fingers reflexively felt the edges as it dug into my palm and the tighter that I gripped it, the more the pain was pushed back from the front of my brain.

"You are not James," a deep voice filled my head.

"Why are calling yourself the 'Prisoner?'" Getting information before he made my mind explode was my only goal. "You never told Jim your name. Why?"

"Bold of you to demand answers from me as the grip on your mind is so tight." He grew quiet and more pressure filled my mind as tendrils of thought burrowed into my skull. "Ah, you are a fighter. A soldier. I fought in that war, too." More slithering in my skull. "It would seem I fared better than you did."

Trying to change the subject and push the feelers from

my mind, I repeated the question, "Why did Jim call you the 'Prisoner'?"

"It is what I am. Atticus Miller is the body. I am the mind. A prisoner in your world. A prisoner in your primitive time. A prisoner in your flesh. Tell me," the Prisoner's tone shifted, "why are you looking for me?"

I ignored his question. "Why does Barrenstand call you a wizard?"

"You were sent by your government," he worked out. "Why?"

"Making critters appear out of thin air tends to get their attention," I said through gritted teeth. "You can't keep the frontier peace when everyone thinks they've gone crazy."

The Prisoner sighed. "That is an unfortunate side effect."

"A side effect?" I forced my eyes open and tried to peer through the night. Atticus had seen me at the board. He had to be close. "Side effect of what?"

"Go home, soldier," his mental sigh conveyed his annoyance with my investigation. "These people will survive. I am not your problem."

It was tempting to believe this voice in my head. He was hobbling me with his thoughts. How was I expected to stop him when I couldn't even see him? It would be easier to just move on to the next job.

Except that wasn't why Captain Fitz gave me my commission. Easy was the path that I tended to avoid.

Easy roads were paved by evil intentions.

"Even without orders, I don't think that I could do that," his disappointment radiated in my brain. "You claim not to be my problem, but you never told me what your crime was. Why are you a prisoner? In my line of work, people don't get imprisoned for no reason. Sometimes the wrong reason, though. Maybe tell me what you did, and maybe I can be on my way."

"Why," his violation of my mind intensified, "is your primitive brain not panicked by - oh," something like laughter threatened to knock me cold, "you hold no fears of the strange. You have seen the things from beyond." His laughter continued. "You are enlightened for a primitive."

The burning pain was becoming too much. Tears blurred my vision and the world shook.

Spit flew from my mouth as I said, "I am coming for you."

"This is your last warning," Atticus responded. "Leave."

Something slapped my forehead and the pressure from the Prisoner's presence vanished. I collapsed to the ground and looked up to see Buford holding something to my head. I grabbed his hand and the thing inside of it.

It was his badge.

"Thanks," I gasped. He helped me to my feet and we both looked in every direction for Atticus Miller.

"What are you doing here?" I demanded.

He shrugged. "Not enough booze in that bar to help me get to sleep with biting worms floating all around me." He nodded toward my still clenched fist. Blood dripped from it. "Seemed a smart idea to follow you in case you needed backup."

I pried my hand open. Blood pooled in my palm underneath my Cavalry badge. My grip had been such that the corners of the star had burrowed into my hand in much the same way that the Prisoner had been burrowing into my mind.

After seeing that I was alright, Buford brought up his pistol and scanned the night.

"Was that him?" he asked over his shoulder.

"Yes," I drew my gun and joined him. "If he's as smart as he thinks he is, he should have ducked out by now."

"Back to the saloon," Buford said. "Let's get you bandaged."

We ran back to the bar, Buford grabbing a bottle from the bartender and smiling back at me. "To sleep with all the things in the air."

Sleep failed to come easy, even with Buford's libations. Ignoring the space worms, we still had to concern ourselves with Miller's mental powers. Buford came up with a less-than-elegant solution that only could have come from his booze-addled mind. Per his suggestion, we took the bandanas that we had previously used for the fog and tied them to our foreheads. Underneath the bandanas, pin out, were our badges, placing the protective ward of the Elder Sign directly against our flesh.

It bought us at least a few hours of decent sleep, but I still woke less than well rested.

By morning, I could see the worms from beyond floating around the room.

Worms was a generic term that, while I could understand how the town got to calling them that, didn't fit these creatures at all.

They were long, wrinkled bodies of pink flesh with large openings where one would assume a head should be. The openings were filled with teeth of different sizes. Covering the bodies, and what made them the least like worms, were a mixture of limbs and none of them matched. Wings, arms, legs, tentacles, and things I had never seen before made these abominations seem even less like beasts of our world.

I tested touching one of them as it floated by my bed. There was only a small bit of resistance as my finger passed through it. They weren't solid, yet, so I still had time before I was driven as mad as the rest of the town ought to have been feeling.

I started when realization dawned that I was being watched. Buford sat at the end of my bed, his feet up on the edge while he waggled a piece of bacon at me.

"Up and at'em," he tossed the bacon at me. "We've got work to do."

The bacon only made me hungry for more food, but Buford was right. I would have to eat on the run.

"Where'd you get the bacon?" I demanded. My head throbbed and I doubted it was from the booze I had used to fall asleep. Whatever the Prisoner used to talk to my mind was less than gentle.

"Nah, you don't get the wonderful breakfast I just went and cooked up unless you're up with the asscrack of dawn," Buford smiled at me with bacon still hanging from his mouth.

"Don't be a shit," I looked past him and saw the plate on the table. "Did you use the kitchen downstairs?" I asked as I made myself a sandwich with the toast and bacon. There was one egg left, and I appreciated that he saved me that much. Buford wasn't a small man and saving me any food was an immensely generous offer.

He nodded, "They offered me a job."

"What?" I waved my hands around to indicate the alien worms behaving like spirits as they passed through us and the walls of the room. "You would leave behind all of this majesty and wonder to be a cook in a saloon?"

Buford laughed. "The idea crossed my mind." His face sobered up. "We heading over to meet Ms. Watts?"

Nodding, I finished getting dressed by tying on my holster. "Miller knows we're here, but she's still the best option for finding out what direction he might be hiding in."

"I don't like the prey knowing we're hunting," Buford let out a sigh. "It ain't right. It makes us the prey."

My hat was resting on the end of my bed. I scooped it up and slapped Buford on the shoulder. "Don't count us out yet, brother." I smiled. "This dog knows a few more tricks. We'll flush him out."

Anna Watts was still opening her shop up when we came into the general store.

"You boys can turn right around," she said the moment she saw us. "There's nothing I can say that will help you with whatever you're doing, and I don't want no trouble in my shop."

"Excuse me? Ms. Watts, is it?" I asked. "I'm Hiram Cart—"

"I know who you both are," she cut me off. "You're the Marshals who came to get the wizard."

Buford raised his eyebrow at me. "Does everybody know more than we do?" he said under his breath.

"That's more or less accurate, ma'am," I said. "We don't want any trouble, either. We just wanted to ask you some questions and then we'll be on our way."

"Like you questioned Jim?" She put her hands on her hips.

"Ms. Watts," I said, resisting the urge to place my hand on my holster, "we only wanted to talk to Jim. He pulled his gun on us, and we defended ourselves."

Buford nodded. "You can ask Mr. Ben, at the saloon. He didn't draw his gun on us, and he's enjoying a late morning at the saloon."

"Jim was a piece of shit," Ms. Watt's features softened, "but he didn't deserve to die."

I nodded, "No, ma'am. In my years, I have come to the conclusion that most people don't deserve to die. It just happens to find them in the end."

She returned my nod, but I doubted she was listening so much as weighing the truth of our story against whatever rumors she had already heard that morning.

"Ask your questions," she waved at the shelves, "and buy some goods or you're wasting my time."

I handed the last of our cash to Buford and waved him toward the shelves.

Anna Watts was a wiry woman a little older than myself. She had thick blonde hair and wore long clothes. She also kept a pistol in the back of her apron. Judging by her demeanor, she knew how to use it.

While Buford attempted to shop, I questioned Ms. Watts.

"What do you know about this wizard?"

"Nothing anybody else can't tell you," she shrugged and continued stocking the shelves. "He showed up, dreams started happening," she pulled back her thick hair and revealed a bite mark on her neck, "bastards started biting me."

She poked me in the chest then. "Tell me something, Marshal. Am I crazy, or are these wrigglers real?"

"They seem real to me," I answered carefully, "but maybe not in a sense we are aware of."

The corner of her mouth turned up in a grin. "Now you're the one sounding crazy."

Her words made me shudder. My everyday worries were that I might be insane.

"The doctor says you saw the two men that went missing?" I said to change the subject and move the questioning along.

Anna shook her head. "They didn't go missing, and if our sheriff was as good at his job as he was at gossip then you might not be needed." She pointed out past the window toward the saloon. "They were taken. The wizard came up in a wagon and …" she stopped, seemingly not trusting her own memory.

"And?"

"Well," she almost seemed angry at having to say it, "he waved at them and they fell over. He didn't have a gun but they just fell. I don't think they were dead." Ms. Watts pointed out the window at the revelers in the street. "And they weren't none of his worshippers either. Those go with him willingly. These were just normal folks who had too much to drink."

"Then he took them?" I asked.

Anna nodded, "As if they had no weight to them. He just picked them up and tossed them into the wagon."

Buford was suddenly beside us, his arms filled with various groceries. "Which way did he go?"

"Anyone in town could tell you where he is," she sighed. "They are all too scared."

We stood there, watching her, waiting to see if she would tell us.

"He went north," Anna said finally. "He's staying at the old Wright place. Everyone knows it," she waved her hands toward the saloon again, "but they know he makes people disappear, too."

Buford dropped everything he was holding onto the counter and came back with a map and a piece of charcoal. "Can you show us where this Wright place is?"

We left Ms. Watts' place once she had finished marking the map. I told her that if she was feeling unsafe, she could find us at the saloon. She was less than enthusiastic about our security.

"You go after that wizard," she had said, "you'll be dead by morning."

Buford and I didn't wait. We went to the stables and gathered our horses. Antilles was antsy to get a move on. The years in the war and travelling the middle states had made him an animal who did not enjoy the stables.

Before we left, we checked our guns and secured our badges. The Prisoner had already showed us he was willing to defend himself. We couldn't let him catch us unprepared again.

We rode three miles north of town before we came across anything of notice. The map showed the Wright cabin still ahead of us by more than two miles, but what we found was certainly the work of the 'wizard.'

"What am I looking at?" I asked out loud.

Buford reached down from his horse and poked it with his

shotgun. "Looks like somebody stitched a bear with something."

"There's no stitching," I said. I hopped down from Antilles and got closer to the dead thing.

It was a mix of animals. Buford was wrong about the stitching, though. This was one animal. It had the body and size of a bear with large wings. Even with how big the wings were, there was no way they could lift this body from the ground. The head was a mix of bird and human in a horrific way. The eyes were human, and the rest of the face was bird with a beak that had teeth that belonged, again, to a bear. Feathers came up from the neck and shifted to course hair that wasn't human.

This mix of hair and feathers covered the entire body in uneven intervals.

The largest oddity was the hands, or paws. The thing's hind legs ended in human feet with the toes ending in claws, or talons. I couldn't tell which. The front paws didn't match at all. The left paw was a human hand ending in more claws. The right paw was the most normal bear thing on the entire creature which made it stand out.

"What is it?" Buford gagged. "Why does it smell like that?"

I shook my head and looked up at my brother. "It's not natural."

"The Prisoner did this?" he asked me.

"That would be my guess," I answered. "He made some sort of mix-and-match monster."

"But why?" My brother shook his head at the idea.

Then he brought his shotgun up to his shoulder, aiming directly at my head.

If anybody else had done that I would be dead to rights. This wasn't just anybody.

This was Buford.

He wouldn't aim his gun at me.

I spun and drew my pistol in one move. The mix-and-match bear thing loomed over me.

I got two shots off before the human hand with claws grabbed me around the neck and threw me directly up and into the air.

It might have been a mostly human hand but it was bona

fide bear strength that tossed me.

As I hit the branches above us, I heard Buford shout and fire two shots from his shotgun.

I hit the ground hard and didn't have a chance to recover before the bear-thing pounced on my back. My mind went blank as the wind left my chest. Its claws pierced through my jacket and into my flesh as it crushed me with its weight.

Another explosion of sound and the pressure disappeared from my back. I didn't wait for it to jump on me again and rolled to the side. Somehow, during my flight and landing, I hadn't let go of my pistol.

Buford stood on the far side of the bear-thing, blood covering the side of his head. He pumped his shotgun, fired, pumped, and fired.

I took my time, aimed at the body of the beast, and then shifted up. With the thing's focus on Buford, I emptied my gun into its head.

It collapsed almost exactly where we had found it the first time. My brother shot it twice more at the base of its man-bird skull.

Buford stood there, not lowering his gun, breathing heavily.

"What are you panting about?" I demanded. "At least you stayed on the ground."

"It-it..." he was struggling to speak. "It flew at me, Hiram. With wings." He pointed at a cut along the side of his head. "Tried to eat me."

"Why'd it look dead when we got here?" I asked.

Buford was in no place to answer. The idea came to me as I stared at the corpse.

"It was dying." I said.

"That thing wasn't dead." Buford finally lowered his shotgun and moved to collect his horse.

"Not dead," I answered. "It was dying, then food showed up."

"I ain't food," Buford shouted. "I ain't never been food. I won't ever be food." He handed me the reins of his horse and walked over to shoot the mix-and-match bear-thing again. "Not food," he screamed at it.

He was not handling our encounter well.

I collected Antilles while Buford whispered crazy at his horse. I approached him once he had calmed down enough to climb up and into the saddle.

"This shit ain't gonna get calmer before it gets worse," I said to him. "Can you keep it together?"

He nodded at the monster, "I stayed cool. It died. I ain't gotta be alright with being eaten."

"No," I agreed. "You don't."

"If it gets worse," he said calmly but with a steel in his voice, "I will deal with it." He looked me in the eyes, "Nobody is eating you either."

I couldn't help myself and my laughter filled the surrounding woods.

"I won't let anyone eat you either." I climbed onto Antilles.

We continued our ride north and discovered what could only be more evidence of the Prisoner's unusual experiments. Pits were dug without any predictable pattern throughout the forest. Trees would be almost side by side and a hole would be directly between them. We were forced to tie off our horses and continue on foot so as to not risk breaking their legs.

We bent and inspected several of the holes. Each one had a pile of what looked like fine ash inside it.

I pinched some of it and sniffed it.

"That's ash," I confirmed for my brother.

"Are these graves?" he asked.

I shook my head. "This Prisoner isn't a person like we are. His methods aren't ours. It's unlikely we'll have any understanding of what this really is."

"Are you entirely incapable of instilling confidence?" Buford was frowning down at me and not even looking into the holes. "This Prisoner knows we're coming. He has power beyond human reckoning. He has space worms biting everybody and hodgepodge monsters at his command, and now you're telling me we can't even call his ash-holes graves?"

I shrugged in response. Everything my brother listed was accurate. "It's our responsibility to put a stop to him."

"How are we going to do that?" he demanded.

I stood and patted my gun belt. "We have guns and our badges for protection. That's more than we had in the War Eagle Caverns. That battle raged for days, and the Cavalry survived without guns at all."

"You're just saying shit to make me feel better." Buford rested his shotgun on his shoulder. "It isn't working."

"Toughen up, buttercup," I smirked.

The holes were everywhere and, while they were shallow, they were deep enough that we would break our own ankles if we didn't pay close attention to where we stepped.

By our understanding of the map, we had less than a mile to go before we would be at the Wright place. The boy at the stables had mentioned the place was mostly avoided long before the Prisoner had moved in. Everybody thought it was haunted on account of the weird things that happened to the Wright family.

He implied they had all gotten sick and died and would not get into it further. It wasn't long after they died that the 'wizard' moved in.

That bear-thing had human features.

Puzzle pieces were showing themselves, but no matter how I wriggled them, they weren't falling into place.

We took our time moving through the trees. After about an hour more of walking, we came to the edge of the Wright property.

The property was surrounded by an old fence that had not seen upkeep in years. The house fared no better. Smoke poured from the chimney and the porch looked like it was about to collapse.

Buford and I stood at the tree line and took stock of the situation. We had no doubts that the Prisoner was in there, but he was not alone. Ten to fifteen armed men stalked the property. From the descriptions we had of the two vagrants that the Prisoner had taken, it was clear that they were not among Miller's followers.

"What makes you think they're more religious nuts and not hired on?" Buford asked when I told him my thoughts.

I shrugged. "One way or another, he's a being from another world making monsters and summoning ghost worms. Do you know anybody who would throw in with that?"

"There's all types," my brother chose to dismiss the conversation. "What's the plan?"

If I were still with Captain Fitz and the rest of the Cavalry, the entire plan could be laid out and understood by all our members by saying two words: Devil's Crossing. They would remember how we approached the hideout at Devil's Crossing, silently taking out the members of the gang one by one until the numbers were more manageable for a frontal assault.

That was not the case anymore. I had been tasked with expanding the United States Esoteric Cavalry beyond the war and into the west, and the only permanent member of the new Cavalry was my brother.

And he had not been at Devil's Crossing.

"Silently," I explained. "We move in quietly, careful to stay out of sight. No guns, just knives."

Buford pulled his hatchet from his belt. "Or this?"

"That'll do," I agreed. At that moment, I remembered who I was talking to. "If you can't do it without being seen, then don't do it. Hide the ones you kill." I smacked his arm and repeated, "Quietly. If you can't do it without being seen, then don't do it."

My brother was obviously annoyed. "I understand. Can we get started already?"

Even if he hadn't been my brother and someone who I knew better than anyone else, he had a look in his eye that haunted the eyes of every kid on the battlefield. He was eager to get started. He had his own plan.

After the way Buford reacted after the hodgepodge bear-thing attacked us, I decided to try one more time.

"Stick to the plan, Buford," I gripped his arm and used what he had referred to as my 'soldier voice.'

He nodded and stepped over the fence. He crouched and ran toward the front of the house. I followed before diverting to the back of the house. Before he fell out of sight, I saw him drive his hatchet into the neck of the man closest to where we were starting. He was a short man and was scraping his boots on the siding of the Wright place. He never saw Buford coming.

I stopped at the corner and looked around it. I started as a bright purple worm with spider legs floated into my face and through me. It took everything to not let out a yelp of surprise. The worms never bothered us on the entire ride into the Wright place and had slipped my mind almost entirely.

I focused my nerves and turned back to the task at hand.

The back of the house did not have a porch. Instead, it had stairs with a railing and not much more. An overgrown plot showed where the Wrights must have kept their garden when they lived here.

Two of Miller's followers stood back there, cradling rifles and a pistol on their hips.

I drew my knife and kept close to the house as I moved in.

My knife went in the first man's neck at an angle. He gurgled, clutched his throat, and fell over. His brother in the church of alien convicts spun on me the moment he noticed something was happening.

Before he could bring up his rifle, I twisted and tackled him around the waist. My arms pinned the rifle to his side and down so he could not use it on me. Once I was on top of him, I drove my knife into his windpipe.

That was when I noticed the third man walking up from the far side of the property. He saw everything I had done and was running at me with a pistol raised.

Wasting no time, I leaped to my feet and threw my knife as hard as I could. It hit him in the eye. His feet kept moving as he fell backward, slumping into the long grass.

Thunder erupted from all around me. Every window that I could see shattered with the roar. I fell to the ground and quickly recovered, leaping back up to my feet and drawing my pistol.

The noise surprised me to the point of confusion. Confused or not, I didn't have time to ponder what it meant.

The back door burst open and a line of six men came running down the stairs.

The first three collapsed, shot dead, in the dirt before they realized I was standing there. The two in the back dove over the railing and sidestepped to the sides of the house, firing wildly in my direction. The one still on the stairs stood his ground and shot at me rapidly.

Sprinting, I met up with the dead form of the man who had been coming up to the house. I grabbed my knife and pulled his body over me just as bullets slammed into it.

Firing around my cover, I hit the man on the stairs but was wide on the two spreading out from the house. Then one of them went down, but not from anything I had done. As he fell forward, I saw the hatchet sticking out of the back of his head. Buford was there, pulling it free before turning and shooting the final member of Atticus Miller's congregation.

Buford came over and helped me to my feet.

"What was that noise?" I demanded.

Buford looked back toward the house. "One of them had a box of dynamite."

"So, you were seen, and they tried blowing you up?"

My brother shook his head. "Nah, I snuck up and lit it."

I punched him in the chest.

"We had a damned strategy," I shouted at him. "You almost got me killed."

"Your way," he wheezed, "was boring."

"My way," I countered, "wouldn't have alerted our target to us being here."

He straightened, still trying to catch his breath. "Alright," he said, "that's a fair point." He shrugged and looked back at the house with its windows shattered and the smell of fire coming from wherever the dynamite had gone off. "Maybe he didn't hear it?"

The smack that I delivered to the back of Buford's head was not nearly as strong as he deserved.

The back door to the cabin burst open again as I finished reloading my pistol. This time it was with such force that the door ripped from its hinges and fell to the ground.

An older man stomped down the stairs. He was bald except at his temples and had a long and wiry beard. His clothes were stained in dark greens and reds. He looked frail in body while his spirit and the look behind his eyes looked stronger than anyone I had ever crossed before.

Each of his steps looked purposeful and well thought out. He moved with speed but had to expend mental energies to control the forward momentum of his body. When Ben had said that Atticus Miller had an odd gait, this was what he had meant.

Even with his pale skin, he still looked entirely human. The only sign that this was our quarry was the thick scars covering every inch of his exposed flesh. It looked like a bear had mauled him.

Buford brought up his shotgun at the same time that I brought up my pistol and we fired at the Prisoner.

He kept walking at us as the bullets hit him. We didn't see any blood, but we didn't stop shooting, either.

When he was within arm's length of us, Buford swung at the Prisoner with the butt of his shotgun. He ducked the swing with the grace of a much younger man and quickly placed his palm on my brother's forehead. Buford collapsed.

As my brother fell, I kicked out. My boot connected with the Prisoner's chest and sent him back a few steps. My gun was empty at this point, and I couldn't let the Prisoner touch me.

On the other hand, I couldn't just run and leave Buford with this wizard, either.

"Screw it," I grunted before lunging at the Prisoner's midriff.

I was pleased to hear him wheeze as the wind was knocked out of him. His body hit the dirt hard with me on top. I flipped my empty pistol over and started beating him. As his hands reached for me, I beat them away.

For all my pistol-whipping, there was no blood or sign of injury on the Prisoner's face.

He finally decided that trying to grab my face was a waste of time and instead turned to fighting back. The would-be wizard brought his arm back and punched up and into my chest.

The world went white.

I hit the ground, wheezing through tears as I struggled to breathe. The force of his blow had launched me off him and sent pain tearing through me.

My vision returned just as the Prisoner reached for my skull.

The white was replaced with black.

We woke up in what I suspected to be the former Wright home. Buford and I were tied to a beam in the main room. The only furniture was a table taking up the length of the wall. It was covered in bottles of things that I could not make out. There were two other rooms on the right side if you faced the front door. I couldn't see what was in those rooms.

The room we were in had three holes carved into the floor and then into the dirt under the house. Each hole went about three feet deep, and they were wide enough to fit a corpse if you folded the legs up to the chest.

I knew this last bit because two of the holes were already filled with the bodies of who I assumed had to have been the missing drunks that Ms. Watts had seen with the Prisoner.

I was tied up, facing the holes and the front of the house. Buford was tied to the other side of the beam with his back to mine.

"You awake, Hiram?" he wasn't whispering as he asked.

"Yeah," I answered. "He got in our heads."

"He left through the door on my side a few minutes ago," Buford explained. "I've been working at the knots but they're tight. Can you see anything?"

"I found Ms. Watt's drunks," I said and then proceeded to explain what I could see on my side of the house.

Buford then did the same.

"There's some sort of kitchen on this side. A stove and cupboards, but everything looks empty."

I strained my neck to see what he was describing. The edge of the stove was visible, but not much else.

"Shit—" Buford yelped as a door behind me opened.

"Ah," Atticus Miller said, "you're awake." Buford grunted as the Miller kicked him. "You are both of hearty stock. Scars do that." He kicked Buford again. "Your body," he came around to me and grabbed me by the chin, "and your mind. Scars all over you both."

His breath smelled like nothing I had ever come across before. The rancid smell of rot combined with a sweet smell of something new that I couldn't place. His voice was akin to rocks being ground together. How he made that sound without hurting his throat, I did not know.

When he let go of my chin and stepped back, I saw what was in his hands.

He was carrying a bucket that had fog pouring out of it.

"What are you doing to the town?" I demanded.

Miller set the bucket down between Buford and me, out of our reach. The fog continued to pour out and surround us.

"My plans have accelerated now that your government knows I'm here," he explained. He indicated the fog bucket. "As far as the town is concerned, that's the good news. Life will return to normal for them as the transformative wears off." He grunted and I couldn't tell if it was a laugh or a sound of disgust. So much of the way he moved and sounded came out as if he didn't belong here. "Unfortunately for you, that is where the good news ends."

That sickly smell continued to fill the room, almost as if it was part of the fog surrounding us.

Without the mask, Buford and I began inhaling the fumes. We were so close to the source this time that the room began filling with those devilish creatures within minutes. As the critters floated around us, I heard Buford yelp.

I soon saw why.

The worms were becoming more real as we breathed in the fog. We had realized before that the fog let us see these things, and now we were seeing them as if they were in the room with us.

Then one bit my arm.

I screamed as uneven rows of foreign teeth bit into my flesh through my coat.

Atticus grabbed the worm. Seeing him touch something that had previously been intangible was almost enough of a shock to distract me from the bite.

Almost.

Whatever he was doing, I needed to keep him distracted. If I could buy us some time, Buford or I might be able to loosen our ropes and tip the scales.

"What is with the religious doctrine?" I demanded.

Atticus still held the squirming creature but stopped to face me.

"Humans need something to believe in if they are to be," he tilted his head to consider the correct word to use, "useful.

They saw the," he made a noise I couldn't have repeated if my life depended on it that must have been the name for the worm things, "and assumed, maybe correctly, that they were demons from their Hell. I needed help. They provided, as long as I promised to protect them." He shrugged, and the very human gesture looked entirely alien on the Prisoner's stolen body. "Useful."

He returned to the pits and used both of his hands to tear the creature in half.

"Is this it?" I asked.

"What is he doing?" Buford hissed. He twisted as he tried to see what I was watching.

"I don't know," I answered. "Atticus," I repeated, "what is all this?"

The Prisoner held his hands over the pit on the left. He dropped the winged half of the worm thing. He shouted a noise that sounded a lot like what he had called the creatures. Bright light filled the pit and smoke mixed with the fog.

"I cannot escape," he clawed at his face, drawing blood in long streaks, "this, but I can leave. I can get revenge for being put here."

"How?" I shifted as I pulled at my bonds. "How are you going to leave? What did they have to do with this?" I nodded toward the corpses in the hole.

"Experiments," he answered. "I need to test the process on them before I try it on myself. There's no going back."

"The bear in the woods," Buford put together. "You're mixing critters so you can leave? Where would you go?"

"Out," Atticus shouted as he dropped the second piece of the worm creature into the second pit. He barked the word and light filled the second pit. More smoke mixed with the fog.

"The stars," I translated for him. "He wants to go home."

"What?" Buford asked. "Oh," he thought about it. "The bear had wings. Is he trying to mix the space worms with people?"

"I think so."

"When broken down to their essential salts," Atticus spoke to no one in particular, "they can be reconstituted. Mix those essential salts between species and you can share traits between them."

Buford and I understood. Atticus Miller wanted to mix the different parts of the space worms with people to see if he could use them to escape our world and go home. Now we just had to stop him.

My brother's hand brushed mine. He was free.

"How are you going to do it to yourself?" I needed to get myself free. Buford slid a knife into my hand.

"The process is in place," Atticus grabbed a pitcher and poured a red liquid into each of the pits. The smoke grew worse, and the room filled with a smell of rot. It was then that I realized that burning the drunkards, or whatever he had done to them, hadn't created any stink.

The pits swelled and bubbled over before retracting back and forming into fleshy shapes.

My ropes snapped. I jumped to my feet and spun to Buford.

I might have been facing Atticus and his creatures, but Buford was facing our guns.

He tossed me my pistol and belt. Atticus Miller was occupied watching his monsters grow from the goop. We reloaded our guns and turned them on the Prisoner.

Whatever power he was using when we first fired on him wasn't in use now. Our bullets struck him and knocked him down toward the goop monster on the left.

Bullets or not, he roared at us from the pit. Then Atticus barked the word that burned the bodies before. He was brighter than the sun. We didn't stop shooting.

The Prisoner collapsed in the light, taking whatever had been growing in the pit with him.

He was still holding the pitcher when he collapsed. The chemicals in it went to work immediately and the pit frothed over again.

We had no time to see what was going on with that.

The creature in the pit on the right finished coming together.

Standing in that pit was a mostly human naked thing. It was a mix of human skin and pink worm muscle. The former drunkard's head was a mix of eyes and gray hair. The eyes were still human but the mind behind them looked mad. Where the mouth should have been was a large hole of teeth.

"Look at those arms," Buford gasped. He was right. There were two elbows on each arm and they stretched to twice the length they should have been. Instead of hands, each arm ended in two wiggly bits like fat sausages.

"What is it?" Buford asked.

I shook my head. "Tough. It looks tough."

We turned our guns on it next.

The beast jerked and writhed under our attack. A mixture of blood and some sort of gas leaked from every wound. Every hole we put into the monster's body only seemed to annoy it.

It was easy to see that whatever had been left of the man had become replaced by the insanity of combining a person with a creature not from our world. It clawed at its face. New life, rebirth, or whatever the hell was going on wasn't something it was happy to be experiencing. In a fit of rage, it roared and ran at us.

I had figured the thing would use its huge mouth to bite us, but it didn't act like it knew it even had it. It grabbed at us with those tentacle fingers and ignored our bullets punching holes through it. Its long fingers felt like they had no bones as they wrapped around our chests and threw us.

The force of the throw would have killed us in a younger house. We crashed through the wall of the kitchen. A bell sound followed by an urge to be sick took me a moment to understand. Grass was clumped in my mouth. I spit it out and looked around. Buford was climbing to his feet, and we were outside where I had killed the men in the back. The stove pipe from the kitchen was lying next to me and it took me a while to connect that to my aching head and dizziness.

My gun was a few feet from me. I must have lost it as the monster demolished the kitchen wall with my body. I crawled to it and reloaded it, noting that my ammo was running low. We needed to put this beast down.

Any remorse that I might have had for killing one of the townspeople was not there. Atticus Miller, or whatever he had become, was responsible for that. This would be putting down a man who would not want to live.

Buford was shouting at me. My head was still spinning. I

shook my head and looked at him.

"-is my shotgun?" He was crawling in the grass too. Behind him, the tentacled fingered thing was crawling from the mess of the kitchen and moving toward him.

I didn't see his gun anywhere.

An idea sprung up somewhere in my hurting mind.

I dug into my jacket. I pulled out a pack of matches and threw them at Buford.

He caught them with a look of complete confusion.

"I said my shotgu—" he stopped when he realized he couldn't keep secrets from his brother.

The monster's mouth opened wider, and I worked on emptying my pistol into it again. Buford needed a minute to get ready. My bullets weren't stopping it so much as pissing it off. It turned away from Buford and ran at me.

Sometime since we were in the Wright kitchen, this thing had learned what its mouth was for. It grabbed me around the gut and drew me in. I shoved my pistol in and emptied it again into where I hoped its brain had been.

It dropped me and rocked back just as a lit stick of dynamite landed at our feet.

I turned and ran, spinning to see what the monster was doing before the stick exploded.

The beast still had a human mind somewhere inside of it. Looking down at the stick of dynamite, it connected to what it had once been, and its eyes went wide.

Then I saw something that surprised me. The surprise disappeared and it sat down still about two feet from the stick of dynamite.

The explosion was bigger than I expected. That, or the noise had mixed with my still-rattled brain. I fell to my knees and collapsed on the ground. Darkness filled the edge of my sight.

The ground was rocking. It wasn't a quake, but like I was lying in a rocking chair.

I opened my eyes to see Buford, holding a pistol that didn't belong to him in each hand and rocking me hard.

"You gotta get up, brother," he stood and fired out of my sight. He was mumbling something. I could not make out what it was until I was finally to my feet.

"Damned demons from the pits of Hell. Space worms and then demons."

I turned my attention in the direction he was looking. The first thing I noticed was the crater filled with body parts where the monster was before. He had seen what he had become and chose to end it during a brief moment of lucid thought. It was desperate and unfortunate, but it was also the right choice to make.

I don't know that I could have made the same choice in his place, and I hoped that I would never have to find out.

The mess of carnage wasn't why Buford had shaken me back to the waking world.

Breaking out of what was left of the kitchen to the Wright place was something from my nightmares. It had three arms, two of them on its left side. One arm on either side had a second elbow, and each hand carried a few extra fingers. Its head was crowned with teeth surrounding a mouth positioned at the top of its head. Four mismatched eyes and no nose marred what would have been a human face in another situation. The face was mostly Atticus Miller's, but I could still make out the features that didn't match and belonged to the other drunk from Barrenstand. The entire body was an odd pink color. It looked like the worms from before.

The thing that made my brother mumble about demons while he shot at it with his weapons pilfered from the dead worshippers of this false prophet was that it had huge fleshy wings.

They were the same wings that the little worms had in various styles, but these matched the size of the beast holding them. Atticus looked like a demon nightmare straight from the pits of Hell and I couldn't help but remember that story of him being an angel escaped from Tartarus itself.

Atticus Miller, or what was left of him, let out a sound that was a mix between a train whistle and a bear.

"Home," he shouted. His voice still a mix of that shrill pitch and animal but he voiced it. "I can feel it. I can go home."

As he said it, I could see his arm beginning to fade from our world.

"He can go invisible?" Buford asked.

"No," I answered, "his plan is working. Those worm things can travel between worlds. He somehow mixed himself with one and is trying to leave."

My brother lowered his gun. "Then let him. I don't know about you, but I am done fighting giant monsters that want to eat me."

I shook my head. "He's called the Prisoner for a reason. Whatever he did, they locked him up down here to stop him from doing it again. We can't let him escape."

Buford's jaw tightened. "They ain't our problem. We have got plenty right here to worry about."

My brother was reacting much as I had at the beginning of the war, when I had first joined the Esoteric Cavalry. If the evil wanted to leave our world, then let it. Except that's never how it worked.

"Evil begets evil, Buford," I explained. "If we let him go and he starts killing in another world, what's to stop them coming here to retaliate?" I pointed at the still-fading Atticus Miller thing. "Or how about justice? Forget him and his alien crimes. This man tortured a town and killed at least two innocent men. We can't let him get away with that."

Buford's eyes softened and his shoulders tensed. "Alright, stop your preaching. You had me convinced with the justice thing. How do we stop him from disappearing?"

I shrugged and returned to firing my pistol.

My hope had been that to use his new magics, Atticus needed to concentrate. He might be an alien mind with more knowledge than we had, but a fish can't walk and whatever Atticus had been didn't know how to be what the worms were.

The mouth on top of his head roared in frustration as our bullets distracted him from his work. His body snapped back into our reality, but not completely. His arm was missing some of its fingers.

"Hey," Buford shouted as his pistols barked at the monster, "our bullets are making holes this time."

He was right. When Atticus Miller first came running out of

his borrowed cabin to confront us, our bullets had bounced off of him or somehow missed their target. We couldn't hurt him for nothing. Not so much, now. Holes opened in him with every shot we took.

Our heads were empty of his mind powers as well. Either he was too distracted with his escape and our bullets to attack us or, more than likely, he had lost that power when he combined with the thing from space.

Atticus Miller was not going to stand there and let us shoot him. He began tossing the nearest corpses at us, scooping them up as if they weighed nothing and throwing them. Buford jumped over one and I stepped to the side to avoid another. When Atticus ran out of bodies, his many-fingered hands grabbed at pistols. The ground was covered in the dropped weapons from his fallen congregation, and in seconds he was firing at us with four separate weapons. On the demon's back, his wings began to shudder. They weren't flapping, but Atticus still lifted from the ground. Whatever propelled his demonic flight was not from this world.

Buford and I took cover as much as we could. My brother dove behind the nearby fence that surrounded the property and I ran. It looked as though I might have been running away. I took off toward the side of the house and circled around to the front.

Atticus didn't have full control over his new body yet and was only able to get about as high as the roof. He didn't have a shot with me at the front of the house, so he rained down his lead and gun smoke solely on my brother.

The front of the house was mostly in one piece. Buford's stunt with the dynamite took out most of a wagon and there were just about as many bodies on the ground as there had been in the back. We had obviously miscounted from our poor vantage point.

I ran to the front porch, which looked to be as simple as the back, except with a roof and railings around a small landing.

The railings made for an excellent ladder as I used them to climb up high enough to pull myself on to the lower porch roof. The slant wasn't that bad and soon I was standing and pulling myself up onto the roof proper.

From this angle I could see Buford struggling to not get shot. He was a big man hiding behind the post of a short fence. I moved quickly across the roof until I got to the kitchen. When Atticus had burst through the wall, he had taken some of the roof with him.

I stepped back toward the center of the roof and ran at the broken edge. I drew my knife and leaped from the roof top.

The blade of my knife sunk into the back of the Atticus-demon, but it didn't want to stay. I grabbed at his wings to hold on as his arms twisted around to fire at me.

I pulled myself up onto the critter's back and wrapped my legs around his waist. Atticus's head was bending back to put that tooth filled mouth on my own. I stabbed up and down into his neck before he could.

When Atticus figured out that his arms couldn't reach me, he spun in the air. I wasn't sure he knew how to direct his flight, and we began to fall.

I only had one chance to stop this thing and bring justice to whomever he had wronged.

He spun fast enough to finally toss me, and I crashed back into the kitchen of the Wright home. I stood and pain shot through my left leg, where a hunk of wood had been lodged.

I pulled the wood out and tried not to ignore the rush of blood and pain as I stood and limped down the stairs toward the squirming critter.

"What is it doing?" Buford was walking over with a new pistol raised and aimed at Atticus.

The thing that had been Atticus Miller, and then the Prisoner, and was now this mixed-up monster from beyond the stars writhed in pain on the ground. Its body was vanishing and reappearing in parts as Buford and I traded looks.

"What did you do to it?" Buford asked me.

"I played a bet," I explained, "and it looks like it paid off." I stepped closer as Atticus roared. His yell of pain bounced around in my head and made me shake with the pain. Between that and my leg, I almost collapsed. "You showed me how to stop him," I told Buford. "The Cavalry badge was able to stop his brain powers. It's in his neck right now."

It was possible that this wouldn't kill the Prisoner. The plan had been to stop him from leaving and it was working so far, but we weren't done yet.

Just as I had the thought, Buford went over and put his new gun to the demon's and pulled the trigger. I had thought his new gun was a pistol that he grabbed from a corpse. Instead, it was a sawed-off shotgun.

The first shot put a hole in Atticus's head. The second removed it completely.

We stood there as the odd pink blood poured from the headless corpse.

"Now what?" Buford looked around at the bodies on the ground and then back to Atticus's demon corpse. "Can't just leave them here."

"Nah," I knelt to take the weight off my leg, "we can't just leave them here."

That was when Atticus's body began to shake before fading away, particles of whatever he had been floating on the breeze. It only took a moment for the demon body to disappear.

"Hiram?"

"Yeah?"

"If those space worms have huge mouths in the front," he tossed the sawed-off shotgun to the ground, "then where do they keep their brains?"

I stared at the spot where Atticus Miller's body had just been and wondered the same thing that Buford was likely thinking.

Did the Prisoner escape?

We lined up the bodies and went back to town. Our horses weren't far. We called them and rode back to town. The sheriff didn't ask for credentials when we told him who we were and what he would find at the Wright property.

He grabbed his hat and a pistol, but otherwise didn't seem to care.

We let Doctor Warren know that his overabundance of patients would be slowing down soon. He told us that he would believe it when he saw it.

Buford rode next to me as we made our way to the edge of town.

"What's the plan now?" he asked as I stopped and climbed down from my horse. "What are you doing?" He stopped and shook his head when he saw where we were.

"We need to telegram Captain Fitz," I explained as I walked to the front of the telegram office. "And get our next set of orders."

BROKEN SINGULARITY: SEQUENTIA SECUNDUS

BY DAVID CONYERS

"**W**ake up, lazy bitches, lazy bastards! Time to work. Time to live!"

Eyelids fluttered. Dry air carried no scent. Icy chills prickled Harrison Peel's naked skin. Frozen muscles shook without control.

"Move it! Move it!"

An artificial cocoon split like unfolding petals and tipped him forward and out onto a metallic ribbed floor, and he landed hard. The impact hurt, exactly as he had remembered from the previous time. Muscles felt stiff and old. Attempts to suppress today's moans of pain failed, and still his voice came out croaky.

The same darkness. The same encircling halo of light. Peel rubbed his bare chest again for warmth and danced on near frozen feet. He looked upwards, waited for the pooped spacesuit, so he could dress and warm his skin. The cold bit like needles.

He noticed three figures expel from cocoons around him, expressing confusion and fear. One he identified as Chusue. Net, but instead of a single leg injury replaced with a thin stick-like cybernetic limb, she had also lost an arm and it too was now a full metallic extension graphed to her fleshy shoulder. Her eyes shocked Peel more, with the burned tissue around two black inky orbs that resembled both artificial lenses and two pools of thick oil.

The two other figures were men, each muscular with blue tinges to their skin. They were unscarred, but also hairless, including an absence of eyebrows. Eyes were cat-like with their vertical slits, and expressionless faces remained fixed like stone. What united all four was they all shivered in the subzero temperatures.

"You want to live? Then work to live." Came the disembodied voice from all directions. "Bitches and bastards. Hesitation is a rookie mistake. Grab your suits. Work for a living."

As the suspended-animation cocoons retreated into the shadowed ceiling, the slurped organic black blobs fell at their feet. Without hesitation, Peel stepped into his blob, so it morphed around his skin, enveloping him with a new carapace-like spacesuit.

Chusue.Net and the two men watched, then followed Peel's lead and allowed the blobs to suit them.

Peel nodded at the woman, but with her void-like eyes and scarring, it was difficult to know if she recognized him. If he could detect any emotion, it was that she appeared to be in shock. Probably Chusue.Net had undertaken missions since their last pairing, working with other teams while Peel had remained in suspended animation, explaining her injuries and pale complexion.

"Tools and tanks, boys and girls. Tools and tanks. Oxygen privileges expire in sixty seconds."

The spider-like chromatic limbs fitted transparent head shells and air tanks to their bodies. Soon, Peel's suit temperature warmed him to what felt to be a comfortable twenty-five degrees, just as it had the last time the disembodied voice had revived him.

He looked at his companions, seeking to build a bond between them. The men expressed confusion, and Peel guessed this was their first time to be awakened in this prison on a dead, distant planet far from the Solar System where they had presumably all originated. There would be much explaining to do.

"Resting is for the dead, bitches and bastards. Its... work time."

The same sequence of events followed, with the air sucked out and replaced with vacuum, adding evidence to Peel's supposition of an automated voice, non-sentient, and pre-programmed with a series of predicable commands.

The vast, metallic door ground open from the center, as Peel knew it would. The view was the same, of an airless, crater-pocked planet of gray rock, and a dim but prominent red dwarf star in the sky, and a backdrop of distant galaxies.

Peel stepped outside. His three companions followed. When the door closed behind them, Peel turned to the woman and said, "Chusue.Net, what happened to you?"

The inky pools of the substitute eyes perfectly reflected Peel in their eerie deadness. "How do you know me?"

Peel chuckled without humor. "You know how. We did all this before, together."

"When? Where are we? What is this place? And I don't know you."

Peel shuddered and stepped back. Had their captors erased Chusue.Net's memories between missions?

Then Peel shuddered again. If that were true, how many times had they erased his memories? How many times had he explored this world before today, and the previous day? Dozens, hundreds, or thousands of times? And not just this version of him, but all his clones as well.

His legs became like jelly, so Peel steadied himself and took deep breaths until he calmed his inner turmoil. He couldn't have survived here for hundreds or thousands of iterations of the previous day—odds were against him surviving anywhere near that long on this bizarre alien planet. He would resemble Chusue.Net by now if he had. A jigsaw puzzle of flesh and cybernetic parts as the hostile planet slowly broke him apart. Or more likely, he'd be dead long before it came to that.

Then he remembered his interrogator, nothing more than a head and an arm and now a permanent fixture of the disembodied systems and infrastructure that maintained and operated their bizarre prison. Peel remembered she had told him about a cable with a round socket, which he had removed before his induced slumber. Was that the data feed that erased his memory every time he returned to the cocoon? How many times had she told him about this cable in the past? How many times had he pulled it out, and how many times had he not?

Unable to control his fear, Peel retched, but thankfully nothing expelled from his stomach, because there was nothing inside him to expel.

Chusue.Net stepped close to Peel and shook him. "How do you know me?"

"I'll explain, but not here," said Peel as sweat ran down his face. "Suit, slave all three suits to mine, and send us into orbit, one klick above the surface."

The suit responded, firing them into the sky using an unseen force, Peel guessed, that was a type of repulsive gravitational effect. Tech far beyond the understanding of the historical era that had produced him, but useful. The acceleration crushed bones and muscles against his organs and blood vessels, but not powerful enough to render him unconscious or permanently damage him. When they reached orbital velocity, the forces vanished, and the four floated effortlessly through the inky black of space.

"My name is Harrison Peel. I'm a former soldier from Earth, circa early twenty-first century. Don't ask me how I got here, I don't know. All I know is that this is not the first time I've explored this world, and it's not the first time you have either, Chusue.Net."

"How do you know this?"

Peel paused, sensing panic in her tone.

He wondered if the intelligent entities behind the disembodied voice listened in on their conversation. Then Peel figured he'd likely already given the game away that his memory of the previous mission remained intact. A problem their jailers could easily remedy next time they forced him into a sleeping cocoon. He'd have to avoid that fate at all costs within this iteration, and find a path to the spaceship he had noticed last time he'd orbited this world, and somehow use it to escape this torturous prison.

"We've all been here a while... I guess," Peel said, recognizing that he likely spoke the truth. "What I've figured out is we work for a day, exploring the surface and reporting what we find. When we're done, they put us back to sleep, and then erase our memories. Each time is like waking for the first time, and they make us perform the same routine repeatedly."

After further explanation and details about their previous mission together, Chusue.Net accepted his explanation, including how he had avoided memory eraser in this iteration.

Their two new companions, Renault-87 and Renault-14, two mining engineer clones with identical pre-life memories and personalities, didn't question him either. The pair told him they were once Belters from Earth's twenty-second century, and had spent their entire lives extracting rare metals from the dwarf planet Ceres in the Solar System's asteroid belt between Mars and Jupiter. But back then, they were only one person, and their captors had cloned him.

Peel wondered if he too carried a number designation.

"What exactly do our captors hope us to find?" Renault-14 asked.

"I don't know. I'm guessing it's 'something' on or in this world our captors know is here, but they can't locate it. Whatever that 'something' might be, they want it desperately enough to establish this elaborate imprisonment process we find ourselves in."

Without warning, forces soon pressed against their bodies, decelerating them. Their spacesuits gently returned them to the surface, landed them on another vast gray and dusty surface covered in craters and tiny hills.

Peel wondered why.

The scene appeared as serene as it was possible for it to be on the surface of a dead, vacuum-shrouded world pockmarked with meteor craters, until Peel spotted the rhinoceros several hundred meters from their position.

"That thing," Peel spoke to their companions via their radio communications, "is fucking dangerous."

"A rhinoceros!" said one of the Renaults. Peel couldn't tell them apart anymore. "They went extinct in 2049."

"How is it breathing in a vacuum?" asked the other.

Peel ducked and found cover behind a low rise. "Except it's

not a rhino. It's a fucking polymorph sentinel. An automated killing machine that will soon be hunting us."

His companions showed enough foresight to hide with him.

Peel hoped the sentinel hadn't seen them, allowing them time to plan their next moves. But he couldn't rely on luck alone. They had to act quickly and decisively if they were to escape unharmed when it decided to attack.

Chusue.Net said, "It's standing over some kind of vertical shaft."

Peel looked up and back at the seemingly innocuous rhinoceros and couldn't see what Chusue.Net had reported, but he didn't doubt her modifications made her better than him in all physical attributes, including visual sensors. He thought perhaps that the Humvee might have parked over a similar shaft when they had encountered it during his previous sequence, or that the Humvee and the rhinoceros might actually be the same creature.

"You've fought these before?" asked a Renault.

"How did you defeat it?" asked the other.

Peel swallowed. "We didn't. Chusue.Net and I barely escaped with our lives. Our two companions died, and not well." Peel described the encounter, shared every detail he could remember.

While he talked, he watched to ensure the rhinoceros hadn't moved, and thought back on that terrifying moment with the Humvee. He felt certain there had been a shaft underneath it that time as well. Whatever they were upon this world to discover, perhaps it lay beneath the sentinel they now faced.

"What do we do?" asked a Renault.

Peel waited for someone else to answer. When no one did, he said, "We wait and watch. If it comes for us, we ask our suits to shoot us back into orbit." Then Peel had an idea which gave him hope. "Suit, provide me with a weapon?"

Nothing happened.

"I knew I was getting too optimistic."

They waited, hidden behind their low rise, for what was probably two hours, watching the rhinoceros wander around and do what a normal rhinoceros would do; graze for grass, poop, and shake its head to scare off buzzing insects. Only there was no grass, shit, or bugs. There was only the rhinoceros, and it never moved far from where they had first discovered it.

Peel considered perhaps it would only attack if they came too close. "What if we approach it from four angles? It might come for one of us, allowing the others to race into that shaft?"

Chusue.Net said, "Why attack it? What benefit is there for us in doing so?"

Peel looked into her inky black eyes and saw his haunted and aged features reflected back at him. "I'd rather die than return to that prison and forget again everything that I know now. Whatever we need to get off this planet... that rhino is protecting it."

A Renault said, "Your plan will probably result in one or all of our deaths."

"Maybe," said Peel, "but every time the Boss Man returns us to the big sleep, we could forget again why we are here, and face off against its next shape with no idea what it is. In this iteration, we at least know something of its capabilities."

His three companions considered his proposition, then one by one agreed with him.

Chusue.Net said in a whisper, "Statistical calculation suggests your plan is sound, but high probability at least two of us will die during the process."

Peel tensed. He had hoped for his companions to challenge his plan and present more viable options. The futurists were too accepting, too clinically emotionless in their logical responses. But this was his team, and he had no better ideas to share. He also knew at a deep, emotional level, doing nothing was worse than performing a reckless act. "Very well. Whichever one of us the polymorph sentinel chases, they run long enough to distract it while the rest of us drop into the hole. Then command your suit to send you into orbit."

The group split without wishing each other luck or sharing last words of encouragement.

Peel headed in an anticlockwise direction, first marching with Chusue.Net, then leaving her to trudge to the opposite side of the rhino. The mimicked alien beast showed no interest in their activities but it raised its head often to sniff the vacuum, as if sensing them. Or perhaps it merely replicated a normal rhinoceros on the lookout for predators such as lions or hyenas back where it was supposed to belong, on the grasslands of Sub-Saharan Africa.

In half an hour, everyone was in position.

Peel felt his hands shake and sweat bead on his face and shaved scalp. He'd faced death many times, often against weirdness of the variety he faced today. He'd grown used to the idea that with death came the emptiness of nothing and a timeless peace—which he would welcome. What he feared was not dying, but becoming trapped in a surreal alien dimension where he suffered an eternity of fear, desperation, pain, and confusion, looped like a discordant horror movie on repeat. Whatever awaited in that pit might bring him to such an end. Now he hoped the rhinoceros came for him.

It was then he spied a book lying half buried in the airless dust.

Peel picked it up, discovering a curvilinear script imprinted on metallic sheets of flexible paper, bound in a bronze-textured front and back cover. He'd seen this script before, in the Australia Outback, during an early period of his career when Peel led security on a research base studying an ancient alien metropolis unearthed in the desert. The city had a name, Pnakotus, and its former inhabitants were a species that had conquered space and time, the Great Race of Yith. In the time Peel had spent there, he had learned some of their history, but not enough to make sense of this discovery today.

"We're ready," said the Renaults, distracting Peel.

Chusue.Net expressed similar sentiments.

"Okay," said Peel, feeling his Adam's apple run up and down the length of his throat. He left the book where he'd found it, deciding if he survived this encounter, he'd come back for it, not that he had any chance of reading or deciphering its contents. "Let's move."

They each advanced. Light steps taken towards the mimicked African megafauna.

Peel kept willing it to look his way, to chase him so he could fly away, but it didn't.

Then he remembered it probably didn't use the rhinoceros's biological senses to perceive its environment.

When they were each within a hundred meters of the creature, it reacted. Bone-like rods burrowed out of its gray fleshy hide and fired as missiles towards all four of them. The missiles didn't move fast, so Peel had time to drop into a two-meter-wide crater and hope they fired over him.

He lay still for several seconds and realized he was still alive and unharmed.

Then he noticed the silence, interrupted only by his own breathing and heartbeat reverberating inside his face shield.

No sounds from his companions carried through their suit communicators.

He looked up. The rhinoceros charged not towards Peel, but toward one of the Renaults.

Peel leaped to his feet and sprinted for the hole, knowing he had to at least try. His own breath and heartbeat sounded like another person screaming inside his head, and they were the only sounds.

From nowhere, two space-suited figures also ran towards the hole, but one seemed to chase the other. Peel thought he recognized a blue face in both bubble helmets. Then the lagging figure propelled itself into the air like a monkey and landed on the back of the second runner.

Both shapes merged, then twisted and separated as a dozen cubes of flesh, spacesuits and compacted organs now compressed into square-sided contraptions, all of which bounced around like surreal nightmares warped by twisted, higher-dimensions a human mind could not accurately perceive.

Then the cubes bounced towards him.

Of the rhinoceros or Chusue.Net, there was no sign.

"Suit, run me faster."

It complied, and suddenly Peel's legs were not his to control, but moved with such speed he had not believed possible, and within seconds he reached the circular opening.

"Drop me inside!" Peel screamed before the suit propelled him onward.

A smooth, circular tube opened up beneath Peel and he

fell like a stone dropped from a tall building. Darkness soon enveloped him as he accelerated. His breathing and heart rate became noticeably louder, because sound became the only sense afforded to him.

Then a world opened up.

A vast, circular chamber, of gray- and slate-colored veins on a black rock like the undulations in a human brain, that was the inside shell of this world, presenting a spherical chamber several hundred kilometers across.

An eerie orange-red light permeated the interior, concentrated in the sphere's center, which Peel now fell towards. He noticed it as an odd, twisted vortex that seemed to exist in all of his vision while simultaneously seemed edited from his perception. Encircling this singularity, beams of light twisted and formed into shapes of burning matter. But not all matter was gas or rock. Much of it appeared to be living, twisting, eye-polluted and tentacular-infested shapes of aliens, orbiting the central, dimensional mass.

Encircling and falling in and out of the central swarm mass were long, wrinkled worms of pink flesh, with various openings filled with teeth of different sizes and shapes, and random protrusions that resembled wings, arms, legs, tentacles, pincers or organs. They wrapped and twisted around each other, as if trying to climb upon their brothers and sisters, to gain height and escape the maelstrom, but none had the energy or strength to affect an escape.

Peel realized he was falling into it.

"Suit! Put me in orbit! Now! Around whatever that is!"

Gravitational forces twisted Peel first into parabolic arcs that brought him close to the unholy central pit of flaying worms, where deeper still lay an undefined black realm where watchers guarded whatever lay on the insanely curved surfaces with no conceivable purpose and following no conceivable geometry.

During his long parabolic orbit, Peel zipped past a creature with charcoal skin the texture of porridge, multiple randomly-distributed eyes like green stars, and tentacles and mouths that thrashed and slathered. As Peel drew close to this creature, he recognized it as a Shoggoth, a monster encountered too often in his terrifying past. Closing in, it seemed to speed up. Mouths and tentacles bit and twirled at an accelerated rate. As Peel raced away from it, the creature slowed again. Then it seemed to fall, ever closer to that sphere of worms above the undefinable central shapeless point, but never quite fell into it.

Peel saw himself, multiple times from multiple directions, all moving in perfect synchronization.

Then he noticed every creature and rock and ring of hot dust also replicated multiple times from multiple directions.

As his orbit sped him through the mélange of monsters, he thought he recognized other people. Or at least creatures that vaguely resembled a human form.

Now he raced back towards the inside shell of putrid gray- and slate-colored veins of rock, up out of the gravity well. Everything beneath him slowed again, and soon most of the alien monsters and people from lower down appeared not to be moving at all. Those closest to the central point moved the slowest.

He passed the floating shell of a wrecked AH-64 Apache helicopter with empty tubes for Sidewinder air-to-air missiles. It looked to have crumpled under the whack of a gigantic, whale-sized tentacle.

A minute later, the gray corpse of a young woman, dressed as a flapper with dark hair and bulging eyes, drifted past. Her dead face expressed a fear Peel could not describe, and didn't want to.

Then he recognized that spit drifted from her mouth. She must have died recently, and there must be some kind of atmosphere inside this shell. Had she died in a vacuum, her blood would have boiled away, leaving her as an emaciated and shriveled husk.

"Suit!" he shouted inside his helmet. "Keep me orbiting as high as possible." He didn't wish to fall back towards the central point, where all the monsters, wrecked helicopters and dead people had collected and frozen in time.

His suit performed as commanded, and kept him in a circular orbit about the strange, central pulsating blob of what appeared to be a conglomerate of people and monsters, of twisted light, and also of nothing, as if folded outside the confines of space and time itself. And yet, everything inside this shell of a world seemed to fall towards it, and the closer they were, the slower time seemed to pass.

After a few orbits, Peel recognized various holes in the roof of this sphere, similar to the one he had fallen down, all dark and uninviting, but likely the only paths to the surface again.

He realized he needed a plan, and that plan needed to include his escape from this world before he too became permanently trapped here. Peel suspected he could ask his suit to fly him out, but that would leave him with only one option: to return to the base to face his captors, who would force him back inside the cocoons for memory erasure.

The problem was the suit. It trapped him, for without it he would die in a vacuum, yet he had no control of its functionality. All control lay with the Boss Man.

He needed another spacesuit.

Peel kept orbiting and asked his suit to bring him close to any human in high orbit.

The first body they passed by was the beaten remains of what appeared to be a Victorian era male cowboy, complete with a ten-gallon hat, spurs, and two six-shooter revolvers secured in hip holsters. He wore a sheriff's badge, but of an unfamiliar design, resembling a pentagram with a single human eye in its center. Peel grabbed the corpse as they swung past each other, then transferred the ancient revolvers to his own belt. Antique weapons were better than no means of defending himself.

Later he passed the corpse of a man in a 1940s suit and tie, fedora and scuffed shoes. This thin individual looked to have died only recently, for two bullet holes in his chest bled fresh blood that hung around him like tentacles emerging from his insides. His expression was of shocked surprise, as if he hadn't seen his own demise coming. The body zipped past Peel and was soon out of reach.

More disturbing were the implications of the recent dead. They were all fresh kills, yet from seemingly distantly separated periods of time. And they had all materialized here, not only in this distantly remote corner of the universe, but had all arrived in this location, in or around *the same time period!*

Peel tried not to focus on any of this, and instead find what he needed.

After many orbits, he found a human wearing a spacesuit Peel could understand. The United States flag stitching on the armband was a bonus, but the corporate logo next to it Peel did not recognize.

The emasculated man inside looked to be over a hundred years old, with wrinkled skin and a hairless scalp, and liver spots everywhere. At first Peel wasn't certain the man was alive, then he saw him breathe sharply, as if taking in oxygen his lungs desperately needed after holding his breath for too long.

Peel grabbed the old man and together they spun through the shell chamber, with the weird pulsating shapeless mass in the center, dragging all of them around it at rather considerable speeds.

The man opened his eyes. He seemed surprised, then spoke in a gasping croak Peel couldn't understand.

They touched helmets, so noise could pass between them.

"Single..."

"What was that?"

He said again, "Single..." then started choking. "Enter..."

Peel had hoped for a corpse like every other human he'd encountered that floated in their orbital maelstrom. A living man in a spacesuit was no more help than no spacesuit at all. Peel couldn't very well take it from the man by force, resulting in his death only to save Peel's own skin.

The ancient man tapped a pocket on his side, then smiled as if he had just arrived home after being away for many months or years. Then he pointed towards the dimensionless anomaly.

Peel looked, then heard a popping sound, and air escaping.

He turned and found the man had unclasped his helmet. Unable to breathe, his eyes rolled up into the back of his head. He seemed to shrivel, like a mummy in its tomb, recently unearthed and opened, reacting to chemicals in the atmosphere that dehydrated him suddenly. The man had taken his own life, and Peel couldn't understand why.

They kept orbiting, with Peel holding onto the corpse.

In time, he found the courage to strip the suit from the man, then let the shriveled husk float away to join all the other peculiar visitors trapped in this surreal contraption.

Inadvertently, Peel read the name on the spacesuit's stich pad.

H. PEEL.

He was almost sick inside his suit. The man who had just given up his own life was Peel, only a much more ancient version of himself.

Was this how Peel himself died, sacrificing himself so a youthful version of him could live? And Peel had discarded the old man with no care or mourning for his passing.

Peel remembered his future-self had touched a pouch on his suit's thigh. He looked now, and discovered an inflatable oxygen tent.

The future Peel had known the solution to present Peel's predicament; the only means to change suits was in an environment where Peel could control the atmosphere, and the oxygen tent solved that problem.

The U.S. spacesuit showed the tanks were at 62%, able to provide one hour, thirty-two minutes of operation under non-strenuous use. Peel hoped that would be enough time to make his escape.

"Suit," he spoke aloud to the imprisoning carapace garb that kept him alive. "Take me back to the surface."

The carapace suit obeyed and manipulated Peel's trajectory multiple times until his position allowed him to float up through one of the circular entry points. It might have been the same one Peel had entered by, but he couldn't be certain, as the interior of this shell held no distinguishing features across its undersurface.

The darkness enveloped him, and within seconds Peel shot up above the dead planet's surface, noticing only momentarily a contraption resembling a giant metal spider with a gun turret for a head, guarding this entry point. The carapace suit moved too fast for the polymorph sentinel to attack. Or perhaps it didn't care, for Peel was leaving, not trying to break into the shell interior.

The suit quickly returned Peel to the imprisoning complex. The same door spread with great effort and took far longer to open than it had the last time he had returned here.

Peel thought of running, finding somewhere to hide and inflating the oxygen tent to change into the spacesuit once belonging to his ancient self, but he realized he didn't know how to remove the suit he wore, and that it might not let him do so of his own volition. With no obvious solution to that predicament, Peel instead stepped inside, waited for the door to ground shut and for breathable air to fill the chamber.

"Bitches and bastards, back I see. Information you bring, better be good."

The voice again, inside his suit. Then the ceiling-dwelling metallic mandibles snatched his helmet and air tank. His suit dissolved and flowed into holes opening in the floor.

Peel stared down along his bare chest and arms, aware that the old U.S. spacesuit remained in his hands. He could slip into the suit now, but how would he open the door to the outside? He likely only had one chance at this ruse, so his mind pondered the various courses of action he could take.

"Lazy bastards. Lazy bitches. Work time hasn't ended. Time to report in."

The Boss Man had spoken again, repeating the same words from Peel's last awakening. The air carried the same warmth and humidity as it did last time. He looked for the opening airlock to dilate open, and it did, spilling an inviting light that beckoned him from the dark chamber of slaves trapped in suspended animation. Peel recalled the woman with only a head and an arm, the only individual he'd encountered in this strange world that he had felt any emotional connection. Could he save her, too?

Peel decided the risk was worth the effort. With the spacesuit and oxygen tent bundled under his arm, he walked naked into the interrogation room. Again, it was tiny with metal walls, structural beams and grills inlaid into the cladding, a metal desk built into the wall and one metal chair bolted to a pole jutting from the ground.

He sat, and when a portal opened in the wall, it was Chusue.

Net's head, neck, shoulders and bare breasts that appeared, the rest of her body absent. She lived only because her flesh attached to a robotic limb that presumably pumped blood and nutrients into what survived of her body. The eyes were as Peel remembered, two black orbs, like pools of inky oil, surrounded by scarred flesh. Chusue.Net looked to have aged decades, for her skin had wrinkled and dried.

"This is a surprise," she spoke in a voice that Peel didn't remember as being her own. "Inventory tells me we exhausted our contingent of Harrison Peel clones."

Peel shuddered, felt the room recede from him while he recognized this as a shock response and nothing more.

"You've been gone a long time, Peel-49."

"How long?"

"Three hundred and seventy-nine years."

"What?" Peel felt his throat and fists tighten. "But you and I... we..."

"We, what, Peel?"

"Our tactic, to distract the polymorph sentinel disguised as a rhinoceros, it worked."

Chusue.Net turned her head left, then right, then back again. "That incident occurred three hundred and seventy-nine years ago."

Peel shuddered, trying to understand the disparity in time. For Peel, the encounter with the alien rhinoceros was an experience from earlier today. "That's not possible."

"It was how I became an interrogator. The polymorph sentinel's bone missiles cubed the rest of my flesh. What remained of my carapace suit returned me here, three hundred and seventy-nine years ago."

Peel wished to slip his mind into a self-imposed oblivion, because he didn't wish to ponder the implications of what Chusue.Net was telling him. "Where is the woman you replaced?"

"The Pilot?"

Peel nodded.

"We retired her. I am more efficient in this role than she ever was."

He nodded again, not sure how to respond to that depressing revelation. "I found a way in."

"Into where?"

"Into this planet's interior."

He described what he had seen and experienced, the many orbiting human corpses from multiple time periods, and the monsters such as the circle of worms and a shoggoth. The only detail he left out was the Yithian book he would go back for later if given the chance, and the discovery of an ancient Harrison Peel, who had passed on a spacesuit which Peel still gripped in his tense hands. Chusue.Net hadn't mentioned it, so Peel wouldn't either.

"You said creatures seemed to slow down, relative to how close they were to the central mass. The singularity where angles and dimensions made no sense?"

"Yes," Peel answered with a whisper. "Time dilation. Is it possible that I flew by a black hole, one without an event horizon? Black holes accelerate time?"

The inky black eyes reflected Peel's distraught face back at him. "Possible. If it is a true black hole, its gravity would have collapsed everything on this moon-sized world long ago. Perhaps whoever built this place bleeds off most of its gravity into alternate dimensions, but its other effects remain unchanged."

He nodded and tightened his grip on his stolen spacesuit.

"What you say makes sense, Major Peel. The Riders, imprisoned in a broken singularity, can project only a part of their essence across space and time, but they can't fully escape it. A prison of time, space and gravity, all bundled up into a compacted knot of dimensions. They can't perceive it, but you can. A human. You found what we came here to find."

"What did I find?"

"Irrelevant. We are both redundant. Mission, completed."

Expressing sudden and welcomed relief, Chusue.Net's head and upper torso seemed to wither and die before him, collapsing as dried, mummified flesh that turned to dust as it hit the floor. The mechanical appendage twisted and fell, it too devoid of life.

Peel felt the air temperature drop. The air felt stale.

The lights extinguished.

Peel slipped into his ancient spacesuit, sealed all the joints, then pumped oxygen into his helmet. Years earlier in subjective time, NASA technicians had trained him in the operations and maintenance of spacesuits similar to this one, allowing him to travel to alien worlds far beyond Earth. That experience now saved him, for the outside environment thinned into vacuum, and the temperature had dropped to deadly, frigid extremes. He knew because his suit reported on the external environment. No atmospheric pressure, and an ambient temperature of minus one hundred degrees.

The only light originated from his suit. All other tech had shut down and gone offline. He shined the torch attached to his arm, tracing its dull beam across the dark, tiny room. The door into the larger chamber with its crypt of suspended animation units remained open. When Peel glanced inside, passing the torch beam over the interior, he noticed dozens, if not hundreds of corpses had dropped from the pods above and had crinkled and frozen solid in the frigid temperatures. Peel's discovery in the planet's core, it seemed, had brought an end to this station and its purpose.

He paused momentarily and became aware of his rapid and shallow breaths. His head felt dizzy, and his chest felt tight. Examining his feelings, he recognized he feared loneliness, for he was hundreds of thousands of light-years from the nearest human and had no viable means of escape, stranding him here. But that might be a moot point anyway, as his suit only provided him with an hour and a half of oxygen, or far less if he kept hyperventilating in his panicked state.

He stared back to the interrogation room and remembered the Pilot. She was the first human he'd engaged with who'd expressed human emotions Peel could understand. What had Chusue.Net said, that the Pilot had been 'retired'? That could mean anything.

Peel pulled at the many panels. Soon enough a panel dislodged, then another. In minutes, he'd stripped all the walls, disposing of the metal sheets in the suspended animation chamber out of the way. Behind the walls were circuits, pipes, gears, valves, junctures, and structural support elements. He set about dismantling this secondary layer, snapping pipes that fired gases into the vacuum, before crystalizing as solids and falling to the floor.

Soon he found what he searched for, the Pilot's head inside a cylinder that resembled the suspended animation units, but suitcase sized. To his surprise, readouts flashed, that noted the Pilot was not dead, but in an artificial slumber, running minimal biological processes.

Peel sobbed, uncertain if he felt despair, or relief, or a little of both.

He checked his suit's oxygen readings. Fifty-eight minutes remained. He needed to find the spaceship witnessed on his first remembered day and see if it could take him far from this nightmarish planet.

Exploration of the suspended animation chamber revealed other doors, but they were all locked and too heavy to forcibly open.

He checked his oxygen readings again. Twenty-seven minutes. Far less time had elapsed since his last reading. In his panicked state, he was wasting oxygen.

With no other viable plan, Peel pulled apart the panels adjacent to the nearest door. After several minutes, he exposed the piston-gear contraption that opened and closed the portal. Snapping off a pipe, he used it as leverage and after much effort, jimmied the door wide enough for him and the Pilot's head to slip through. Air from the other side rushed past him as he worked.

The other side was a corridor. His suit told him the air was a mixture of nitrogen and oxygen. Peel checked his suit. Only seven minutes of air remained inside his suit.

Placing the Pilot's head upon the metal floor, Peel took his oxygen tent from the pocket on his spacesuit and adhered it to the open door. The tent included many adhesive strips which Peel used to forge an airtight seal across the opening, halting the escaping air.

Breathing rapidly, Peel slid down the wall, feeling his exhaustion and lightheadedness.

The air inside his suit reported it would only last two more minutes.

The air outside was seventeen percent oxygen, survivable, but not enough to engage in strenuous activities. The temperature was a cool five degrees, also survivable with his suit.

Peel disengaged his helmet, breathed in the outside air, and sat for a moment, just to recover from his ordeal.

Lights flickered down the corridor.

Red strips of illumination lined the floors.

He heard a voice.

A man's voice.

The Boss Man.

THE BODY SNATCHERS

A Harry Stubbs Adventure

BY DAVID HAMBLING

"There are certain groups of searchers—certain cults, you know—that might misunderstand …some of them have damnably curious ideas and methods."
HP Lovecraft, *The Thing on the Doorstep*
"That corpse you planted last year in your garden,
Has it begun to sprout? Will it bloom this year?
Or has the sudden frost disturbed its bed?"

TS Eliot, *The Waste Land*
London, 1928

CHAPTER ONE: SMITH CALLS IN A DEBT

There are certain dark rumours concerning me, which can be traced back to a case which culminated one night in West Norwood Cemetery. I would like to say I am not a grave-robber as some have implied; nor was I hammering in a stake in a deluded attempt to put down some imagined vampire as others suggest. The truth is stranger and darker than either of those fables. For those who want the truth and nothing but, and who possess strong nerves and strong stomachs, I set it down here.

The hour was approaching five o' clock, and the girls packing crockery outside my office were slowing down. They had finished their last orders for the day and were not going to start anything new. They were tidying up, sweeping up the sawdust while Kitty worked on the books and tallied what they had achieved, so many sets of china dispatched. In the background I caught the welcome sounds of spoon against teapot and a gas flame being lit.

I was winding down myself. Being your own boss is not as easy as those in more traditional occupations assume. I had known this since I was a boy when I saw my father working all hours keeping his butcher's shop going. He was up well before us, whistling as he sharpened knives and laid out the day's arrangement on the cold slabs, and still cheerful at the end of the day when he brought down the shutters and went through the day's takings. He did not finish until long after the office workers were back with their families.

I sometimes wondered out loud whether he wouldn't rather have chosen an easier life. All the people we saw in the shop seemed to start work later, and finish earlier, than he did. Also, their trades did not involve intestines or pig's blood, or the frankly disgusting business of making sausages.

"Harry, my boy," my Pa told me, "It always looks like the grass is greener and everyone else has an easier life. But believe you me, if you could see anyone else's problems, you would not trade places with them in a million years."

And he went back to his butchery, having never wanted anything more out of life.

I might say that my own life was in some ways enviable, although with the caveat that, if I did not keep my wits about me, it might get cut short at any time. My financial situation verged on the precarious, but in terms of adventure and excitement, not to mention downright fascinating exploration of the unknown, the benefits were more than adequate.

A polite tap sounded at the door, and I was not a little surprised to see Smith. He had changed out of his attendant's uniform but the smell of the lunatic asylum clung to him. Smith is not a good-looking chap by any means. He has the features of a weasel, and bowlegs from childhood rickets. Not that I, with my caveman brawn, am a delight to the aesthete; we might tie for last place in any masculine beauty contest.

Smith's previous occupation was as a thief, and that's what Smith looks like. There's something about his natural expression that sets you on your guard and makes you put a hand on your wallet.

Looks aside, I was not exactly pleased to see him. Things between me and him had been peculiar. We met as enemies; in our first encounter, in the Horniman Museum, I held Smith's arms while my associate Skinner threatened him with a knife when we caught him following us. Since then, things had changed, and at this point I owed him a debt of gratitude. I cannot say I felt much by way of warmth or trust toward him though, merely obligation.

It was incumbent on me to make him welcome. His timing was perfect, and we were soon facing each other across two steaming cups of tea.

"Got anything to sweeten it with, Stubbs?" Smith asked. "They always do in the books. Bottle of rye whiskey in the bottom drawer."

"That would be if I was an American 'gumshoe'," I said, "rather than a British insurance investigator."

"Insurance investigator, my eye," he scoffed.

The sign on the door said, 'Lantern Insurance.' It was one room rented from a concern selling china sets by mail order and it was, in theory at least, a legitimate business. It was no great secret that little of my time was spent on insurance affairs, and while Smith was not privy to my main occupation, he knew my reputation as a ghost-breaker. There were plenty of stories floating around. I chose not to confirm or deny any.

"Nevertheless," I said, deciding on generosity, "I do happen to keep a little brandy by me for medicinal purposes."

I produced the bottle from behind some books and uncorked it.

"A little *fine and dandy?*" said Smith. "Don't mind if I do, Mr Stubbs."

I poured a good slug into his tea and awarded myself a similar amount to be companionable. Polite society might not approve, but I sensed serious business ahead.

We talked a little about my Sally, and Elsie, his lady love, and some mutual acquaintances at the asylum, but he wanted to get down to business.

"We had an emergency admission today," said Smith. "You might want to take some notes on this."

"I remember those admissions," I said, opening my notepad.

In the majority of cases, a patient was transferred to the asylum via an unhurried process of assessment and referral, when it was deemed necessary for the safety of the person or those around them. In rare instances though, when someone snapped without any warning, they would come in unceremoniously. Most of those afflicted with insanity are rather drab people. Screaming madmen are the exception, not the rule.

"The coppers brought him in. He's spent the night in a cell after they picked him up on the streets in the early hours. An old boy in robes, waving a sword and shouting."

"A not entirely atypical case," I said.

The asylum saw more bizarre manifestations of delusional behaviour on a daily basis. Smith leaned forward in his seat and spoke with deliberation, a witness on the stand.

"He gave his name as Eddie Haywood, carpenter by trade. He was pleased to see the bluebottles, said he'd been drugged and kidnapped, and taken to a strange house by two men, and all he wanted was to go home." He was watching me to see if my notetaking was keeping up and matching his pace of speech. "They couldn't smell drink on him, and he seemed quite docile, so after relieving him of the ironmongery they escorted him to the address he gave. That being a shared flat off Salter's Hill, which this individual said he shared with two other men."

Smith slurped his tea, pausing to savour the kick of the brandy. The story was coherent and to the point so far. Whatever else, Smith is not scatter-brained.

"And what do you think they found when they got there?"

"That the flat did not exist," I said. "Or rather, that it had been demolished twenty years earlier?"

This sort of thing happened quite frequently, with older patients who had reverted to an earlier stage of their lives and forgotten that the homes they had once occupied were buried in the past.

"They found the place alright," said Smith. "And after a bit of bell-pull hauling and hammering on the door they gain admittance, and a bleary-eyed fellow opens up."

"'Thank goodness it's you', says the old man. ''Let me in, Bob.'

"And Bob just stares back and says, 'Who the blazes are you, old man?' only not so polite.

"Bob's mate Gus comes to the door, and they have exactly the same exchange. "Let me in Gus'—'Who are you?'"

"So at this juncture even the rozzers are thinking to themselves that there's funny business going on somewhere, and maybe the two have got something to do with the kidnapping, or someone is playing a practical joke on them. And just as things are getting heated, a third bloke comes to the door.

"And the old man lets out a cry and points his bony finger and says, 'He's an impostor!'" Smith imitated the gesture. "The reason being, is because this one is the actual Eddie Haywood, thirty years younger than the greybeard being escorted by the law, and this one hasn't left the flat all evening. He's as mystified as anyone else.

"The old man goes into a rage. First he tries to attack Eddie Haywood, and then he gets into a fight with the police and will not calm down even when they get him in the cuffs."

"And there's nothing else to do with the old man but bring him to an institution," I concluded. "Until they can trace his family."

"Got it in one, Stubbs" said Smith, taking another slurp. "So the poor chap is handed over to our tender mercies."

"I see," I said, to show I had followed this and was wondering what it had to do with the price of fish, or, more pertinently, what it had to do with Harry Stubbs, Esq.

"So far, so routine," said Smith, as if apologising for the story's lack of color. "Until the patient sees yours truly, at which point he bursts out with 'Smith! You can vouch for me!'"

Like me, Smith had a face you remembered. Though in this case he would have preferred not to have been recognised.

"And could you?" I asked.

"Never seen him before in my life," he said. "But I wasn't going to say that. I said I'd be happy to oblige, and what would he like me to vouch?"

Smith was one of the less physically robust attendants. Most of them are strapping types, like me, who would not be out of place keeping the door at a rowdy pub. Smith, though, is about half my size, a bantamweight at best, but does well with what you might call a psychological angle. He enlists the sympathy of the patients, getting them to behave themselves with patience and understanding rather than main force. It is an admirably effective technique, not to say humane, as this case was to show.

"He goes into a long ramble about how I must remember him as he'd spent such a long time working at the Knight's Head last month, refurbishing all the window frames and putting a new top on the bar, and he'd seen me come in every day. And how Elsie wasn't half a hard taskmaster and would not let him have so much as a glass of half-and-half until knocking-off time, and how he'd gotten into a fight with some bloke who'd stolen a hammer out of his tool bag, and on and on."

Smith leaned forward to deliver the punch line.

"The thing is, Stubbs, *every word of it was true*! I did remember a carpenter called Eddie, and all of the old boy's recollections were spot on, point for point. Elsie had such a time with that idle beggar. But even if you took thirty years off him and added three stone, this wasn't Eddie. Of course I smiled and nodded and said I would put in a word with the proper authorities, but that the paperwork took a bit of time and he'd need to be patient."

"Plenty of inmates think they're someone else," I said. "There used to be a brace of Lord Nelsons, and they say there are plenty of Napoleons knocking about."

This was caginess on my part. The case was already starting to take on a familiar shine.

"But a carpenter...?" he started.

"There has been the odd notable carpenter who has inspired imitators," I said, but he waved this away. "Alternatively, might it be possible this is just something he could have picked up from overhearing a conversation and acquired as they say, an *idée fixe* that he was Haywood?"

"No, no, Stubbs," he said, shaking his head with a look that made me half-ashamed to be evading his point. "He had an inventory of Eddie Haywood's memory, down to every last detail. And his manner, you know…it reminded me of something you once said: maybe it's not so much a question of not being in his right mind, as not being in his right body."

"Mental transference, or metempsychosis. Modern psychic theory admits such a thing as a possibility," I said. "At least in theory."

Conan Doyle had a comic story about the effect, *The Great Keinplatz Experiment*. But it was more than a theory. The individual who called himself Roslyn D'Onston claimed to have mastered the art of swapping his mind with another person and wrote of spending a day inhabiting the body of a friend—even going so far as to make love to the friend's fiancée. My encounter with D'Onston, described elsewhere, had borne out the truth of his claims.

"Let's assume the theory is accurate, Stubbs," he said quietly, with a look that told me not to hold out on him. "And let's see where that gets us."

I stayed silent. Smith had more to say.

"That American woman psychologist, Dr de Vere, she takes an interest in certain cases. I expect she'll hear about this one before long."

Hearing her name gave me a chill. Smith did not know it, but Miss de Vere was my *de facto* employer. It was not a happy working arrangement, as I did not undertake it voluntarily. It was a choice of working for her or against her, and I took the former.

Like many at the asylum, Smith had guessed that Miss de Vere was more than she seemed. Some of the cases she took an interest in were whisked away in an unmarked van. None of them were ever heard from again, as far as the asylum staff knew. Everyone knew it was wiser not to ask questions or be seen to be taking an interest.

Miss de Vere and her associates were part of a shady outfit

calling itself TDS, a kind of secret society. As I understood it, they had taken it on themselves to stamp out incursions by other-worldly entities. Their policy of strict secrecy extended, not infrequently, to ensuring that nobody connected with such beings survived. It was a brutal, but effective, scorched-earth policy.

"That might put you in the position of being a man who knows too much," I said.

"You catch on quick, Stubbs."

Smith was a witness to something extraordinary. He knew to the point of certainty that a genuine mental transference had taken place. A man who knew that might pick up the thread and follow it to some very dangerous knowledge indeed. Smith was not the man to do such a thing, but he might pass what he knew on to others, and Miss de Vere would not be happy about that.

Working in a place like the asylum, there were all sorts of things that might befall Smith without there being any undue suspicions. It had happened before.

"I owe you a debt," I said. "How can I help?"

"If Haywood were to escape, there'd still be trouble," he said. "So that's out. And I'm not ready to disappear myself yet. So how do we put things right?"

The ball was in my court.

"Let us assume that the person now passing as Eddie Haywood is the original possessor of the body now in your custody," I said, doing no more than stating the obvious. "And, from his actions when confronted, let us assume that this transference is a deliberate act of larceny."

"What the Yanks call a 'highjacking'," Smith agreed. "Only he stole a body instead of a truck loaded with booze. How do we get him to give it back?"

"You want me to apply the necessary pressure to persuade him to reverse the exchange?"

Again, this was caginess on my part. D'Onston's writing suggested that the transfer was a temporary measure, and that souls always returned to their natural containers in the normal course of events. Maybe I would not need to do anything.

"Exactly." He drained his cup and put it down. "Apply a bit of pressure. When can you start?"

"Just one or two details more," I said. "These 'kidnappers' Haywood chased with a sword—what happened to them? Who were they?"

My suspicion was that they were accomplices who failed in their job of securing the body with its new occupant and let it escape. But one man, even if he is a wizard, is easier to deal with than three. Smith held up his hands.

"I don't know a thing. I've told you all I know."

"Do you have the address for Edward Haywood, and the approximate location where the police picked up the old man so we can find where he came from?"

As I was taking them down, another point occurred to me.

"Presumably the asylum took charge of the inmate's personal effects, as per usual," I said. "Did he have anything on him indicative of his identity?"

"No papers," said Smith. "First thing they looked for. Empty pockets, all he had was a ruddy great sword."

"I don't suppose you saw this weapon...?"

"All the lads had a look when it came in." He chuckled and I could imagine them passing it around, pretending to be Errol Flynn. "It's a proper old sword, Robin Hood and his Merry Men type-of-thing. But blunt, like a stage prop, with fancy markings down the blade."

I turned to my shelf of books, drew out one on ritual magic, and located a picture of a sword used in certain magic rites. It was in the style of a medieval longsword, and the blade was inscribed with zodiacal symbols.

"That's it," said Smith, stabbing the picture with a forefinger. "Or very like it anyway."

He seemed to be impressed.

"And a robe?"

"Fancy dress, scenes-from-the-Bible garment, not this season's Paris collection."

I turned a few more pages and showed him a photographic plate of a man wearing robes, inscribed with mystical symbols like the sword.

"You've got his number," said Smith. "What does it all mean?"

"Double, double, toil and trouble," I said. "Do you want to know any more?"

He looked down at the book, and up at me. A lot of people will plunge headlong into adventures involving the occult. I have seen them come to some bad ends.

Smith was a native of the walled-off area called Norwood New Town, a lawless place which the police rarely entered. He had learned caution, and the value of not seeing or hearing any more than was good for you.

"Where ignorance is bliss, 'tis folly to be wise," he said. "You sort it out and tell me when it's all done. And discourage this Merlin from any further 'presto-chango' business, or who knows where we might end up."

We shook hands and there was a cordial exchange of greetings to be passed on to our respective womenfolk. I advised him to keep an eye on his patient and watch out for signs of a sudden change of personality. Smith was a good deal more relaxed when he left than when he had arrived. Some of that was the brandy, but some was the confidence that he had placed his troubles in the hands of the right man.

I hoped his confidence was not misplaced.

CHAPTER TWO: A PLAN OF ACTION

Wizards, if you wish to use such a florid, fairy-tale term in the age of aeroplanes and electric lighting, are not a homogenous group. Even more so than other professions, practitioners of the esoteric arts span the range from the rough-and-ready street-corner types to the highest in the land. At the lower levels there are those who have, or believe they have, psychic gifts, and whose activities are strictly of a non-commercial nature, who tell fortunes and the like. I was acquainted with at least one spirit medium of this type.

Further up the scale were those with a family tradition, with both natural talent and accumulated knowledge passed down from generation to generation, like the late Mr Whately who lived over in Dulwich and was of settled Romany stock. He had quite a reputation for finding lost items, telling fortunes, and removing curses—and placing them too, according to rumour. They tell me he came to a bad end while doing some funny business in the churchyard. Even those who think they know what they are about can come undone.

At the highest level, you have the scholars and book-learners. Most of these are university students who fancy themselves as great black magicians in the mould of the infamous Mr Crowley, more interested in seeking sensations beyond fast cars and cocaine than actual knowledge. A few take matters further and spend years devoting themselves to obscure arcana, like Mr Yeats and his circle.

The texts they pore over are mainly harmless nonsense—so I am assured by Captain Cross, my friend in the arcane book trade—while others are shrouded in such layers of obscurity that a lifetime of study will not extract more than a teaspoon of enlightenment. But some, like the works of Paracelsus and a certain mad Arab, are Pandora's Boxes that can be unlocked by an astute or talented individual.

A degree of scepticism and a hefty pinch of salt are always needed when dealing with such people. When you boil it all down, most of their great workings rarely amount to much that cannot be explained by a willingness to believe.

A very small minority have genuinely succeeded in contacting beings from another plane, as you might say, and producing, in reality, the effects so often claimed by spiritualists. Just as the psychic medium may allow their body to be possessed by a spirit for the purposes of communication, they may also be able to send their spirit out to possess another.

What I had heard of the Haywood affair reeked of incompetence. When attempting to exchange bodies with an unwitting or unwilling subject, surely the first thing to do would be to ensure your body is secured by a servant or assistant to prevent the exchangee from making mischief. It seemed the preparations had been inadequate; Haywood had not only escaped from the room where he had been confined but had fought off two men and made it out of the house, to liberty and into trouble.

The ceremonial sword and the robes also gave me grounds for doubt. These things were stage props, more often found among those who wished to impress than serious practitioners of the occult.

I read through D'Onston's original account of his exchange of personalities with a German colleague. The process seemed simple; taking charge of a new body was as simple as driving a new motorcar. As with cars, the vehicle had its own tendency, and the body retained its old habits and proclivities. In his German body, D'Onston experience a craving for, and subsequent delight in, wurst and sauerkraut, which had previously disgusted him, as well as desire for his friend's fiancée which had not troubled him hitherto.

I suspected the transfer was accidental or at least unexpected. Why the wizard would have chosen this particular carpenter I could not even conjecture, although I could see why he wished to cover his tracks and masquerade as Haywood after he had succeeded.

My hope was that I would not need to do anything and that everyone would find themselves back in their right bodies by morning. Perhaps it had just been something in the nature of an experiment with no harm intended, although to carry out such an experiment with an unwilling participant was a dubious practice.

There was also the possibility that the perpetrator wanted to borrow Haywood's body for some sinister purpose, such as the commission of a crime.

My first act was to dash off a telegram to Captain Cross and take it to the post office on Westow Street. The saying that it is a small world is partly true: each of us does tend to inhabit their own limited circle. Cross was in the business of esoteric and forbidden books, and if anyone bought or sold such items, he might have a record of them. I looked at the street map of where Haywood had been picked up and took down the names of the eight nearest streets.

If things did not revert to their proper places, then knowing the address of the wizard might be important in resolving matters. As an afterthought, and an even longer shot, I asked Cross if he could recommend a means of reversing the magic.

I would have liked to interview the man in the asylum and find out what he knew, but that would be difficult to arrange and was unlikely to be fruitful. Partly because of his distress and confusion, but mainly because he probably did not know anything beyond what he had said. He must have seen his new face in a mirror, and if he had recognised it he would surely have told Smith.

This left the most obvious approach: tackling the fake Haywood and letting him know that the game was up, that he needed to return Haywood's body to its rightful owner or face the consequences. He might brazen it out and laugh in my face. Nobody was going to believe me and proving an offence had been committed under English Law would be impossible.

If he took me seriously, it might go worse. The man might

possess other occult powers—perhaps the ability to paralyze someone with the evil eye, or kill them with a word, as D'Onston claimed to be able to do. Such characters needed to be approached with caution.

On balance, the false Haywood might still be a reasonable man. So often in life we assume the worst of people, and that creates friction which leads to unnecessary conflict. An open mind and a friendly word can see things settled quickly and peaceably.

In this optimistic frame of mind, I took myself to Northwood Road and one of the streets that ran into it. The area is a warren of Victorian terraced housing, painted front doors, scrubbed doorsteps, window boxes, and neat front gardens. The sort of place that intellectuals decry as characterless suburbia, and ordinary people celebrate as 'home, sweet home' in framed embroidery with floral embellishments.

I straightened my tie and knocked on the door. It was early evening and just getting dark. There were no lights on in the windows and my knocking echoed through an empty house. It seemed everyone was out for the evening, and no telling how many hours before they came back.

I saw a passer-by with a small dog looking at me and gave him a friendly nod. A man of my type—one of my proportions— loitering about is rather conspicuous. At best, the neighbours would assume I was collecting a debt, which would not endear me to anyone.

A woman in a shawl opened the door.

"Yes?"

Some people can convey volumes in a single word. I surmised that she was irked at having been interrupted at whatever she was doing.

"Harry Stubbs, madam, of Lantern Insurance," I said, proffering a card.

"I'm with the Pru," she said, making to shut the door.

"I wish to speak with one of your lodgers," I said, "about a matter of business."

"The lodgers all went out to the pub," she said. "And no, I don't know what pub where. Who's in trouble, anyway?"

"Nobody. Just a small matter of settling an insurance claim."

This was an outright lie, but people are always more co-operative when they think money is being doled out. From her expression I doubted she believed me. I have the look of one who collects money rather than delivering it.

"Oh yeah? I'll let him know."

She took my card and, in the same smooth movement, shut the door in my face. Without even asking which lodger she was to inform.

I could have scoured the local pubs, but that was a fool's errand. There were far too many in easy walking distance, and it was fifty-fifty whether she was even telling the truth. On top of which was the equally serious problem that I did not know what the man I was after looked like. Asking around for him would be more likely to give him warning than turn him up.

A more dedicated man might have pressed on, but I decided to call it a day and return to my own affairs. I went back to my lodgings for dinner and a read of the papers, penned a brief letter to Sally, who was spending the evening visiting, and rounded off with a pint and a game of darts at the Conquering Hero.

With a little luck the exchange would have worn off and everything would be back to normal in the morning, with no need for me to exert myself. Sometimes masterly inactivity works wonders.

My sleep might have been more troubled if I had known just how wrong my assumptions were, and just how dangerous an opponent I was facing. By no means the gentlemanly explorer of the arcana I had imagined, he was something far more dangerous. And, had I but known, he was not even the worst of my problems.

CHAPTER THREE: THE WIZARD'S LAIR

In conversation, my friend and associate Captain Cross is apt to digress into unexpected territory and lose you in a tangle of past adventures. Telegraphic communication with him is far more efficient. Over the wires, he is as concise as everyone else who pays by the word.

In answer to my first question, he sent me an address on Belvedere Road, with the name Balthar and the information that the gentleman had purchased Gnostic texts on three occasions, thirty years ago. Most people would have moved in that time, but I felt in my water that we had our man. Not that I had any clue what Gnostic texts were.

To the second question, on whether there was a way to reverse the transfer of minds, he stated: DO NOT ATTEMPT MAGIC STOP EVER STUBBS STOP PACKAGE TO FOLLOW STOP

Not long ago, I would have had to go to the Upper Norwood library to find anything out. Now, I had my own small stock of reference works and I can tell you that the Gnostic religion, if it can be called such, is largely mysterious to outsiders, and deliberately so. While run-of-the-mill religion spreads itself far and wide, and ardent believers are nowadays apt to buttonhole you on street corners and share their Good News, the Gnostics keep their religion away from prying eyes.

Things are confused by the fact that the Gnostics are fragmented into warring sects. At any rate, their texts are secret, forbidden. That gives them a certain glamour, especially for young people, and ensures their books are valuable enough for someone like Cross to pursue.

The heart of Gnosticism, as far as I understand it, is that this world is an evil place, created by a subordinate deity rather than the genuine author of creation. Heavenly souls are lured here and trapped in mortal clay, unable to escape until they gain secret knowledge and understanding, which only Gnosticism offers. But while the Church of England and its numerous competitors democratically offer salvation for all and sundry, the Gnostics are more selective. In their version, salvation is only available to those with a particular level of refinement, leaving the rest of us gross creatures stuck here until Kingdom Come.

One strain of Gnosticism, the Sethian, is strongly associated with magical practice. There is a whole area of study of magic papyri written in late Egyptian, using a combination of Greek script and something called kharaktêres—which are just 'characters'—of an angelic language. I was starting to compare this to examples of other scripts I had come across from genuinely alien languages, when I realised an hour had passed and I was getting side-tracked.

Sufficient to the case was that the subject appeared to be a wizard in the Sethian Gnostic tradition, or at any rate might have been thirty years ago.

Belvedere Road is a select address, a road of mansions built in the last century, and the place was as grand as its neighbours, quite the towering masterpiece. Approaching, I noted two things: that there was an upper room with large windows in which the brass tube of a telescope could be seen, pointed heavenwards, and that the place was shuttered, stout bars set across every window.

It did not have a friendly air. A fence of tall iron spikes ran round the property, although the defences were imperfect as the gate was ajar.

From the gate I could see that the front door was nailed shut. Someone had done the job hastily but thoroughly, nailing four planks across the entrance. The work looked to have been carried out recently.

Next door, in the area outside the windows below ground level, a woman was beating a rug as though she held a grudge.

"They've cleared out," she said, pausing in her labour to

scrutinise me. She was a small woman of around sixty, hair covered by a scarf, wearing a full-length apron and rubber gloves. A cigarette adhered to her lower lip.

"That's a pity," I said.

"Not a friend, are you?" she asked.

"I'm here on business," I said, and came down the steps to proffer her my business card and tip my bowler. "Harry Stubbs, Lantern Insurance."

"Oho," she said, taking the card. "Insurance investigation, eh? I wouldn't be surprised, I would not be surprised one little bit."

"Excuse me, Mrs…?"

"I'm Mrs Spinney, Mr Stubbs." She smiled and then jerked a thumb disapprovingly at the house next door. "I'm his neighbour. The things I have to put up with!"

I surmised from the layout of doorbells and letterboxes at the entrance that this property had been divided into flats, and that Mrs Spinney was the occupant of the basement flat.

My enquiring look was all she needed to keep going. "Well, there's the Romanies for a start. I've got nothing against them myself, but they're not used to living in houses, are they? Not *clean*."

"And who would these Romanies be?" I asked.

"His servants," she said. "Why can't he have proper Christian servants? Each to his own, but you want a servant you can trust with the silver, I would say."

"Very true," I said.

This sort of prejudice is universal among those who do not know better. Having had dealings with Romanies, who form a significant segment of the boxing community, my main conclusion is that they are neither better nor worse than anyone else. I would only say they are remarkably tenacious in the ring.

"They're a husband and wife, the servants. Unfriendly. No point going round there to borrow a cup of sugar! And that German boy—well, he looks like butter wouldn't melt in his mouth, but if you ask me, he's a spy."

"To be honest with you, Mrs Spinney, my business is with Mr Balthar himself."

"Him!" she said, crossing her arms under her bosom. "He's aloof. Wouldn't give you the time of day. He's got a right to his privacy, we all do, but he's downright secretive. And there are comings and goings at all hours."

Mrs Spinney kept tabs on her suspicious neighbour, rattling off his misdemeanours as though consulting a list of charges.

From failing to keep the weeds in his garden in check until they spilled over into hers, to not sending a Christmas card, to being negligent in the matter of the Resident's Association, he had offended in every way possible. He had never been seen in church on a Sunday morning, but he had been seen regularly walking round West Norwood Cemetery, which was hardly acceptable.

He did not work, as far as anyone knew, and nobody knew where he got his money from, which to her was highly suspicious. Equally damning, he did not have any family or if he did, they never visited, which was just as bad. He was not foreign, or if he was, he spoke very good English. Apart from that he was, in her eyes, barely respectable, for all that he owned a big house and kept staff.

Spilling the beans to an insurance investigator was not an act of revenge so much as an unloading of grievances nobody else would listen to. The cigarette adhering to her lip continued to burn without ever quite coming to an end.

He talked loudly with his friends late at night and kept people awake and, furthermore, inside the house it was not normal at all.

I cocked an eyebrow at this. Had Mrs Spinney been inside? Before I could ask, she assured me she had never been invited to set foot in there—and was not sure if she wanted to. She had spoken to a gentleman who had been carrying out some carpentry work in the place, and who took his tea-breaks outdoors, and according to him the house was full of locked rooms, strange pictures, and display cases full of old bones, and stone and things. Mrs Spinney did not mind a neighbour having his interests, but none of it was exactly normal, now, was it?

I was forced to agree.

Not that the carpenter was an unimpeachable source: she

had smelled drink on his breath, and caught the tell-tale clink of a bottle in his tool bag when he left for the day.

"He wasn't the most reliable type," she said, "but from what he told me, Mr Balthar is a very queer fish."

"That's very much the impression I'm getting," I agreed. "Did you catch the carpenter's name by any chance? Edgar Hayman, something like that?"

"Edward Haywood," she said at once. "You talked to him?"

"He's someone I'd like to talk to."

"He keeps animals in the cellar—him next door, that is—now is that allowed in the by-laws?"

"Animals?" I queried.

"Pigs. I hear 'em snorting and snuffling around at night sometimes. I've complained, but he won't do anything. I say pigs, I've never actually seen them, but who knows what he has?"

"Who indeed?" I said, feeling called on to say something, and not being able to suggest anything worse than pigs.

"And then last night," she said. "There was screeching, and banging about, and carrying on at four o'clock in the morning. I was going to put another note through the door when I saw they'd nailed it all up."

"Was there a removals van or any such?" I asked.

"No such luck," she said. "I expect he'll arrive back late one night and wake the whole street up again."

"It must be very trying for you, Mrs Spinney," I said.

"Very trying," she said. "This insurance investigation—would that be about the fire?"

"I'm afraid I'm not at liberty to divulge the details," I said. "But I can tell you confidentially that we have our eye on Mr Balthar."

"Do you really?" she said, with a kind of thrill.

I nodded significantly.

"This fire—?"

"All I know—all I know is one Thursday afternoon about six weeks ago, they had a big fire. Smoke was pouring out all the upper windows! Mrs Black on the first floor said it was more like steam, but you'd need a locomotive to make that much steam! I went round and asked about calling the fire brigade, but the Romany answered, and he told me there was nothing to be done. And he was not polite about it neither. Is that the one you're investigating?"

She was bursting to find out more about her neighbour's infractions, but in my guise as an official I would not give anything away.

"I dare say Mr Balthar has made a few claims," I said gravely. "And if anything comes out in court, you'll read it in the papers."

"It'll be in the papers?"

"It has been known. It's been very interesting talking to you, Mrs Spinney," I said, tipping my hat. "Thank you for your assistance."

"Anything to oblige, I'm sure," she said.

On the continent, governments maintain secret police forces. In this country we have neighbours like Mrs Spinney.

I paused for a closer look at the iron gate. The bolt which should have secured it was cut through. The severed end looked melted, which was odd. From the makeshift padlock on the front door, I surmised that the lock had been disabled.

Walking away, I reflected that if you are going to carry out any sort of clandestine activity, it is advisable to maintain good relations with your neighbours. A few friendly words and the odd gift to Mrs Spinney from Balthar would have kept her complacent. Instead, she had catalogued his every move as assiduously as a private detective, with particular reference to everything that was out of the ordinary for suburbia.

I did not doubt that, given another interview, one could have teased out all sorts of details of Mr Balthar's activities, but everything she had said suggested one who was enmeshed in the study of the occult and remained apart from mundane things.

She had mentioned one male servant and a German boy, as well as a female servant. Possibly those were the two kidnappers Haywood had fought off, but I was forming a different theory. It seemed to me that someone had cut the bolt on the gate, then cut through the lock on the front door with the same tool. That was what necessitated the boarding up afterwards.

Following which, there had been a ruckus in the house, culminating in Mr Haywood, occupying an unfamiliar body, chasing away two attackers with a sword before being apprehended by the police. At which point the rest of the household had decided to decamp.

Walking back towards the high street I sensed I was being followed. A couple of times I tried to get a look at my tail, but he was too canny and maintained a distance. On the third effort, when I tried to double back, he was wise to me and disappeared down a side street, leaving an impression of dark clothes and a cap but nothing else.

The plot was, as they say, thickening.

CHAPTER FOUR: AMBUSHED

The information from Mrs Spinney made me consider the mental transfer in a different light. Rather than being the result of a deliberate plan, had it been the desperate act of one who, cornered by his enemies, had taken the only escape route open to him? Having forged some connection with Eddie Haywood while he had worked in the house, had Balthar been able to switch bodies at short notice?

Stealing a man's body is still a low thing to do, but if this was not a pre-meditated theft there was every chance he might be persuaded to switch back. Of course, I would need assure him I was not in league with his pursuers.

At this point I made doubly sure I was not still being followed, taking a bus first in one direction and then another before heading back to my true destination, a return to Northwood Road. While the gothic pile that Balthar inhabited might be the stuff of ghost stories, this was comfortingly suburban. The delivery boys sailed past on their bicycles and mothers pushed prams in a sane and ordered world.

Or so it seemed.

The door was answered by the same woman as before, wearing the same shawl and the same stern expression.

"You," she said, and turned and shouted upstairs that the insurance man had come back.

"Send him up," someone shouted back. She let me in and directed me up the stairs, following at a short distance.

The upstairs smelled of old cigarette smoke and unwashed laundry. The landing door opened into a living room which had seen better days. Stained and mismatched rugs were arranged on the floor, and the sofa and two armchairs were worn and battered. Discarded clothes and newspapers were scattered about, and empty bottles sprouted from every available surface, with a particularly fine collection on what might have been a coffee table.

As I came in, a man was rummaging through a large toolbox, with another holding the Picture Post at his side. It looked like he was trying to conceal something under it, and I was on my guard.

"Mr Haywood?" I asked, looking from one to the other, business card ready in my hand.

The man with the toolbox looked up at me, smiling. He was a stocky, ruddy-faced man. The smile did not look normal on him.

"I think there's been some sort of misunderstanding here," he said pleasantly. "Why don't you take a seat?"

"I'm sure you're right," I said. The atmosphere felt wrong, and my suspicions were confirmed when he brandished a sharp-looking chisel and the man next to him dropped his paper and raised a mallet.

"Get him!" he yelled, and the next thing I knew everything went black.

I had been ambushed by someone hiding by the door. He had thrown a canvas bag over my head and was trying to draw it tight around my neck, and I sensed the other two advancing on me.

One hand went to my neck in an instinctive act of self-preservation. I retained enough of my wits to realise this was not the greatest threat, and at the same time I lashed out with one boot and kicked the underside of the coffee table, sending a dozen bottles and assorted other items into the air and raising a shout from my assailants.

With my free hand I reached behind me and seized the man's shirt front, leaning to one side and hauling him around. As I had assumed, I had a good advantage in weight, with the added benefit of surprise, and had him off-balance.

He flailed at me to not much effect, and I heaved him in the direction of the others and heard them collide within arm's reach.

I stepped back, using both hands to try and free the bag around my neck, when someone crashed into me, and I fell over backwards with him on top.

Punching down from above puts you in a greatly superior position, partly because of the benefit of gravity, but more because you can swing your arms, whereas the unfortunate below has limited freedom of movement. I moved my head about though, and the presence of the bag must have made it more difficult. He hit me with bruising force, but no great accuracy.

The one advantage of this situation was that I did not have to see to have a pretty good idea of where to aim, and in terms of weight I was punching guineas to shillings. I struck out freely, and after a couple of good body blows, he was off me.

This all took place to the sound of a woman screaming.

I got the bag off my head just in time to see the mallet descending. My reflexes saved me again, though I still took a numbing blow on the shoulder. On his next swing I caught his wrist and we grappled, falling to the ground together.

As I struggled, I saw Haywood looming over me, blood running down his face, holding the chisel in both hands. I used the man I was wrestling with as a shield, even as he was attempting to knee me in the groin.

A moment later Haywood was gone, and I delivered a series of jabs to my attacker's face with my left hand. The first checked him, the second dazed him; at the third he let go of my right hand, at which point he was in a purely defensive position. I was able to direct swift lefts and rights to his body, neck, and head with sufficient conviction for him to roll over and curl up.

The woman was still screaming as I bounced to my feet, ready for the next round, but besides the man at my feet there was only one other person facing me in the room. He did not look like he wanted a fight but was staring through the doorway through which I had entered.

"What's going on?" he asked.

"You stay here," I instructed, hurrying out and down the stairs, past the landlady who looked like she might scream again. She pointed a shaky finger towards the back of the house.

I barged through the back door in time to see the gate bang shut. The gardens backed on to a path leading to the road. My quarry had enough of a lead to make it to the road before I could catch sight of him. I was left standing on the street, looking left and right.

A good amount of traffic occupied the road, and a few pedestrians going either way, but nobody was running away. He had either ducked out of sight or had the good sense to walk normally and blend in with the background, perhaps on the other side of the road where he would be partially obscured by the traffic. Maybe he had climbed on to the double-decker bus which was even now passing.

"Which way did he go?" I asked a woman with a basket full of groceries and a small boy in tow.

She just looked away though, as did the others I tried to make eye contact with. This is one of the perennial inconveniences of being my size, build, and general demeanour: folk are apt to assume the worst of you when you are pursuing a man who is smaller, lighter, and less rugged. My dishevelled appearance from the fracas would have done nothing to impress them with my respectability, come to that. Grazed knuckles are not a good signifier of peaceful intent.

I set off one way at a trot. Seeing nothing after fifty yards, I quickly changed my mind and went back on myself. I could feel every eye on me, including the mother and child. So much so, that I went around the long way to the front of the house after I had given up on the search.

"If you try to come in, I'll get the police," the landlady informed me, standing outside her door. Faces looked down on us from the houses on either side.

"You'd be well within your rights to do that, madam," I admitted. "But I might suggest first asking your lodgers their opinion on the matter, and whether we can't all settle this peaceably and without application to the law, who I believe were here the other night."

She looked at me as though I might be about to attack her if she looked away for a moment.

"Madam," I said, "I am the injured party, having come

under unprovoked attack the moment I stepped through the door, without any discussion, as you witnessed."

She looked as though she would have liked to argue, but found my logic unassailable

"You wait here," she told me and disappeared inside. The door closed, the key turned in the lock and the bolt shot across. She was taking no chances.

Some of the faces at the windows melted away at my look, while others—the very young and the very old—stared boldly back.

Waiting on the doorstep, I set to wondering how I might track down the false Mr Haywood or Balthar. He did not have many resources to call on that I could tell. He had been forced to flee his original home in the dead of night, at short notice, and had again been evicted. He was a man alone, on foot, with precious little by way of financial resources. He might have fled to the locked-up house I had visited earlier, but without the servants he would have trouble getting in. Also, there was a good chance it was being watched.

The bolt rattled, and the door opened.

"You'd best come in," said the landlady. "No more rough stuff, mind."

"I won't be the first to start anything, madam," I assured her.

We repeated the same procedure as before, only this time she came with me to the upstairs flat, which was rather the worse for wear, with two chairs and the coffee table all broken. Some ashtrays had been upset, and a thin film of grey ash settled over the scene like a dusting of snow.

Two of my assailants glowered at me from the other side of the room. Both wore fresh bruises. The one with a moustache held his hand in a way that suggested a sprained wrist. Probably from inexpertly punching me.

"Now then," said the landlady, standing between us, and looking from me to them and back. "Perhaps somebody would like to tell me what all this kerfuffle is about."

"Eddie told us they were on to him," said the one with the moustache, who was looking very sorry for himself right now.

"Who were?" asked the landlady.

"He didn't say," supplied the other. "He wanted us to hold them back a minute so he could get away. And being mates, well, we wanted to help."

"Of course we did, Robbie," said the moustache.

"And you thought his attacking me with a chisel was reasonable behaviour?" I asked. The chisel itself was displayed on a side table with some other odds and ends, as part of the first stage of tidying up.

The two men exchanged a look.

"Well," said Robbie with a half shrug. "Pop a bag over you, knock you on the bonce so you're out cold and Eddie would be off and away, that was what he said."

"We didn't know he was going to stab you," said the other, who must have been Gus. "Honest."

"What were you planning on doing afterwards?" asked the landlady.

"Nothing much," said Robbie. "We didn't think he'd be interested in us."

"Allow me to hazard a guess," I said. "Mr Haywood has been acting strangely since last night—since around the time of the police visit. His demeanour since then has been highly unusual and you have had reason to wonder at his mental state."

"He does act funny sometimes," Robbie said. "Sometimes he's not himself. But Eddie's a drinker."

"But had he been acting especially strangely?"

"Writing those letters," said the landlady.

"There's that," said Robbie. "After the police visit, he was up writing letters all night. And he never writes anyone, usually."

"He had to borrow envelopes from me," said the landlady. "I don't expect I'll get those back."

"And he took the letters to the post office himself to send them," said Robbie. "Wouldn't say who he was writing to, or even let me see them."

"Overseas, I think," said Gus. "I offered to sell him some stamps, but he said it wasn't enough."

"And would I be correct in saying that Mr Haywood offered you some inducement to waylay me—that you were bribed?"

"Maybe he did, maybe he didn't," said Robbie, but he shifted on his feet as he said it. I hope for his sake he stayed away from the poker table.

"I bet he offered you everything he had in the flat," I said.

"What are you getting at, Mister?" asked the landlady.

"In our situations, we don't necessarily have the luxury of turning down that sort of offer," said Robbie, somewhat sourly.

Robbie was eying my shoes. They were nearly new, well-polished, and, as he perhaps could tell, made to measure, which is sometimes a necessary thing with feet my size. His own footwear was scuffed and sad. These were not easy times for many working men.

"Too true," added Gus.

"Exactly so," I said, taking out my notebook and pencil. "But, given there is no real harm done on either side we can forget the matter, if you don't mind obliging with some information."

"What about my furniture?" asked the landlady.

The debt recovery trade had given me a smart appreciation of the value of second-hand furniture. When you have to recover a certain sum, you need to know what's worth having if it comes to taking possession, not to mention whether a household in its entirety can cover the value of a debt.

The cost to repair two chairs and one table of that quality should not be more than eight shillings, and that was on the generous side.

"I can see my way clear to covering that, madam," I said. "If these two gentlemen wouldn't mind helping me."

"That's very good of you," she said, impressed by the unexpected generosity, her gaze turning harder as she pointed it at her two lodgers. "I'm sure they'd be happy to help. If they want to carry on living under my roof, that is."

"Just a few details about Mr Haywood," I said. "Approximate height and weight, distinguishing features, and what he was wearing when he went out that door."

There followed a three-way colloquy while they assessed Haywood's vital statistics. The men had not noticed his clothing, but their landlady gave me a pretty good account.

"Not carrying anything?" I asked. "No bag or holdall?"

"There's a suitcase in his room," said Gus. "He was packing, but you caught him on the hop."

"So you knew he was going?"

"*I* certainly didn't," said the landlady.

"It was a spur-of the-moment thing," said Robbie. "He has been sort of quiet. "

"Very quiet," corrected Gus.

"Not saying much, but listening to everything. After breakfast we heard him banging about in his room and when we opened the door, he was packing."

"So you knew he was going," I repeated, leading up to the big question. "But did he give any indication where he might be going?"

They exchanged that look again.

"Away," said Robbie when I had let the silence grow. "He said he was going away and didn't know when he was coming back."

"What about the rent he owes?" asked the landlady, voice rising an octave. "He was just going to skip out on me, was he? You mean to say he's gone for good?"

"Mr Haywood is not currently in his right mind," I said, replacing my notebook. "But if we can locate him, there's a very good chance he can be treated."

"I'll treat *him*," she said.

"And if you don't find him?" asked Robbie.

"If you were hoping to divide his effects, you might be disappointed," I said, guessing that was what he had offered them. "He'll be wanting them back when he's in his right mind. You have nothing to gain—so let me know if you remember anything."

I had heard similar speeches from police officers, and I think I delivered it well enough. Unfortunately though, these two did not have any more information to give.

"I'll leave this here," I said, laying my business card on the mantelpiece. "And I'll send a carpenter round to fix the damage."

"A better carpenter than Eddie Haywood, I hope," said the landlady.

After locating my bowler in the wreckage, I dusted it off and knocked out a dent, placed it on my head, and bade them good day.

CHAPTER FIVE: STRANGE DREAMS

I spent the rest of the day pursuing a few leads and deciding how to make my next move, but things developed in an unexpected direction. That night I was visited by an unusual dream. Each night, every one of us visits a strange world of which we remember little, those of mine that I can remember are coloured by some of my stranger experiences. It is characteristic of dreams that, however strange the situation we find ourselves in, it never occurs to us that we are dreaming until afterwards.

In this case I was in a crowded railway carriage, and it did not seem strange that we were speeding through clouds rather than across fields. This was in fact a variation of a dream I had had many times before. I took my seat with some difficulty, railway seats being on the small side at the best of times. The travellers around me were all disapproving undertakers, each carrying a small rectangular black case.

I was wondering, as I always did at this point in the dream, whether I was on the right train and whether I had the right ticket, but also whether the brown paper package I had was allowed, or whether the conductor would order me off the train. I was trying to hide it, but there was no room under the table, and the parcel shelf was just out of reach, however hard I tried.

Two dark objects, somewhere between fish and birds, flew by the window and there was a double thud against the side of the train. A shower of orange sparks erupted in the corridor outside, and as it subsided two figures could be seen looking in.

They were looking for a seat. I was trying to signal to them that they were out of luck when I realised that the carriage was now empty. Nothing had happened to the undertakers, they just were not there anymore.

The door to the compartment slid open. The first to come through was a woman wearing spectacles with silver frames, and iron-grey hair. She was dressed in a man's black suit. Her expression reminded me of the more severe type of nurse. Or, rather, since she had an air of education and authority, one of those female doctors you meet in the army, who won't take nonsense from any man regardless of his rank.

The companion who followed wore similarly dark clothes, but was an altogether larger individual, who might also have been a heavyweight boxer. He looked to be the size of a bull, far too big to fit in the carriage, but he came in alongside the other without difficulty. His face might have been drawn by one of those modern artists who try to get in several angles at once. This grotesque visage changed and flowed as he turned his head but, this being a dream, it did not seem particularly extraordinary.

"Sorry to disturb you," said the doctor, more an introduction than an apology, as they seated themselves opposite me.

"I'm dreaming," I said, making the realisation at last, and wondering why I did not wake up, as dreamers usually do at this point.

The doctor put a hand on my arm.

"Please stay with us," she said, as though to detain me from standing up. Something told me I would not wake from the dream until she released me.

"The name is Harry Stubbs, of Lantern Insurance," I said. "I don't believe we've met."

"You're taking it well," said the man, talking more to his companion than to me. "That makes communication easier."

I produced a business card. Neither of them took it or offered one in return as etiquette demanded.

"What are you after, Mr Stubbs?" asked the doctor.

This was a dream and she might have been asking about anything, but I knew perfectly well what she meant.

"I'm trying to return things to their proper places," I said. "Things and people. Keeping the peace, no more than that. And yourselves?"

"That's not what we usually hear from TDS," said the man with the cubist face.

"As a matter of fact, TDS are uninvolved at this point," I said carefully. "It's just me."

"You're an independent agent then," said the doctor. "Well, if you give us what we want, we'll see what we can do to smooth things over."

"None of us wants for things to be disturbed," said the man, and glanced upwards. "It's better for all of us if there is no trouble."

While the doctor seemed much less sympathetic than her words, the grotesque man was the opposite. Instead of a threat, this sounded like an appeal. Despite being a hulk with the face of a monster, he did not feel as dangerous as the woman.

"We are looking for this," said the doctor, holding up an object the size of a deck of playing cards, made of clear green resin or glass.

She passed it to me and I found that it was contoured, with smoothed edges and a series of indentations. Embedded in the material were egg-shaped blue objects, the size of marbles, which turned and quivered like compass needles. I could not tell how they could be encased in solid material and move—but this was a dream.

"What is it?" I asked.

"Something from outside," she said. "Contraband. Balthar has it; we need it."

"It doesn't belong to him," chipped in the big man, as if this would persuade me. "And I need it."

"Just that," said the woman. "Find it for us, and we'll go."

"And who are you, if I might ask?"

She sighed. "Questions are a burden for others; answers a prison for oneself."

"We are like Balthar," said the man. "His tribe, more or less, you might say. Similarly imprisoned here."

"The dream is fading," said the woman. Through the carriage window was the Egyptian Hall of Crystal Palace. In fact, the big window, and the carriage, now appeared to be part of the Crystal Palace itself. "Find the item and we will see that everything is put back as it was."

His companion had already opened the door. He raised his hand in a parting gesture, and they were gone.

There was no door now, and I was trapped in a room with glass on all sides. The people outside were walking past, not seeming to notice me. I was torn between trying to attract their attention and fearfulness about what they might do, and what the label said on the outside of my cage.

And then, of course, I woke up.

I turned on the light and located a notebook. I generally keep one beside my bed for those fleeting thoughts that occur to you in the midnight hour, and which you can never remember the next day. Dreams fade quickly, and I was determined to make a record of this one. I am no great believer in the premonitory power of dreams as many are. Communication through the medium of dreams is practically a mainstream theory in psychology these days. I believe the great Dr Sigmund Freud himself has documented cases of dream telepathy and lectured on the subject.

This one did seem to have a particular significance to it.

I added a life-size sketch of the glass object and notes on the appearance of the two interlopers.

Contrary to my expectation, I fell asleep again as soon as my head hit the pillow. Equally surprisingly, although the other dreams of the night evaporated from my mind as thoroughly as morning dew, the encounter in the railway carriage stayed with me as though it had really happened.

Something almost equally unexpected occurred over my breakfast porridge. My landlady brought in the post, which included a small package. The return address showed it was from Captain Cross. It contained a box, two inches square, such as jewellers use for rings.

My landlady, who must have expected something more relevant to my forthcoming nuptials, was disappointed to see it contained just a blue stone the size of a kidney bean.

"Prevention is better, or at any rate easier, than cure," the captain had written in an accompanying note. "This amulet gives some protection against possession, but I do not guarantee its effectiveness. Be careful. Capt X."

The stone was strikingly reminiscent of one procured from Whately as protection from the evil eye, which I had lost in unfortunate circumstances. It was also identical to those embedded in the resinous object I had handled in my dream.

Which was not just a dream.

CHAPTER SIX: A DEBT REPAID

Life produces unexpected twists and turns. Getting from A to B you may have to travel via F, K, and X. For example, on some occasions you want to make a cup of tea, and you find the gas-ring will not light, forcing you to descend to the cellar to turn the gas tap—except one of your house mates has the key to the cellar door, and someone else has to tell you where he is, so you can get it, open the door, turn on the gas, and make your tea…if you still want it.

So it was in this instance that circumstances carried me by motor-van to a furniture restoring concern on Brickfield Road, the site of much of the area's light industry. I was there to do Arthur Renville a favour, knowing he would use his considerable resources to grant me a favour in return.

"Reckon this is it," said my driver, an American by the name of Bear. If anything, his accent had grown stronger during his years in England.

"I believe so," I said.

"We gonna have any rough stuff?" he asked, half smiling. "You gonna have at him with your quarterstaff?"

Bear and I had worked together before. His joke was that we British were still medieval. He was not entirely wrong.

"Not by choice," I said.

The business had an open courtyard, with the workshop on one side and two warehouses forming the other two. An apprentice was laboriously sanding down a huge bedstead in the middle. It was one of those dark old Victorian relics; without the mattress and bedding it looked like the skeleton of a dinosaur. As the van drew up, the apprentice's head turned, and his lips moved as he called to someone.

A door opened and a man looked out. I had never met Mr Stamford, but knew him by reputation. He was in his late forties, balding but with no other signs of physical decline, with the steel-hard, steel-bright gaze of a man who knows what he wants. He waited in the open doorway, coming no further.

"Best if you wait in here," I told Bear, opening the van door. "Don't get ready to load up until I give the signal."

"I'll sit tight and watch the show," he said.

I nodded politely to the apprentice at his sanding, who ignored me. Stamford looked me up and down as I approached, in an exaggerated way that suggested he did not think much of what he saw.

"Is it such a sum of money Renville needed to send a big bloke like you to bring it?" he asked, with a sneer.

"My name is Harry Stubbs, Mr Stamford," I said, removing my hat. "As you've surmised, Mr Renville has sent me with payment for the safekeeping of certain goods, and to collect said goods."

I produced a brown envelope from an inner pocket, weighing it in both hands. The young man continued to sand away beside me.

"If I open that,"—he nodded at the envelope but did not approach—"am I going to be disappointed?"

"The payment is based on the previously-agreed and long-established per diem rate for the relevant number of days," I said.

"That's not what I'm asking for," said Stamford. "As you and Renville well know, I've upped my rates for this consignment. And he can either pay up or say goodbye to his loot."

Arthur Renville is a consignment man, one who acquires ship's cargoes which have been damaged or written off for some reason, but which may still retain significant residual value. When goods are damaged by water, or perishable goods perish, the underwriters tend to dismiss the lot with the strike of a pen. But a captain knows better than the insurers when not everything is equally rotten or water-logged, and that intact goods remain. Hence there is a trade in the disposal of commodities which may be in legal limbo.

The exact details of where such consignments have come from and the lawful ownership thereof are often tricky, and it is preferable not to open the discussion with anyone in authority. Hence, Arthur Renville often had a pressing need to store large quantities of goods without too much publicity. People with spare space, like Stamford, made a tidy profit acting as bonded warehouses.

Except that Stamford had welched on the deal and was holding the goods hostage.

"A consignment of Scandinavian furs," said Stamford. "Some very nice stuff. I shouldn't have much trouble finding a buyer for them."

I continued to weigh the envelope in my hands.

"A deal is a deal, and Mr Renville has always been fair to you, always paid promptly, always kept his word," I said.

"Oh yes, he's a regular angel, Renville is," said Stamford, his mouth twisting. "You've never done time, have you? Never been inside. I have, and all because of that wonderful Mr Renville."

"I don't know about that," I said. Now he reminded me, I could see the prison-look on Stamford, the deep-cut lines in his face, the suspicious eyes. He was probably younger than he looked, too. Prison ages a man.

"Of course you don't. Two and a half years I served, on a charge of handling stolen goods, on account of some of Renville's boxes in my warehouse." He looked me in the eye to see that I understood. "Thirty months at His Majesty's pleasure, in a stinking cell in the Scrubs."

I gathered he had only returned from stir a few weeks previously, and the resentment still burned hot. I guessed that his family had been looked after during this interlude, and that he had been able to resume his business exactly where he had left off, but it seemed this was not enough.

"I want paying," said Stamford. "And if Renville thinks he can send a gorilla to take those furs without paying what I'm asking, he's got another think coming."

"I'm not proposing to do anything without your consent," I said.

"You certainly ain't," said Stamford, stepping back into the doorway and deftly picking up a shotgun leaning against the doorframe out of sight. He raised the weapon, levelling it at my face and pulling back both hammers.

Shotguns have a larger bore than other firearms. While the standard military rifle has a calibre of just under a third of an inch, a twelve-bore shotgun is more than twice that. Looking into two such barrels at close range was like seeing a pair of black eyes stare at me from an abyss.

Satisfied at the effect he had produced, Stamford lowered the weapon to point at my ankle region.

"I picked this up second-hand," he said. "I'm well ahead of Renville, tell him that. Gun beats gorilla: checkmate, muscle man. Now, clear off."

At the edge of my vision, the apprentice scuttled past and disappeared through the still-open doorway.

I am not much at home around guns. There are those, like my friend Captain Cross, who treat them as casually as pocket-knives, but in truth they are far more dangerous, both to those who carry them and those around them. Firearms mean trouble.

I could not tell if the weapon was loaded, but I had to assume it was. Stamford was not the sort to make empty threats. While his hands looked steady enough, there was the risk of a reflex-action trigger-pull if he was startled.

"As I say, I did not come here with the intention of coercing you," I said. "Rather, I wished to smooth things over between you and Mr Renville and ensure the continuance of business as usual."

Stamford had played his ace, but if he had been expecting I would fold and leave the game he would be disappointed.

"What?"

"I was given to understand the source of your grievance, and I can sympathise, Mr Stamford. As it happens, I am no stranger to involuntary confinement myself. I have an idea what you might be feeling."

"Is that right?" He sounded curious, in spite of himself. "What was it, the Glasshouse when you were in the army?"

"Worse than that. It's a story for another day. Suffice to say, I know what it feels like to hear the key in the lock from the other side." Maybe my tone conveyed more than my words, because Stamford did seem to soften a little. He did not lay down the gun though.

"It seemed to me that a little detective work might be helpful. I think you've been harbouring a grudge against the wrong man. Who you should really be complaining about is the one who tipped off the authorities to search your premises."

"What are you talking about, 'tipped off'?" said Stamford, eyes narrowing.

"The police came with a warrant, issued on grounds of reasonable suspicion," I said. "Because they had been tipped off by an informant, who happened to be a former employee of yours." Moving slowly, I extracted a second envelope from an inside pocket. "If I may read you?"

"Go on."

I took a single sheet of notepaper with a brief scrawl on one side.

"'I fixed Stamford good and proper, and taught him a lesson he won't forget. He'll be inside for years. See, I'm a man who won't be crossed. Chew on that if you want to get served the same way.'"

"What is that?"

"It's an attempted blackmail by the letter writer," I said, holding it up for him. "If you compare the handwriting with your files, I believe you'll find a match. You used to employ a man named Vaughn as a clerk."

"I remember Vaughn! Young fellow, caught him with his hand in the till," said Stamford. "And you reckon he had something to do with it?"

I placed the letter on the bedstead in front of me. "Confirm it for yourself. This was addressed to another gentleman who was also involved in the storage of goods in transit. It seems Vaughn was having trouble getting further employment after you sacked him. It was his revenge—nothing to do with Mr Renville."

"I'll talk to that Vaughn," he said, knuckles whitening around the trigger.

"Not this side of Judgement Day," I said. "He met with an accident not long after. Seems he fell under a tram. Practically cut him in half."

The newspaper clipping giving an account of the accident was in my pocket, but I did not feel he would want to see it.

"Renville must have known about this," he said. "Nobody breathed a word to me."

There was resentment in his tone, but not disbelief. I did not tell him that nobody knew just how bitter he would be. They thought he would just take his medicine like anyone else in the business.

"To protect you," I said. "If you knew about Vaughn—even if it was only after the event—if the topic ever came up, people would wonder. Your enemy, the man that put you in prison, coming to an untimely end…they'd wonder what you knew about it."

"You mean whether I'd arranged it," he said. "I suppose *somebody* did arrange it."

"Cause of death was an accident."

I was not going to go into that. Although there were several someones who wished ill on Vaughn, his death was not all it seemed. Nobody had pushed Vaughan under that tram, but he had not ended up there by accident. Vaughan had been involved in murkier matters than blackmail even, and as so often happens in my experience, those who think they can make a fast buck out of the occult end up as cautionary tales.

"Well, that's all very interesting, and it's certainly food for thought. Your problem is," he said, a note of self-satisfaction creeping in, "you've got nothing to bargain with now. You've given everything away."

"I'm not bargaining," I said, opening my hands. "I've given you the information as a goodwill gesture. Mr Renville is a man of goodwill. I think you are as well, at heart."

"What about my money?"

"Nothing can compensate you for that lost time," I said, "and Mr Renville is hardly the party at fault. He lost his goods too, that time, remember? *He's* not the one that owes you damages."

"Ahhh," said Stamford, as though spitting out something

distasteful. He looked like he wanted to shoot someone. "You're just the messenger, ain't you?"

"I am," I agreed. "Now, I've said all I came here to say, Mr Stamford, and you've been good enough to listen, for which I thank you. What message would you like me to take back?"

Stamford swore and started on another rant.

"Thirty months in prison, banged up in the Scrubs! Unless you've been there, you don't know, can't understand what it's like. It's brutal! Prison turns men into animals! Fighting over scraps! Beating each other half to death over a cigarette butt…"

There was much more in this vein, and I nodded to show I was listening. As I expected, he ran out of steam after a bit.

"This isn't doing us any good, is it now," he said, as though I was the one who had started the confrontation, and lowered the gun. "I'll tell you what—I'll tell Renville what." He held out his hand. "You give me that money, and clear off with those boxes of furs, and we'll call it quits."

"I'd be happy to do so, Mr Stamford," I said, handing over the envelope.

"What about this?" he held up the shotgun in one hand. "I wasted money on this."

It looked to be a Holland & Holland, and fairly new. It would certainly have some resale value.

"I'll mention it to Mr Renville," I said. "He might be able to help you."

"Good thinking," he said. "Yes, if Renville pays for it, we'll be all square, tell him that."

The point about prison is not so much loss of liberty, *per se*, as loss of power. The prisoner is no longer master of himself. He does not have the power to decide if he stays or goes, much less to dictate terms to anyone else. Being able to dictate terms to the nearest thing to an authority figure gave Stamford back his freedom.

Another man might have bought the gun off Stamford then and there, and some might think me a fool for passing up an opportunity to arm myself with something more powerful than my customary knuckledusters. As things happened, I might have saved myself some trouble if I had availed myself.

"Consider it done," I said. "May I start loading the goods?"

"In the shed at the end. It's not locked," he said, already admiring the contents of the brown envelope. Money is not as good as freedom, but freedom plus money is a happy combination.

I thought Stamford might have tipped me for aiding such a neat resolution, but I was not too offended when he just waved me away.

CHAPTER SEVEN: AN INTERROGATION

The man inhabiting Haywood's body had not fled Norwood as soon as he could but had stayed at the same address, only packing to leave when he heard someone was looking for him. He must have had reason to stay in the vicinity. Maybe with a view to taking back possession of his property or keeping an eye on it. Maybe something else.

A manhunt of the area was needed. The police could not be called on to track down the fugitive, but there was a much better organisation for the job. The informal network of individuals that comprised Arthur Renville's associates spanned the entire informal economy. Arthur could summon a veritable panopticon gazing across South London, casting a net with a very fine mesh over the whole area.

A couple of early reports told me Haywood was still around. But when I did get word that the net had closed on someone, it was not Haywood at all, but a different and very odd fish indeed.

In addition to Haywood, I had mentioned the two Romany servants and the German described by Mrs Spinney, just on the off chance.

Three men showed up at the china-packing floor. Two of them were colleagues from the days when I used to load boxes on vans at the dead of night, escorting a smaller, slighter figure. He looked a little rumpled, as though he had slept in his suit, and had maybe endured some rough treatment.

He was blond and blue-eyed enough for an alpine travel poster, with a peach-smooth complexion that must have belied his true age. He attracted some looks from the women packing cups into crates as his minders marched him to my office.

"Does his mother know he's out?" Kitty asked one of the others in a voice meant to be overheard.

He had something of the choirboy about him, of having led a cloistered life, away from the outdoors and the rough and tumble of boys' play. His complexion was pale because he had not been exposed to the sun, packed away like precious china in tissue paper. But although he had been shielded from the sinful ways of this world, there was something not altogether wholesome about my visitor.

"He's all yours, Stubbs," one of the escorts told me. "Says his name's Schmidt. Says he's Swiss."

He did not sound like he believed either the given name or nationality.

"Mind you don't break him now," said the other.

"This is Stubbs," one of them told him. "You be a good boy now and tell him what he wants to know."

I could have asked them if they had checked him for concealed weapons, but he might have the sort of weapons which would not be found by any physical search. I suspected my visitor might be a far more dangerous man than his appearance suggested. I rolled the blue stone Captain Cross had sent between my fingers and placed it in my watch pocket. That might help, but wits might be the best protection.

They left him in my office and wandered back out. I heard them exchange some words with the girls, and laughter as they went.

"Make yourself at home, Herr Schmidt," I said, indicating for him to take a chair. He looked at it doubtfully. "Would you care for a cup of tea?"

"No," he said. "Just water."

He was sullen and irritated, but not afraid. He had more the air of one obliged to attend a tedious public function, making the best of a bad job.

Kitty put her head around the door, and I requested a cup of tea and a glass of water.

I knew I needed to put him at his ease, but that was easier said than done. Things had not gotten off to a good start. By the state of his clothes I could tell he had been pulled about a bit, and I now saw his lip was swollen.

"My name is Harry Stubbs, and I am, well, I am an investigator," I said. "I bear you no ill will, Herr Schmidt. In fact, I believe we have interests in common, and that we may be able to help one another. I'd like to talk to you. I don't mean to detain you any longer than strictly necessary."

"*Ach, so,*" he said, or something like it. "I thought those men were the secret police, but they were common thugs. They said a man called Stubbs wanted to see me."

His glasses flashed as he spoke. He had a deal of courage, considering his situation.

"They were asked to bring you here," I said. "I'm sorry if they were rougher than they need have been, but we're all friends here. There's no reason we should not have a frank and fair exchange of information."

Now he was looking at me with interest. Information meant something to Herr Schmidt, but he clearly did not trust me.

"Tell you what, I'll trade you question for question. How's that?"

"Certainly," he said, and continued without a pause. "My first question is: when you will let me go?"

I always prefer to work out my questions in advance and have them written down in front of me. This interview would be more like a boxing match, and I would have to think on my feet.

"Just as soon as this conversation finishes," I said. "Which I do not envisage taking more than half an hour, unless we get to talking and extend it by mutual consent."

"One half hour," he said, looking at his wristwatch. "You may ask your first question."

"Thank you," I said, flipping open my notebook. "I do believe you, by the way, when you say you are Swiss rather than German. Paracelsus was Swiss, if I recall correctly."

"That is correct," he said, less fazed than most by my dropping the name of a celebrated sixteenth-century alchemist and reputed wizard. As I had expected.

I could also have told him that Paracelsus expounded

Gnostic ideas which he had apparently gleaned from an Italian called Ficino—but Schmidt already knew all that. My hope was that he might assume I was well-informed, too. I wanted to get some idea of what he knew before I closed in on the crux of the matter.

"You were in the employ of Mr Balthar. My first question is if perhaps you can shed some light on what this occupation entailed?"

Schmidt inspected the desktop in front of him before replying. Perhaps he was taking in the fact that I knew about Balthar, and that he had been seen entering and leaving the house by talkative neighbours.

"I am employed as his general assistant," he said carefully. "Now, who is paying you?"

"Nobody," I said, almost laughing. "As a matter of fact, I am not being paid a penny for this. But, to make things clear, a man has been displaced from his rightful body into another body—that of your employer—and that's not right."

He was not puzzled, or even surprised by this outlandish claim.

"This is an inconvenient situation for some friends of mine, so I want to see things put back," I continued. "When I tried to discuss this with the man whose body had been swapped—or rather, his body, now occupied I believe by your employer—he tried to kill me and ran off."

That might have been a revelation to Schmidt, but he nodded as though it was expected.

"Well then," I said, "can you tell me what is going on?"

"You have already said what is going on," he replied. "Two men have exchanged bodies." He made a switching gesture with his two hands. "This is a thing which is possible, though few have the imagination to realise it. My question: what sort of investigator are you?"

Schmidt was sharp at giving short answers and getting his questions in quick. If this was a sparring match, I was losing on points.

"An investigator of strange occurrences," I said. "Of impossible happenings. Of things above and beyond the imaginings of ordinary men. Dark and dangerous things some of them are, too: creatures that don't belong on this world…"

"You are a *dilettante*," he said, pronouncing the world with an accent, and what might have been a smile of superiority. "Just a dabbler, an enthusiast."

"If that's what you like to call it. Whereas you are a professional: what we might call a real-life sorcerer's apprentice, come here from Switzerland to learn the secrets of the trade. That's not a question, by the way," I said when he opened his mouth to answer. "Maybe you can tell me what happened on the night of the peculiar exchange?"

"I can tell you almost nothing," he said. "I was in my room. I stay in my room at night from six PM onwards, always."

My look must have showed disbelief, and this time he gratified me with some amplification.

"My existence is one of study and contemplation," he said. "It is what people call an ascetic life, a monastic life. I do not go out at night in search of pleasure. When my daily duties have been completed and I have attended to my bodily needs, I return to my room—my sparse room, you might say—and I consider what I have learned. I do not have a gramophone or a radio. I do not take magazines. Sometimes I read books—not novels, you understand, but books of philosophy and meaning."

There was no mistaking the pride, the sense of superiority over us mortals who wasted our time on trivial things.

"That does sound like a very dedicated existence," I said, although perhaps 'obsessive' would be a better fit.

"You know something of the other world," he said, pushing back the lick of blond hair from his forehead. "You understand something of what I am seeking."

Of course I did. I had met other scholars before, men who had been sucked in by the fascination of the occult. I suppose it is something that niggles at a tidy mind, like an uneven floorboard that they keep tripping over until they are driven to hammer it down, that one little mystery they have to make sense of.

Little do they realise that in trying to make sense of it, in trying to hammer it back in line with normality, they will twist and warp all the other boards until the whole floor gives way, and their sanity with it.

Perhaps there are happy students of the occult out there, but I cannot say I have ever met one. In the ordinary mind like mine, or I dare say yours, the flooring is so uneven anyway that a few extra warps make no difference.

"I do understand, I do," I said. "As you say, I'm a dabbler, with the vaguest appreciation of how much there is that I don't know."

"You are on the first step," he said. "If you have the will, you might rise higher than that."

"My question, though, was what you can tell me of what happened on that night, rather than what you can't tell me."

At this point Kitty entered bearing a cup of tea and a glass of water, which she placed before Schmidt.

"Thank you, Miss," he said, not looking directly at her.

"Pleasure's all mine, sir," she said in a husky voice before sashaying out.

We waited until the door shut behind her.

"What I can tell you is almost nothing," Schmidt said, but he knew he had to say more than that. "I was working on a geometric exercise when I heard a loud commotion downstairs. A sound…*kreischen*, perhaps you would say. Screeching, but not animals. When I looked out the window, I saw sparks at the front gate."

"You weren't inclined to investigate?" I asked, accidentally asking a question out of turn.

"My door is locked each night, from the outside," he said, not noticing the slip. "For safety. At night, there are things in the house which it is better not to see or hear. Then another screech, not the gate this time but the front door below me. Then raised voices, then nothing. Shut in my room, I was helpless."

He was re-living the tension, knowing something was badly wrong.

"The door burst open and two men came in. I could see at once they were enemies. They overpowered me, held me on the floor and asked questions I did not understand. I thought they might kill me, but instead they let me go. Then they asked me in English who else was in the house, and they were taking me down the corridor when a man attacked them with a sword. It was my employer—but not him, I saw at once."

"He had switched bodies with another man," I said.

"I seized the advantage and hit one of them from behind with a wooden stool," he said. "There was a fight and they ran away, with the swordsman chasing them. That is all I know and all I saw. I ended up outside, on the street, running in the other direction."

"Very interesting," I said, jotting down notes furiously.

This appeared to confirm my original theory that the house had been subject to a break-in. The intruders had cut through the bolts securing both the gate and the front door with great speed, forcing Balthar to flee by metaphysical means. I had little time to consider the ramifications of these facts.

"My question: what do you know of my employer?" he asked.

"Almost nothing beyond his name and the public record," I said, echoing his own words. "But I know that he is a student of the occult, and of a Gnostic bent. That he has lived in that house for some decades, keeps to himself and keeps a couple of Romany servants, whose present whereabouts are unknown."

"You will not find them," he said with something like contempt. "Like rabbits, they go back into their holes when they are scared."

"My turn, I think," I said. "Speaking of whereabouts, do you know the current location of your employer, or have you a way of contacting him?"

The double question was a cheat, but Schmidt just shook his head.

"No, that is why I am lost, wandering the streets. After the commotion, I went out after them, and I saw the police arrive and arrest him. I followed for a little, but then I was worried about getting lost—I do not know anything of this city beyond my room—and I went back to the house. Already it was locked, and the servants were gone."

"Leaving you out in the cold," I said, thinking he had done well to stay on the loose for as long as he had.

"Yes. Now, what do you know of mental transference?"

For answer, I flipped open D'Onston's book on my desk, to the place I had saved with a leather bookmark.

"I have been spending some little time studying this in the past day or so," I said. "What did you want to know?"

He took the book, inspected it, and passed it back with the look of a schoolteacher who has found his pupil reading a comic-book.

"Popular nonsense! What I mean is, do you have personal experience of it?"

"That's another question," I said. "But I will answer anyway. I have seen a man who exchanged bodies with another. He described himself as an adept in the arts. He was an evil man and is no longer with us."

"Who—?"

"Not so fast," I said, raising a finger. "It's my turn. Can you tell me what this item might be?"

I showed him the page of my notebook where I had drawn the object from my dream. "It's made of something like green glass, but with these blue ovoids set in it."

"*Schmuggelware*," he said, and this time he did look just a little surprised. "It is something that has been smuggled—you say, contraband. Something from outside."

"Not allowed by whom?" I asked. "Outside what?"

"It is my question," he said, tapping the picture with a finger. "How do you know about this thing?"

"I was contacted by two individuals using dream telepathy," I said, hoping to throw him with the outlandishness of the reply. "They told me they are looking for this."

Schmidt nodded again, taking communication between unconscious minds in his stride. This was bread-and-butter stuff for him.

"Of course. They found you too. That explains much. And now we know what they want."

He seemed highly satisfied by this. Perhaps it was everything he wanted to know. My list of questions kept growing, and he would not stay around to answer them if I had nothing to offer back. I would need to be cannier about how I played this game.

"You did not actually answer my question. Herr Schmidt," I noted. "You said it was contraband, but that's a broad class of item. I'd press you for an actual answer, or I'll have my turn again."

He almost pouted, then spoke grudgingly. Schmidt was a man of his word. His code compelled him to tell the truth, but he would tell as little of it as he could.

"It is a key," he said at last. "For my question: what is your source of information on me?"

It was a hurried question, asked off the cuff. Asked, perhaps, as a distraction.

"Mrs Spinney," I said.

He frowned when he saw I would not go on. "Who is she?"

"That's another question, but as we're getting on so well, I'll give you an extra bit for free. She's the lady in the basement flat next door. She keeps pretty close tabs on you and Balthar, and is not greatly enamoured of either of you as far as I can tell."

"That dog's tongue," he said. It seemed an odd thing to say, but I did not have any questions to spare. On looking it up later, I find this is an uncomplimentary German expression for a gossip.

"This key," I said, choosing my words with some care. "Would it be to do with opening the door to another man's mind?"

It was not a good question, but it was lucky, because it struck Schmidt's weak point: his intellectual superiority, his pedant's need to correct error.

"No, it is the exact opposite!" he snapped. Then, realising he had given too much away, but that there was no point in trying to backtrack, he went on. "It is for locking that door to make transfer, or further transfer, impossible."

"I see," I said. "So your employer is in possession of this key, which is prohibited by some third party and sought by these two interlopers."

"Yes," he said. "Did they say where it is?"

"Only that Balthar had it, and they wanted it," I said. I furrowed my brow to give the impression of concentration. I was hoping that he might be more talkative when discussing generalities if I could flatter his scholarship. "This exchange of minds—is it something like telepathy, or hypnosis? I don't really understand it."

"Few do," he said. Instead of leaving it at that, as he might have done, he was off and running. "The relationship between mind and body has troubled philosophers for millennia, though it was not really addressed in the exoteric world until René Descartes, two hundred and seventy years ago...Descartes believed the pineal gland was the connection between body and mind, but he never tried the experiment. The real answer comes from the works of masters of the esoteric arts."

I continued to furrow my brow, hoping he would elaborate.

"Because it is the experiment which proves it," he went on, even more excited. "Theory, yes, there are many theories, and I have studied every one of them. A theory can be logical, complete and consistent, but still *wrong*. It is the experiment which proves it. When your mind is transferred to another body, you see the world through other eyes, see your reflection in the glass and a strange face looking back at you, then you *know*. It is the intoxication of true discovery beyond books."

A smile played about his lips.

"This is beyond my powers, but my Master is highly accomplished in the Art, and can transfer to the most difficult bodies with much less preparation than others. Because he can make these transfers, he can make exchanges so I occupy another body. For example, if the subject is a woman called Eve, first we secure my Master's body and bind it up. He exchanges with Eve"—that switching gesture with his hands again—"and then, he exchanges from Eve to me, so I am in Eve's body, breathing in with her lungs, touching the world with her fingers!"

"A rare privilege."

"These are not joy-rides for entertainment," he said. "The contrast enhances the understanding of the relation between mind and body. The experience of transfer also makes the mind more supple and flexible, so it will be more easy for me to transfer myself when I have learned the technique." His voice dropped almost to a whisper. "And it can be...not a punishment exactly, but a warning."

"A warning?" I said, unable to restrain myself. Luckily, the interruption did not break his thread and he carried on.

"On one occasion I had…displeased him. To demonstrate, he switched his mind that of a rat, and then with me, so I was in the rat's body." Schmidt held up his hands as though penned into the smallest of cells. "The darkness, the oppressive confines of that rodent brain! You cannot conceive what it is to be trapped there in such a place. Your mind is cramped, you cannot fully think human thoughts in that rodent brain. A rat's body is not a natural home for a human mind, and the pressure-differential drove me back to my body in a matter of seconds. But if you were locked in with the key, you would be trapped in such a horrible form…!"

His expression was one of joy and wonder rather than horror. The experience had terrified him, but Schmidt was not thinking that he would be subject to such a fate, but what he could do with this power. I recalled tales of witches turning people into frogs and mice.

I thought also of whatever lurked in Balthar's cellar. But I had too many other pressing questions to pursue that line.

"A remarkable experience, to be sure," I said. It sounded like the ravings of a madman, but I did not think that Herr Schmidt was insane. Not yet. "You'd be respectful of someone who had that sort of power over you."

"Without a key, exchange is of short duration," he went on. "It depends on compatibility between each host and guest, the psychic force of the two entities involved, and other complex factors. Habituation, also, can make it easier, when the ground is prepared, when the mind is supple, made easier by frequent occupation…but I will never, never go inside a rat again!"

Schmidt came back to himself and looked at his watch. I knew I had lost him.

"The time is up," he said, rising to his feet. "You will not stop me from leaving, I think."

"Can I help you at all?" I asked. "Do you need to borrow money, a place to stay or anything…?"

"I can manage for myself." His smile was cold, and I saw a more composed, more dangerous character than the one who had been brought in. Then, he had been biding his time, gleaning information. This was more like the real Schmidt. "Now we have had our conversation, you will not send thugs after me again—or it will be the worse for them."

"Understood perfectly," I said. "Now, if I had your address I could keep you informed if I locate Mr Balthar…"

But he had already taken his leave and was at the door, without having even offered to shake hands.

I heard a sarcastic female 'cheerio' as he departed.

I was vexed to be taken for granted, that Schmidt should simply assume I would not try to follow or detain him, but his intuition, or whatever mind-reading skill wizards possess, had been correct.

The interview had not been entirely satisfactory but it had told me some of what I wanted to know, and I could fill in some of the rest. It was interesting that Balthar had not attempted to contact Schmidt, nor to exchange bodies with him. Perhaps Balthar suspected that Schmidt was under surveillance, and perhaps he was right.

I suspected I would be seeing Schmidt again before the matter was closed and that the next encounter might not be so easy.

CHAPTER EIGHT: A BREAKTHROUGH

I was on my way to meet Sally for a brief engagement before we went our separate ways for the evening. I was going to the boxing gym, while she and some friends were going to see the latest Hollywood production. It was well past dark, and the traffic was sparse. I was a little chilly, and I was wondering about a meat pie later on, when my attention was caught by the metallic ring of a bicycle bell.

I turned, instantly alert to danger.

"Oi—Stubbs!" A cyclist glided to a smooth halt alongside me. "There you are, hold up."

It was Smith, his bowed legs more awkward than ever on the bicycle.

"Hullo there," I said, in wary greeting.

"Stop here a minute," he said, picking up his machine and wheeling it onto the pavement. "I've found a clue."

His tone was lighter than I might have expected.

"This is relating to the business with Mr Haywood?" I said.

"It certainly is. I went out for a breath of fresh air on my lunch hour, get away from it all, and this German bloke is waiting at the end of the drive. I bet you know the one."

I did not have Smith pegged as a nature-lover, but it seemed he was a man of parts.

"Face of a cherub," I said. "Talks like a Prussian officer."

"The same. Didn't take too much to figure out this was the German you've had the whole borough looking for. He says he's a friend of our guest Balthar and could he possibly ask something? He wants to retrieve something of religious importance which is currently languishing in our store rooms."

"The sword?"

"No—the robes the old chap was wearing," he said, and I raised my eyebrows. "That's what I thought. Very important robes for religious ceremonies, et cetera. Says he can't go through the approved channels because he doesn't have the right paperwork, but If I could oblige he'd put silver in my hand."

"What did you say?"

"I played dumb, but I told him I'd see what I could do. Anyway, what I'm thinking is, 'robes, my foot.' *There's something else he's after.* My first guess was it was something in the pockets, but you know what? No pockets in those robes."

"Good thought anyway."

"But a bit of poking and prodding about, and I found there was a piece of paper sewn into one sleeve—this piece of paper." He produced a sheet of thick, creamy vellum, the size of a piece of writing paper, folded over several times into a narrow strip. "That's what he wanted."

I took the proffered paper, covered with neat but indecipherable squiggles.

"Written in Chinese," said Smith. "Or it might as well be. I thought I'd give this piece of evidence to you, see what you made of it."

"I don't make anything at all of it on first acquaintance," I said. "I will have to consult my cipher books."

"Keep it, keep it," he said. "I reckon I'll give that German his robes tomorrow too. He'll never know who took that." He winked, mounted his bicycle, and rode it from the pavement onto the road, and away.

I do have cipher books, but breaking codes is not for the amateur, unless you have some idea what you are about, which in this case I did not. My assignation with Sally, however, turned out to be more useful than I expected. We met at a bench in Westow Park—our bench, as we thought of it—and I told her of my encounter with Smith and the mysterious coded message.

"That sounds like one of those things you used to carry in the War," she said. "Didn't all of you soldier-boys have one?"

"One what?" I asked, feeling slow.

"One of those letters 'to be opened in the event of anything happening to me'," she said. "One of those things you tear up afterwards. He kept it on him because he didn't want the other man knowing what was in it unless he was dead."

That made sense. Being sewn into the robe, it would not have been something he could get at in a hurry, but would always be kept safe close to him.

"Like the address of who he should contact when his Master died," I said. "Or some other secret he would not reveal in life."

Such as the location of the key which could help him transfer bodies after death, perhaps.

"You know the easy way to find out," she said. "Show it to Lizzie. She can break any code."

Of course. Miss Frey was the first person that popped into my head at the mention of a code. She is a young girl with an uncanny talent, and can fire off answers to crossword puzzle clues faster than you can write them down. She had a real skill when it came to decoding, but it should be said that Miss Frey sometimes needs to be handled with care. But it should also be said she has blossomed into a different person now Sally has taken her under her wing.

"No harm in asking," I said. Lizzie Frey liked a good puzzle, and could usually be induced to play along. "Are you seeing her soon?"

"In about fifteen minutes," she said. "She's coming to see *Seventh Heaven* with some of the girls, and a fish supper afterwards. Walk with me and you can ask her yourself. She'll crack it in two minutes."

I rather doubted that, but I could at least see if she would be game to give it a try. We stood up and, arm in arm, headed towards the Rialto.

"I did not think romantic melodrama was exactly Miss Frey's cup of tea," I said. I knew nothing about the film, except for the posters.

"There's no need to take that tone with me, Harry Stubbs. She's a young woman and growing up fast," said Sally. "It's part of her education."

"I'd better not give her the original," I said, aware of how dangerous such things could be. "But she can have a look at it and I'll post her a copy in the morning if she thinks she might be able to crack it."

"Two minutes," Sally repeated.

"Cryptography is not a party trick," I said. "I expect she will need to do some transcribing and drawing up tables and whatnot."

"Well I say she'll do it in two minutes. And if I'm right—you have to come and watch the flick with us."

"I'm expected at the gym," I said, though we both knew that with my erratic lifestyle nobody would be surprised if I did not turn up. "And—if she can't solve it, what do I win?"

"I'll come and see *The Sea Beast* with you on Saturday."

"That's more like it," I said. I was going to see the new John Barrymore film anyway—it looked like a cracking tale from the trailers—but I would enjoy it more with Sally beside me. She had been resistant to the idea, as her taste runs more to Valentino and his ilk. "But why do you want me to see that slush?"

"Because you need an education, too. Every man should be forced to watch something romantic once in a while."

"It's a bet," I said.

Miss Frey was a different figure to the one I had known earlier. For one thing, her self-mutilated hair was concealed under a fashionable hat, and her clothing looked less thrown-together and more carefully chosen—possibly Sally's influence. She did not look out of place among the pickle-factory girls. There was still something of the hunted animal about her, but when one of the others made a joke she laughed with the rest, looking for a moment like any other girl.

"Good evening, Mr Stubbs," she said, a little archly, clearly enjoying her new status as one of the girls.

I saluted her and was partway through explaining my request when she snatched the piece of paper out of my hand. Miss Frey is a direct sort. If she has not quite mastered certain social niceties, she does not let them delay her. She had deduced what I wanted and was untroubled by whys and wherefores.

"Not like the last one," she said, flashing a smile of relief. "But it's a complex cryptogram. A treasure map, maybe?"

"Maybe," I agreed.

"Because, you see, these lines here are not writing, they're a diagram—turn left, fork right."

"If you say so," I said. Now she mentioned it, the items she was pointing to were different in style to the other characters.

"Oh that's an *easy* one to solve," she concluded after a second, handing it back to me with an impish look.

"You can't just decipher it by sight," I objected.

"I don't need to. It's in English—or at least the important bits are."

It felt like a conversation out of *Alice's Adventures in Wonderland*.

She giggled at my obvious lack of comprehension, and placed a finger on the page. "See, this word here is in the Roman alphabet. B-E-S-S—"

She was right. I had missed the fact that some of the characters were in distorted but recognisable English, twisted like letters in a medieval manuscript.

"Bessemer," I said. She pointed out another word two lines down. "Bessemer again."

"And that tells you where to go," she concluded. "If you happen to know."

"I don't happen to know, so perhaps you should give me a clue."

"Go on, give him a clue," Sally interjected. "He needs it."

"Shall I?" She placed a forefinger on her lip. "It's the last place you'd want to go. But people are dying to get in."

It sounded like a riddle. Luckily, Sally had heard it.

"A cemetery," said Sally.

"Quite right," said Miss Frey.

"West Norwood cemetery," I said. His neighbour had said Balthar went for walks there. "Something buried in West Norwood cemetery."

"And it is a treasure map," said Miss Frey. "Treasure is buried between Bessemer and Bessemer. If you go through the main entrance, turn left and fork right, as it says they're a little way up."

"How do you know all this?"

"I go for walks in the cemetery," she said. "It's ever so much more peaceful than the park. And after a while you get to know some of the names. Like Bessemer and Bessemer, the same name repeated three graves apart."

"That's a little bit morbid," said Sally. "Though I suppose there's a sort of High Gothic fashion for that sort of thing."

"There's a lady poetess called Claudia who walks there for inspiration," said Miss Frey. "She always wears black. She looks like a vampire, but she's my friend."

"Just a minute," I said, trying to get them back on the subject. "So you're saying X marks the spot in a grave between these two Bessemers?"

"I don't think there's a grave there," she said. "Just the remains of an old one."

The cemetery is less than a hundred years old, but still some of the memorials have crumbled or tumbled or sunk into the clay. A disused grave site, one the family would not open for further internments, and no visitors to notice disturbance, would be the best place to bury something.

"Well done, Lizzie," said Sally. "I knew you'd solve it. I think Mr Stubbs has just lost his bet. And I think he'll be buying you a box of chocolate creams as a reward for your help, at the very least."

"Oh, definitely," I said, feeling in my pocket for change. "I'd better get myself a ticket for *Seventh Heaven* then, if they still have any."

"I already got tickets for the three of us," said Sally, holding them up.

I did not pay too much attention to the film performance, though it was pleasant to sit in the semi-darkness, holding hands with Sally. I only had part of her attention though. She was engaged with pointing out actors and explaining the nuances of the plot to Miss Frey. I was turning over in my mind the revelation that had just been delivered.

It made a great deal of sense that Balthar would keep something valuable hidden away from home. As events had proven, his house was not secure and raiders, either surreptitious burglars or overt armed robbers, could gain access easily enough. Stashing it away was a safer option, and a graveyard is, as the poet said, a fine and private place.

Tomorrow night I would go on a little expedition.

CHAPTER NINE: ANOTHER STRANGE FISH

I was more than half hoping that the next day would bring news that either the man in the asylum had reverted back to being Balthar, or that Haywood had been apprehended. Apparently, that night a couple of lads had visited a rooming house which had recently taken in someone of Haywood's description, but he had given them the slip. And I was sure Smith would have let me know of any changes from the asylum.

I went on a little preliminary scouting mission round West Norwood cemetery. The place indicated was an empty plot between two others, roughly midway between Henry Bessemer—known to all schoolboys as the inventor of the Bessemer Process which had driven the Industrial Revolution— and Alfred Bessemer. This latter was his ill-fated grandson, also in the engineering line until his career was cut short by either a bizarre accident, an undetected murder, or a peculiar suicide, having been found hanged from the cord to a skylight.

I was on my way back from this reconnaissance when I noticed a man walking towards me wearing a cap spattered with varnish or something like it. Just the sort of thing a carpenter might wear—and under it was Eddie Haywood.

He must have seen me at the exact same instant, because he executed an abrupt about-turn and took off at speed, his cap flying off.

I may be big and heavy, but my legs are long. Anyone who has seen the prop forward in a game of rugby will know that big men can move if they are trained to it. Running is part of any self-respecting boxer's training regimen, and my time for the hundred-yard dash has surprised many.

When Haywood ran down the street I was after him like an express train.

At the same time, I was thinking about what might happen if I were to catch him. If cornered, Balthar might be a dangerous character with who-knew-what powers to defend himself. As I ran, my hand went to my watch pocket and extracted the small blue stone Captain Cross had sent me. It might not provide sovereign protection, but it was the best I could muster.

Haywood took off down a side street, with me getting closer every step, and then into a builder's yard where he ran down a narrow alley between stacked timbers. At the end he hesitated, then went left, dodging my grasp by a hairsbreadth.

I half-expected him to turn on me, but when he looked back I saw the whites of his terrified eyes, and I knew he was not going to fight. He swerved and stumbled and this time I caught him by his coat, swinging him around and slamming him against the pile of wooden beams, which wobbled slightly under the impact.

This was not the first fugitive I had pursued, but I rarely managed the act of catching one and knocking the fight of them with such aplomb. Sometimes you wish there had been an audience.

"So, we meet again, Mr Haywood," I said, panting but entirely in control of myself, not looking in his eyes. "If you're contemplating assaulting me with any carpentry implement, I advise you to think twice."

He was dazed, and not just by the force of being stopped.

"Don't hit me," he said weakly. "You've—you've got the wrong man."

What persuaded me was the look he had about him, the look of a man run down out of the blue by a huge assailant of whom he had no prior knowledge. I suspected I did indeed have the wrong man.

"I'll be the judge of that," I said, still cautious. "Perhaps you might tell me who I have the honour of addressing. "

"Ah, well," he said, with an ingratiating smile. "You've probably been deceived by my face. Everyone tells me I've got Eddie Haywood's face."

"His face, his coat, his trousers and his shoes," I said. "I daresay you happen to have his wallet too."

"I dare say," he agreed weakly. His eyes slid sideways, a sign of a man thinking about making a run for it. I enfolded his skinny shoulder in my hand to quash any such notion. "But I'm not him, whatever he's done!"

"Most people would not believe you. But maybe I do."

"You know what happened!" he said, his eyes growing wide. "Who are you? How do you know?"

I was able to relish the rare pleasure of being the man in the know. I had information that this not-Haywood wanted. I removed my hand from his shoulder. His need to know would secure him better than the latest-model handcuffs.

"We have not been properly introduced," I said, producing my business card. "My name is Harry Stubbs. If you'll accompany me back to the corner house without further escapades or skylarking, perhaps we can have a bit of a chat about matters relevant."

We retraced our steps, pausing to retrieve the cap. Five minutes later we were ensconced at a table in a café that was otherwise virtually empty, this being after lunch and before the afternoon tea crowd showed up.

The man was not, it seemed, Eddie Haywood. The individual I was facing told me, not without hesitation, that his name was Jimmy Pennington.

"I'm in the horoscope racket," he said, with a kind of defiance. "It's a perfectly legal trade, more or less."

That told me a lot about this Jimmy Pennington character. Horoscopes are an old game, but still a highly profitable one for the none too honest.

You may have seen small advertisements for personalised astrological readings in the columns of the newspapers. They aim to persuade the reader to send their date of birth and a postal order to the PO box specified, and receive in return a star chart revealing the mysteries of the zodiac and what they foretell for the reader's future. The best of them are quite fine; the worst are blurry, cheap reproductions. What they have in common is that they are all functionally identical, with the same diagrams, observations ("you have a kind nature, which people may take advantage of") and predictions ("October could be a lucky month for you, financially.") The only difference is the name and birthdate printed on the front.

Pennington been involved in this sort of malarkey for many years, and many adjacent schemes besides. There are plenty of gullible folk willing to pay up for such things. His chosen area was the mystical and magical, which had the advantage of being perfectly legal without being susceptible to any sort of scrutiny. If a lucky charm does not work or a horoscope does not come true, there is no legal redress. This peddler of bogus magic had run into the real thing.

"I woke up suddenly last night," he said. "It took me a minute to work out whether I was asleep or awake, or something between the two, because I was lying in my bed and at the same time I felt myself being sucked towards a whirlpool."

We have all woken after a few drinks to find the room rotating around us, but I forbore to joke. I had my notepad out and was jotting down the key points.

"There was a whirlpool in your room?" I asked, without a hint of mockery.

"Not exactly," he said. "But I was in the whirlpool. Or rather, it was gathering around me. There was a great force of suction, a vacuum, and a rotation, and everything was going down into it. Or rather, bits of me were going into it."

"Bits of you…?" I prompted. "Arms, legs…?"

"No, no," said Pennington, trying to make sense of his own words. "Like, what woke me up was when my dream was sucked under. And my memories were going too, all spilling out and running away down the plughole. And even the thoughts I was trying to think, they kept disappearing before I could put them together properly."

"Were you scared?" I asked.

"Scared—I was petrified!" He was a picture of honest fear. "I thought I was dying…I don't know what dying is like, but that was a foretaste of it, I'd bet anything. The only thing that made me think I was not dying was when I saw the face. Everything was going around and around, and then I saw this face looking down at me through the ceiling."

He was reliving the experience in front of me, his eyes fixed on something horrible. I said nothing, letting him gather his thoughts.

"It wasn't human," he said. "Not a devil neither. It had eyes and a mouth, but it wasn't anything normal. Like a…I dunno, like a fish or something." he glanced up at me quickly to see how I took that.

"Definitely not human," I said, making a note. "Well, that figures."

"I felt like something under a microscope," Pennington said. "And that thing was controlling the whirlpool. All I could do was lie there as I felt myself getting sucked down, out of my own body, like water draining down a plughole. Like being squeezed through a very narrow hole, with this great roaring sound like a waterfall."

"And when you woke up," I said, "you didn't know where you were."

"I never passed out," he said. "But I was flailing about, sort of. You know what it was like? When you've already got several layers on and you're struggling to put on an overcoat and you can't get your arms in the holes properly. And then, suddenly, everything fell into place and I was kicking and thrashing, and I fell out of bed. Except it wasn't my bed, or my room.

"I found the light switch and when it came on I was in a cheap hotel room, with peeling wallpaper and cigarette burns in the bedside table. I did not recognise it at all—I didn't know what was going on, whether I'd been drugged or hypnotised, or if I was going mad. The first thing that struck me was my knee hurt, and then there was something wrong with my arms.

"The room was full of steam or fog, but as it cleared I saw the washstand, and the mirror was covered by a sheet of paper with writing on it.

"There was one word written on the paper in big black letters—'RUN!'—and when I picked it up to see if there was anything on the other side, I saw what was in the mirror and I got the biggest shock of my life."

"A different face to your usual," I said. "A whole different body."

He nodded.

"That moment I heard a disturbance downstairs, voices raised. I would've known it meant trouble even without that note. I was out of that room like a shot, down the corridor and into the bathroom. I lay down in the bathtub, with the light off and the door ajar, so nobody would see me if they looked in."

"That was very circumspect of you," I observed. It sounded like Pennington might have had to resort to a similar bolthole before. He was a more slippery character than Haywood.

"Pays to be circumspect," he said. "As soon as they were past the bathroom and banging on my bedroom door, I was down the hall stairs and out through the scullery window."

"These people who were looking for you—"

"The hue and cry," he said. "Mr Renville's lot."

Of course, they had been looking for Haywood. Balthar must have seen or heard them at the door and made his exit via Pennington's body in a matter of seconds. Maybe he had to prepare the spell in advance, like an escape hatch he could slip through when he was threatened.

Haywood had been lying low all morning. What had brought him out of hiding was a sudden need for a drink.

Pennington seized my lapel, suddenly agitated. If he thought he was going to have trouble explaining what had happened, he was wrong. My taking it so casually was what bothered him.

"I told you what I know. What's going on?" he said. "Who did this? What do you know about it? Who's this Eddie Haywood? And why is Renville after me?"

Perhaps I should have been entirely frank, but I felt an indirect approach would work better.

"I don't suppose you've ever met a Mr Balthar," I said.

His face looked like an adding machine when the numbers spin round and stop as the calculation is completed.

"Balthar," he said. "So—he really is a Master?"

"And able to exchange bodies at will," I said. "Though I believe he needs some sort of connection first. How did you come to know him?"

"Only in passing. A business transaction, a few weeks ago. Unsuccessful, as it happens, but it got so far as me visiting his place on Belvedere Road. You know it?"

He was the one fishing now.

"I've been there," I said, telling the literal truth. "And I've met Balthar and Schmidt, though not on the best of terms. Would I be right in assuming that you were selling something which Mr Balthar was not buying?"

"I sell all sorts of things to all sorts of people," said Pennington. "And Balthar—he's more particular than most. There's two sorts of people in this business, those who are fooling others and those that are fooling themselves. Usually you just have to work out which they are. It seems like Balthar was neither."

Pennington would have assumed that Balthar was another mark he could fob off with dragon's teeth, unicorn's horns, or whatever other magical paraphernalia he was dealing in. It would not have taken Balthar long to test Pennington and find him wanting in anything but superficial verbiage.

That must have been what gave Pennington away . Anyone else might have expressed surprise, or confusion, or indignation, but Pennington's was the blank face of the practised confidence trickster, momentarily caught out but trying not to spill the beans.

"And was there any suggestion of anything out of the ordinary...?"

"You mean, did he put a hex on me or something?" Pennington was doubtful. "No, nothing of that sort. A servant brought us tea, we talked about matters various, he showed me a few things..."

Unfortunately I was blundering in the dark. I did not know whether the magic required a lock of the subject's hair, or capturing their image in an enchanted mirror, or whether it was something more scientific like scanning with instruments, taking measurements and calibrating. Whatever it was, Balthar must have performed the operation on both Haywood and Pennington, and perhaps others.

According to Mrs Spinney, Balthar did not have many

visitors except those secretive types who came and went at odd hours of the night. Perhaps he primed every other visitor he had as a possible subject for bodily exchange, just as a precaution.

I remembered the pebble I was still holding in my palm, and put it back in my watch pocket. I was aware of Pennington's attentive eyes on me, although he said nothing. Did he know about the evil eye and protection from it?

"Now, tell me about Haywood," he said.

In a few words, I explained how Balthar had made the exchange first with Haywood and then with himself, and filled in a bit of background on the life and times of Eddie Haywood, carpenter.

"So this carpenter is now the magician," said Pennington, quickly getting to the nub of it. "And I'm Haywood. And the magician, Balthar—he's me?"

"In a nutshell, yes," I said. "So what I need to know, Mr Pennington, is where and who you are when you're at home so we can track you down. I need an address, and a description."

"This is bonkers," he said, cracking a smile. "You want me, sitting here, to tell you what I look like?"

"Height, weight, hair colour, distinguishing features, if you please," I said, pencil at the ready.

"And when you find me—what are you going to do?" he asked, still wondering at the strangeness of it. "Don't go punching him on the nose—it's my nose!"

I suppose there was a lighter side to it, if you looked at it that way. His expression turned serious.

"So what would happen if one of us were to be killed?" he asked.

"I don't rightly know," I said.

"You haven't picked up any hints?" he said. "I mean, if I die now in this body—do I go back to the old one? And if my other body dies—do I l keep this one for good? Or what?"

Something about the way he asked, casual though he tried to sound, made me wonder if Pennington might just be contemplating murder himself. He had regained what I suspected was his habitual confident manner.

"I sincerely hope that nobody will get killed at all," I said.

"But how can you stop a man like that?" said Pennington. "What if you put your hand on his shoulder, and he just takes your body—sucks you right out of it like an oyster out of a shell—and you're the one that gets a beating?"

"I don't think he can effect an exchange quite that easily," I said. "Not without preparation. And, as I say, minds will be reunited with their suitable bodies sooner or later. Though I don't know what effects deaths would have anywhere along the chain."

Pennington was looking past me now, on to something else, as if deciding he had extracted all the information he was going to get from me.

"That's all very interesting, very interesting indeed, Stubbs," he said, standing up. "Thank you for bringing all this to my attention.

"And where are you off to?"

"Where I please," he said. "You've got nothing against me—I've broken no laws."

He looked at me as if daring me to attempt to detain him again. Like Schmidt, he had perhaps divined something of my personality, and the fact that as a sole operator I was not equipped to put him in a dungeon somewhere.

"Perhaps you might care to help with the case in hand," I said. "Seeing as how this third party has stolen everything you own, not to mention the body you were born in."

"Fair exchange is no robbery," he said, smiling slyly.

"Where can I find you?" I asked. "I don't want to have to run you down again."

"I'll be about," Pennington said, with a wink and a wave of his hand. "Just ask Renville's boys. Thanks again."

Trying to capture Balthar seemed increasingly like an exercise in futility. Any attempt to lay hands on him and he would skip to the next host-body, creating ever more confusion, slipperier than an eel. Though, like a man in a comedy routine attached to an elastic cord, he could only run so far before he would be brought back...unless he could get hold of that key and lock himself into a new body for good.

My appointment at the cemetery could not be postponed.

CHAPTER TEN: GRAVE MATTERS

Perhaps I could have made the effort on my own, but that did not seem advisable. Two pairs of eyes are infinitely better than one for this sort of task, especially when one pair are engaged in looking down while digging. I needed a lookout man, and there was only one person I could reasonably ask.

"Why rope me into this?" Smith asked.

"Because you know all about it already," I said. "And more pertinently, this whole exercise is being carried out on your behalf and for your benefit."

"I didn't sign up for this." Smith eyed the open tool bag on my desk distrustfully. "There's laws about burglary, and penalties stipulated for being caught with the tools of the trade for the same, and some of us don't have quite such a clean sheet as you."

"I'm not fool enough to do this on my own."

"You ain't scared just because it's a graveyard after dark, are you?" he said, trying to make it sound like a joke. "I mean, what could happen?"

"If nothing could happen, you won't mind accompanying me," I said. "If something could happen, then your presence as sentinel is mandatory. It's one or the other."

"You're quite the logician, Stubbs," said Smith. "You've got me fair and square. Very well then, I'm your man."

As always, preparation was the key. First off, we made a complete circuit without encountering any of the constabulary or anyone else likely to cause trouble. There was a night watchman at the cemetery, who in theory patrolled the grounds at intervals, and had a telephone-line to call the police station.

He was an old fellow called Tommy who had been there for decades, and was known for turning a blind eye to any goings-on. You do not get much watching for what they paid Tommy. From what I heard, if we wanted trouble from him we'd have to go into his hut and wake him up.

A cemetery at night when there's a sliver of moon is a poetic place, if you like your poetry dark and gothic. The angels do not look exactly sinister, but carry a certain foreboding. The gravestones lie at odd angles with spreading pools of darkness between them, as though you could stumble into an open grave and be gone forever if you missed your step. Branches do not wave any more than they do in the daytime, but every movement attracts your eye and makes you think there was something slipping away from it, something you did not quite catch.

I was not fearful, but I was certainly wary. Say what you like, there is rarely, if ever, such a thing as a simple job in this business.

"How's your night vision?" I asked Smith as we came around to the main gate.

"Works better in daylight," he said. "But I can see enough. Miserable place."

"Like most cemeteries, I suppose." I was thinking about the last funeral I had attended there, the friend I had buried and the woman in black who must have blamed me for some of what happened.

"There are pieces of me buried in there," he said. "Friends and relations."

The cemetery is bounded by high stone walls for some it its perimeter, and a fence of tall iron spears at other sections. At one point there was a length of spear which could be removed and replaced to give access out of hours. This was my entry point, and where I wished Smith to keep watch.

"They might come in another way, if they do come," said Smith. "Or they might be in there waiting."

"Or they might not come at all," I said. "All you need to do is keep watch and if you see anything, make a signal." I held up a whistle of the sort used by referees. "Two quick blasts."

"And then run like the blazes," he said.

He took the whistle and held my hat and coat, which I removed to squeeze through the gap. It was still a tight fit.

"You watch yourself, Stubbs," he said. "And listen for the whistle."

There was no sense in trying to be furtive and creeping among the gravestones. That would be a short route to a twisted ankle at least. Instead, I walked up the path that leads from the main entrance opposite St Luke's, down an avenue of fine sepulchres, and up in the direction of the catacombs.

This was a sort of hallowed ground to me, to any boxer. West Norwood Cemetery is uniquely gifted with the mortal remains of many of our greatest pugilists.

I could show you the grave of Tom King, 'the fighting sailor' as he was known, who was renowned both as a bare-knuckle man and in the more civilized age of gloves. King always downed a tot of gin before a bout.

Then there was lightweight Johnny Broome, who was never defeated in the ring, and his heavyweight younger brother Harry, who at one time was the champion of England. Not to mention Jack Burke, who went by 'the Irish lad,' and was also English champion a few years later.

I have a special affection for Tom Spring, heavyweight champion of England a century ago. Spring was the first of the scientific boxers. He lacked the sheer physical force of his contemporaries—one opponent called him a "lady's maid fighter" for his weak punch—but Spring was the master of the art of defence. He was also master of the cunning left hook and a technique he called Harlequin Step, which enabled him to get within reach of his opponent and avoid their blow while delivering one himself.

Mainly though, I admire Spring because he was the subject of a short story by no less than Sir Arthur Conan Doyle, which is surely a high form of immortality. That was before Sir Arthur was chained to his detective, whom he apparently despises, but whose adventures he seems doomed to chronicle until he dies.

All those boxers fought in the days when matches carried on until one man was down, or gave in. It was a matter of endurance, and Broome's forty-two-round fight with Hannan is unimaginable now. In these more enlightened times, there is less public taste for seeing men destroy themselves. Tom Spring's seventy-seven-round match against Jack Langan was legendary, especially as Spring, the smaller and lighter man, won against the odds.

While their mortal clay may rest in the West Norwood necropolis, I refuse to believe that it was a quirk of the physical frame that made any of these men unique. There was something more that drove them on, far beyond the limitations of frail flesh, some inner fire. That was what audiences paid to see in those days, those superhuman feats of endurance and tolerating pain. It was their souls, not their bodies, that made them champions.

Feeling thus uplifted by the shades of the past, I walked briskly, taking the right fork where the path split, and then a side turning on the left. Off the path, in among the headstones and the trees around them, it was considerably darker.

This was what you might call one of the more desirable residential districts of the cemetery, for the upper orders, with accommodation ranging from family tombs the size of a cottage and vaults bigger than a wardrobe to shared graves with headstones like bedsteads and crosses with life-size angels, stone urns, and broken pillars.

I counted off the requisite number of headstones and flicked my electric lamp on for just long enough to confirm the vacant site between two headstones was the correct spot. Things look different in the dark.

Shielding the light, I poured out markings of chalk dust to indicate the area that needed digging. Even without direct lighting the white markings were discernible, so I could work without artificial illumination.

I laid my overcoat and jacket over a headstone, balanced my bowler atop them, and got down to work. I thrust the spade down, put my weight on it, levered up a shovelful and tossed it to one side, then repeated the action, and again.

Slow and steady was the way to win this race. My brother and I had earned pennies digging our neighbours' vegetable patches as boys. Two strapping youths, we had been a great help to some of the elderly or widowed residents of our street, and could probably have made a deal more money if Pa had not put strict limits on how much we could charge.

I did a plenty more digging in the army. We may not have been in the front-line trenches, but you have to shift a prodigious amount of earth to dig a gun position, and the engineers with their mechanical excavators always had more urgent matters to attend to. So, along with the other artillerymen of my company, I spent many days getting well acquainted with the rich, loamy soil of Belgium and France.

Norwood soil is another matter. It is heavy, clayey stuff. After the first few inches of topsoil you come across thick, glutinous matter that sticks to the spade in a single, solid lump until you help it off with a shake or a boot, or a scrape on a handy headstone.

This must have been the same as the scene those years ago when Balthar did his own burying there. He was not a muscular individual by any account, and I was hoping I would not have to dig down far before I found what I was looking for.

It is possible he had magical assistance. Wizards, from Merlin onwards, have been credited with wonderful powers when it comes to earth-moving. However, modern archaeology now informs us that the ancient earthworks said to be built by wizards or giants were all built by patient human hands. The fact that a modern steam-shovel can quickly shift more dirt than the ancients could imagine may suggest that, in this regard at least, magic may not be all it is cracked up to be.

According to the cemetery's record, the now-vanished headstone for this plot was for one of the earlier internments, circa 1839. While many of those surrounding it were family plots or vaults which had been used many times over succeeding generations, for whatever reason this one had never been revisited. The effectively empty plot was a convenient site for anyone with something to hide.

My concern was that I might be looking for a needle in a haystack. I would not miss a coffin, but a smaller container, one big enough for the mysterious glass key, would be easy to miss in the dark. It might even be small enough to be encased in one of those great lumps of clay I was tossing to the left and right.

Maybe magicians can sniff out these things with a sixth sense, but I was hoping Balthar had made the prize obvious to mundane senses.

Twenty minutes in, and I had dug over the whole grave to a spade's-depth and was on the way to working up a good sweat. My arms were aching, which was no concern. What was worse was that I had forgotten to bring gloves, and I was starting to blister. I improvised some padding from a handkerchief and dug on. A quarter moon had risen above the rooftops to spill ghostly light on the scene.

The hum of the city was still present, but individual sounds were muted. Motorcars puttered by on their way.

My spade struck something hollow.

"Hello," I said.

A little scraping and scooping quickly confirmed my initial impression. I had come upon a coffin, and in a very shallow grave indeed.

As I cleared away the final tangle of roots, I thought I heard a distant whistle. Just one. Maybe it was a train whistle on the Liverpool Street line. Or was it Smith? Nothing followed.

I quickly cleared all the earth from the surface of the coffin. It was a cheap pine affair, and of no great antiquity. The place where a brass plate bearing a name would have been attached was blank. It might be a few decades old, but no more than that. This coffin was an interloper, a squatter, illegally occupying ground in someone else's patch.

The question was what, or who, was in it. I could only guess why Balthar would wish to secrete bodies in this place and if the key was here at all. I resigned myself to the task of opening the coffin and searching through the grisly remains to find the object I was looking for. Not that I have any particular horror of dead bodies, but there is a deal of difference between a cadaver on a mortuary slab in daylight and one found in a graveyard at midnight.

I dug swiftly around the coffin and then, with a grunt of effort, heaved it free from the embracing earth and slid it on to the grassy verge. At that point I saw something which had escaped me before. A small metal box was fastened to the top of the coffin, something like a cashbox, close to the head of the occupant. It was fastened with a stout padlock, now clogged up with earth.

That looked promising. The box was the right size to hold the 'key' I was looking for—but calling for another key to get to it. The only recourse would be to physically break the little box off the board it was attached to, entailing a certain amount of damage to the coffin. And, if I was not careful, an undesirable amount of noise. I leaned forward and cupped a hand around my torch to get a good look, working out the best angle of approach while still not touching it.

Just then, there was a scraping sound from inside the coffin.

I jumped backwards faster than a cat. Perhaps it had just been the contents settling after being hauled out of the ground, but it sounded very much as though something was moving inside.

I let out a slow breath. I did not relish the thought of contact with a reanimated corpse. A quick check suggested the coffin was still nailed securely shut, but it was hard to shake the conviction that if I came too close something would leap out at me like a ghoulish jack-in-the-box.

I hesitated, nerving myself up. After all, there was nothing else to do. I just had to detach that box, which presumably held the key I sought, and leg it. I could not imagine following my original plan of reburying the coffin.

"Good work, Mr Stubbs," said a German-accented voice, as two figures emerged from the shadows. "We thought you might do the work for us."

The smaller figure on the left was recognisable from his hair, which shone white in the moonlight, and the glint of light from his glasses. He carried a shovel jauntily over his shoulder. The one next to him was harder to place, but he walked with a deliberation that suggested both age and strength.

"Step aside from the coffin," said the second man. He regarded me for a long moment. "You know, the wisest thing you could do now would be to run away and not come back. You have my word you will not be pursued—in spite of the trouble you've caused."

"I don't believe I was the one that started the trouble," I said. "I assume I have the honour of addressing Mr Balthar."

"Now the digging is done, we no longer need you," said Schmidt. "Go, *schnell!*"

The flick of his hand was especially galling.

"I had some sympathy for you before, Herr Schmidt," I said. "I saw you as the innocent victim of this whole business."

"Victim?" asked Balthar.

"Of course," I said. "The whole thing is clear as daylight. A man, a wizard who has the power to jump from body to body, must find a new shell every half-century or so. Rather than just picking someone willy-nilly, he has years to select and nurture his victim."

I looked from one of them to the other. Neither seemed inclined to interrupt.

"Obviously he chooses someone young and healthy," I said. "He chooses a man who has no friends or family who will ask inconvenient questions—a foreigner in this country. He gets this man to live in his house, so his face is known to the neighbours and to his associates. And then—"

I was going to explain how the whole pose of being a wise Gnostic teacher was simply to draw in Schmidt, a screen for Balthar's real powers and purpose. I had the whole story figured out. But Schmidt was well ahead of me—and had carefully positioned himself a step behind Balthar. He raised his shovel and brought it down with an audible thump on the other man's skull. Balthar crumpled at once. Schmidt was immediately fastening manacles around the unconscious man's wrists.

"You nearly 'gave the game away' too soon, as you say," Schmidt said. "But you gave me a distraction, so again you have been helpful."

My hope had been that the scales would fall from Schmidt's eyes and the ensuing conflict between them would give me opportunity to at least escape, but he was more worldly-wise than either I or Balthar had assumed, and had planned for this moment. Before I could formulate a response, a small automatic pistol appeared in his hand. I raised my hands.

You might say it is a pretty poor sort of magician who needs a gun—it bespeaks a lack of faith in their own talents—but that did not make the weapon any less dangerous.

"Knowledge is power, Mr Stubbs," he said. "Which is why it must be possessed only by those who can be trusted with it."

That he had not shot me already meant he still wanted something.

"I let you go, remember," I said. "I treated you fairly."

His smile was hard in the moonlight.

"Your mistake." The pistol was a small-calibre weapon, but any gun will kill you at close range. "This time we will not have evasions. You are not a lone agent; you have a master, a superior. The name, please?"

My mind went to Miss de Vere. Betraying her would be very dangerous indeed.

"Gunshots at midnight attract attention," I said. "Even in a cemetery. Put the gun away and we can talk."

"One shot sounds like a backfire," he said, making no move to lower the weapon. "And I assure you I will only require one shot. The name, please."

"I don't see how any name I give would mean anything to you," I extemporised. "I mean, the name I have probably is not even their real name. It is not like I am in any position to check. As you must know, having been in a similar situation yourself with Mr Balthar, who obviously kept secrets from you and in fact tried to deceive you about his true nature and purpose."

I was babbling because I was distracted. It was difficult to be sure, but I was now positive there was movement behind Schmidt. Something darker shifted and blocked out patches of lighter vegetation as it moved. It looked very much as though someone was creeping up on him from behind. I thought it might be Smith, but I was wrong.

"Either you tell me the name," he said. "Or else—"

He turned abruptly, just as a figure emerged from the dark behind him. I recognised the stern expression and steel-rimmed glasses of the woman I had decided was an army doctor. There might have been someone else behind her in deeper shadow.

"What do you want?" Schmidt demanded.

"The same as you," she replied. He started to raise the gun, but the movement and his reply were both cut off suddenly as the two of them locked gazes.

In folklore some call it the evil eye: the power to freeze someone with a look. The psychologists call it neurotic paralysis and say it is merely a trick which affects the susceptible and weak-minded, like stage hypnosis. I can only say that I have been subject to its effects myself and can attest to them. No doubt the process of negating someone's control over their own body is a preliminary stage in displacing them from it.

Schmidt and the doctor were engaged in a battle of wills. The advantage of age, experience, and psychic strength no doubt lay on her side. On the other, all Schmidt needed to do was find the power to move one finger and he would shoot her dead in an instant.

The contest was settled by a third party, as the doctor's companion came out of the dark and grabbed hold of Schmidt with two massive hands. I could not see him well, but I had the same impression of muscular bulk as in the dream. He was a wide, lumbering figure, not fat, but a great block of muscle, less than six feet tall but so broad he had the proportions of an overgrown baby.

A friend of mine is a keen angler. I spent an afternoon with him at South Norwood lake, catching nothing. He reeled in a few though, and always dispatched them the same way: holding the wriggling fish by its tail, he brought its head down with a hefty whack on a convenient rock. It was as quick and humane as any slaughterman could hope for.

What I witnessed here was the same. The acolyte, as slight as a schoolboy, only had time for a faint whine as he was raised up and brought down, his head smashed on a waist-high stone tomb with a sickening noise.

The hulking figure raised Schmidt again before letting the lifeless body fall to the ground.

"You killed him!" I said, in a state of shock. "There was no call for that!"

"He would have shot you, and us," she said. "And Balthar, when he had interrogated him."

The wizard still lay unconscious and manacled on the ground.

Her companion moved beside her, and I could see hm a little better. I still could not make out his face, but his bulky body gave the impression of deformity and constrained movement.

"You should have run away when Balthar told you," she said, taking an object from an outer pocket. Not a gun—something made of dark metal crudely welded together.

I was in the difficult position of being a witness to a killing. Maybe they would have called it self-defence, but all three of us knew that it was never going to court.

"You can get what you want," I said slowly. "And this can all be settled. I think you'll find it right there."

I took a step forward and gestured to the box attached to the coffin. In hindsight this was a great mistake, as it might have looked like I was going to make a grab for it. That must have been what they feared above all else.

The big man came at me in a lumbering charge. I say lumbering, but that only applied to his first steps. He accelerated like a charging bull. Maybe he saw me draw back and could tell I was not going to steal the box, but by then he was committed to the attack.

I had no real chance to weigh him up and assess what sort of adversary I faced, but some facts were obvious even by shadowed moonlight. He was substantial, wide rather than tall, and his feet pounded heavily on the ground. You can tell something of the power of a boxer's punch by the thickness of his wrists, and this one had wrists like tree trunks. His charge was determined and utterly fearless, as though he expected to run right through me.

I could have turned and run, which might have been the sensible thing against an unknown quantity. As I have said before, only a fool steps into the ring without knowing who he is up against. I could have squared up and aimed a punch to catch him as he came in, as he did not appear to have even a basic defence.

Instead, I adopted more cautious tactics. As he came towards me I took up a boxing stance, shifted left, and then leapt to the right as he bore down, so he hurtled past me like a runaway train, crashing through the undergrowth.

I half-stumbled as something splintered beneath my right foot. I had trodden on the coffin, breaking the lid. I hastily moved away from it before I could trip over the thing. I had more immediate concerns to deal with, as my assailant had wheeled round and was crashing through the undergrowth towards me.

This time he crossed a clear area and the pale moonlight revealed more of him, his form swathed in an overcoat, his face concealed by a balaclava helmet. The contours though, suggested horribly misshapen features. Only his hands were visible, but what hands they were! Bloated and almost cartoonish, stubby fingers with great thick fingernails, knuckles like cobblestones. It looked like elephantiasis, but was all muscle and bone.

He was human, but some experiment or accident had left him looking like something in a medical exhibition. Perhaps it was simply the mismatch of mind and body which had triggered some rush of glandular secretions and this unnatural growth, but if ever there was anyone who might be looking to switch bodies, it would be this fellow. He made me look like Michelangelo's celebrated *David*.

His approach was slower than before, but determined, giving me less chance to move aside. I had the measure of him though. He was big, but still a good few inches shorter than me, nor did he have my reach. Also, that coat would restrict his movement. I did not wait but moved forward and threw a straight right to his jaw.

Scientifically speaking, a knockout occurs due to the movement of the brain within the skull cavity. Stories about blows to the chin being conducted up through the jawbone are nonsense. What actually happens is that the head snaps back under the force of a blow, and it is this acceleration that causes the damage. The chin is the point of aim, being a convenient fulcrum, but what really matters is the stoutness of neck.

If your neck is solid, even a blow to the chin will not cause any motion, and your brain remains undisturbed. Hence the secret to having an 'iron jaw' is nothing to do with the jaw but everything to do with neck muscles and how well they are conditioned. Chin tucks, neck bridges and other exercises are regular parts of a boxer's training to this end.

There are plenty of toughs out there who have impressive biceps from manual labour and fancy themselves as fighters. These characters are bullies who invariably lack any kind of neck conditioning, and for all their size and strength, possess a glass jaw so that any fight with them can be finished quickly at no more expense than a skinned knuckle or two.

My assailant received a sixpenny shot right on the jawbone. He certainly felt it, but he failed to collapse as I had hoped. His neck, even untrained, must have been a formidable thing.

He tried to grab me. I slapped his hand away and gave him a body blow to his upper right quadrant, which would sap some of the strength from his right arm. After that, I lost track of things and relied on instinct and good reflexes for a bit. It was more roundhouse style than the noble art, but I know that one too; I can dance in any style my partner requires.

Punching him was a fruitless occupation, and I quickly gave ground, backing and circling, putting gravestones between us and making him do all the work while I figured out what to do next.

The doctor was watching us with an uncertain expression. She was no fighter, that was for sure, but she might have thought about picking up that gun. However, he seemed more interested in the coffin and in Balthar, who was starting to stir.

My opponent came for me again, both trying to keep our footing as we danced around the gravestones. I caught him off balance and landed several blows in succession. He fell against the stone slab wall of a vault but came back, awkward and angry but not greatly damaged.

I was overconfident in my ability to wrong-foot the hulking, faceless figure, and as I dodged around a tomb the size of a garden shed, sure I had sent him the other way, I practically ran into him. He grabbed two handfuls of my jacket, and with phenomenal strength threw me into a raised headstone as easily as if I had been a straw dummy.

I clearly remember flying through the air, seeing stars whirl above me, and having time to think the same thought over and over: *that's it, I'm dead now.*

It felt like I flew fifty feet. In truth it was probably a quarter of that. The anvil on which I was to be smashed was one of those family markers on which the lives of several generations of a family are recorded, a stone slab standing six feet above ground and four feet wide.

The gradual effects of rain and shifting clay undermined by generations of worms, perhaps assisted by poor positioning, meant that it was not rooted deeply or firmly enough to resist the lateral force of Harry Stubbs being hurled into it. I was not splattered against it like a tomato on a brick wall. The thing simply toppled over under the impact. I felt like I had been hit by a bus, but I still kept enough momentum to roll into bushes beyond.

I regained my feet before the pain hit, as I knew it would. My hip and left knee had taken much of the force. Being back on my feet meant I was still in the fight though. My opponent had briefly lost sight of me in the shadows and undergrowth. He loomed into sight again, moving purposefully towards me. Next time he would know to throw me at something more substantial.

The pain flashed through me, so intense I could not localise it, but felt a single pulse of agony across my legs and hips.

I sucked in a breath. Pain is something you never get used to you; every time it surprises you afresh. My opponent, for all that I had hit him, showed no sign of injury, and I suddenly began to doubt whether I was up to this. The first instinct of a hurt animal is to avoid being hurt any worse.

But I am no animal. Something lifted me up then. The medical men might say it was the release of glandular secretions that nullify pain during a fight. I prefer to believe it was the spirits of my forebears interred in that ground who carried me along. Johnny Broome, and Jack Burke, and Tom Winter, perhaps they extended their aid from whatever heavenly boxing gym they look down from, and loaned me the strength to fight on, come what may.

The big man was coming for me, and I made a split-second decision. I feigned befuddlement, but when he grabbed me again, I grabbed him. We both tried to heave the other in an upwards direction. While he may have been many times stronger than me, he was not blessed with legs as long, and his toes left the ground.

On the first try I only lifted him a few inches clear and dropped him on his feet again—he felt like he weighed a ton at least—but he was so surprised he did not do anything but clutch me more tightly. As soon as he touched down, I heaved him up and away from me. He did not exactly fly as I had done, but he underwent some rotation and so landed almost horizontally across a tomb that stood about knee high.

They do say that that the bigger they come, the harder they fall. My hulking opponent fell very hard indeed, and did not have as soft a landing as I had. Nor was I about to give him the opportunity to rise again, as I would have done if it had been a properly conducted match. No, we were back in the days of bare-knuckle rules, which meant no rules at all. The prohibition on not hitting a man when he's down hardly applies when he is trying to kill you, and I made free use of my boots until he was out for the count.

The doctor was leaning over the coffin. With a fizzling sound, a giant sparkler lit up in her hand. It was a bar of light, throwing out brilliant orange sparks in all directions, which redoubled as she cut into the lid of the coffin. The doctor was lit up as though she had been standing in an orange spotlight, a look of concentration on her face, as the device cut through the hasp securing the metal box. The lenses of her glasses had darkened to blackness, and it belatedly struck me that I should not be looking into the bright light.

A moment later the sparkler went out, leaving dark blobs across the centre of my vision. I heard but could not see as she fished around on the ground. And then she saw me.

"Stubbs," she said.

"You got what you wanted," I said. She was holding something that glinted green in one hand and Schmidt's pistol in the other.

"That's mine," said Balthar, standing up, holding his bound hands in front of him.

She moved the gun from me to him, then back to me as I stepped forward.

Under other circumstances I might have appealed to them to be reasonable, but not when two people have a grudge that might go back several lifetimes. I could only wait and see how things worked out.

She said something in a language I did not understand, something sharp and guttural. He replied in the same.

In just about another minute she was going to lose patience and shoot both of us. My hope was that, as he was closer to her and the bigger threat, she would shoot him first. That would give me a fraction of a second to run. Should I run away from, or towards her?

My injured knee was hurting considerably. I hoped it would not give way when called on to perform sudden and extreme maneuvers.

While the doctor and Balthar were arguing, they did not notice, as I did, what was happening at their feet. It was beside Balthar and out of his field of view; as for the doctor, I wondered if her glasses had not adjusted back to the dark. Howsoever it happened, they did not see what I saw.

The broken coffin lid slid slowly aside, and something rose up from the interior. A shaft of moonlight caught the shrouded head, though in truth it was more like a skull. The flesh had shrivelled on to it like a desiccated apple, all juice gone, leaving a skeleton wrapped in leathery skin.

The living corpse moved awkwardly, in a jerky, unnatural motion. There were still eyes deep in those black sockets, and they were focused on the object in the doctor's hand. It crawled forward like a lizard, craning its neck and moving on all fours.

So intense was the doctor's dialogue with Balthar—while keeping one eye on me and moving the gun between us—that she did not see the corpse-thing until it touched her.

The doctor gave a sound that might have been a yelp and fired at it by reflex, three shots, crack-crack-crack. Then Balthar was on her, grappling her gun hand with both of his bound hands until she dropped it.

I stepped forward and kicked at the fallen gun, booting it

into the dark. The doctor still clutched the green glass key in one hand while fighting off Balthar. In her other she was struggling to bring the cutting tool to bear. It fizzled up with a shower of orange lights, and now it was Balthar who was fighting to keep her from bringing it down to slice through his head.

"Enough!" I ordered, grabbing the cutting tool out of her hand and sending it spinning through the air, a Catherine wheel throwing out sparks, until it suddenly went dark and disappeared from sight.

While avoiding looking directly at either of them, I seized the green key and shoved them both, sending them sprawling to the ground, when they clawed at me to get it back.

The object was exactly as it had been in my dream: green, translucent, slightly warm to the touch, with those little blue stones rotating inside it like the dials on a scientific instrument.

"Give it to me," said Balthar.

"No," said the doctor. "I need it."

With the ghastly creak of bone scraping on bone, the corpse thing came to a kneeling position and reached up to me like a thirsty man begging for water. Fortunately I could not see its face.

Sometimes intuition is your only guide. Trembling from exertion and maybe something else, I passed the glass key to the living corpse.

Balthar gave a groan, but the doctor put a hand on him and stopped him from trying to intervene as the thing from the coffin moved its rotting finger bones over the device. It seemed to be trying to speak; its shrivelled lips were moving, but nothing intelligible emerged from that blackened mouth. I could not see just how the manipulation was done, and there was no external sign that it was working, until mist suddenly rose around us, as suddenly as dry ice used in stage effects.

The cadaver slumped to the ground, and a moment later Balthar let out a strangled sound and fell to his knees. He flailed at the mist as though trying to wave it away from himself, like it was some insubstantial creature he was fighting. The doctor watched with detached interest as he succumbed and lay inert.

Silence fell over the cemetery, making it easy to hear the footsteps. The hulk I had beaten was limping towards us.

"You have your wish, everyone is going back," said the doctor. "I would have done it anyway, you know. I'm so sorry my friend panicked. His brain is not good."

"Was this Balthar's original body?" I asked, indicating the corpse. I was assuming that was the first link in the chain, but it might not have been.

My guess was that the cadaver, the not-quite-dead-thing, was the body Balthar had previously occupied. With the key turned, his mind would be sucked back into it, and the sequence of subsequent displacements would be undone one by one. The corpse-person would find themselves back in the body in the asylum, displacing Haywood and so on to the unconscious body in front of us, which must have belonged to the horoscope-dealer Mr Pennington.

"Questions are a burden, answers are a prison," said the doctor. "Please do not ask me anything."

It seemed to me that she did owe me more than a few answers, but sometimes you are better off not knowing, especially as Miss de Vere might want to question me on the matter. I leaned down and picked up the key, sending my back into a spasm of pain. I would get the Swedish masseur at the boxing gym to fix me up.

"Here," I said to her. "You'd better take this. And find that sparking thing too or someone will pick it up."

Another man might have claimed it for himself. Why, I could have gone into business breaking into bank vaults, with an oxy-acetylene torch small enough to fit in my pocket. But I have seen enough to know that wonderful magical gifts can be dangerous things for those who do not know what they are doing, and also how people like Miss de Vere tend to find out about it and descend on them.

The hulking figure approached. He did not seem to be much hurt, and maybe be would have gone for another round, but the doctor gave some signal and he moved to her side.

"We do not want trouble," she said, with a glance upwards. "You won't see us again, be sure of that. But we will need to clear things up here."

The three of us did what was necessary, bundling the shrouded corpse back into its coffin, and burying it again, with Herr Schmidt's remains alongside.

"He was a dangerous young man," said the doctor. "Not just to you or to us. If he had secured the key for himself…he would have done a lot of damage before they stopped him."

"I'll take your word for that," I said. I was careful not to turn my back on them. "And Balthar, what about him?"

The corpse had not been moving when we moved it, but maybe it took more time and effort to figure out how to work a body that was dead.

"He'll stay in the ground until Kamog's people get him out," she said. "It will keep him out of trouble."

"This Kamog," I said. "Are they likely to take this personally?"

"Oh, you have nothing to worry about," she said. "But for ourselves, we will be departing very soon."

As always, I am aware that I am not inconspicuous, and anyone asking around would be able to ascertain my identity without any great difficulty. Nobody yet has marked me down for vengeance, but it is always a possibility. Hence, partly, my desire not to start a feud with these two and their allies.

"You're safe," said the big one, the first time I heard him talk. His voice was distorted as though through a speaking-tube. "But don't you come looking for us, or any of our kind."

"I shan't," I said. "But you know, you can't go taking bodies…"

I did not wish to start an argument with them but stealing bodies—whether from a graveyard or by mental transfer—is a bad business.

"Do not worry," said the doctor. "We will not make trouble. We are always careful with our choices."

"No trouble," said the other, with that same glance upwards.

The doctor cut the manacles from the wrists of the one who had been Balthar, in other words Mr Pennington. The little device cut iron like a hot knife through butter. As she finished, he moved and started mumbling something incomprehensible.

"Back with us?" I said. "Take a minute to recover. Everything is back to how it should be."

"I don't half feel strange," he said, sitting up with difficulty. "Like I've been turned to dust and sucked up by a sandstorm."

The other two were moving quickly back into the shadows as though afraid of being seen. Coming to and finding yourself in a moonlit graveyard must be disconcerting at best, and when he saw what we three looked like I could have understood if he had run away screaming in terror. Instead, he just seemed completely stunned.

"You've been through quite an experience," I said. "Don't worry, I can de-brief you."

Mainly, I was thinking, make sure he knows that he's not supposed to breathe a word of this to anyone—not that there was much danger anyone might believe him.

He looked at me with wonder and, it seemed, gratitude.

"We will finish here, you get him away," said the doctor, and I did not argue. I walked the dazed man with me down the path that led to the cemetery gates, and the gap in the railings where Smith was waiting.

"Stubbs!" he said with obvious relief. "Thank heavens! I signalled—I saw them cutting through the fence over there—"

"All settled," I assured him. "Now let's get our friend here to the Electric Café."

"Bacon sarnies all round," said Smith, and I actually heard my stomach rumble at the thought of strips of salty meat between slices of white bread with generous addition of brown sauce.

The café is scarcely more than a quarter-mile from the cemetery and stays open all hours most nights. We soon saw its cube of light shining before us.

Pennington stood by the plate glass front of the café and froze. It took me a minute to gather that he was not hypnotised by the sight of the place, or the menu above the counter, not even by some familiar face among the clientele. What had struck him was the reflection of his own face in the glass. He raised his hands to his cheeks, and grimaced when the man in the glass did the same.

"Something wrong, Pennington?" I asked.

"My face," he said. "And what did you call me? My name's Eddie Haywood."

The face, the body was certainly that of Jimmy Pennington, peddler of horoscopes. But it was occupied by Eddie Haywood, the carpenter. Something had gone wrong.

EPILOGUE

"**B**ut it's all over now," said Sally, anxious for reassurance. We were in the foyer of the cinema for a Saturday evening performance of The Sea Beast. She was dressed up and looking very fine with her hair done up and her best silver necklace.

"More or less," I said.

The body residing in that unmarked grave was now occupied by Balthar, as far as I knew, and that was the main thing. Though it was quite possible that further exchanges had taken place and his soul had cascaded down through a series of ever-more-decomposed remains back to its rightful place in some other cemetery.

"And they let that poor man out of the asylum," she said.

"He was three parts mad, as you might expect after being buried alive for who knows how long," I said. "But he had enough of his wits to say the right things for them to let him out, with a little help from Smith."

The old man had given his name as Wayland, which may or may not have been his true identity. Smith did not get much from him, but it appeared that he had been another sorcerer's apprentice, a young Gnostic like Schmidt who thought Balthar held the key to all the mysteries—rather than the key to locking him away in a mouldering body. Wayland lacked Schmidt's devious streak and suspicious mind. Smith had found a place for him at a religious institution which took in men recovering from drink, and Wayland had seemed grateful. I wondered if he would adapt to modern life in whatever years remained to him.

"He's a good sort underneath it all, that Smith," I said.

"I don't like him," said Sally.

"He looks like a weasel, and he's not exactly charming," I said, "but—"

"He kidnapped me, remember," she said, a touch sharply.

"Fair point," I conceded. "I'd like to apologise on his behalf and hope there's no harm done. And vouch for him being a reformed character."

"And what about Haywood and Pennington?" she asked, showing that she had been keeping track of everything with her usual acuteness.

"Things resolved themselves," I said.

When the other exchanges took place, Pennington had somehow clung on to Haywood's body, leaving Pennington's body as the only empty vessel, which Haywood's mind had gravitated towards.

I had expected this situation to reverse itself in short order, but Pennington must have improvised some sort of psychic defence from what scraps of lore he might know and the two had remained swapped.

Haywood remained in Pennington's form, and the carpenter was literally a new man. For one thing, the taste for drink had left him; for another, he had lost much of his carpentry skill along with all his tools. For a third, he had some run-ins with characters who had a grudge against Pennington. Mainly though, he was healthy and several years younger, and decided that fate had given him a second chance in life. He took passage to South Africa to work on a ranch, and that's all I know about it.

As for Pennington, I have a suspicion.

A small fleet of pantechnicons had arrived at Belvedere Road. The workmen opened up the boarded-up front door with crowbars, and then spent several hours packing up every stick of furniture in the place. This, I suspected, was after one of Balthar's correspondents who wired on a regular basis had found their messages were no longer being returned.

I dropped by to ask Mrs Spinney if she had noticed anything—as if it was likely she would have missed something. To her obvious disappointment most of the items removed were under dust sheets or in packing cases, and she never did get to find out what Balthar was up to.

Mrs Spinney also mentioned was that she had found a cap in the back garden, which she showed to me. The sort of cap a carpenter might wear, flecked with varnish. The sort of thing a man might lose while going over a garden fence on a mission of burgling a wizard's house for all the wonderful things it held. My guess was that Pennington/Haywood had succeeded in getting into the house, but not out again.

Those bars might have been meant to prevent exit as much as entry. I never did find anything more about those mysterious pigs in the cellar, and Mrs Spinney could not enlighten me.

She mentioned, though, that one of the removals men had let slip—no doubt under cross-questioning—that the house contents were being taken to a cargo ship at the Port of London, at a dock used by ships plying the North Atlantic route.

"And we all know who we are," I told Sally.

"But you never know," said Sally, looking into my eyes. "Who is in there, eh? Are you really Harry Stubbs? How do you know I'm really me?"

The thought had occurred to me that I could never be entirely sure of anyone again. If minds and bodies could be exchanged so easily, there was no telling who was friend and who was enemy. But that way lay madness.

"I'd know you anywhere," I said.

And, as nobody was looking, we sneaked a quick kiss.

BROKEN SINGULARITY: SEQUENTIA TERTIUS

BY DAVID CONYERS

"Wake up, lazy bitches, lazy bastards! Time to work. Time to live!"

Peel followed the rasps of the Boss Man, echoing off metallic walls stretching deep within the labyrinthine corridors of this extensive moon-world base. As he advanced, he drew one of the Victorian era six-shooters and held it ready in his gloved hand. His limbs shook, a physical manifestation of his fear. He didn't believe he could shoot straight, but held the weapon in a firing stance regardless.

"Move it! Move it!"

Every room and corridor he explored was dark and empty, despite the dull light that shined from dim recesses, or lines of white light that traced patterns over consoles, data screens, electrical cables and pipe racks. He heard water dripping from far away, and the fain hum of machinery. Occasionally, he imagined slurping noises, like a slime mold transmogrifying in fast motion.

"You want to live? Then work to live."

Data typed out in blue lettering on black screens. Diagnostic reports perhaps, but compiled in a language Peel didn't understand or recognize. The tech and ergonomics were definitely human. Too many elements and aspects he instinctively understood, despite not understanding the specifics of what any of it was for.

"Bitches and bastards. Hesitation is a rookie mistake. Grab your suits. Work for a living."

Ahead, emerging from the pervasive darkness, a human-shaped figure slumped in the shadows, strapped to a large seat that looked to belong inside the cockpit of a fighter jet. His back was to Peel, and he wore a spacesuit too big for him. The hair on his head was flaccid and lifeless. Beamed lines of blue text illuminated across his forehead and crumpled spacesuit.

"Tools and tanks, boys and girls. Tools and tanks. Oxygen privileges expire in sixty seconds."

Peel raised his weapon and pressed it against the side of the Boss Man's head.

The head rolled and dropped to an unnatural position against the chest.

The head was nothing more than a skull with traces of hair and desiccated sinew that were once muscle and skin. Blue streams of indecipherable words illuminated across the corpse at the same speed as audio devices projected the speech throughout the base.

"Resting is for the dead, bitches and bastards. It's... work time."

The words didn't originate from the corpse.

The words were an ancient recording.

Peel asked himself, had the Boss Man lived during Peel's first remembered waking in the suspended animation crypt, or had the process always remained automated? If always automated, why the need for monitors, joysticks, keyboards, seats, doors and ventilation shafts?

The conclusion was obvious, that this place was once the domain of—and under the control of—humans. Peel didn't believe that to be true anymore.

A monitor flickered, then showed a projection into a crypt similar to the one Peel had first awakened from. On the screen, pods opened, and bodies fell out, three naked women and one naked man. All corpses, desiccated and brittle, they snapped at the joints and shattered into husky fragments as they hit the metal floor. They looked to have been dead for hundreds of years.

"Wake up lazy bitches, lazy bastards! Time to work. Time to live!"

Peel noticed a pistol holstered to the Boss Man's suit.

Taking it in his grip, Peel discovered it was a projectile weapon similar to automatic pistols from his own era, but with a larger caliber and twenty bullets in the magazine. After stripping and rebuilding the weapon, Peel fired it into the darkness.

The explosion was sudden and jarring, momentarily lighting up the control room in orange light and casting sharp shadows everywhere. The blowback was too intense for the fragile bones of the nearby Boss Man, and his barely-held-together skeletal remains collapsed as dusty fragments upon the metal surface.

In the aftermath, Peel detected movement. He heard a noise like crumbling parchment.

The same slurping noises he'd heard earlier.

With his new weapon raised and ready in one hand and the Pilot's detached head still gripped in his other, Peel advanced through the shadows towards whatever slid almost silently in the deep shadows.

Screens lit up, projecting moving images seen through eyes from distant pasts.

Peel watched imagery of a gothic cemetery at night, lit by a sliver of Earth's moon, with gravestones at odd angles and angels resembling demons more than heavenly messengers. Two men, dressed in garb from the first half of the twentieth century, explored the cemetery. There was a foreboding sense they were not alone.

The second image comprised a woman with silver-framed spectacles and iron-gray hair. She dressed in a man's black suit, business shirt, and a narrow tie. Behind her stood a humanoid creature molded in severe angles, resembling a walking, living statue.

The third comprised two cowboys, tied to beams within a sizeable ranch, but devoid of furniture other than a table. Earthen holes dug in random spots held corpses. A fog spilled out around the two men, and from the wispy trails appeared ghostly worms with wings, similar to those Peel had seen circling the naked singularity in the planet's core.

Another image formed, a man in a suit whose face seemed to fall into a whirlpool of his own flesh, before multiple human hands and arms emerged through the newly-forged orifice...

"You... understand."

The startling voice echoed behind Peel, sounding more like vomiting than speech.

Peel turned, his upgraded weapon raised and pointed at the black, viscous sludge that had crept along the metallic walls and dead machinery. Oily faces, human and those of alien origin, floated in the wet mass. Thousands of pseudopods resembling snail ocular tentacles waved and twittered in the quivering monstrosity.

"You... see... what we cannot see."

Peel fired his weapon again, and another explosive round disintegrated a portion of the wall where the creature oozed. The burning light again was sun-like and the smoke was acrid, causing Peel to blink, cough and splutter as the blowback gases entered his mouth and lungs.

When the smoke and flames dissipated, more of the slime oozed forward from the carnage as more oily faces appeared, reforming the space he had destroyed. The weapon had done nothing.

"We... are... everywhere."

Black ooze seeped from the monitors, vents, and joins in the walls and floor.

Peel stepped backwards, then turned only to halt again. Already the creature had blocked the path that had brought him here with more of its viscous, oily-like substance that seemed to exist and permeate all the seams and dark spaces of this futuristic base.

"We... are... the Riders."

"You wish to bargain with me?" Peel kept his weapon raised, and the Pilot's head gripped tight in his other hand.

"The... Yithians... hide their prison from us."

"The... Yithians... make it so we... cannot perceive."

"The... Yithians... trap us inside... the broken singularity."

Many voices spoke from the many oily faces, human-like

and monstrous, all slurping and sliding across the walls and ceilings. Peel kept turning, searching, but they blocked all escape routes.

They had always been here, hiding in the walls and joints and pipes and conduits of this base.

"You… see… the broken singularity."

Peel shuddered. His breath felt rapid and his body shook with spasmodic trembling. "What—? What do you want from me?"

"You… close the singularity."

"You… complete the black hole."

"You… fall into the event horizon."

Peel shuddered and almost vomited. These creatures, the Riders, were asking him to sacrifice himself inside a black hole, the most powerful natural destructive force in the universe. The surface gravity would be the equivalent of trillions of times the pull of Earth's gravity, and at its singularity, its center point, gravity would be infinite. Nothing could survive that kind of force.

"What's the point?" Peel asked, sensing he was out of options, that his life would soon end whatever path he now chose.

Then he remembered his elder-self, Peel fifty or even eighty years from now. Was that him? Or a clone? Peel wore the same spacesuit now, so odds were good they were the same person, and not separate clones of himself. Did a future self suggest he would survive through this day? What were elder Peel's last words?

"The… black hole… is a white hole."

"The… black hole… is a wormhole."

"The… black hole… forges an alternative universe."

The ooze permeated every surface now, leaving only a tiny patch of metal floor for him to stand upon. And somehow, Peel sensed he was only witnessing a tiny portion of this alien monster, for he suspected it spread everywhere throughout the base.

"Close… the gravity leakages into other dimensions."

"Close… the event horizon."

"Close… and we are free."

Peel shook his head. He didn't understand what he could, or should, do here. Why he was important. Why couldn't the Riders solve this problem themselves?

"We… dig a tunnel into the empty core."

"We… let you fall."

"We… let you traverse… the singularity."

Shuddering, Peel had sense enough in him to shout his fears. "I need oxygen for my suit." He held the Pilot's head high, not wishing to endure this unnatural death alone, or if he somehow survived the impossible journey, unwilling to endure eternal loneliness on the other side. "And she is coming with me, with a full body and protected from the vacuum of space."

A count of several seconds passed before the ooze receded, forming a path through the base.

Knowing he faced little choice, Peel followed that path as it opened before him and closed behind. The only light was a dull blue that emanated from the Riders themselves. Otherwise, he would have seen nothing. The darkness was that pervasive now.

He followed the path through many corridors until the Riders led him into what resembled a medical facility. The slime formations didn't follow him inside, as electric lights and monitors lit up the interior, offering a modicum of normalcy to his predicament.

In a tank, bubbling with green-tinged waters, floated a human body, skinless but growing muscles, nerves, blood vessels and lymphatic nodes at a discernable speed.

What the body lacked was a head.

Peel opened the cylinder, withdrew the Pilot's cold, dead head, then dropped it into the bubbling tank.

Immediately, nerves and blood vessels reached out as tentacles to adhere to the severed neck. The nutrients brought color to her porcelain face. Then the eyes flittered open, and the mouth gaped and closed like a feeding goldfish. Peel watched in horror as the skinless body attached itself to the head, and the two dismembered portions grew together as a single living entity.

It took ten more minutes before skin grew across the flesh.

She was perfect, unblemished but hairless, and soon the Pilot resembled a full-formed human. Peel wondered if he had endured this process himself, when they had forged him and his clones, back before the suicide missions had begun.

Fully formed, the Pilot regained consciousness, then suddenly unable to breathe, clambered upwards to escape the tank.

Peel reached in, lifted her body up and out of the green fluids, and pulled her close. She gasped for many minutes, as if remembering how to breathe. He cradled her as she recovered and returned to the land of the living. Despite the warmth radiating off her pinkish skin that didn't match her porcelain head, she shivered. Peel rubbed her naked back and hummed lightly as he gently rocked her.

After a period of perhaps twenty minutes, she had relaxed into his embrace, her muscles no longer spasming and her breathing leveled out to a normal rhythm.

"You came back for me," she whispered, as her unblemished hand gently touched his face.

His skin felt ragged and old compared to hers, baby-like in its newness.

"I did."

The warmth in the chamber had dried the fluids on her skin, so now he noticed the tears rolling from her eyes.

"I'm sorry," he whispered. "Apart from our last meeting, I don't remember you."

"I remember you... Many times."

He looked down at her, and she smiled.

"I feared remaining as just a head and an arm for the rest of my life. You saved me from that fate."

Now tears rolled down Peel's cheeks. "I'm not sure for how long."

She tensed. "What do you mean? Where are we?"

He told her what the Riders had explained to him, in its disjointed, otherworldly voices and mélange of ugly, oily faces.

The Pilot sat straighter but remained curled in Peel's embrace as she held him tight. "I know more than you do, Harrison. Perhaps I can explain?"

"Please do. But before… Do you have a name?"

She laughed lightly. "You really remember nothing?"

He shook his head.

"Hannah. Hannah Stanchfield."

Peel almost wept. A normal name at last. "It's nice to meet you… again, Hannah. How did you come to be here?"

"I was part of the original crew that piloted our sub-luminal spacecraft across one hundred and nineteen thousand light-years, taking us from Earth to this planet, far beyond the Milky Way, near the remnants of the supernova that created the gas clouds that formed Earth and the Solar System."

"What? How? Why?"

Hannah sat taller but remained in Peel's lap. "I forget, you are from a time much earlier to me."

"Where are you from? Or when?"

"Originally, latter twenty-first century. But after our initial test flight, twenty-fourth century. I was one of the last full biological humans ever to exist. There weren't many of us left by then."

Peel shook his head, feeling it ache with the information he had trouble processing. "So much I don't know."

"I've only been able to piece it together through fragments drawn from my own disjointed memories. But let me explain."

"First, how do we know each other?"

She shuddered. "Through the Boss Man. We explored this world together many times, searching for the key to the prison that holds the Riders here. Like you, they kept erasing my memories, but after you saved me when a cliff face collapsed and crushed most of my body, the Riders no longer felt the need to keep me ignorant. I remembered it all after that, and how I came to be here, and what they forced me to do upon arrival. What they forced all of us to do."

"You are a pilot?"

"Kind of."

Peel held her, not moving or speaking, while Hannah told her story. "I was born in Montreal in 2038. As a kid I was always interested in the stars, so I studied mathematics and physics, and eventually secured a double degree in astrophysics and engineering. I joined a project funded by multiple governments and corporations to build humanity's first sub-luminal spacecraft. A rocket powered by energy sources collected via microscopic wormholes tapped into the Big Bang, or the primordial nuclear chaos of the universe's center—"

"Azathoth?" Peel asked, remembering his experience with the Outer God from a time long in his past. Azathoth was a kind of deity that represented the potential of all uncollapsed wave functions in the universe, and one of the primary 'cosmic' gods that were the fundamental building blocks of the universe he lived in.

Azathoths's brothers and sisters were many, and included Nyarlathotep, the messenger particle of quantum mechanics, consciousness, and the conservation of information in the universe; Shub-Nigguarth, the source of all-life, evolution, and self-replication; Yog-Sothoth, the curvature of space-time, dark energy and the vacuum energy comprising virtual particles; Last was Cthulhu, a naked singularity like the black hole Peel now faced, and the breaker and destroyer of all the fundamental and universal structures the other Outer Gods projected out across the universe.

There were likely countless more Outer Gods Peel was ignorant to, but were the very structure of reality that allowed him to exist and be aware of his existence.

Hannah shuddered. "Yes. How did you know?"

"One of your financers: was it NASA? When I worked for them, they had tapped into Azathoth. Back then, we called it the Infinite Eye. I thought I'd shut down its connection with humanity, but it seems I had not."

"Well, it worked, the sub-luminal Azathoth drive. Physics tells us the energy needed to accelerate a gigantic mass across vast cosmic distances at near light-speed is effectively infinite energy, which Azathoth provided easily. I was on the test flight, to our nearest star Alpha Centauri, but during an accident where we flew too close to a primordial black hole no one knew was lurking out there gravitationally time dilated what should have been a ten-year journey into a three-hundred-plus-year journey. We returned to Earth in the twenty-fourth century, only to discover our home was nothing like we had left, alien to us and… horrific."

Peel squeezed her, a non-verbal signal he understood, as he remembered the various individuals he had explored this world with, and how strange they had all been.

"Humans were no longer human, more machine and emotionless than what we are, or were. In fact, consciousness was being bred out of us. We were existing, just to exist."

"That sounds horrible."

"It was horrible, and why I signed up with the rest of my crew from the first mission to leave the Solar System. A group calling itself the Rider Corporation had a scheme to head out across the Milky Way Galaxy and beyond into empty space, where they had discovered the black hole produced in the supernova that created the dust clouds that formed the Sun, Solar System and Earth four and a half billion years ago. A one hundred and nineteen thousand light-year journey, but on our sub-luminal starship, a journey of only twenty-three years and almost all of that spent in suspended animation."

"But why?" Peel asked.

Hannah shrugged. "Do you understand quantum entanglement?"

"Spooky action at a distance?"

"Yes. Two particles that have interacted in the past become entangled so that if one particle changes a fundamental property, that other particle instantaneously changes its property in a known way, even if separated by light-years. Even hundreds of thousands of light-years."

Peel felt struck by a moment of searing clarity, understanding now why so many human-elements existed and orbited the interior of this world. "You are saying the Riders, who permeate this base now, originally funded the sub-luminal drive project?"

"Yes."

"We are talking about the creature that oozes through the walls, right? But how?"

"I don't know, but they did."

More pieces of the puzzle fit together. Peel said, "The Riders became trapped here in the broken singularity, whose properties disallow them to see what traps them. But while they can't escape their prison, they can project their minds across space and time. Quantum entanglement would explain why they project their ethereal selves towards the Earth, through the entanglement of particles here and back home. So that would be why aspects of this connection can also manifest itself here."

Hannah stiffened as her bare arms and legs wrapped tight around him. "Who are the prison wardens, so to speak? Who imprisons the Riders?"

Peel remembered the book discovered on the moon's surface, with the metal pages and curvilinear script, and his conversation with the slime creature. "I think they are a species called the Great Race of Yith. You heard of them?"

"No."

Surprising them, the oily creature of waving tentacles and humanoid faces seeped into a corner of the medical bay.

"Sorry, Hannah, but our time is up." Peel said, noting the Riders return as he helped his companion to her feet. She struggled with her balance as she adjusted to her new body.

A drawer opened on the wall. Inside were spacesuits similar to the one he wore. She dressed in a fresh suit while Peel replenished his oxygen tank.

The faces spoke to them.

"You… fall into the singularity."

"You… enter the next universe."

"You… restore the event horizon."

Hannah's stares widened. "What does that mean?"

Peel shuddered. He hated these moments of clarity that sometimes struck when the weirdness of the universe made sense to him, but those moments also always reminded him how utterly cold, terrifying, and depressing reality was. "The Riders believe if we restore the gravity bleed-off around this black hole, it will free them of their prison. The singularity will close."

"What…? But that means… Falling into the black hole?"

Peel swallowed. "Yes. I don't think we have a choice."

Sensing the air pressure and temperature dropping, they sealed their suits as the oozing Riders filled the room.

"You… go now."

The door leading outside the medical bay opened. All surfaces beyond were again smeared with the black, oily sludge of the Riders' combined projections.

Herded by the expanding alien biomass, Peel and Hannah advanced inwards, until they looked downward into a new intrusion built into the base, a tunnel that was kilometers deep, a vertical shaft that dropped into the shell interior. The Riders had been busy drilling into the planetary surface while the medical bay grew Hannah a new body.

Peel took Hannah's gloved hands in his. "The Riders brought humans here because they can't perceive their prison, but we can. They needed us. Still need us."

"Yes… I guess it all makes sense now…"

Further tears rolled down her cheeks, but he couldn't wipe them away because of their sealed helmets.

"Hannah, are you ready for this?"

"No."

"Me neither."

She took his hand, and they jumped.

The fall was sudden, silent and direct.

They passed into the shell, raced past the many human corpses, the broiling shapes of Shoggoths, and the ring of flailing worms.

They fell into the singularity.

But they didn't crush into a point of infinite density and zero dimensions.

They kept falling.

The universe became like a Mandelbrot set, as every visual sense around them exhibited elaborate and infinitely complicated boundaries built from the massive structures of the universe, that revealed progressively ever-finer recursive detail at increasing magnifications.

Peel realized he was seeing the entire universe all at once, stretched to the infinite and encompassing all creation. He witnessed the cosmic Outer God structures fundamental to the existence of everything. Azathoth. Cthulhu. Nyarlathotep. Shub-Niggurath. Yog-Sothoth. His mind should have exploded into its fundamental components from witnessing their terror, but he was no longer a separate, diffuse biological entity. He was both an infinitely minuscule droplet of the universe and also the entirety of all the fabric that bound the composite dimensions of time and space at the same moment.

Everything and nothing.

He glanced at his hand.

He still held Hannah tight in his grip.

Peel watched them both as they became their own Mandelbrot sets, infinitely repeating as magnifications of their own existence repeated at the cellular, particle, string, and at deeper quantifiable measurements.

The fall seemed to last forever, and it passed by in no time at all.

They must have transgressed the universe that had produced them, as the singularity removed them to a place beyond and outside every experience and entity they had ever encountered.

They should have collided with the singularity by now. They should be a nothing-point of infinite everything.

He should have died. And so should have Hannah.

Instead, he stood intact on a beach, by a bungalow, with the waves of a tropical ocean lapping at his bare feet.

LENG'S LABYRINTH

BY JOHN DELAUGHTER

"Battle not with monsters, lest ye become a monster, and if you gaze into the abyss, the abyss gazes also into you."
Friedrich Nietzsche, "Beyond Good and Evil."

"I rejoice that you traffick not so much with Those Outside; for there was ever a Mortall Peril in it…"
Edward Hutchinson, late of *Salem-Village, Massachusetts Colony*

"By my manner, you assumed I was a Guardian…by your manner, I knew you were a Prisoner…"
Number 6, *The Village, Whereabout Unknown*

CHAPTER ONE: FOREIGN EXCHANGE

All lives are filled with their share of shadows. In sunlight, shadows multiply like weeds. They sprout everywhere, evidence of the substance of the objects that cast them. And like weeds, people seldom give a second glance about one shadow over another.

The only time shadows are generally given more thought than that is when the sun is scorching the earth from high overhead. Only then does a shadow become a life-giving, cooling shade.

Even in the dim light of dusk, the shadows shine brightly for those who have eyes to see.

In the depths of the night, those that cast shadows largely go unseen. Only the sound of their nearness, if they are clumsy or casual, alerts others of their presence. And sometimes, by their scent, you can count them nearby.

My name is Francois Luc DeLapont.

Once, to me, a shadow was a shadow. I was innocent, but not naive. I was young but knew some things about the big wide world that belied my age. I was trusting, but not gullible.

I turned to the shadows when I became interested in my own shadow, the essence of the sides, the heights and depths of my life that were not known to me.

I was young and the idea that such self-knowledge would liberate oneself was a heady drug. I was, like many of the young, an idealist who believed in many people and many answers given inside academia and outside by society.

Some things are understood in this world and some things are not understood.

Now, I know of things that I wish I could expunge from my memories. I have seen things not meant for human eyes. I have heard things not meant for human ears. I realize that shadows bear more substance and reality than meets the eye. Many shadows in this world bear no resemblance to the objects that supposedly cast them.

Then, I lost my anonymity. Once, I was a nameless, faceless member of the human herd. I was one shadow among an anonymous many. There was nothing in me that inspired a second look from anyone in officialdom or among other entities, prefects, and predators, not of this world nor our epoch in time.

My journey of discovery and disaster began far away from home, in France.

I was a foreign exchange student, smart beyond my age, taking the introductory courses a person usually takes during the first two years of college, except my school was a branch campus of the *Université D'Orléans*, ninety miles south of Paris, France in the ancient town of Chartres, capital of Eure-et-Loir.

In time, the aura of Chartres came not only to haunt me, but possess me with a compulsion to act on impulses and follow courses of action that I would have never considered "proper" given my staid, New England, upbringing.

My basic understanding of French grew, from a stammering tongue to one that spoke like a native, albeit with an accent, a reality that marked me as an outsider.

At that time, I was bewitched. I abandoned any thought of an afterlife under the enchantment of the new religion, science. I exchanged one propaganda for another. One promised a never-ending tomorrow, unverifiable, unpredictable. The other promised no such fantasies to inflate the ego that wishes to live on, though its death is inevitable. But then its gift to its adherents was no afterlife, but an empty life.

Though I toed the materialist's line; I was not one to stray far from the chalk lines they drew around my still-living corpse.

Why France, you may ask? Some of my relatives originally came from France, under the banner of the Huguenot faith, a persecuted minority when they did not tow the Romish church's prattle. My progenitors, the DeLaponts, a father and two sons, volunteered to serve in the American Revolutionary, as part of the French Expeditionary Force under the Marquis de Lafayette.

At the end of that war, the DeLaponts stayed in the Americas, as the promise of religious freedom and opportunities to own their own land were intoxicating.

I desired to unearth, as my studies allowed me time, any details of my family from its ancestral homeland.

Then, that ominous first day came. That day started no different from any other. I had un croissant et du cafe-au lait for breakfast, at my normal morning cafe haunt, *La Table du Marche*. But it marked the beginning, one of many fated days that forever changed my life. I must set down the chain of events before the darkness envelopes me. You, my readers, beware. I cannot be held responsible for your safety or sanity, if you read further.

Perhaps, my attempt to chronicle the events that forever changed my life reflects a desire to return to the privacy of my once placid existence. And to resume what semblance of sanity I still retain before my life ends, sooner unnaturally, I fear, rather than naturally and much later.

My initial study of all things "DeLapont" began in the Chapter Library of the Chartres Cathedral.

To approach the Chapter Library, one must first enter the Chartres Cathedral itself.

A hush of antiquity, a feeling of untold ages left me feeling flush as I traversed the sacred space of the cathedral. I entered a world of stained-glass rainbows as the outside light filtered into the hallowed halls. The soaring, cyclopean heights of the cathedral's steepled sun spire and moon spire echoed with ghostly Gregorian chants perhaps piped in to heighten the sense of otherworldliness that permeated the arch-lined heights and many candled depths. The Sacred Vestiges of Holy Forebearers, lifelike and vibrant, formed heavenly patterns here, there, and throughout the cathedral. Such was the great cloud of faithful witnesses who followed my meandering tour of the church.

I grew faint as I came to the great labyrinth. My booted foot offered me no protection from the sense of timelessness that radiated there, a relic whose mythical origins were clouded by the miasma past. Then and there, I decided on a whim, to celebrate October thirty-first by walking the labyrinth. Intuitively, I sensed the fronds of the labyrinth were reminiscent of the lobes of an eerie brain, thin-sliced by an MRI scanner.

I had to sit in one of the many pews that surround the multi-columned hall of the labyrinth. As I caught my breath and the dizziness subsided, I watched men and women, old and young, follow the course of the maze, each lost in the moment and their own little worlds. Was the labyrinth some type of multi-symbolled curse, unified into one mysterious emblem that lulled its devotees into a disturbing doom?

How was I to know that the Labyrinth was a symbol for the sacred womb, or of what evil that was to be birthed there?

Was there a secreted pagan geometry woven into the sacred design of the cathedral? Did thus the ancient Celtic-Gaul druids, who I later found to have once worshiped a mother god in the place that is now the crypt of the cathedral, have the last laugh on the zealots that desecrated their holy grounds?

Hiding the pagan in plain sight, such was the subterfuge of one of the unknown architects who penned the cathedral's plans centuries ago. His name was forgotten during the one hundred and fifteen years, 1145 to 1260 AD, it took to complete the church, one of five worship centers that, one time or another, had occupied that site.

Why spend millions on SETI (the *Search for Extraterrestrial Intelligence*), on the remote chance you might contact others from elsewhere? Here lay an immortal portal to the unknown, by which an ingenious man might lay hold of all the mysteries summed up from untold ages and uncharted infinities.

Such were my playful thoughts, dark though they be.

If the still greens that surrounded the cathedral were meant to mirror the ancient, legend-bound Garden of Eden, the church was meant to be a hallowed meeting place between today's Adams and Eves and their deity.

Religious attendants, brothers from the Augustinian Order, asked me a series of questions to help me define the parameters of my search. Enamored with my youthful zeal, they agreed to comb not only their records but other genealogical sources available to them via the internet.

All they asked for in return was a bottle of choice vintage from the nearby *Jean-Karl Louis Vins et Conseil*.

That was a Thursday, and Brother Bertrille promised they'd have results for me in a week.

Strange, as I left the cathedral grounds, I sensed I gained a stalker, though not one I could use my finger to point out among the milling folks that walked by the church. It wasn't a feeling of butterflies in my stomach. Instead, it felt like bats clanging around in my belfry.

As I drove back to *Université D'Orléans*, I wondered what that was about.

CHAPTER 2: THE CHARTRES LABYRINTH

I waited and the promised date of my genealogy's completion passed with no word, nor phone call from Brother Bertrille.

I wondered why that was the case. Were the brethren holding out on me, for additional bottles of their favorite vintage?

It was fall in France, and according to the Pagan calendar that the *nouveau idéaliste* idolized because it was the "in" thing to do, it was the season of Samhain, October 31 to November 1. It was a time to usher in "the dark half of the year," a season when the veil between our world and other worlds is at its thinnest, transparent, and permeable. That which dwelt on our side of the quantum fence was date-stamped, categorized, filed, and inexhaustibly defined.

What of the denizens that dwelt on the other side?

In my youthfulness, I hadn't given much thought to another side.

As to my planned celebration, officially, the cathedral was open daily, 08:30 AM - 07:30 PM. But the witching hours did not follow the sanctioned Romish hours, so I and Mahmood Le Fey, the accomplice to my sacrilegious deed, planned to unsecure a little-known egress to the cathedral prior to our advent into the church.

It never entered my mind that, should we be caught, any genealogical research Brother Bertrille and company may have conducted would be terminated. Such was the cast of my young mind, never considering in the least the potential consequences of my actions. Why was I so unwittingly compelled to drive a nail into my coffin?

Oh, my innocence in the face of the darkness I might release.

I wish I knew then what I know now.

How obsessed had I grown over the planned celebration? Given the few euros to my name, a poor student at best despite the small stipend supplied to me by a campus job and the student exchange program, I purchased from the cathedral gift shop a replica of the Chartres Labyrinth. The purchase price made sure that I would forgo a meal or two, as I added my own layer to the myth of starving students.

Little did I know that the priest who blessed that replica was not of any holy Catholic order. Or that for me, this perversion of the Chartres Labyrinth amounted to a Ouija board.

Mahmood and I parked a few blocks away from the cathedral, arriving there separately at around 11:00 PM. Moonlight stirred up the shadows all around us, as we gathered our bundles in small shoulder satchels. My paranoia had grown since we first hatched the plan, so we kept what we carried to a minimum. The only obvious out-of-place item, should we be stopped and questioned by a *gendarme*, was a crowbar in my possession.

What motivated Mahmood to follow my madness? I don't know. At the time, perhaps it was the adrenaline rush so many of the young are addicted to. Breaking the law involved many of the same emotions incited when one broke a record, landed a date with a young lady out of one's league, or dared the loss of control while driving a speeding car. I had no more insight into his behavior than I had of my own.

We moved as quietly as possible, making ourselves part of the shadows. We plied business alleys where possible, using hand signals to communicate. Vehicle traffic was sparse, though once a *gendarme* drove by, flashing a fender-mounted spotlight toward Mahmood's general direction. Had he moved, the proverbial jig would have been up.

Providence, at the time, seemed to smile on us. The *sûreté* squad car drove off to more violence-prone parts of Chartres, leaving Mahmood and me to our felonious appointment.

We encountered a noticeably-cooler locale as we reached the green commons that surround the cathedral. There was no wall, as the church was meant to be a place of the people. The air smelt of rotting leaves, as many bared tree branches forked toward the heavens. A waning, gibbous moon stippled the land as the wind blew loose leaves in circles around my feet. Mahmood hid behind a stray bench, lost in its shadows, as I peeked around another. We alternatively bounced, ducked, and zig-zagged between tree boles, other benches, and sporadic shrubs.

I flashed my red-lensed torch, chosen to yield minimal light to others, along the low, ground-level windows, among which Mahmood had unsecured one the prior day. The selected portal opened onto the stairs that led to the cathedral's crypt, as a smile broached my partner's face. He slipped through the window feet first, as I pulled myself tight against the building, looked around—not a soul was in sight—handed Mahmood first his satchel, then my own, before I too plunged feet first through the window, my gloved hands holding fast to its frame.

Why gloves, you might ask, during the commissioning of what amounted to a sophomoric prank? It was the thrill of being a well-prepared burglar that drove this detail. On the other hand, Mahmood, who was not one given to such larcenous flights of fancy, bare-handed things. As for me, I entertained no vandalous, nor sacrilegious thoughts against the sacred grounds.

It was Friday, so the chairs that normally obscured the labyrinth were removed (as was the case from the start of Lenten season—around the end of February—to the Day of the Saints, the first of November).

While Mahmood kept watch, he turned his red-lensed flashlight against the lobes of the labyrinth, staining it blood crimson. Sitting on a crude bench, one that skirted the archways surrounding the labyrinth, I removed my shoes, intending to perform a walking meditation. I took a deep breath, calmed myself, donned a ball cap with a rudimentary light reddened by crepe paper, and reached into my bag for the final piece of the puzzle.

I stood up, taking my place at the central node of the labyrinth, in hand a Tibetan singing bowl and mallet. I placed the mallet at an angle against the bell of the bowl and began to drag it in circles around the lip of the bowl. The point of the ritual? The bowl symbolized the "void" and its echoes helped empty its wielder of "containments" of this lower realm.

Mahmood set up and lit four candles at the cardinal points of the compass within the labyrinth's outline. He also started a large battery-powered "white-noise" machine to mask the peal of my Tibetan bowl. We heedlessly pushed the limits; this was our celebration of All Hallows' Eve, and, were it not for Mahmood's nominal faith, we would have toasted the moment.

I was caught up in the ambiance—the gibbous moon peering through the soaring, stained-glass skylights above, the moaning of the bowl drawing "hungry ghosts" from near and far, the candles invoking a flickering separation between the scant light and the sea of shadows. What slipped within the shadows I invited to seep into me, as I slowly treaded the petals of the lotus-like labyrinth. Mahmood cared not for my ritual; he simply reveled in the casual moment, the chance mood, and changing moonlight.

Then, a strange shift stirred the air, the same shadow that fell on me before, the day of my visit with Brother Bertrille on my genealogical quest. I stood unsteady, overcome by a wave of nausea, as weird angles in the moonlight emerged, shifted like a satellite was somehow descending outside the cathedral, and strange crimson pillars stirred in the flittering shadows.

Mahmood looked like he stood on the other side of a gigantic aquarium's wall, vague and fluctuating, like an image in a fun-house mirror. He stood looking this way and that, more concerned about discovery, oblivious to my deterioration.

Of the formless crimson pillars arising near the four flickering candles, three began to coalesce amid a dark, many-columned edifice, not of this world, that soared beyond sight into the heavens. Archetypes of my ancestral unconscious, I wondered as I glanced at one, then another of the three.

A bent-over, slack-jawed brute, clad in rough animal skins, slumped leering all around to my left. Behind me, a coiffed, white-wigged, ghoul-faced, linen waistcoat, high knee-breeches, white hose, and black-buckled shoed man stood, proud and preening. Immediately before me, a lantern-jawed, high-foreheaded man with enormous eyes and silver uniform arose a meter taller than me.

Nearest to Mahmood, the largest pillar whirled like a dust-devil, crimson-shadowed and peppered with short flashes of forked lightning. A dread sense of peril filled me, as in the spinning darkness I briefly thought I saw—of this image, I cannot be certain in the adrenaline-fueled instant—huge, clicking pincers and enormous, lantern-like eyes.

I had no time to think. Mahmood suddenly floated into the air, his face a mix of awe and confusion. His limbs then jerked spread eagle, as if bound between four stallions charging in opposite directions. A piercing shriek broke from Mahmood's terrified face, before he came apart in a fountain of blood, his limbs, head, and torso hitting the labyrinth with a hollow plop and splat.

I dropped my singing bowl, which clanged loudly when it hit the floor.

As the spell broke, the vision vanished and I impulsively yelled for help. Mahmood's head, his face a rictus grin, his eyes ghostly and empty, stared up at me. His pool of blood turned into a steamy morass, reeking of sewage and sulfur, before the labyrinth face sucked it up till only my friend's carcass remained. When I snapped out of my stupor, as I heard a distant siren, I grabbed my bag and bowl before I dashed toward the basement crypt, its open window my only escape.

I quickly made my way back to the faraway parking lot, dodging any building with lighted windows or passing cars, where we had parked our cars. I started my wreck without gunning the engine, and rolled slowly away from Mahmood's car without lights until I reached the A11 highway.

I decided spending a few nights away from my boarding house in Chartres might help throw off my part in what happened at the cathedral. I bought a bottle of vodka and found a cheap inn for the night.

As I lay on the hard mattress, staring up at the ceiling, unable to sleep, I said to myself, "What the hell happened tonight?"

CHAPTER 3: THE DELAPOERS

In my mailbox, *La Poste*—the one part of the vast French bureaucracy and semi-private companies that are essential state monopolies—had delivered a package officially marked with a Chartres Cathedral logo. I guess Brother Bertrille decided to forgo his bottle of vintage for some reason, though I would keep my promise to him, I was a man of my word, even back then.

I let the package set for several days in my flat, going about my duties as a student, attending classes, taking notes, and occupying my mind with enough busyness to avoid thinking about the labyrinth. I also waived my normal habit of scanning various news websites, especially those with a local focus, for fear of hearing about Mahmood's death from third parties.

I succeeded, to some degree. It was in my idle moments that the abject horror seeped into my brain, lifting an edge of the curtain that my instincts of self-preservation had strung up, a trick of the reptilian core of my mind from ages past erected to maintain my sanity.

I needed company but avoided it. I craved the nearness of others, but whom could I tell about the circumstances that burdened me so? What would be the first topic of the conversation, "Have you heard about what happened to Mahmood? How terrible…" And what if I shared what I thought was "safe" about the affair, without the gory details that might incriminate me? Would one of my more observant friends intuitively link two and two together, and ask me, "How did you know about that facet of poor Mahmood's story?" Or would they forgo grilling me on the subject, and simply rat me out to the local *gendarmes*?

Fear of discovery haunted my every step. I felt relieved as days passed and no one had tracked me down to learn of my whereabouts on the night of October 31st.

Then came the moment a week later, while drinking a cup of coffee, that I opened the package from Brother Bertrille. There was no cover letter as I would have expected. Perhaps the informality of my request led to an informal response. Perhaps, the keepers of the Chartres Cathedral archives thought it a mark of ego to sign the fruits of their labors.

I read through the page upon page of scholarly notes, discoursing several rather dull confirmations of what I already knew about the DeLaponts. It frankly read like a genealogy from the Bible, line-upon-line, rote-upon-rote, detailing a rather somber list of people, marked by few standouts who distinguished themselves above the rather common folks who were born, lived, and died in obscurity equal to the DeLaponts.

The exercise served its purpose, another pointless distraction to my pointless existence.

Then my eyes chanced upon an obscure scion of the DeLaponts that branched off into England, around the time of the Roman Invasion and occupation of that isle. Over time, the DeLaponts became the DeLapoers according to the local idioms and enunciations. Rather than recite the rote details about that offshoot of the family, it repeated in short vignettes the dark rumors that grew up around the DeLapoers over the intervening centuries, from devil worship to demon possession, from classic in-breeding to cannibalism, foraging on the nearby country folk. It seems at some later point, one of the DeLapoers killed every one of the rumor-haunted line in a mass-murder and suicide event. Rather than treat the affair as a tragedy, the locals celebrated it as a day of liberation from a curse brought on the region by the blasphemous DeLapoers. Only members of the DeLapoers that migrated to the new world escaped the massacre that bordered on genocide.

The last entry recorded how, at the end of World War I, one of the surviving DeLapoers returned to their ancestral seat at Exham Priory, without knowledge of his family's dark legacy, in the hopes of erasing the scars that the war inflicted on him by reinventing and reinvigorating the priory's past glories. Somehow, for the scholars recounted fables rather than facts concerning the DeLapoers, the ancestral madness that afflicted the cursed family fell also on that last DeLapoer, who, after being caught in the very act of a cannibalistic ritual reminiscent of his horrid ancestors, lived out his days as a rambling madman writing lunatic word-salads in an undisclosed asylum for the criminally insane.

I noted that these entries were penned by a psychologist, Dr. Leopold DeLapont, in the footnotes. I wondered if we were related in some way.

I paused, letting the genealogical research fall to the floor in a heap. I felt a gnawing presence standing before me. It was only a fleeting sense of nearness, perhaps a hovering in the sunlight, I do not know. But the ramifications of what I had just read bedeviled me. Had the shadow that fell over the DeLapoers also darkened the more ancient DeLaponts?

Was the horror in the cathedral rooted in the dark deeds of my ancestors?

I felt afresh the terrors of that titan night. My mouth went dry, as terror seized me. I felt like lashing out in anger with no enemy near at hand. I felt like running to escape, but where could I go to escape the horror recorded in my mind?

I thought that Mahmood had died at the whim of some unknown, paranormal presence that night in the cathedral. Did he? Or did he somehow die at my hand, and my mind came up with some insane delusion to mask that fact?

I tried to comfort myself with the notion that, if I were entertaining those types of questions, I had not killed my friend.

I sat still until the dizzying feelings subsided. Lucky for me, it was the weekend, and I could do so without having to skip a class. My semester would be over in a month. The rigors and routines of student life would mechanically carry me forward. I sought additional hours at my meager employment to dim the violence I witnessed with the dumbing down of dreary duties.

I pondered as I picked up the scattered papers and stuffed them back in the large envelope, a courtesy of Chartres Cathedral.

What would I do next?

CHAPTER 4: BASALT TOWERS

I awoke to stabbing pains piercing my person in many places. I was broken and I could not focus on my whereabouts. A roaring wind filled my ears and a whiteout blinded my sight.

I sensed I was on my right side, wherever that might be. I know I wasn't laying in my single bed, boarding with a local family in Chartres, with access to my own hutch of a kitchen, small shower, and separate pot to pee in. An open window in the depths of winter and a night of hard partying could not duplicate my surroundings.

Dust, debris, and loose piles of "snow?" slid against my back from above and behind me. Was it an avalanche? Was I somewhere in the Alps or the Pyrenees? How did I get here, I mean there? Was there someone on a ledge above me, intending harm?

The noisy wind languished for a moment which, in turn, lessened the blinding snow that blew into my eyes. I tried to rise, but the pain overwhelmed me. What little I saw, I could not believe. A brief ledge, barely wide enough to hold my person? And my clothing, from what I spied from the waist down, a hairy, knee-length, blood-stained buffalo robe? And raw, homemade hairy boots to match?

Had I assumed the person of the stooping, skin-clad ape man from my labyrinth night terror?

I turned to look out, away from the mountain, wherever it was, whoever I was. For what was I to make of my getup? Whatever shadow hung over me, I was no longer Francois Luc DeLapont, at least in the flesh.

Suddenly, a deep rumble shook the mountainside I lay

upon to its roots. More debris bounced down the slope behind me, many of the larger rocks bounding off a higher ledge and cascading upward into the sky.

At the shaking, a thousand needles of pain pierced me; I almost passed out.

Then, a cyclopean, spinning red-hot object, most like a manhole cover crisscrossed by a girder-beamed "X" flew upward into sight. In moments, it sailed in an arc away from my cliff perch into the near curtains of swirling snow, a true UFO—I'm sure I was mistaken as to its identification.

Besides that, four immense towers of basalt of different heights, with one or two of them missing their dark crowns, stood windowless, snow enshrouded, and imposing. The soaring, rigid monoliths swayed slowly amid undulating blankets of snow, as their table-rock foundations shifted like glaciers fracturing adjacent to the Antarctic seas.

Below me, I heard an enormous train whistle multiplied once, thrice, four times over, slowly rising from the earth. The roar ascended from the same location as the flying fiery sewer grate.

Unable to move, I was a captive audience as it rose into sight, like a hovering black helicopter, yet it emitted thundering whistles from countless locations across its body, for the thing was organic, polyp-studded, grey, glistening, and visibly quivering.

The object defied description—I'm sure my agony influenced my impressions of the thing that loomed like madness before me.

Lace-like tentacles spread-out from its many-ridged circumference, fragile-looking, undulating, alive as if each limb were motivated by a mind of its own. More steam escaped from previously unseen orifices, so loud the pulse, I tried to, but could not cover my ears. It had no visible eyes but erupted into a mass of searching, gaping maws, each surmounted on rope-like feelers.

How could the thing hang there, effortlessly in the heights, with no visible wings or artificial contrivance to bear it up? Did my growing instability—for I must be teetering on the brink of insanity in a padded cell somewhere—give this living nightmare the ability to soar in the updrafts?

The dark whistling thing slowly drifted toward me. I screamed, my head palpitating as blood-filled visions jammed with bursts of forked lightning, alien squeals, and teeming with lantern-like eyes, poured into my cranium.

I could not move, I had nowhere else to go. A mountain floated, whistling as it made its way toward me.

I shrieked, an ear-splitting falsetto. So, this is death, the existing pain undeniable, lost on an unknown mountainside.

I screamed myself awake, bolting upright in a sweat-drenched bed, my eyes blinded by sunlight, rousing not only those with whom I shared the residence but also the surrounding flats.

Panting, I heard feet charging down the hall.

Next, there was one, then many fists pounding on my door.

"Francois, Francois, what is happening in there? Do you need a *Médecin*?" shouted the voice of Roger Blanchet, my landlord.

The incident at my flat almost brought a swift end to my lease. Though always a bit of a vagabond, my recent brush with death and the inexplicable incident at the cathedral brought my survival instinct into sharp focus.

I sat at my desk, the cursor blinking at the top of the Word file, nothing but a blank screen and I had a term paper due on Friday. I could no longer concentrate on my studies. I took small steps on the path to keep progressing. But those paths ended up going nowhere.

I missed classes and was running out of excuses and understanding professors for such absences.

My credentials and career as a foreign exchange student were in dire jeopardy, as it depended on my finishing out the semester with at least a "B" average.

I had to do something. I could not sleep most nights since Halloween, and when I did, I had dreams like my nightmare on the cliffside a few nights ago. I could not presume on any goodwill with my landlord.

I needed someplace to go, somewhere to resolve the issues associated with the shadows that invaded my waking life. I needed to make a decision, one that amounted to self-preservation. Was any of it real anymore? I had trouble navigating the difference between whether I was awake or asleep. Was my world the real thing, or had I vividly hallucinated the whole nightmare on that Samhain night, the one forever burned into my memory?

I chanced on an idea.

It centered on the psychologist who penned the history of the DeLapoers, Dr. Leopold DeLapont. Did the good doctor know more about the clan than he let on? And, was he only interested in paranormal research, or did he provide counseling services too?

I checked the internet to see what I could find out about Dr. Leopold DeLapont. It seems there were two listings for Dr. DeLapont. One, a Dr. DeLapont was listed as an Adjunct Professor in Psychology, at the *Université de Tours*. Tours was about one hundred and fifteen miles from Chartres, if my wreck would hold together that far.

Now, what about that other listing? It seems Dr. DeLapont was also the head of the prestigious *Institut Jungien Pour L'étude des Mémoires Ancestrales* (the Jungian Institute for the Study of Ancestral Memories), also of Tours.

In that role, did Dr. DeLapont do consultations or see patients? I called the Institute's number and got a busy signal. I tried again and got a multiple-choice, press one if you are a healthcare provider, press two, if you are calling about making co-payments on your account, etc. Ah, there was a choice about a consultation. I pressed that number and got to leave my number for a call back and possible appointment.

I got a mid-morning appointment for the next Tuesday, the one day a week I had nothing going on.

It was a consultation with an associate of the Institute. Dr. Leopold DeLapont did not regularly take on new patients, I was told.

I felt an immediate relief of the tension in my body. I sensed a dark cloud lifting off me, not literally, but something shifted in me.

I experienced a new head of steam. A bit buoyant, I attacked the same term paper whose deadline now stood only three days away.

CHAPTER 5: LIBRARY STACKING

It was Saturday, one of my weekend workdays at the *Université D'Orléans'* campus library. I got up and drank a cup of coffee. It was supposed to be a rainy day. I didn't dither by digging for distractions on my computer.

Saturday was re-file day, for the books that the regular staff did not have the time to replace into their correct position on the shelves of book collections, the general library shelves, and the special references. The volumes that belonged in the special references were rare, one-of-a-kind tomes from antiquity. Some are even supposed to be cursed or forbidden in some past age when the mother church ruled society, sacred and secular alike.

It would be a slow day. I looked forward to times such as these when the rhythm of university life beat steadily and helped synchronize my own senses to that relative calm.

Since Leopold DeLapont had some standing in academia, I wondered whether he might have penned a book or other memoir? Perhaps, if such a volume existed, I could acquaint myself with the mind of the man before meeting him. I did intend on meeting him somehow though the professor insulated himself against meeting the general public; his "associates" represented the gatekeepers to the man.

I entered my *salle de bain* for a quick shower and shave. That ritual each day served as a transition point, where I left the problems of my private life behind and entered the social world of others, and the wider sane universe of routine.

I peered into the mirror; my face too lined with concerns for a man my age. Did I see right? I drew closer to the reflecting glass to inspect myself. Was that a touch of grey at an age when I wasn't that advanced beyond the baptism of adolescence?

I grabbed the sides of the sink to steady myself. "This isn't happening," I muttered, as I looked down at the sink trap. Had my mirror become a metaphorical *Picture of Dorian Gray*?

I looked back up and… What's this?

Instead of the bland backdrop of my landlord's bathroom, with its soap-stained chrome fixtures and crumbling desert-hued plaster walls, there was a gaseous, dark background flooded with twinkling stars, all jammed together like a starry path to nowhere. The vision, whatever the hell you might term it, moved slowly as if I were peering out the portal of an ocean liner, except the cruise ship was coursing its way through a lone nebula somewhere in deep space. I remember seeing Hubble Telescope stills like this one, but none had the quality of moving, the starry panorama inching past my mirror, err portal.

I felt my knees grow slack and I giggled nervously, an insane, unfiltered moment, a window into my inner confusion and craziness. I looked down at the yellow-tiled floor, scuffed from use and weathered by age. What lunacy was seizing me now?

I struggled with myself, wondering if I turned, would there still be a doorway there, through which I might escape this madness? But an intense, bordering on obsessive curiosity also dogged my thoughts. What would I see if I simply looked again at the mirror?

What harm could there be in it?

Against my better judgment, I stopped my hasty exit from the bathroom and looked up from the floor at the mirror again.

There was a shifting glitter that faintly sparkled metallic in a grey and red cloud that hissed and shifted within the mirror frame. Again, there was life in the reflection, but was that life a lie, a hallucination? Slowly through the chaotic curtain peered but for a moment, enormous, lantern-eyes followed by huge, clicking pincers that slid forward, in and out of the hazy miasma.

I next found myself walking behind a rickety cart chock full of books, the rasping noise of its neglected wheels waking me out of my stupor.

How did I get here? I felt along my person, found my face unshaved. Thank the heavens, I was otherwise clothed, though my shirt and pants were a screaming mismatch.

What time was it? I checked my pockets, I didn't have my cellphone, but my watch said 11:00 am.

Was it still Saturday? I would have to check something electronic to know for sure.

Or maybe I didn't want to know.

I continued to push the cart, dropping off its literary passengers at their appointed Dewy Decimal reference address on varied shelves. I needed normal, even if it was an act.

But in my right mind? I had suffered alcohol-induced blackouts in the past, though they were few. My actions during those times, when my consciousness left my body to its baser desires, were contemptible. I was lucky the friends that steered me through those unknown times kept me from penalties and prison. I cut back on my beer rations considerably, though in a country where wine was as common as water, toeing the straight and narrow was a difficult task.

No alcohol led to this blackout.

I vaguely remember from an "Introduction to Student Life" class that undiagnosed epileptic-seizures were the organic basis of some blackouts. But my body didn't feel like it had experienced a grand-mal seizure, where my body went stiff.

I categorized the situation and the last event I remembered prior to my stumbling around like a zombie in the library.

I feared asking anyone about what happened, between now and then. I guess one or another person would come forward, if I'd done anything out of the ordinary.

I clung to the shadows that lined the library's halls. I tried to stand outside myself, observing my creeping body from somewhere in the heights of the library's open floor plan, for its first floor opened to a second floor ringed by a continuous balcony, spacious and airy. From that vantage point, from what I could see, I was until now, normal, my life no more checkered than most students.

From here on out, I didn't know returning to my body.

I trod robot-like through a side door that led to the reference and reserve aisles. The last twenty or so books went into these guarded stacks, though some books weren't necessarily ancient, they just cost more coppers than those volumes lining the shelves in the main library.

Sensing a slight change in my otherwise panicked mood, for the walking helped calm me, I looked through the reserve books, seeing if any were bound for those aisles nearest me.

"Oh ho, what do we have here," I said as I pulled a book out with a familiar name on it.

Talk about a synchronicity, I thought as a sense of bewildering déjà vu struck a chord deep inside me.

Maybe, I picked this up when I walked unconsciously through the earlier part of my day at work.

It was a book by Dr. Leopold DeLapont, monographed on the book's spine. A greyed, but distinguished-looking chap with a sharp nose, holding a pipe and wearing a scholar's tweed jacket graced the back cover. Its title was intriguing, but read like a scholarly work, *The Ghayat al Hikam: A Jungian Look and Fresh Interpretation of the Latin translation and Arabic Original Picatrix.*

So, the good doctor was also a linguist, having more than a working knowledge of Latin and Arabic. Dr. DeLapont was looking more and more like a bit of a renaissance man. And the *Picatrix*? According to my meager understanding of the book, the veracity of that Grimoire of Astrological Magic was a hotly-debated topic among occultic practitioners, Latin and Arabic scholars alike.

What was Dr. DeLapont's interest in magic and its interconnected worldview?

Suddenly, I felt a deep tingling and twitching at the base of my skull, where my head was attached to my neck. It felt like an unseen surgeon poked an index finger into my head and pressed down on my brain stem. That was the only way to describe the weird sensation.

Quickly, a parade of the events in my life flashed like time-lapse scenes before my eyes.

For the life of me, I know I watched too many science fiction movies and television shows to have an unbiased reference to the experience. I felt like I was being psychically scanned, but by whom or for what purpose? Or was this sensation an onset symptom of a grand-mal seizure and another blackout episode?

I tried to calm down, when the fight-or-flight instinct inside me screamed otherwise. I stood there for an eternal instance, slamming my clenched fists against my hips. My knees almost buckled as I steadied my quaking frame with the rickety book cart.

Then, just as quickly, the crawling sensation inside my head ceased.

I stood panting for a while, thinking. Was that a near-death experience? The reel of my short life being played out in rapid succession, what was that all about?

"Monsieur," a voice shouted, as someone ran toward me, "Monsieur? Do you need assistance?"

A young raven-haired woman came into view. She wore a black and white checkered beret, denim jacket, and matching pants, worn through at the knees and the thighs, and matching, checkered sneakers. She grabbed my free hand and looked me squarely in the eyes.

"Monsieur, I saw you almost faint before you grabbed your cart." She pulled out her phone. "Do you want me to call an ambulance?"

"No," I said weakly. "No, I'll be ok in a moment, Mademoiselle. What's your name?"

The young woman guided me to a chair, where she indicated for me to sit down. Still drained, I followed her lead. I didn't think she was the type that would take no for an answer.

"Monsieur, we can exchange pleasantries in a moment, once I'm sure that you're better..." she said with an air of authority.

I settled into that wooden seat and found myself out of breath. Perhaps I had been in a brief denial, too much time spent in my own head. The young Mademoiselle snapped her fingers in front of my eyes—the action broke me out of my introspective spell.

"Monsieur, what just happened to you? Do you have a medical condition?" she asked, still withholding her name.

Her eyes, I saw the world in her eyes, in a moment—they were a strange blue, like the sky, with a wholly different world spinning beneath that sky.

There was something else about her eyes, the lenses of her corneas were extremely convex, though beautiful, almost fish-like in aspect.

"No, Mademoiselle, no. Not that I know of…" I replied as I tried to snap out of it, the spell her eyes cast on me. "I'm sorry to have troubled you, I think I've had a bit of the flu in recent days."

"And since you won't give your name, I will mine. My name is Francois, Francois Luc DeLapont," I said, reaffirming my identity to the world, this woman, and the universe.

She pulled a chair up beside me and took my hand.

"Monsieur Francois Luc DeLapont. That is a good, solid name," she said, her eyes leaving mine for a moment, but not her hand in mine.

Or was my hand in hers?

A warmth seemed to surround me and her, apart from the atmosphere in this temple to learning.

"Monsieur Francois…" She started to say.

"No, please just call me Francois…" I reasserted myself.

"Francois, perhaps a cup of coffee will bring you about…" she said, shaking her head, her long raven tresses reaching out, entangling me.

"May I ask who is inviting me to coffee?" I asked her while thinking how uncommon it was for a woman not to give her name.

"Me Monsieur, I am Luka," my mystery woman finally revealed, "Luka Saint-Laurent…"

"Luka, I like that," I replied, then thought to ask.

"By the way, Luka, what day is it? Saturday?" I smiled at her.

"Why, it's Sunday, Francois…" she said, smiling back at me.

I decided to leave things alone and not overthink what happened in my missing, roughly thirty, hours.

To change the mood, I took my lunch break and escorted Ms. Saint-Laurent to the nearby student lounge and snack bistro.

I brought Dr. DeLapont's book with me, what better way to protect it?

We passed the library parking lot along the way. I wondered if I had driven to work in my blackout.

Coffee might change my mood if the company didn't.

CHAPTER 6: FRENCH ONION SOUP

We ended up skipping the coffee.

I sat across a smallish table from the fetching Ms. Saint-Laurent, placing Dr. DeLapont's volume on a third chair, tucked under the table's edge.

I bought her a huge hamburger and fries, sort of a large meal for a rather petite young woman. I had a more modest dish, French-onion soup, with a hearty crown of mozzarella cheese and little chunks of prime rib.

We each had a Diet Coke, which we used to begin our meal with a toast.

"Let me propose a toast, Mademoiselle Luka Saint-Laurent," I said, extending my bottle to my new companion. She returned the gesture likewise.

"Monsieur Francois, we haven't much to toast to, as we have only just met," Luka said nonchalantly.

"But if we do not celebrate our meeting, then let us toast the fates for aligning our lucky stars this day," I replied, smiling at the novelty of my own thoughts.

"You are so easily amused, Monsieur," Luka said, as we tipped our soda bottles to each other.

"Cheers then," I said, as she placed her bottle on the table and turned her attention from exchanging banters to focusing on her food.

I felt a passing but strong revulsion toward Luka, as the sense of alienage about her broke through the brief infatuation that initially mesmerized me.

Her face broke apart from top to bottom, abnormally wide, where her jaw and skull met. One-third of the hamburger disappeared in a flash of serrated teeth, it happened so quickly, I blinked and saw no more of what I thought I had seen.

"Is there something wrong, Francois?" she said, daintily dabbing her lips with a napkin and taking a sip of diet soda.

I blinked again.

"No, just the glare of the sun in my eyes for a moment," I replied, unsure that I had seen anything in my present state of nerves.

A sense of unreality returned to me.

I took a heaping spoonful of the French onion, one of my favorite dishes at the Lounge and Bistro. I ate here often with the library being nearby for my campus meals. Though, I seldom had company in recent memory.

Luka took another bite of her hamburger, this time her portion more realistic, human-scaled, the size a female might take were she watching her manners.

Maybe I imagined what I saw in Luka a moment ago. I'm pretty sure Luka was real. My wallet was lighter a few Euros.

"How is your soup, Francois?" Luka paused as she exchanged glances with me.

I felt an uncertain hunger behind her glance, as if she were a predator and some prey animal loomed up large, but invisible behind me.

"Even though this is campus food, it's one of the best French onion soups served in Chartres, at least nearby..." I smiled, hoping to lighten my somber cast, "...haunts where a student hangs out."

She laughed and took another bite of her burger.

"What are you studying, Francois?" she asked, her eyes twinkling with interest.

Luka's hypnotic eyes made my thoughts a stutter.

"Uhm...I'm still a sophomore and I'm torn between something practical like business administration and maybe an interesting social science, like political science..." I replied, before enjoying another spoonful of my soup.

"Political science, Francois? Do you plan on being an *Avocat*, an ambulance chaser no less?" Luka said, as if expressing a proletariat shock at my seeming Bourgeoisie motives for getting a degree.

"As I said, I'm a sophomore, Mademoiselle," I replied, with a bit of chagrin in my voice, "Sophomores are averse to commitments..."

"...Averse to commitment?" Luka asked, for the first time broaching what might embody a romantic interest, "Is loyalty a liability to you?"

I enjoyed the pivot, a verbal turning of the tables. I was young but had a wee bit of experience in the dating game.

Was she toying with me?

"My dear, commitment to one thing closes off the chance to experience a whole spectrum of sensations in another," I said smiling, while a bit of a pout crossed her face. "Variety is the spice of life, *N'est-ce pas*?"

Luka got quiet for a time, eating her meal like it was a duty to get through, rather than a highlight to enjoy; the French normally savor a meal, as they do life.

"Are you disappointed in me, Mademoiselle?" I asked, rebreaking the ice, which had frosted over the lake between us.

"Mon Dieu!" she said, exasperated and glaring at me. "You Americans are all the same, afraid of making choices, always playing both sides against the middle. Ah, you think I didn't know? Your French, though good, comes with a noticeable accent, perhaps the East Coast region, no?"

I felt a bit dizzy at this point and nauseated. My earlier weakness returned in spades. Luka appeared to flicker in place, like an old VHS tape skipping in frame, from being played one too many times. I blinked, once, twice, trying to steady my fluttering vision.

Immediately, Luka noticed the change, as her scorn changed to concern. She rose from her chair and came to my side, again grabbing my hand while her eyes quickly searched me for signs of sickness or fainting.

"I'm sorry, I'm feeling a bit sick again," I said, pushing my remaining soup away. I hadn't the stomach for it.

"Do you live far? Did you drive to work today?" Luka asked, eyeing me for a decision. "Do you want me to drive you home?"

I scooped up Dr. Leopold's book and stood up.

"I got a ride from my landlord this morning," I said, not

knowing whether it was true or not. "I can walk, but appreciate your offer of a ride. I'll take you up on it, and return the favor sometime…"

"Too sweet! No, you will not, I am helping a comrade in distress…"

Then she said with a sly smile, "We can work out how you can pay me back, later…"

While her last remark piqued my interest, my normal enthusiasm burnt on a low flame. I blinked at Luka again, as an unnatural shimmer clung to her curvaceous silhouette even in the bright sunlight.

'Strange…" the word briefly crossed my mind.

We left the dishes on the table as I shuffled alongside Luka out the automatic door of the café. The ground was moist after a fresh rain, the sky still felt wet to walk through.

Luka kept up with me, or without my ego it would be more accurate to say that I kept up with her.

We arrived at the half-occupied, thirty-stalled parking lot after a ten-minute walk, barely a word passed between us.

I wondered if she reconsidered her offer to what amounted to me, a complete stranger.

I half expected my red jalopy to be there.

When it wasn't, nothing could surprise me at this point. I turned and asked Luka, "Having second thoughts about giving me a ride? I can get a taxi…"

"Nonsense," she replied with a bit of a pout on her face, "I do what I say, a promise is a promise, Monsieur. Were you to faint from your 'flu,' and were I to find out, well…"

"Ok, Luka, you've convinced me," I said, almost putting my wrists out for the cuffs my companion seemed to be putting on me, "Which car is yours, ma chérie?"

"That one, over there!" Luka said, pointing toward an older, light green Renault Zoe.

In the front seat, I was pretty sure I could fit. I could also fit in the back seat, if I stuck my feet out a side window.

She climbed into the driver's seat with a smile and a tap of the horn. I opened my side, and tried to slide in—the last rider to use the passenger's side must have been five-foot even. I held my breath until I adjusted the seat all the way back, then gave Luka a thumbs up. Like an aviator, she slapped on flight gear sunglasses and slammed on the accelerator.

I nearly lost my stomach due to centrifugal force in some of the curves on the way to my boarding home.

"Thank you, Luka," I said, as I tried to work myself free from her smallish rocket sled on wheels and retrieve Dr. DeLapont's book.

"You are most welcome, Francois!" she smiled broadly, "May I see you again, once you're feeling better?"

"Do you have a pen and paper?" I asked her, to which she dug around, pulled a briefcase from the back seat, opened it, and quickly handed me a notepad and pencil.

I jotted my name and number down, then handed it back to Luka.

"Ah, Francois, I will not forget your name…" Luka said, "Au revoir, mon ami! Till then…"

Luka's Renault sped off, as I waved at her, an image in the rear-view mirror.

Luka's phone rang as she drove away from dropping Francois off at his off-campus boarding home.

"Bonjour, yes, this is Luka…" She said to the caller. "Oui, yes…the youth called Francois is the one you saw in your dreams!

"But even more, yes, mon dieu, I sensed he's seen the Master! No, no, I don't know where or how…The intuitive sciences are sometimes so imprecise on this point…Oui, oui, He might lead us to the breakthrough and breakout!"

"Agreed, we must know more!"

A time away, a world apart, the air was incredibly cold, the land around the place an arid waste of snow, not sand, and encircling the plateau, a jagged ring of lofty, white-capped spires. There stood a palace, ageless and inhuman, old when the stars were young, called a stone monastery by some—the uninitiated, the unholy, the untrue.

In the universe, there exists a yin and yang, heads and tails, light and dark, shape and shadow, up and down, east and west, here and there, yesterday and today. Therein, the absolutes were given full expression without a teetering middle ground of sights, sounds, and sanity.

Magics were woven there, counsels were sought there, mighty Merlinus Ambrosius—Myrddin Emrys to the Welsh— once tread its primal, frescoed labyrinth, seeking answers of worlds beyond the limitless cosmos and its unnumbered dimensions.

A corpse-eating cult worshipped them, the eight and the one, all dark on their onyx dais, of this world, but not of this world alone.

It was sanctuary for the *Unknown Nine.*

They were the purpose in the madness, the course in the chaos, an aim in the aimless, the reason behind the random universe.

In absolute night, for the sunlight of day never broached the bewitched boundaries of the building, a flare arose in a sacred fire, kept fueled by fresh corpses, atop an obelisk altar of curious and exotic design.

Their nine black thrones stood tall in a circle, with one higher than the others positioned nearest the obelisk, set around the yawning maw of a bottomless pit, Abaddon of Old, the Ultimate Gate. A fresh thought entered the cloud of incense, where minds mingled and melded, as the stench of sacrifice enshrouded the nine.

Human in outline, they were. Human in biology, they were not.

"Lord, I sense an unmasked movement of the renegades, one thoughtless and reckless…"

The most high priest, from eternity secreted behind a yellow, silken mask, shifted in place, the immovable moved for the first time in a thousand years.

"Our prey grows restless; they roam to and fro behind their cage bars with nowhere to go…They tirelessly pursue dead-end trails, filled with hopes that that false prophecy of old is true…."

"Go, I send you forth to divine whether there is a reason behind their restlessness…" decreed the voiceless prophet of the paradoxes.

A shadow on one of the lower eight thrones shifted, stood, then vanished as it left Leng's circle.

In a nearby cavern, above and behind the high throne, for a moment, illuminated by flashes of dull purple twilight, an ant-like army of mephitic devotees attended an incredible amalgamation of bewildering technologies forged in breathtaking proportions.

The immense, dazzling, bejeweled tree shimmered and whirled silently as a spectral dervish, while a priceless fortune of gem-fire burned up its luminous trunk and down its crowded limbs.

No echoes resounded in the empty expanse, as the high priest returned to its contemplation of on-world and off-world events.

CHAPTER 7: DR. LEOPOLD DELAPONT

Rain poured down on the roads as I made my way to the *Institut Jungien Pour L'étude des Mémoires Ancestrales* in Tours. My windshield wipers occasionally slapped in time with a song or two on the radio. I tapped my thumbs on the steering wheels, keeping time.

I could not help but think about Luka. Obsession, no. I had not blown up her phone with calls or texts after our meeting. I did dream of her one night since Sunday. It was not the kind of dream one would normally associate with a young man over a young woman he just met.

Yet, dark my dreams had been of late.

I saw her not as I had seen her on the weekend in her checked beret and matching sneakers. Nor did my dreams turn into a cornucopia of pornographic scenes starring her and me. Though she was attractive to me in a hypnotic but peculiar way—I was not in a committed relationship with any woman at the time—I initially had no designs on her.

No, in my dream, I walked beside Luka, in the same fashion as the day I walked her to her car. Simple enough, a processing dream, my mind running a review program before our meeting was filed away in my unconscious.

No, it was not that simple, not that plain, just more in the stream of my growing insanity, I could not trust the series of visions, were I to remain sane and in possession of myself. Nor in the possession of someone or something else.

Not that I attached much importance to dreams…until they

grew troubling, obtuse, and those that served as reminders of my troubled consciousness.

As of late though, I've often felt that dreams are answers to questions I haven't yet figured out how to ask.

Halfway to Tours, I reached Vendome, nestled alongside the river Loir, home to the *Abbaye de la Trinité* and an exquisite baked *camembert*, but I digress.

Again, I was walking beside Luka, but then the dreamscape changed from the grassy lawn, manicured trees, and asphalt trails between older buildings on campus. Luka and I entered a woman's clothing boutique, walking now hand in hand through aisle after aisle of woman's clothing and accessories of every style, from goth to glam, from noir to nouveau riche, they were all there, some in drips, others in droves.

Luka didn't try to make up her mind, she just marveled at the selection. And on some level, I felt she needn't decide on which ensemble to coordinate or purchase, for she seemed to own them all. She acted confidently, as if she would never have to wear the same outfit another day of her life.

Then, the clothing boutique went dark and the air grew frigid, like an arctic blast blowing across the southern Canadian border.

I felt a swaying suddenly under my feet. All around Luka and me stood the shadows of shifting passengers, standing and holding onto train-straps aboard a crowded commuter train. Men, women, children, the shadows were indistinct, genderless. Some were unquestionably alive, some were not. There was an undeniable stench of pungent, rotting flesh in the air, drifting from among the riders. *Could one identify smells in dreams?* Luka seemed to have lost interest in me, eyeing the shadows as she had first eyed me.

Then, I was no longer beside her, but found myself among the shadows, a shade with them. I was one of them. Had I symbolically passed from life to death?

Furthermore, I felt my feet leave the ground, hoisted aloft by an invisible titan like a bag of potatoes, hung on an unseen hook. I was a sack of meat hung freshly in a walk-in refrigerator, ready for a butcher to slice off the choice pieces.

I hung like that for a moment, then looking down on my person, I saw I was naked. All the other people, male and female alike, hung there, shadow people like me. How could I tell each person's sex? The angle of the ice box's lights illuminated many lower torsos. which, in turn, undulated in the shifting shadows.

Then I was walking beside Luka while simultaneously hanging among the shadows. I bounced back and forth like a tennis ball between my two shells. I could describe it no differently; those were the words that came to mind when I first awoke.

The end of the dream? The words Luka said, her face shrouded by shadows, her voice a clicking parody of the human tongue, standing among fresh meats of every size, shape, and color.

"…I choose…"

I wondered how Herr Sigmund would have interpreted that one as I pulled into the *Institut Jungien Pour L'étude des Mémoires Ancestrales* parking structure.

"I guess Herr Jung will have to do, instead…" I muttered, as I looked for a stall closest to the street.

I drove down one level below ground and drove by an older, light green, Renault Zoe beneath a "Reserved" sign that hung above the stall space.

I shook it off as a coincidence. I had larger things on my mind, much bigger fish to fry.

As I parked my car two levels below the street and stepped out of the vehicle, a new wave of nausea overwhelmed me. My heart pounded wildly, my palms began sweating, and dizziness spun me around. Colors of the parking garage, though not painted in bright pastels, visibly shifted to hues of black and white.

I leaned against the side of my car, vomiting until I was empty. I stayed like that for a time, needing to continue so I could get my foot in the door. Maybe therapy held some answer, though I was beginning to wonder if there might be an organic basis for my state.

My watch read 12:30, and my appointment was at 1:00.

Maybe a quick soda or something else might help my stamina, once the spinning went away.

I sucked it up and decided to gut it out. I set one foot in front of the other—avoiding my puddle of puke as I did so. "Inch by inch, anything's a cinch…" I muttered aloud, thinking, 'Hey that self-help mantra worked for some televangelist.'

I made it to the stairs, then kept going, my gait a bit unsteady, lurching onward and upward. I sweat with the effort, as my touch of nausea passed.

Strangely, as I paused at the top of the stairs to catch my breath, now at street level, though the rain stopped and overcast remained, the world was still painted in black and white. The few people on the street in the early afternoon moved in a strange synch, almost in choreographed unison, a slow pace in comparison to my own tottering stride.

I stood on the street corner and looked for the Institute's building, as people walked past me, oblivious to me. At once, I saw a flowing, swirling, stream of blue and white veils sail through the crowd, virtually through several people.

The swift maelstrom knocked me down, hovering but for a moment, its huge blue eyes in an otherwise featureless blur, stared down at me. Then it flew away at break-neck speeds. *And no one but I noticed its flight, a harbinger of the proverbial Valkyrie!*

A banshee maybe, but it made no chilling scream? Or a ghost, but it made no suffering cry? It disappeared as quickly as it had appeared. The colors of Tours were bright for a moment in its wake, then the somber drabness returned to everyone and everywhere the eye could see.

"Did you see that?" I asked an older man with massive grey-eye brows and a tattered brown coat, as I picked myself up. The man didn't look up or stop to hear what I said, he simply walked past me.

"Mademoiselle, Mademoiselle …" the younger woman in a purple pants also ignored me, as I avoided her almost stepping on my feet.

I looked up by accident and, "Excusez-moi, what's this?" I blinked and gazed up again, between some buildings.

Strung between the two structures, like a clothesline full of peasant outfits, hung a flight of pigeons. I said "hung," for they hovered in complete stillness there, no wings in motion, defying natural laws.

"Is anybody seeing this? Are you not hearing me?" I screamed, as no one took offense, none nodded in agreement. In a crowd moving past me, not a person screamed in hysterics or shrieked in panic at the sight, not over anything that bewitched and bewildered me. The people walked past me, with a few in silent conversation with each other.

"Why can't I hear what they're saying?" I said, going down on one knee in the middle of everything, but somehow separate from it all.

I began to laugh, inexplicably, uncontrollably.

Why the hell I looked at my watch made no more sense than what happened around me.

A glint of sunlight sparkled off my watch crystal on what was an overcast day. I looked up and sunlight blinded me. My ears suddenly throbbed with the sounds of a busy street. Car horns sounded, engines sped up, and a train rolled noisily on a nearby track.

Another flock of birds flapped their wings overhead—what kind, who cares—and *gendarmes* shouted their traffic signals from the centers of crossroads and roundabouts.

Tours was alive to me, alive, breathing, and its lifeblood pumped again.

An approaching teenager grabbed my outstretched hand and pulled me up, off my one knee.

"Bonjour, Monsieur, did you slip on something?" the kid asked, sporting a scruffy beard as some attempt to add age to his cherubic face.

I burst into more laughter, which startled the young man.

"No, just my own clumsiness..." I remarked with a smile, trying to calm my accidental companion, "I was rushing to keep an appointment..."

With that, I shook his hand, and said, "And there's where I need to be..."

Off, I left my rescuer, in the one direction I hadn't looked until now.

I stuffed my feelings over this latest experience, at times being in control and other times, like the past few minutes, not.

I wondered how much of this should I share with the associate. Better still, how much could I share and stay out of the madhouse?

I sat across from the Jungian Associate, who introduced himself as Mathéo Archambeau. He had been with the Institute for three years, under the supervision of Dr. Leopold DeLapont himself.

This was of course after an exchange of small talk, and the filling out of forms, authorizing the Institute in what it needed to treat me and obtain what medical records, few they were, that might assist in their work with me.

In hushed tones, I tested the waters with Mathéo, sharing my least-troubling recent experience with him, about my dream with Luka—whom I called "Simone" to protect her identity. I wanted to see how he handled my concerns. I wanted to know whether he could be trusted with my darker experiences.

"I want to share a fundamental belief for those who follow Carl Jung's teachings in their therapy sessions," Mathéo said, thirty minutes into our appointment.

"What's that?" I asked, because I had only a passing knowledge of Jung.

"Jung once said," replied Mathéo, as he flipped over a page in the notes he took:

"'Have you noticed that all your foundations are completely mired in madness? Do you not want to recognize your madness and welcome it in a friendly manner? You wanted to accept everything. So, accept madness too. Let the light of your madness shine, and it will suddenly dawn on you. Madness is not to be despised and not to be feared, but instead, you should give it life…If you want to find paths, you should also not spurn madness, since it makes up such a great part of your nature…Be glad that you can recognize it, for you will thus avoid becoming its victim…'"

"So, what's the bottom-line in what you just quoted me?" I

asked Mathéo.

"It's clear as day," Mathéo's face glowed as he spoke. "Your dream, and the other things that bothered you enough to bring you here, to seek some sort of resolution to. Instead of shunning your shadows, trying to eviscerate them, or denying them through some sort of psyche-numbing of that part of yourself, I say embrace your darkness! Don't fear your phobias, explore them, and shed light on them when they shun such exposure. Only when the unknown becomes the known, can you feel liberated from your fear!"

I sat in my chair, trying to take in what Mathéo was asking of me.

"So, how do we best approach that ideal, your 'embracing your darkness?'" I pressed him for answers.

"There is no one technique that works in all situations, Monsieur DeLapont," Mathéo said. "But, Dr. Leopold has pioneered an approach that helps you go deep into the psychic stratums where not only your traumas lay, but also those you inherited from your forebearers. Those later disturbances arise in your person from the ancestral unconscious your inherited from your forebearers."

"What technique is that?" I asked. "And what if I don't believe in an 'ancestral unconscious?'"

Mathéo smiled.

"You don't have to believe, for what is there is there, whether you recognize it or not. Talk therapy can go on for years without strongly affecting a person's psychosis. I would suggest in our next session," Mathéo continued, "if you are up to the experience, that we employ one of the Institute's suspension tanks, where you are removed from any normal distractions. Through an applied version of hypnosis, we can journey backward in your life story, revealing the shadows most directly that are causing you pain.

"We are taking the physiological pathways to your earlier consciousnesses, a pathway to the past, a time machine to your ancestors' selves, to their memories, to their experiences, to their truths, that in our modernity you and I have forgotten. It's all there, buried in the DNA libraries, billions of years old, vast and all-encompassing that, all together, constitute the corporate you. One gram of DNA alone can store two hundred and fifteen petabytes or two hundred and fifteen million gigabytes of data. Energy is eternal, it doesn't change, it's the everlasting ink and glue that are stored in your DNA, the records, the recordings of God, eternity, and all your ancestors interacting as one, their legacies, their inheritances left to you…

"Forever our species had searched for the infinite outside themselves, elsewhere, hoping to find the Alpha and Omega at some point in the starry heavens, atop tall mountains, at some holy point, or in some holy person, past, present, or future. And all along that pathway was inside, not outside ourselves…

"And as we journey into your past, if we see one of your ancestors crossed paths with one of the gods, so much the better for you."

"I didn't quite catch that last thing you said about 'the gods,' Mathéo…" I suggested.

"Don't worry yourself," Mathéo replied as he grinned again. "It's an inside thing we disciples of Jung often joke about amongst ourselves."

I naively smiled at his explanation. Unlike him and others in the Institute, I hadn't memorized the works of Carl Jung, like some did the Bible.

I could appreciate a psychological approach with humor, that was able to laugh at itself. There was way too much seriousness in the biz.

My time was almost up and the drive home to Chartres weighed heavily on my mind.

The technique's strangeness also weighed on my mind, but then so did my slowly-unraveling life, ever since Mahmood died that night at the cathedral's labyrinth. I agreed to the novel therapy session and set an appointment later, after Mathéo said his adieus and picked up another patient from the waiting room.

The Institute conducted its suspension tank therapy sessions on Saturdays. I booked one for the coming weekend and called the head librarian at the *Université D'Orléans* to take the day off.

The next few days passed without the growing routine of psychic drama I had experienced before my first therapy session. I'd hoped to read Dr. Leopold's book by now, but it seemed a bit too intense for a casual scan. Instead, I began reading some internet articles about Post Traumatic Stress Disorder (PTSD), a malady many soldiers or others suffered due to overwhelming, psyche-scarring circumstances, where an individual was thrown into out-of-control situations.

Detachment and a sense of unreality were a safety mechanism of the brain to protect itself, a reactive byproduct of our pre-mammalian evolution centered around a self-preserving instinct. Not induced by recreational drug use.

I felt it might be another option to explore.

I read more from the Institute's website about this bringing the past into the present through a form of hypnosis without intervening external stimuli.

Then the day came, and I found myself at the Institute, troubled but trembling inside at the potential relief it offered me.

I wore light swimming trunks and was a tad embarrassed as the young attractive female technician, who served on the monitoring team, attached waterproof electrodes to my chest, back, and elsewhere. She next fitted on my head what can best be described as a diving mask, with built-in, interactive blinders and a communication suite. I could talk to my therapist and they could talk back to me.

"Now, I just want to go over a few things. On your intake questionnaire, you checked off 'no known phobias.' But I must ask this anyway, have you ever found yourself afraid when you were in close quarters, like an elevator?" my therapist, Mathéo, asked.

I thought for a moment.

"No, not to the best of my recollection, why?" I replied, as I was further fitted with a harness for floating without effort in the chamber.

"This sort of situation can ignite past feelings, negating any therapeutic value it offers," Mathéo answered, while going through a flip chart.

"If you feel threatened or should you want to end the session, there are two panic buttons, one on each side of your dive helmet. Press either one, and we'll get you out of there," Mathéo said. "Just breathe normally, the system automatically adjusts to your breathing rate."

"Do you have any questions before we begin?" He further asked.

"The website spoke of an injection?" I replied.

"It's a mild muscle relaxer that helps loosen you up in the water," Mathéo said. "Nothing in your medical history contraindicates its usage."

"One more question," I said, as we walked to the chamber and the table beside it where I would initially lie down, before being hoisted, first up, then down into the pool horizontally. "How do we begin?"

"A simple progression of descending numbers and corresponding tones, synchronized with visual cues. Just listen to my voice and follow my lead," Mathéo said, before he did a soundcheck. "Testing one, two, three."

I gave him a thumbs-up, as I climbed onto the table and prepared myself for the joyride ahead.

One of Mathéo's associates retrieved a syringe from among many related instruments on a small table, set strategically in the immersion tank area. The orderly picked one syringe from among the others, tapped it to remove any bubbles in the suspension, swabbed my left shoulder with alcohol, and jabbed me. I felt no immediate effect from the injection.

I was told there were three such suites in the Institute, all situated in an open-air theatre arrangement, much like an operating theatre, which allowed other doctors and specialists to observe surgeries as they were performed. Everything was an antiseptic white, except where alternative colors were called for, and those were done in soft pastels.

I think the neutral décor was an attempt to prevent the settings from having any impact on a patient's healing experience, positive or negative.

Slowly, I was raised by the small windlass setup above the suspension tank. I felt the weight on my body on my neck, shoulders, hips, and knees—the four attachment points of the harness.

Then, I was lowered into the water.

"How's our snorkel system working out for you?" Mathéo asked, as the water enveloped me, and the shutters on my breathing helmet went dark. "Breathe deeply, expand your lungs with the air, feel the buoyancy it adds to you. Then exhale, I want you to become more conscious of your breathing. It helps you avoid hyperventilating and panic in this environment."

I tried the pattern Mathéo suggested.

"So far, so good…" I said.

"And how's the temperature? We try to adjust it to your body heat, it's at 31.4 degrees Celsius so it blends into the background as a neutral thing," Mathéo asked, his voice a bit mechanical through my headset.

"I'm fine with that," I stated. "I hope I don't go to sleep on you. I haven't been resting too well recently…"

The electrodes recorded physiological changes as they arose in my person, I felt no ill effects from the sites where they were planted.

"Stand by for action…"

"I'm going to now start some music we've found effective over time in our therapeutics. Start by visualizing yourself at the top of a long set of stairs that lead downward. I want you to gradually count out one step at a time, as you put one foot, then the other, and head downstairs…We begin at one hundred… ninety-nine…ninety-eight…" Mathéo's voice drifted into the background music, as I counted out the next step, then the next.

I stood in a pool of darkness everywhere around me, except on the surface of the water. There one, two, three swirling patches of light came to life, mimicking in their bewildering, twirling lines and dramatic colors—vivid yellows and oranges, the bluest blues and greenest greens—the turbulence in Vincent van Gogh's *The Starry Night*.

I felt alone in the maelstrom, apart from the vortexes, bound by time in my person, eternal in the moment, a lapsing bit of consciousness, soon to be submerged again, a brief expression of the finite in the infinite.

Suddenly, I heard a roar, like a jet taking off from a runway. Before my eyes flashed a bewildering choice of different panoramas, dense forests of ancient trees, luxuriant fields of heather in swaying purples and pinks. The roar changed and I saw sandy seashores with boiling surfs of greens and blues, which melded into the dim inner recesses of dark caverns.

I tried to communicate with Mathéo, but found I could not hear my own voice. Nor his voice, if Mathéo were talking back to me.

I next stood on the pinnacle of a cold peak somewhere gazing into the star-strewn heavens—for it was abruptly night in my journey—thinking out loud, "Where should I go from here?" I felt an intense draw toward the stars, a definite point somewhere between Hydra and Argo Navis. In my delirium, I feverishly laughed and looked for some means to ascend, some stairway to heaven.

I leaped into the air, once, twice, thrice. The last time, I caught myself when I landed, for I near jumped off the pinnacle, on a side bordered by a sheer drop-off whose bottom I could not see in the shifting shadows below. I wondered what might happen, were I to leap into the darkness. But something within, perhaps a survival instinct, held me back.

I felt the pinnacle shift beneath my feet, then the mountain top caved inward. I found myself falling downward, inward, not sliding down a hole, but freefall, as rocky debris and dirt bounced off the sides of the black shaft and against me.

Sometime, somewhere far below, for a small patch of starlight sky floated above the yawning gap in the distance overhead, I awoke in the shadows. My landing, how I got down there and came to the bottom, I had no memory of it.

Dozens of red, glowing eyes broached the shadows and shambled slowly toward me. An overpowering stench filled my nostrils as I gagged and almost vomited. For an instant, as I raised my spinning head, I beheld among the approaching shadows huge, clicking pincers and enormous, lantern-like eyes, many times larger than the others.

Just as quickly, that monstrous vision faded into the shadows. A single flame flared to life, as if among the ravenous horde, an intelligence struck a match. Further, a large candle was lit and, in its light, I saw. Mon Dieu, what I saw.

"Monsieur, what are you doing here?" asked a white-bearded herdsman in a strange accent, dressed in a ragged, filth-stained, once-ochre robe, knotted with worn rope at the waist.

Around his staff leaped chest-high a flock of fungous, flabby beasts, whose breed was a blasphemous conflation of swine and human. I could not believe my eyes. The hoary herdsman slapped them away from his person and his light, which now illuminated our surroundings.

We stood in a deep layer of stinking excrement, amid an immense and high twilit grotto, flung haphazardly with dung-stained ruins that cancerously filled its breadth, length, height, and depth in all directions.

The aged herdsman kicked a path through the nauseous beasts, their squealing protests a deafening cross between human and inhuman terror.

The white-bearded man motioned for me to follow him. I did without question, as my feet had their own minds about this thing. As we strode through the ruins to an unknown destination, every low arch we passed beneath and massive pillar we trod by was unmistakably Roman, with worn inscriptions like, 'P.GETAE. PROP ... TEMP ... DONA ..." and "L. PRAEC ... VS ... PONTIFI ... ATYS ...' and 'DIV ... OPS ... MAGNA. MAT ...' in abundance everywhere.

Then as the herd thinned, we came to a newer building, from which emanated an intense sensation of evil and stench of wickedness, both travesties of the human condition. The filthy herdsman smiled, his bearded face missing several yellowed teeth.

He motioned me forward. My feet obeyed under their own compulsion, as I wandered through the yawning maw of a door.

Inside, the smell of decay reached its heights so far in my experience. I found in the casern a row of ten moldy stone cells with rusty bars. Three had tenants, all human skeletons in various states of disintegration.

I walked past the barred blasphemies in horror, while on the other side of the jailer's hall hung meat hooks, from a few dangled more incomplete skeletons, some obviously swine, while others, I shuddered at the thought of the others.

Beyond the hall was a larger room built within a separate cavern of the grotto. It was lit by several ashy sconces littering the irregular walls.

Here, the stench of the pits of Hell made me vomit until I could retch no more than dry heaves. Black piles of carrion waste—of sawed, picked bones and opened skulls—choked off either side of a raised dais, with the reddest throne. Was it glowing?

Atop the throne sat a coiffed, white-wigged, ghoul-faced, linen waistcoat, high knee-breeches, white hose, and black buckle-shoed man. In his hand, he bore a skull-topped and ruby-encrusted scepter, which he extended toward me.

I approached the crimson throne in horror, my feet again possessed, past the piles of dismembered humanity, taking me to that mockery of a human's side.

In a broken, barbarous French, the ghoul said, "Mon Dieu, you have finally come..." Then, he laughed, a demonic cackle echoing in the heights of the killing fields.

The primping peacock looked at me with an evil eye, it could be called nothing other. I dared not look back at him, in fear and almost overcome by terror.

Then, I saw myself as if from the heights above, looking down on my near-naked person, clad only in swim trunks, my legs covered in swine filth. My own head below raised and looked up at me, as a demonic grin crossed my face and intense exaltation filled my eyes!

I tried to scream, but it was not the me below that screamed, it was me, now clad in the body of the primping peacock who screamed until my ears bled.

Inside the suspension tank control room, a few select personnel heard Subject 359 scream and twist in his harness within the isolation tank

Three people conferred together, the young lab coat-clad Mathéo Archambeau, the shorter, denim-wearing Luka Saint-Laurent, and a taller, high-foreheaded, distinguished-looking man wearing a pin-striped business suit, with flowing grey hair and matching Van Dyke beard, standing in black, wing-tip shoes—Dr. Leopold DeLapont.

They stood behind a panel of flashing lights, whirling dials, and a dozen monitors, enough equipment to run a standard starship, were humanity to that point in its scientific evolution.

"See, what did I tell you about him?" Luka said, as an unnatural smile breached her otherwise human-like face, "He bears the sacred genetic markers deep in his DNA, signs that one or more of his ancestors served as a host."

"I administered the dosage of Amanita muscaria you recommended, Leopold," Mathéo chimed in as Dr. Leopold considered what he saw in the readings and heard from his colleagues.

"His temporary possession by one of the sorcerous DeLapoers in his deep time experience also proves he is a candidate for a present-day habitation by one of us, should the necessity arise."

"Good, good," Dr. Leopold nodded at the fresh finding concerning Subject 359.

"What of the Master? Was there any solid indication as to who possessed him, or where his present self saw the Master?" Dr. Leopold asked.

Both Luka and Mathéo looked at each other, perplexed.

"I thought not," Leopold answered his own question.

"Dr. Leopold, given time and better technologies than these infernal human machines at our disposal, I believe we could isolate the synapse where that experience is stored, and follow the lead to its source, good or bad," Mathéo said, summing up the situation.

Dr. Leopold drew to his full height and made a decision concerning Subject 359.

"There is no means here, in this branch office, to prove whether the sighting of the Master is real or another fake, planted by the enemy to waste our time and valuable resources.

We established local divisions of the Institute to screen for those among the human herd that possessed the sacred genetic markers and who had sufficient mental and physical acuity to host one of us, a prisoner in this time," Dr. Leopold explained. "In exceptional cases, our institute was meant to be no more than a transitional step on the way to the K2 Compound. We will send Subject 359 there, under the guise that he is possessed of extraordinary raw telekinetic and psychic powers, which may only be developed to their fullest potential there..."

"And while there, the *Elder* can further test him and ascertain the validity of his encounter with the Master," Dr. Leopold stated.

"Agreed," Mathéo and Luka said in unison, before returning their attention to the writhing man in the isolation tank below.

I awoke from my trance, for what else could I call it? But not where I expected to, and with whom sat with me.

"What the hell am I doing here?" I asked, with a pulse-pounding headache, my limbs feeling empty and immovable, the world around me a sensation of powering forward.

"Here," spoke a female voice.

I knew it was Luka. How did she find me?

"Here," replied Luka a second time. "Here is aboard a Lear Jet, where you and I sit..."

"As to our destination," Luka smiled tersely, "you have a special talent that better serves the world and humanity in the place where we are headed."

"And where's that?" I asked, struggling to move my legs and arms.

"It's what we call in the biz the K2 Compound," Luka said, glancing nonchalantly out the plane's window.

"What biz is that?" I posed the question, my mind a jumbled confusion of conflicting needs.

"We are operatives, if you would, of the FVEY or Five Eyes Agreements. FVEY is an intelligence alliance funded by Australia, Canada, New Zealand, the UK, and the USA. all black, off-the-book budgets, they stand at the fountainhead of our efforts..."

"In time, you will become part of the Psi-SETI Initiative. Our experienced remote-viewers search the heavens, the earth, and other timelines—though that branch is in its infancy—for the existence of extra-terrestrial life."

I shouted in anger, "What about my schooling, my friends and family? I own my life, not you!"

Luka laughed and grew stoically silent.

"It's your kismet, dear Francois. Relax and learn to accept your fate, for it was written in the stars from long ago, before you were born," Luka eventually said.

"We are all prisoners, my dear Francois. Some of us are in cells with windows, and some without. If you cooperate, you will become one of the privileged former rather than the deprived latter."

I tried to move again, but the need to pee overwhelmed my ability to concentrate on anything else.

But I couldn't break free of the stupor.

I looked up in time to watch Luka jab me with a fresh syringe.

Afterward, the world went black.

CHAPTER 8: HIMALAYAS BOUND

I felt the downward angle of the plane descending as I came to. For some reason, my urge to pee had disappeared while I was out.

Luka sat passively, watching me. She barely acknowledged my waking up.

The coming to my assistance at the library after my blackout, the lunch afterward, and the seeming chemistry between us, I felt used. It was all a ruse.

Somehow, she knew about my episode—I don't know how she knew. I just couldn't imagine any other way she could have trailed me, without knowing—maybe she drugged me, and that resulted in my psychotic break, beginning at my flat. But how? I didn't know her, and why? I made my own coffee—it wasn't a boutique coffee "beverage" where someone could have slipped something into my cup.

How did she accomplish what seemed impossible? Plus, there was a commonality to my visions, whatever they were. I saw the clicking chaos that night at the labyrinth and the morning in my landlord's mirror.

Wait, wasn't there another such beast in my recent isolation-tank therapy session?

This was not a local police operation, a sting related to Mahmood Le Fey's death. Otherwise, I would have already been secured behind bars, not in a chemical straitjacket jetting to somewhere in the Himalayas—I remembered from high school that the mountain K2 was found in the highest mountain range in the world. I could be wrong.

The jet hit the runway below with a noticeable "thud," then

a sense of things rapidly rolling forward, until the plane came to a complete stop.

Since Luka and the Psi-SETI Initiative held all the cards, I played along with things. I would find a way to play this thing to my advantage. After all, the goal of the program sounded intriguing. I faintly remember hearing about "remote-viewers" as part of a Cold War CIA attempt to locate deeply-planted Soviet assets. My memory was sketchy at best. Mainstream news played up the narrative that the idea of "remote-viewers" was all a madness that afflicted "conspiracy theorists."

I could move my limbs again, so I stood and looked outside one of the plane's low starboard windows. The landscape was completely alien-looking. Snow blanketed the foreground to the horizon, except where I supposed the plane landed. I had lived in areas where snow was common when I was younger. But this icy, snow-infested world outside the jet was a magnitude worse.

I saw Luka standing before the crew compartment.

"How are we supposed to travel in that?" I said, as I pointed my finger out the window.

"There's a heated umbilical arm rolling to link up with the plane door as we speak," replied Luka. A jolt against the port side of the jet, slightly forward of Luka, shook us both.

"You can follow me," Luka said, as the air pressure popped when the jet's exit door opened.

"And Francois, about everything that happened back in France," Luka stated, as we stood eye-to-eye, before disembarking.

"Yes, Luka?" I said, steeling up my resolve for what lay ahead.

"I was just following orders, I never meant for you to get hurt..." she replied, trying to salve her own conscience, I suppose, if her kind had one.

I paused, looked at her, and said what I had every right to say, given the circumstances, "Just so I'm not being sold to the highest bidder, let's let bygones be bygones."

I sat behind a monitor, where I wore a headset that made my

listening experience private. I was parked in a small meeting room, furnished with a regular refrigerator, a self-service coffeemaker, and a few vending machines that only accepted credit cards or the organization's equivalent.

Playing was a video introduction to the Psi-SETI Initiative, the first point of my "in-processing" into the "Hive" as my coach only known as "Leonard" called it. Leonard was my "interpreter" of all things Psi-SETI, my On-the-Job Instructor (OJI). I garnered during my initial tour that the operation was comprised of seven hundred to a thousand people, based on the size of the facilities. There were several lower levels, into which the personnel could expand and live, if an unknown situation occurred, perhaps like some threat on the Defcon One through Five scale.

This was all conjecture on my part, perhaps I had seen too many spy movies in my younger years. Nonetheless, what I saw impressed me. Though it was permanently snowbound, where that was—North Pole, South Pole, the Alps, the Andres, the Atlas, or the Appalachian range—I hadn't a clue. The Himalayas sounded exotic and isolated—that's the story I had been told. More misinformation should I ever be compromised? If anyone ever had a chance to leave an "operation" like this one, that is.

The video continued, "Welcome to Psi-SETI, a cooperative private and public project. Frank Drake, an American astronomer, was the first scientist in modern times to probe the heavens for evidence of extraterrestrial intelligence (or ETI).

"Drake searched specific spectrums for narrow-band microwave radio signals originating from nearby solar systems in an investigation he called Project *Ozma*.

"Philosophers and formative theorists had wondered about extraterrestrials for more than two thousand years. Drake established the technical parameters, as well as the Drake-equation, which have served as the standard, still followed decades later by the SETI project, also known as "the Search for Extraterrestrial Intelligence," founded on November 20, 1984.

"The Psi-SETI Initiative was founded fifteen years to the day later. The Initiative celebrates Dr. Drake's pioneering efforts, augmenting his traditional approach, enhanced by decades of research and technological advancements, with decades of proven psychic-search techniques. Those psychic sciences were first authenticated by the Office of Strategic Services (later reorganized into the CIA) in its search for fugitive Nazi officials in the Western Hemisphere after World War II.

"You join a crack team of psychic astronomers who employ the technique known as 'remote-viewing.' Its members search the heavens above, the ends of the earth, and new to our program, a few chosen researchers are exploring alternative timelines for Extraterrestrial Intelligence. In whatever level your special skills are employed on our team, we bid you welcome to the adventure, the calling, the vocation of a lifetime..."

I got hungry as the video droned on predictably, given the nature of the introductory material. Part of the introduction included a "How to evacuate the complex reel". These folks thought of everything, though why would the compound, dedicated to the search for Extraterrestrials, ever need such an emergency plan?

Later, the clang of the meal bell went off. Luckily, I was finished with the canned travelogue.

Tomorrow promised to be my first day of testing and training, after I was welcomed by the director of the Psi-SETI Initiative, Dr. Garibaldi Pietro Esposito.

Dr. Garibaldi Pietro Esposito sat in a sanitized room behind a high, white desk, in what best could be described as a "hall of audience," much like those used by high potentates and kings across the centuries. A male office assistant or secretary sat next to the office's door, at a common, office store-issued desk, nothing special to detract from the aura of the director's prominence in the gallery.

The director was old beyond natural, shriveled with age, like a monk who practiced *Sokushinbutsu*, the process of Living Mummification.

"Dr. Esposito, may I present the newest candidate for Psi-SETI, Monsieur Francois Luc DeLapont," said the good doctor's assistant, using a small, stand-alone microphone he picked up off his desk.

A large antique double button carbon ring microphone hung from a wire situated above the director. He pulled the old-fashioned mic down, handling it like a crooner from yesteryear. The director's voice was hoarse, hardly above a whisper,

"Welcome, young Monsieur DeLapont. Let me introduce myself, I am Dr. Garibaldi Pietro Esposito. I have led the Psi-SETI Initiative for the past twenty years."

The director's movements were wooden, stiff, almost as if he were not human, but an animatronic puppet, articulated to pass itself off as alive.

"I would come forward to shake your hand," continued the director, "but, as of late, arthritis has limited my mobility, but not where it's important up here..."

The Director pointed at his head and broached a wooden smile.

For a moment, I thought I saw something different, as if the room were suddenly shifted elsewhere, and a pale white curtain was being drawn aside.

Behind that veil, instead of the old man's veined head, his crabbed fingers, and bluish hands, I swear I saw something else that made me shudder.

The director's eyes became the size of lanterns, and from the sides of his head erupted horn-shaped apertures on stalks. His hands became overlaid with pinchers, like a crab's in shape and color, missing a bit of its serrated, outer edge, but inhumanly enormous.

Just as suddenly, a lone light shone from above, illuminating the small, gnome-like figure in the upraised seat.

The weird shadow that surrounded the director vanished.

"If you have any questions, I'm sure Leonard can answer them," the smallish man said.

"Now, I must bid you a good day, the responsibilities for running a place like this are enormous, and leave little time for further pleasantries. Be off with you now!"

I wondered, as I followed Leonard out of the hall, what I had just seen and why?

I sat with Leonard and about fifty other people enjoying a menu of either veal parmigiana or bangers and marinara, over cavatappi noodles. In the meal room, the observatory crew ate in shifts, much like a military base ran three crews: day, swing, and night. A long set of pressurized windows opened on a rather bleak landscape, a snow-inundated plateau somewhere. There were signs of permanent glaciation along the horizon, interwoven with odd formations, some befitting natural promontories worn by aeons of weathering and erosion. Others left me bewildered and bewitched, for the teetering and towering columns of basalt bore an amazing regularity, many bearing a roughly hexagonal shape—except for the six-sided storm at Saturn's North Pole, nature didn't fashion its handiwork with such civilized regularities.

I wondered why the columns struck me as they did. Perhaps I saw them in a dream that now seemed a lifetime ago. But I could not shake the suspicion, the premonition of danger associated with the ruins, from another world, another time when the snowy desert was primordial, filled with steamy forests of tree-ferns, lofty fungi, and strange creeping fauna of every kind: herbivore, carnivore, and omnivore.

I knew with an unnatural certainty, one not born from my young and few years on earth, but an insight bred from my nightmares, that somewhere beneath that horizon, below its teetering heights, far lower than the deepest borings of the recent interloper on deep time, the shambling primate known as man, there lay massive gates guarding horrors I dared not think about.

"Francois, you are in such deep thought, and we haven't begun the testing, nor training," said Leonard, joining me in looking out the windows into nothingness, as far as he was concerned. "You barely touched your dinner. Did you know our chef is world-renowned? Or he was, at one time, before he became part of the staff. The veal is one of his specialties."

"I've been here before, Leonard. I'm sitting here, and I know there's no logic to my claim. But I have an almost unshakeable knowing in my gut, that somehow and at some point, I saw those crazy rock formations in the snowy distance that look like, for the life of me, ancient ruins of incalculable age…" I replied to my coach, as I unconsciously poked at my food, half-listening to his praise of the menu.

Leonard looked at me, not as if I were some half-crazed drunk newcomer to a country club, but like he heard things in my words that authenticated the reason for my being at the compound.

"I tell you what, Francois. Although your premonitions are unusual for the icy confines of the Psi-SETI Initiative, here in the remote middle of nowhere, they are not unusual for the type of people recruited for the work," Leonard said.

The antiseptic quality of the place oozed from the low tables edged in chrome, the common chairs, and the few wall coverings that were very generic and not dramatic. It could have been a roadside dinner from the sixties, it had that bland quality to it. Or a hospital during times when the medical industry turned into an assembly line, with incredibly short stays for increasingly difficult surgeries. Everything was measured by the buck.

I felt a sudden sinking feeling, like I needed to breathe fresh air, but there was nowhere to exercise that freedom in what amounted to a gilded cage.

"Tomorrow, Francois, we will begin testing you, to sort out what type of training you'll receive and thereafter, what division in this three-ring circus you'll be assigned to," Leonard said, almost emotionless in his delivery, a mere cog in a larger machine.

I wondered if the man dreamed? As the evening ended I retired to my living quarters, a ten-by-ten room, with all the charm of a prison cell.

The next day, with Leonard in attendance, I sat in a room crowded wall-to-wall with a bizarre amalgamation of old radio-tubed devices, hundreds of dials, switches and single-use monitors, and newer use technologies with the more familiar keyboard and flat-screen interfaces. This was the lab where my planned series of psychic tests were to be carried out. A row of ten padded chairs stood at the center of the room, surrounded by iron walls with tri-dimensional monitoring sensors and cameras within the inner chamber to keep track of the test subjects.

"Why iron walls, Leonard?" I asked, as he escorted me into the inner psychic sanctum and stood with me as I sat in one of the padded chairs. There, a team of lab-coated researchers fitted me with enough electrodes to fill me with visions of an electric chair execution.

I noticed some automatic hydraulic devices, best described as partially-hidden clamps, that appeared near my ankles, arms, waist, and chest within the structure of the chair.

"When one deals with the psychic reality of the visible, and the many invisible worlds and timelines that overlap our dimensional space, one can never be quite sure whether one's test subject is the inherent source of their manifesting psychic potentials or…" I believe that Leonard paused for the dramatic effect, "Or if a trans-dimensional being, which priests long ago misidentified as 'demons,' has taken up residence in a person we are interested in."

"Trans-dimensional what?" I asked, having never heard that term discussed outside a fictional setting.

"A being of a different nature, who may have no more respect for a human being than we have for ants or cattle. You're never sure who or what you're facing in a situation like that, though it is rare. Why iron?" Leonard said, as the researchers finished their business and a little rodent of a man in white gave my coach the thumbs-up.

"Yes, why iron? Why not lead, since it can shield a person to some extent from radioactivity? Or why not some other metal?" I asked as the researchers scurried off to other duties, I assume related to my testing.

"Iron is an ancient talisman against such non-human entities. The potential of iron outside its mythic qualities was verified by Dr. Matthew Roney, an English paleontologist, when a pan-dimensional rift in the space-time continuum opened in Great Britain during the late 1950s…" Leonard said, as I noticed his foot tapping impatiently.

"We could spend the morning chatting about the various tests you're about to undergo and the weird scholarship behind some of the more esoteric assessments, I don't claim to know half the science that stands behind some of them," Leonard continued, "but it's a busy day ahead for you, so we'll save the explanations to some of my more learned colleagues for later.

"I'll be back to pick you up in an hour or two. If you need something, press the button on the console under your left hand and speak," Leonard said, as he began to walk out of the iron cell.

The door automatically closed slowly behind Leonard, with a ratcheting rasp and an expelling air, the latter like a corpse giving up the ghost.

A translucent helmet slowly slid down to encompass my head. A hiss of air accompanied its coming to rest.

Thank God for the sedatives, I thought as the room turned into a dark tunnel.

"Time for another psychic sleigh ride..."

"Should we induce clinical death in this one, in order to access the last 'flash of important life events' recording?" asked Luka, as she fidgeted to fit a translucent helmet to her own head, like the one affixed to test Subject 359, Francois Luc DeLapont, who resided in a nearby room.

Dr. Garibaldi weighed his words, a mere shell of the old man kept alive by the intricate mechanisms of his otherworldly wheelchair. His brain stem and arms still functioned, though the rest of his biological support apparatuses were animated by parallel servos and actuating automatons.

"We may still have a use for this one, as a host. So many of our kind were driven into exile, imprisoned in bodies by the cursed rulers and guardians, so as to prevent our comrades from accessing and thereby, using the inherent powers of the Great Race to escape their mortal cells and confines. No, we will try other methods, perhaps a heightening of our combined powers will reveal whether Subject 359 has, indeed, seen the Master and through which, we can ascertain where the Master rests..." Dr. Garibaldi said.

Dr. Leopold DeLapont nodded and spoke, his steely eyes points of scintillating fire, his mane of grey hair a swirl of madness framing his head. "Yes, yes, for a millennium, our agents have searched for the Master's sarcophagus, for since his near-death and the preservation of his life force in the early days of this world, plate-tectonics have remade its face a dozen times over. Even where our hallowed burial grounds remain, the stones are all changed now in nine grounds out of ten. You are never sure who or what you have till you question..."

"And was that notion an old wives' tale, wherein they whispered around ancient chimneys that the Master was preserved or," Luka said, "was it a bit of gossip planted long ago by the guardians to give us a false hope to forever chase, without chance of fulfillment?"

"Even though our kind must by nature explore the endless possibilities, there are times that even we, by choice, must decide to exclude such thoughts, or we will become paralyzed and end our days woefully indecisive among the *apathetics*, hidden among the human's own Alzheimer's sufferers," said Dr. Garibaldi.

"It is agreed, *Elder*, we follow your lead, from the dawn to the dusk," said Dr. Leopold, as he and Dr. Garibaldi each secured a translucent helmet to their own head.

As the trio bowed their heads in reverence, they uttered a strange clicking of their tongues and, in unison, an odd snapping of their fingers. Therein, they joined as one in a language of deep time while a sickly, sinister, violet luminosity began to ooze from the outlines of their persons. Then the eerie miasma melded into a single, unmistakable shifting shadow peppered with shards of lightning, dozens of huge, searchlight-like eyes, and a myriad of ginormous, animated pinchers.

In a stippled darkness, four candles lit the cardinal points of the compass within a labyrinth somewhere. Its location was hazy, shrouded by the trauma and denial of its victims. And in a brief instance, amid a dust-devil—crimson-shadowed and peppered with short, flashes of forked lightning—appeared huge, clicking pincers and enormous, lantern-like eyes.

"The Master! Behold, the Master lives!"

CHAPTER 9: WHAT LIES BELOW

I sat at a streetside café, alone and sipping coffee. I felt like I was waiting for someone or something. There was a crispness to the air, summer was almost gone, and fall was almost, but not quite, here. The leaves on a few trees had died, and I heard their rustling in a breeze nearby.

I often wondered what the atmosphere was like just before a witch appeared, just before a bolt of lightning was about to strike, just before an Olympian god of old approached in an earthly guise.

I stared into my coffee cup and beheld strange reflections of the sky above, like oily swirls of violet, reds, midnight blues, of tempest yellows. One eddy, then two, and a third.

I looked up in time to see one of those whirlpools of rotating lights turn sideways and fly from the sky above to the empty, cobblestone street next to the abandoned café. Not a soul but I stirred there now.

Out of that two-dimensional tunnel of primary and secondary hues of violet radiance stepped a woman of medium height and a large golem of a man. Their features and the facades they wore remained blurred out for a moment, then they sharpened to crystal clarity, as their unearthly egress vanished with an audible crackling in the air.

I thought I might be dreaming, though as of late I began to wonder in which realm lay my dreams and in which realm my realities.

The woman wore spectacles with silver frames, accented by her iron-grey hair. She was dressed in a man's black suit, though its outlines, high detachable collar, narrow tie, and style of buttons spoke of an earlier era; her expression was of one who walked in an air of authority. Clearly of the two, hers was the more commanding presence.

The golem was molded in severe angles, looking more like a walking, living statue. He walked behind her like a shadow.

When the pair approached my table, her accomplice pulled the chair out opposite mine for the woman in black to be seated.

"Who are you?" I asked her as I motioned, but was declined by a shrug, for her partner to also be seated.

She waited for a moment, as if savoring the silence.

"Who I am is not important. You have no internal point of reference to understand who I am. And my companion you are nervous about? He follows my lead, though he has a mind of his own when the need calls for it..." said the doctor, for that's what I called her behind my thoughts, as a simple means to remember her.

"Why are you here then? This is my dream and I doubt you and he are some manifestations of unexpressed scions of myself..." I replied.

In a moment, our surroundings changed. Our conversation in the airy, Parisian café melted away, like peeling wallpaper plastered over a hidden passageway.

The café table, my coffee, and my shadowy guests appeared in a dark, dimly lit cavern, whose soaring heights vanished into the darkness above. My companions became shadows, tinged in a red afterglow that radiated from some source below our feet.

My breath flowered frosty in the cold abyss that encircled us.

"Please, look down," the good doctor said, as the reddish glow from beneath us reflected like the flames of Hell off her severe spectacles.

I saw a huge, black vault of immense size and depths. Over that aperture lay an enormous trap door, sealed down with tremendous metal bands, festooned over with ageless sigils and hieroglyphs, wards of cabalistic protection. An aura of death and foreboding hung over the ancient seal of the gods, over this gate to Hell, which still glowed red in the few vents that pocketed its face, despite its untold ages of closure.

At once, I recognized it from another dream of another lifetime.

"I have seen one of these before, flying upward on a volcanic eruption…" I replied to the doctor.

"Mark it well, for tomorrow the seals of Hell will be broken, and your life will be in danger," the doctor said in grave tones.

A chill ran up my spine as I remembered well the lesson of the mountain ledge, the basalt ruins that Leonard had explained away on the outskirts of the Psi-SETI Plateau. I shuddered at the implications of what I heard.

"Why tell me?" I asked, impulsively, given my audience with demiurge or deity or demon, I knew not what, but that it might never happen again.

"'Why' is not a question eternity often answers," replied the doctor. "For your kind matter little to the Guild or those above, whom I serve."

"Your value to us? When you were psychically violated many days ago, that act revealed the hand of our enemy. You are nothing more to their kind than a number, Subject 359 to be exact. But for that reason alone, you have been warned. What you do is your choice, either for peril or preservation, your life is your booty!"

"Mon Dieu, how I wish I could forget that. The time in the library I take it. I felt like some type of deranged mental vampire tried to suck the living consciousness out of me!" I said, the pain was too fresh to say more to any stranger, much less this one.

"Oh and, one other thing…" the steely-spectacled woman said, ignoring my vampiric outburst.

"Which is…" I asked, wondering, did the doctor's eyes ever blink?

She pushed a small, iron box toward me with a strange, metallic-gloved hand.

I opened the ferrous box, exposing a tarnished silver marshal's shield, circa the Old West, except instead of the standard five points, it was shaped with a more stylized occultic symbol of some kind, and read, "Esoteric Cavalry," on the "O" clasp, while the remaining letters were worn illegible by age and use.

"What's the odd shape of the marshal's badge mean, and its name?" I asked as I fingered the relic.

My fingers tingled at its touch.

"It's the 'Elder Sign,' which probably means nothing to you. But it may help you, in time of need…" the doctor replied as I picked it up, ignored the weird sensations, and slipped it into my front pocket, which insulated me from its touch to some degree.

At that, the doctor and her henchman faded into the firmament, until only the fiery sparkle on her spectacles remained, then that vanished.

I next fell through a shaft of iridescent colors for what felt like an eternity.

I opened my eyes and found myself lying in a single bed, looking at the antiseptic, cream-colored ceiling of my assigned quarters at the Psi-SETI compound. Beside me, I felt the odd marshal's badge, a relic from my nightmare.

My escort, Leonard, was absent this morning. Official duties, the email read. I now had my own official email address, as part of the Initiative, Francois.L.DeLapont@Psi-SETI.gov. I could not use it for external purposes. For security reasons, the compound used an intranet exclusively. A "Fort Knox" of a firewall, I had been told, protected the place.

I carried the "Esoteric Cavalry" badge in my pocket, though it lost its tingling touch in transition from my dreams. Hey, a rabbit's foot is a rabbit's foot, eternal in origin or otherwise.

I decided to check out the small airport facilities employed by the Institute. I was no pilot, so if my dream indeed engendered a prophetic truth, I would need to find a way out, aboard a plane. There were five small Lear Jets, like the one that Luka brought me in on, and there were four Boeing 737s, which each could carry over a hundred passengers.

There was a separate complex of hangars near the facility that handled the visible jets. The aerodrome was restricted; a security checkpoint was manned there by a single uniformed operative—their distinctive orange jumpsuit and black boots were peculiar to the Institute.

I wandered lesser halls, expecting at any moment to be intercepted by one of the orange-suited security types.

I happened on the infirmary, which was closed on Mondays unless an emergency occurred. There was a small, twenty-five-bed ward, quite a modern, cutting-edge setup.

I heard a clicking sound above me. A camera in the corner turned toward where I stood and the light near its lens began to blink red. I thought about waving, but thought better of it, and simply walked away, as if I hadn't noticed the sound.

I questioned how long it would take for the Psi-SETI operatives to catch up with me. I wondered what would become of me; the compound acted as a law unto itself.

I took a sidestep down what looked like a supply corridor. I asked myself why there were no cameras here—this was so unlike the regimented rest of the complex.

Among a hall featuring six doors, three on one side and three on the other, stood an elevator door. More like a utility silo, with a cage-like platform, it wasn't locked with a padlock and chain. So, I slide aside the metal accordion door to a creaking, metallic cacophony. A single light bulb flashed on as I entered the cage, probably activated by an electric eye. After fumbling along the walls, I found a switch centered between two poles. I pushed the lever down and the elevator began to descend somewhere. I held my breath, not knowing what to expect.

The elevator landed in a dark, wide room that edged toward the size of an auditorium, though not in height. It was a hall of shadows, with a few signs lit in red spaces here and there, throughout.

It was a bit cold and I hadn't worn more than a long-sleeved shirt. And again, there was the strong smell of antiseptic, intermingled with other scents.

I reached around the frame that enclosed the elevator's face for a light switch or lightbox. I searched for a moment, then walked forward and bumped into something hanging from the ceiling, then another. I stepped back and jolted against something upright, a podium? As my hands ran over its face, I sensed knobs, dials, and switches, until one felt like a light switch.

I flicked it, to see what would happen.

More red lights went on, and suddenly I knew where I was, though I had never been there before.

I was in a grand room. Hanging on multiple hooks from the ceiling on what amounted to a track-system, like those used in a dry-cleaning store, dangled hundreds of bodies in translucent full-length body bags, with a wild assortment of tubes and electrodes hooked up to each individual.

Was each body alive? I was a bit spooked, not caring to feel for a pulse or signs of respiration. Men and women alike hung there, naked to the world.

Who were they? When I pushed a body aside, above the body I saw the word, "Subject" then a number in red lights, three-digits worth and non-sequential like unmarked dollar bills of various denominations.

At once, I saw a flowing, swirling, stream of blue and white veils sail through the crowd of hanging bodies, which in turn rustled like leaves in a forest. How could there be a wind down here, and why now?

The swift maelstrom next took on physical solidity and knocked me down, hovering over me. A set of huge blue eyes looked down at me from an otherwise featureless blur.

The blur vanished just as quickly as it started. From where I lay, I looked up at the parade of bodies to an empty rung. I squinted, then grasped as I struggled to my feet and decided to put as much distance as possible between this morgue for the living and myself.

For above that empty meat hook and place in the meat sack line, hung the unmistakable sign, clearly outlined in red lights:

"Subject: 359"

CHAPTER 10: BAKER, TANGO, CHARLIE

As the elevator came to a jarring halt, having reached the top of the shaft, and the cage door swung aside, I leaned against the wall opposite the row of doors and waited until my heart stopped racing.

I kept my back to the wall as I edged away from the corridor of doors and back into the main ward of the infirmary. I tried to remember where the cameras were, hoping that I could find a way around their field of vision. Where did they appear to overlap? Where was there a place or path they failed to cover, if such a hole in the Institute's security net existed?

As I made my way out of the wing that included the infirmary, I walked past a bank of windows that opened onto the horizon where the snowbound plateau, ringed in by tall, white mountain spires, stood, intermingled with the towering and teetering basalt tower ruins. What were the bodies being kept for? Were select inductees into the Psi-SETI Initiative chosen strictly to be harvested for their organs and other valuable body parts on the world's black market?

Or was there another purpose for the accumulated bodies, apparently kept alive for some future use? Did anyone ever leave the compound or was it all a ruse?

I stared out the windows as a fresh snowstorm dumped its load on the plateau, pondering such questions, as a growing sense of paranoia intruded on my thoughts. I stopped for a moment there, wondering what my next move might be.

I heard voices in the distance, further down the windowed corridors. The voices bore a sense of urgency, like they were coming to apprehend me. Could I smuggle myself out of the place, as a stowaway on one of the supply jets that must keep the Psi-SETI compound stocked with rations to feed and fuel to heat the place? That seemed far-fetched at the moment, for I was new here, I had recently gone through their induction process, and more than one person daily, like Leonard, was held accountable for my whereabouts.

Then the floor beneath me and the corridor shuddered in place. The thick windows buckled here and there in their frames, some popping and cracking at stress points, not shattering, but a lacework of fractures held in place by thick, flexible plastic laminate.

I looked outside, only to see a series of titanic fireballs lining the horizon. Where a tumbling of once-tottering basaltic tower ruins had stood, one, two, three molten shields, burning red-hot, flew skyward among sheets of driving snow. Just as quickly, they fell to the earth, their impact beyond sight.

A gong began to go off at different points near and distant, and dim emergency lights flipped on instead of the normally bright hall lights. People piled out of their rooms or abandoned their research stations and filtered into the end of the corridor further down.

I turned around, heaving in place as the complex shook again, and saw a locker automatically open to expose a thick parka, matching snow pants, and insulated boots. Was the site going to be evacuated?

I grabbed the snow gear and headed for the airport, just in case the higher-ups issued an extraction order.

I sideways glanced out the windows, and through a relatively intact panel and swirling snow, I saw three military helicopters, AH-64 Apaches if I didn't miss my guess, their wings bristling with a variety of weapons. They flew as a pack, out toward the sites where the titanic explosions first occurred.

'Why warbirds here?' I thought. What did they intend to encounter out there, among the disaster overtaking the snow-blown horizon?

I heard a "whoosh" sound from somewhere behind me, a pinprick near my left ear and…

Luka Saint-Laurent walked up, holding a darting rifle to the tranquilized body of Subject 359. Two burly, orange-suited agents followed her, checked to see if the man was unconscious, picked a dart off his head, snuggly restrained him with zip-ties, and placed him on a stretcher. The push of a button brought forth an automatic veil that enshrouded the man's body while legs with wheels extended below the stretcher.

Luka led them away, wheeling the sedated man through the still-shifting corridor toward the Psi-SETI airport. A hundred panicked voices resounded in the hallways behind the foursome.

A brisk but purposeful, steady pace brought little attention from operatives and psychics alike who stormed the passageway in all directions.

Luka met up with a tall, high-foreheaded, distinguished-looking man, wearing a pin-striped suit and wing-tip black shoes, with flowing grey hair and matching Van Dyke beard.

She made a slight curtsy gesture toward the man with a commanding presence.

"I have him and none too soon," Luka said to Dr. Leopold. "Is there any news about the uproar along the outskirts of the Institute?"

"No, but the vibrations emanating from that sector are unbelievably ancient, but unmistakable. For now, Psi-SETI has served its purpose..." Dr. Leopold replied with a shrug of indifference.

"Yes, this Francois may be the one we've been looking for all these centuries..." Luka said, as the company moved through the airport and toward its gates.

"The way our Gamma frequencies resonate through the unique psychic echo-chamber formed by Subject 359's temporal lobe and awakening pineal gland will help us narrow down the final location of the Master. Or, we can simply interrogate him..." replied Dr. Leopold as they arrived at a waiting Lear Jet and the Elder.

It was midnight, high noon for gunfights and sword duels betwixt forces that favored the light and those that felt most formidable in the dark.

A diagonal line of tank-like whirlybirds flew toward the thunderous snow-blanched field ahead. Smoldering immense holes in the earth, surrounded like teeth girdling a maw, lay heaps of the odd, toppled basaltic formations best described as towers.

Heated chatter filled the radios between Baker, Tango, and Charlie, elements of the Psi-SETI defense squadron. Their orders were to identify the nature of the volcanic upheavals and if need be, neutralize any sentient source of the chaos.

As the trio of warbirds drew near to the festering abysses, they hovered near the glowering phenomenon, but not too close, to assess the situation.

Except for the heaps of eternal snow and the flickering flames below them, everything was quiet as a cemetery on a moonless night.

"Baker to Charlie, Baker to Charlie. Rob, do you see what I'm seeing?"

"Charlie to Baker, over. Yeah, Phil, I'm seeing big circles, who knows how big, lying in the snow. Is that smoke or steam? Metallic, still-glowing red, but how? Exposed to the frigid temperatures lying in all that snow and ice, it doesn't make sense! It's been over an hour since the commotion went off. Charlie to Baker, over..."

"Baker to Charlie, yes. Rob, we need eyes down on those unidentified bogeys. Take your rig down there and see what we got. But don't sacrifice safety for getting to the bottom of these things. Chet just flipped on our Geiger counter, something's hot nearby, and the rad-dial is dancing, over..."

"Charlie to Baker, roger that Phil, my and Sid's necks are important to us, too! Heading down to the deck...over..."

The second copter in the line titled rear up, then descended toward one of the boiling apertures below.

"Baker to Tango, Baker to Tango, Jerome, you got Rob covered? I don't see any hostiles and nothing flickering on radar...over..."

"Tango to Baker, Tango to Baker, yeah Phil, I've got Rob covered like a fly on flypaper...over..."

"Baker to Charlie, Baker to Charlie, hey Rob, can you turn your forward camera on, so we and the folks back home can see what you're seeing?"

"Baker to Red Rover, Baker to Red Rover. Colonel, we got our eyes on, you got a ring-side seat to what Charlie's seeing..."

Nothing but static crackled in reply on Baker's radio.

"Baker to Red Rover, Baker to Red Rover, Colonel Jenkins, are you copying us? Over..."

Still, nothing but static.

"Baker to Charlie, Baker to Charlie, it looks like we're on our own for now. Rob, can you check whether you can reach Red Rover with your radio? Just in case it's just our rig is on the fritz...over..."

"Charlie to Baker, almost on the deck. Will do Phil, as soon as we're in position to assess...Dammit, the things are huge! The shields, this one's about half a kilometer across, and it's crossed with bands shaped like an Iron Cross. Are you getting this? Over..."

"Baker to Charlie, yes Rob, I see it. And parts of the damn thing are still glowing? Maybe it's just so thick that parts haven't cooled due to its size...Dammit, I'm no lab-coated scientist, Rob. But besides the Geiger counter, I'm getting bad vibes from that thing...It must weigh hundreds of tons...over..."

"Charlie to Baker...Or thousands of tons, Phil. We've never made anything like that or lifted nothing that size...I'm talking about our kind, Phil, our kind...Mankind...over..."

A silent shadow rose to the left of Charlie, the hovering scout.

"Baker to Charlie, Rob, off your port, I'm seeing a dark, unknown bogey! The damn thing, it's got no radar signature. Rob, pivot to port and hit it with all you got... Rob, over..."

The lower AH-64 turned sideways in place and launched two Sidewinder air-to-air missiles. The shadow gave off no heat signature as one of the missiles, locking onto the great heat from below, dove downward, detonating in one of the smoldering abysses.

The other flew upward, locking onto the Tango gunship. Realizing what happened, Tango spun away from its original cover position above the Charlie's Apache, shooting out a dozen flares to confuse its heat signature. The second sidewinder flew into the center of mass, the fireball of flares, detonating, sending shrapnel everywhere and striking the near Tango Apache.

"This is Tango, I'm hit, throttle's unresponsive, I'm riding this stallion down to the deck…over…"

Before long, a dim, but bright flash burst against the snow-frocked desert below.

"Baker to Charlie, dammit to hell, Tango got caught in friendly fire…Hit the damn thing with your chain gun, make 'em do a death dance, whatever the hell the thing is…over…"

"Charlie to Baker, I can't get a radar lock, so targeting the beast with my helmet bullseye…Lining it up, getting a lock there…firing…over…"

A hail of thirty-millimeter gunfire, sounding like a foghorn, hit the shadow in short bursts. The shadow changed from a soft blur, sharpening to crystal clarity. Blowing off thundering whistles from countless orifices across its body, the thing was organic, polyp-studded, grey, glistening, and visibly quivering.

The size of a suburban house, the thing defied description.

The flow of lead—depleted-uranium, tracers, fragmentation—flew through the body of the thing without any effect.

"Charlie to Baker, Phil, this bogey ain't real, it's like some kind of projection or something. Otherwise, how the hell could the chain-gun be useless? Over…"

"Baker to Charlie…Rob, try the flamethrower pod we've recently been outfitted with…Just don't get in too close, we've already lost Tango…Over…"

Charlie didn't need any coaxing, as the copter flew straightaway toward the flying freakshow, drawing within less than four hundred feet, then firing an arc of flames at the bogey.

The flying freakshow changed shapes, for it was viscous and pliable, as hundreds of fissures opened across its body, and a combined blast of dense air emitted from the thing blew out Charlie's flamethrower.

The thing then shot another blast of dense air at the Apache's tail rotor, again and again, as if guided by some modicum of intelligence, sending Charlie into an uncontrollable, plummeting tailspin.

"Baker to Charlie, pull out of it, Rob, pull out…"

Charlie element struck the snow-covered field, not far from Tango's smoldering wreckage.

The flying freakshow arose from its engagement of element Charlie. Joining it was a second shadow, then another roused by the skirmish action in the heavens above its point of egress from below.

Three of the unknowns, trumpeting like a stampede of rogue elephants, made their way toward the Baker helicopter.

"Baker to Red Rover, Baker to Red Rover, do you see what I'm seeing? Send reinforcements, we need the reserves…Hello Red Rover, do you copy me? Is anybody out there? Over…"

CHAPTER 11: MIDNIGHT

I awoke handcuffed in the back of an SUV with tinted-out windows, between two large fellows with single earphones and fondling electronic cudgels.

Electronic cudgels? That's what they looked like. I didn't want to experience the trauma-inducing sidearms firsthand.

Psi-SETI owned cutting-edge technologies and I'm sure that extended over into the latest weapons too.

And personal persuaders.

I smiled at each of them nervously, one at a time.

Neither moved a muscle or made a nod of recognition.

In front of me, between the two forward seats, ran a small column of TV screens.

The top screen flashed on, bearing the familiar face of Luka Saint-Laurent, if that was her true name.

"Good evening, Francois. Yes, it is evening and we're back in France now," she said as if reading from a prepared script.

"What's so good about it, Luka? And why am I being treated like a prisoner again?" I asked, loud enough to be heard over whatever electronic conveyance their system used.

"My dear Francois, we could have left you at the K2 compound to face whatever disaster beset Psi-SETI. Or, we could have brought you with us. We chose the latter..." Luka replied, her responses off-script.

"Why the elaborate ruse, Luka? Why the trip to the Psi-SETI compound up north, on Greenland, or wherever it was? Why couldn't we have done all this in France?" I questioned her again.

"None of that is your concern, my dear Francois. What we

did was necessary. That's all you need to know. Now, please observe the screen just below the one where I appear..." Luka said.

In dark tones, a black and white film began to run, choppy in frame. I saw Mahmood Le Fey laying out candles around me, then lighting them at the four corners of the cardinal compass.

The film came to an end.

I tried to keep my emotions in check, yet here was the reason that I sought counseling with Dr. Leopold to begin with.

"Where did you get that?" I asked. My face felt flush and I sensed hot tears rising over the death of my friend.

"We employed an optic-encephalogram to record your visions. Our question to you is where did this incident occur? We were able to narrow the location to somewhere in the Centre-Val de Loire region of France. But where in Centre-Val de Loire?" Luka said, probing me.

"What, are you and your thugs part of the FBI, the DST (France's 'Department of Territorial Safety/Security), or Interpol?" I asked, sensing my options dwindling rapidly.

"Who we are and what we represent is of no concern of yours," Luka said confidently.

"Now, I will ask you again, dear Francois, where in Centre-Val de Loire did your vision of the candles occur? Don't make me lose my patience with you..." Luka continued in a sterner tone.

"What if I don't tell you?" I said, chancing it.

"Then, you leave me no choice," Luka said coldly, like a sociopath. "Take him to the Rhine, Gerald, and properly dispose of our guest there."

One of the muscular thugs smiled at Luka's command.

I reneged on my ploy.

"Ok, ok, I'll tell you where the candles were set," I tried to avoid saying things like I was pleading, though I felt unable to say no to the woman.

Had they doped me with a truth serum like sodium pentothal before I awoke?

"Where then did your vision of candles happen?" Luka asked.

"At the Chartres Cathedral on the night of Samhain…" I muttered, my will gone, a shambles of mixed emotions.

I felt terrified and relieved at the same time.

Someone behind Luka leaned over, as if the grey-haired man were whispering something in her ear.

"Good, good Gerald, there has been a change in plans," Luka said, her face almost a mask of indifference.

"It's ten o'clock now, meet me at the Chartres Cathedral in two hours with Monsieur DeLapont. I have a few phone calls to make, to one of our operatives in the Augustinian Order. We'll want the cathedral free to ourselves, N'est-ce pas?" said Luka, then the screens all went blank.

I guess I wasn't quite dead, not yet at least.

It was pitch dark except for a few torches carried by Luka's brawny hired men. They used me to bring in a wheelbarrow full of shovels, picks, and, if I didn't miss my guess, explosives of some make, and detonator switches. One of the hired goons rolled in an enormous, aged steam trunk.

Behind them arrived Luka Saint-Laurent, Dr. Leopold DeLapont, and Mathéo Archambeau, who guided Dr. Garibaldi Pietro Esposito's motorized wheelchair.

The Psi-SETI professional cadre were all dressed in flowing black robes, decked out in black mass sigils and symbols. Their faces and foreheads were marked with ashes, bearing cabalistic rather than Christological significance. One other attendee I recognized from months ago, Brother Bertrille, though the vestments of his calling had definitely changed.

From the steam trunk, Brother Bertrille and Mathéo Archambeau began setting things up by erecting a huge, grotesquely carved candle-stand in each of the four cardinal compass points in the labyrinth. A quick lighting of the huge tapers, shaped like demons, brought an odd aura to the cathedral. The other Psi-SETI team stood or set back-to-back in a triangle of sorts, their individual faces—Luka's and those of Drs. Leopold and Garibaldi—were masks of intense concentration and ecstasy, their fingers snapping involuntarily in a queer unison.

Of the trio, it was Dr. Garibaldi who spoke first.

"I have not felt a presence so intense, so deep, so powerful since we came to this world from our first world, the mother of all. He was a millennium older than even I. He is the One, the only, the Master."

The old man spoke without thought.

Luka spoke, almost as if continuing the story. "In him, our kind was imprisoned in the past, sentenced to die because they could not leap forward to new bodies, new lives, new hopes. His was the anchor, the guaranteed jump point, the one by which all those deemed malicious criminals and ruffians by the others, could find in any timeline the means to jump forward; he was our first hope, our last hope, our only hope for release from these prisons."

Dr. Leopold then stood in black behind a makeshift lectern, draped in black, a shadow among the shadows, for the place no longer radiated the Comeliness of Christendom, but the raw, rough, ragged days when the site was sacred to other faiths and their untold gods.

Dr. Leopold spoke last, as Luka concluded her oration, "They thought, the Guardians and their human disciples, that by placing untold holy relics of this faith and others—of Saint John's Day Nail, Our Lady of the Pillar, Our Lady of the Underground, and the Well of the Strong Saints—they could dim his potency, that they could stop his resurrection and rule. But friends, and all who are gathered here tonight, they could not…"

"No, they could not contain him, all those centuries beneath this place, satiating himself on the mental smorgasbords presented by the many generations of the pilgrims who trod this labyrinth."

Drs. Leopold and Garibaldi, and Luka began snapping their fingers in unison and clicking their tongues in a unified alien anthem.

Mathéo Archambeau stood awash in the psychic overflow.

I couldn't breathe, the walls and heights of the great cathedral were spinning, closing in on me. I saw in the shadows other outlines, human and inhuman, arising around the lobes of the labyrinth.

I tried to leave, but one of Luka's bouncers stood in my way. Though by the surprised look on his hardened face, I wondered if this tough guy might bolt like a deer.

A few portable chair dollies and light benches were set back against the circle of columns that divided the Chartres labyrinth and nave from the main cathedral and sub chapels. The two henchmen pulled a couple of benches to the outer circles of the labyrinth for themselves and me, while Drs. Leopold and Garibaldi, flanked by Luka and Mathéo, assembled around the lectern.

From two velvet cases with bright, brass hinges, Luka produced one rather rough man-sized staff, while Mathéo pulled another rod, again as tall as himself, bedecked with strange settings of silver, topped by a stylized dragon's head with jeweled eyes.

"With the staves of Merlin and Moshe, we call upon the elementals of the North and South, of the East and West; hear us!"

Luka and Mathéo each took their individual staves and walked one hemisphere of the labyrinth apiece, stamping the heel of their rods as they went.

The pounding pagan rhythm against the stone floor echoed like a danse macabre throughout the complex. Behind them a sickly, sinister, violet luminosity began to rise like somber specters, some human-like while others inhuman parodies—bubbles, octopi, incubus, succubae, living Hindu idols, and intricate Arabesques. These apparitions formed two conga-lines, one behind Luka, the other behind Mathéo, writhing from left to right, howling in the air and hammering the floor in mad processions.

I hid my eyes as the pale, violet abominations drew near. I felt a brief prickling against my right hip.

The marshal's badge? I quickly realized as the eerie caterwauling and daemonic pounding continued, they hadn't searched me.

When I briefly opened my eyes, I saw two circles of the horrors facing me, eyes all aglow and luminous in form, in the near darkness.

"Those from the outer spheres have chosen…"

I felt four huge hands lift me overhead and carry me toward Drs. Leopold and Garibaldi, the latter swinging, in time to the infernal pounding, a scythe-like ornate cutlass with a shimmering blade.

They held me aloft over the direct spot where Mahmood Le Fey had been torn in half and where, even now, a dust-devil, crimson-shadowed and peppered with short, flashes of forked lightning arose, interspersed with huge clicking pincers and enormous, lantern-like eyes.

"No, No!" I screamed, as Dr. Leopold set himself between the two brutes, preparing to cut me in half at my stomach and spine with an overhead stroke.

The henchman, thinking me helpless and hopeless, didn't notice my hand reach into my pocket and hoist the Esoteric Cavalry Marshal's badge toward Dr. Leopold.

The staff-stamping stopped as the badge burned brightly in my hand and a pale, crimson flame snaked its way around the cowering, violet specters and singed the scalps of the Psi-SETI cadre.

Dr. Leopold filled the air with demonic curses as he hid his face from the cabalistic relic.

"Then, if not this one," Dr. Leopold blurted out, repurposing his swing, "…these will suffice."

Dr. Leopold, his face a mask of triumphant exaltation, swung his blade in a wide, horizontal arc beneath me.

Two huge heads and two sets of arms at the elbows flew upward on spiral fountains of blood.

I fell to the labyrinth floor. The headless and armless, bloodied bodies of the quivering, brutish henchmen, softened my crash.

Partially stained in their mingled blood, I stumbled to my feet, backing my way out of the cathedral while thrusting the cabalistic relic back and forth between me and my still-living captors.

I noticed in passing as I left the holy place, the twin pools of spreading blood hissing in place, then being sucked up by the very stone of the labyrinth itself.

The labyrinth was hungry that night.

I ducked out of an open cathedral side door into the dark, cool night, hearing a jubilant cry as I ran for my life.

"He lives! The Master lives again!"

I watched the local news the next day. It seems that the Chartres Cathedral, labyrinth and all, burned down overnight, almost eight hundred years of religious history gone, just like that.

The usual suspects, unidentified religious zealots or right-wing anarchists, were blamed by the city's gendarmerie for the tragedy, as overworked detectives began the effort to sift through the ruins for clues. The Pope and local Papists lobbied the *Sûreté Nationale* for a federal investigation. Their cries for justice reached the ears of the same officials who inconclusively investigated the burning down of the Notre Dame Cathedral a year earlier.

Soon, the world would forget, but I could not. I know who burned down the Chartres Cathedral, to cover up the resurrection of "the Master," whoever and whatever that beast might be.

I had no idea what freeing the messiah of an alien race meant to our world. But, I know what it did to my own.

Oh, and that talisman, a fugitive from the Old West along some timeline? Like Tolkien's Ring of Power, somehow, I lost it—or it lost itself—during my panicked escape from certain death in the labyrinth.

I retraced my steps in my mind and as I could around the cathedral complex, so as not to arouse suspicion. I found nothing; it was like it never existed.

But it did.

I looked up my old landlord, Roger Blanchet, and found my room to be unoccupied, the way I had left it, how long ago? I lost track of the days in all the madness.

School? I would try to go back, the next semester. It was an immediate way to put money in my bank account. But, I felt an empty shell of the man I once was. I continued as a student, for it was my only anchor to reality and my dwindling sanity.

What of them, Drs, Leopold and Garibaldi, Mathéo Archambeau, and Luka… Luka Saint-Laurent? I have not heard from them, though once or twice, I have received phone calls from an unregistered number, where the caller listened to when I picked up the call, then hung up.

They know where I live. As the poet has said, I will "not go gentle into that good night."

But last night, as I looked into my bathroom mirror, the subtle line between my nightmares and my waking memories came to a head.

For when I last looked up into that mirror, I did not see my tired, now haggard and unkempt face, my uncombed hair and beard stubble—I wasn't even twenty-one yet, and my hair was suddenly turning grey.

No, in that mirror, I saw a young, raven-haired woman, her eyes were a strange blue, like the sky, with a wholly different world spinning beneath that sky.

And she said, back to me, through her reflection.

"I choose you…"

BROKEN SINGULARITY: SEQUENTIA QUARTA

BY DAVID CONYERS

"**W**ake up!"
Peel woke suddenly.

He lay in a bed, stretched out on his back.

Support was a soft mattress, clean sheets, and white fluffy pillows. The air felt clean, pleasantly warm, with a hint of humidity. An airy tropical breeze blew in from outside, bringing ocean smells that enlivened pleasant memories.

He shared the bed with Hannah Stanchfield. He wore cotton pants and a loose t-shirt. She wore a singlet top and cotton shorts. Their feet were bare.

Hair had grown on her scalp and eyebrows, forged into fine, shoulder-length strands of red.

Peel touched his scalp and jaw, and discovered both remained bald and smooth, as was his chosen style. His eyebrows remained as he remembered them, so he wasn't completely devoid of hair.

There was no discomfort. No fear, no stiffness, and no aches.

Hannah stirred, her body pressed up against his with her arm and leg over his muscular body. His right arm held her tight against his skin and clothes.

"Morning," she said, waking. She appeared refreshed. Normal.

"Morning," he answered.

Recognizing the strangeness of their predicament, they

sat and rubbed their eyes until wakefulness found them. For several minutes, they did nothing. Their senses explored, listened, watched, smelled, touched…

He tried to form thoughts, perceptions, concepts, and ideas. Nothing stuck.

"Hannah, let's look around."

Their bungalow resembled a tropical resort, but when they stepped outside there was only a beach surrounded by rainforests and a pristine ocean with waters lapping gently upon the fine, sandy shores.

Peel smelled brewing coffee, so they wandered back inside, finding a table laid out with breakfast. Black coffees, fresh fruit, muesli, yogurt, poached eggs, bacon, bread rolls, pepper and salt containers, and orange and pineapple juices. There were also chairs, plates, knives, forks, spoons and napkins for two.

He didn't have any thoughts about any of it.

Taking the hot mug in his hand, Peel drank the coffee.

It was perfect.

"This isn't real," Hannah said. "It can't be."

"No." He looked for faults, breakages in the coding, suspecting this was a simulated world and that he was simulated, too. They might be nothing more than information particles smeared across a computation program curled up inside an infinitely dense singularity. Or maybe they had fallen through the singularity and reformed inside another universe. Either way, higher forms of intelligence must control them. This was not a random occurrence. "What do we do?"

She shrugged. "Eat, relax, and go for a swim." When he didn't answer, she said, "What else can we do?"

His mind couldn't argue with her.

After eating, they stripped and swam out into the clear blue waters. Tropical fish and turtles joined them. Corals of many colors clumped on rock beds. Waves broke on the shore, creating a swell and foam, leaving many colored starfish in their retreat.

"It's perfect," Hannah exclaimed, as they walked without rush to their bungalow, allowing the sun to dry their skin.

They spent their days reading the many books always found on the shelves in the main room. A multitude of movies and television shows were available for watching. In the evenings they drank gin and tonics, or red wine. Food was always there when they felt hungry and comprised a variety of cuisines popular across the twenty-first century. They fell into a pattern of regular lovemaking. They never fought or argued and, despite their lack of contraceptives, she never fell pregnant.

He felt that everything he did was exactly an experience from his past.

Elements were not new. Only how they collated together was new.

After some time had passed, Peel couldn't remember how long they had lived here.

Had time passed?

He mentioned this to Hannah.

"It is odd, Harrison. We accepted it so readily."

"Accept?"

"Everything. We accept everything."

"We did, didn't we? Still do."

Several more weeks passed, or was it perhaps months? It might have been years that had passed before Peel mentioned the anomaly again. Time had lost meaning, and one day seemed no different than another, despite the variety of entertainments and cuisines available to them.

When they lay naked, entwined in their bed after another bout of exhilarating lovemaking, he said, "I'm going to request a meeting with our hosts."

Her fingers traced a line on his hairy chest. "Who?"

"The Yithians."

"Oh, them."

The alien masters of time and space appeared the next morning, although not in a guise either expected. A black shimmering shape vaguely resembling a slender woman, but also resembling a flickering shadow projected on a wall, appeared on the beach. Peel thought to be terrified, but he couldn't feel anything.

"What are we?" Peel asked the shape.

"A record. An archive."

He tried to process this revelation but couldn't.

"Coded information."

Hannah, emerging from the waters after her own swim, wiped the wet from her shining wet hair and skin. The shimmering black wisp of a shape didn't seem to bother her either. She asked a question of their visitor. "But we are self-aware. How can we be a record?"

"Are you self-aware?" asked the Yithian projection.

Peel felt momentarily stunned. "What do you mean?"

"A black hole destroys everything except information. That is all you are now, information. That is all that survived when you fell into the singularity, as you reinstated the event horizon and closed off forever this universe from the last. You think you have consciousness, but that is an illusion. You only exist when we read you."

Peel looked at Hannah, and she stared back at him. The emotions written on her expressive face, of fear and uncertainty, seemed real to him. But was it? He was certain she was self-aware, and he felt the same certainty about himself. But was he self-aware? How could he know?

"It makes no sense?"

"It doesn't need to," said the Yithian. "I am only here because it suits my purposes. Not yours. We created a scenario where, before we activated you, you needed to ask questions. I am studying you to see how you assemble the 'information' you possess. You have no free will. You have no consciousness, even though we programmed you to believe that you do."

Peel felt their microworld recede from him. He half expected it to break apart, for a line of code to pop up as a diagnostic or error window and instruct him to reboot the system. It probably happened all the time, but each time he was powered up, he and Hannah returned to a default or last-saved version of themselves, with the error erased from their memories.

Peel scratched his bald head. "The Riders, we cut them off from the Earth? They can no longer impact our planet?"

"The question shows much about how your minds perceive time. Linear, and always advancing at a set speed. The Riders lived in superimposed positions of freedom and enslavement, both cut off from your planet and projected there within the same time stream, everything they ever did all occurring concurrently. Falling through a black hole, from an outsider's perspective, takes an infinite amount of time to happen. Cutting off the Riders from their influence on your planet faces the same quandaries of perception in your limited human minds."

Hannah clenched her fists, then reached out to tightly grip Peel's hand. "So, we achieved nothing?"

"The Riders, in their base biological configuration, infested our host bodies on the world where you were both imprisoned. We could not have that state of existence persist. Therefore, we created this alternative universe where only the Great Race of Yith could survive and flourish. No other consciousness or ordered information, other than those collated in our archives, is allowed to exist here. This is our new universal design. The Outer Gods, they pollute everything. We traveled through all of space and time in that last universe, preparing for this moment, our plan where only information would join us here. Not consciousness and not self-aware matter. We could not afford for another dimensional being, operating beyond space and time, to destroy all that. That is what the Riders were, a conscious plague, and that is why we trapped them on the singularity. They refused to leave our world, and we refused to take them with us. But even with their feeble attempts to escape through portals of freedom they believed existed on your home world of Earth, they still lost."

Peel tried to listen, to understand, but a deep recess in his mind told him he would forget all this.

The Yithian was correct. He and Hannah were nothing more than information.

He imagined his data file as a tiny crystal, one of trillions stored in one of billions of archival halls, in millions of libraries constructed across the vastness of the many Yithian worlds in a universe tailor-made to suit only their form of life.

He squeezed Hannah's hand, and she squeezed back.

Peel said to their visitor, "But I sense time. I'm aware of cause and effect."

"You think you do," said the Yithian as its shaped seemed to flicker into a more ethereal state. "How long do you believe you two have lived here, together, on this island?"

Hannah and he stared into each other's eyes. There was a comfort between them, a peace and a shared history of adversity overcome. But what did he feel for her, and what did she feel for him? They never fought or argued, but they never expressed feelings for each other either.

"I don't know," said Hannah, her voice barely a whisper.

The Yithian drifted further from them. "You've both been here an infinite amount of time, and there is no time at all. You are only information. There is no time or progression for pure information."

The Yithian faded from existence.

Peel and Hannah, still holding hands, looked for their keeper, but it was gone.

"Is it true?" Hannah asked. "Everything that it said?"

Peel shrugged. "It could be worse. Far worse."

"How?"

His mind tried to form an idea that had never been there before. "I think you and I are the luckiest people in the universe, and we should be happy with that."

Later, when life returned to normal, he forgot this chance meeting, and so did she. They existed only in moments, slices in time and space, but only when others decided there was a momentary importance for their existence.

And it was enough.

ABOUT THE AUTHOR

David Conyers has published over fifty science fiction and horror short stories, won several awards for his writing, and edited five anthologies including one of the first fiction collections to explore the concepts of exoplanets, *Extreme Planets*. For over a decade he was the Arts and General Editor and reviewer for *Albedo One* magazine where he interviewed many top science fiction writers including Iain M. Banks, Greg Egan and Will McIntosh.

His extensive portfolio of Cthulhu Mythos fiction includes his popular Harrison Peel espionage versus the Elder Gods series commencing with *Cthulhu Reloaded*, contributed to *The Last Door* video game, and for more than a decade he was a prolific contributor to the *Call of Cthulhu* tabletop role-playing game.

Today David writes contemporary thriller fiction novels under a pseudonym.

www.david-conyers.com

Matthew Davenport hails from Des Moines, Iowa where he lives with his wife, Ren, and daughter, Willow. When his scattered author brain isn't earning weird looks from the ladies of his life, he enjoys reading sci-fi and horror, tinkering with electronics, and doing escape rooms.

Matt is the author of the Andrew Doran series, the Broken Nights series (along with his brother, Michael), The Trials of Obed Marsh, and Satan's Salesman among other titles. He's also a self-styled student of the Cthulhu Mythos and exercises that influence in his stories and as an editor at the blog Shoggoth.net You can keep track of Matthew through his twitter account @ spazenport. You can also support him and get regular chapter and novel postings at http://patreon.com/matthewdavenport

John DeLaughter lives in Pennsylvania with his wife. His non-fiction Lovecraft works have appeared in publications like The Lovecraft eZine (24 essays) and Vastarien: A Literary Journal. John's Dark Union trilogy tells how, "a haunted bequest opens a dark door beyond tribal myths to doom and danger for two men. who, to save themselves, must likewise, save another world."

His horror shorts appear in publications like, Ancestors and Descendants: Lovecraftian Prequels and Sequels, Weird Tails, Portraits of Terror, Corridors of Carcosa, and Time Loopers: Four Tales of a Time War. Also, his HP Lovecraft & HR Giger: From Alien to the Abyss is an exploration of both Maestros' creativity. Keep track of John's latest news on Twitter @HPL_JDeLaughter, Facebook @HPLJDeLaughter, Instagram@HPL_JDeLaughter, and Amazon @amazon.com/John-DeLaughter.

David Hambling lives in darkest Norwood, South London with his wife and cat. He is a journalist and his fiction, starting with the collection, *The Dulwich Horror & Others*, explores the Cthulhu mythos in his own locale. He continues the theme in a number of novels including the popular Harry Stubbs adventures, set in the 1920s, and the epic fantasy *War of the God Queen*, and has contributed to the *Black Wings* anthologies, *Tales of the Al-Azif, Time Loopers: Four Tales From a Time War* and others.

Keep track of his fiction at the Shadows From Norwood page on Facebook: https://www.facebook.com/ShadowsFromNorwood/

MEET THE ARTIST

Leigh Whurr is a surrealist artist living in the UK. After completing a Masters degree in Fine Art, he now produces and sells digital and traditional oil paintings, as well as extending his visions into 3D animation and experimental films.

Often alluding to themes of cosmic horror, existentialism and dream interpretation, his work explores the disorientating ambiguity of language and its relationship with the unknown and the unfamiliar.

instagram.com/leighwhurr/
Oddly-Spliced@deviantart.com

Curious about other Crossroad Press books?
Stop by our site:
http://store.crossroadpress.com
We offer quality writing
in digital, audio, and print formats.